ONE POOR SCRUPLE

CATHOLIC WOMEN WRITERS

SERIES EDITORS

Bonnie Lander Johnson, *University of Cambridge*
Julia Meszaros, *St. Patrick's Pontifical University, Maynooth*

ADVISORY COMMITTEE

Alana Harris, *King's College, University of London*
Andrew Meszaros, *St. Patrick's Pontifical University, Maynooth*
Kenneth Parker, *Duquesne University*
Michael Hurley, *University of Cambridge*
David Deavel, *University of St. Thomas*

ONE POOR SCRUPLE

Josephine Ward

WITH AN INTRODUCTION BY
BONNIE LANDER JOHNSON
AND JULIA MESZAROS

The Catholic University of America Press
WASHINGTON, D.C.

First published in 1899
by Longmans, Green, and Co.
Introduction Copyright © 2023
The Catholic University of America Press
All rights reserved

Cataloging-in-Publication Data is available
from the Library of Congress

ISBN: 978-0-8132-3602-5
eISBN: 978-0-8132-3603-2

"… the twentieth part of one poor scruple"

—The Merchant of Venice

CONTENTS

INTRODUCTION TO THE CATHOLIC
WOMEN WRITERS SERIES   ix

INTRODUCTION   xvii

PART I.

I.	Half-Mourning	3
II.	Unripe Years	12
III.	Meeting at a Junction	28
IV.	The Home of the Persecuted	39
V.	An Indiscreet Photograph	53
VI.	A Letter from London	70
VII.	A Retrospect	77
VIII.	Dame Mary Riversdale's Portrait	93
IX.	Madge Visits the Vault	100
X.	Benediction	113
XI.	Madge Leaves Skipton	123
XII.	Mark Sings a Hymn	131

PART II.

I.	Laura's Embassy	151
II.	Hilda in London	159
III.	A Dinner-Party	170
IV.	Amateur Diplomacy	180
V.	Hilda's Letter to Her Mother	188
VI.	A Dull Week	193
VII.	Cecilia Appeals to Marmaduke	199
VIII.	The Evening at the Hurstmonceaux	207
IX.	Madge Has a New Fear	217
X.	Two Lovers Confide in Laura	227
XI.	Opportunity	237

XII.	"Rabboni"	243
XIII.	Side-Lights from Celestine	251
XIV.	Hilda Understands	260
XV.	Cecilia	273
XVI.	More about Cecilia	283
XVII.	The Rest about Cecilia	289
XVIII.	The Twenty-Fourth of March	294
XIX.	Silence	307
XX.	Madge and Laura on the Twenty-Fourth	318
XXI.	Lord Bellasis Meets Mark Fieldes on the Twenty-Fourth	325
XXII.	Laura Drives Mark to the Reform Club	331
XXIII.	The Eve of Lady Day	343
XXIV.	A Postscript	354

INTRODUCTION TO THE
CATHOLIC WOMEN WRITERS SERIES

The Catholic Literary Revival was concentrated primarily in Britain, France, and America. Spanning the hundred years between the late nineteenth century and the late twentieth century, the movement saw an unprecedented quantity of writing by and about Catholics emerging after a protracted absence of Catholic faith and culture from the public sphere. In Britain the catalysts for this flourishing of poetry, prose fiction, and nonfiction were the beginning of the Oxford Movement, John Henry Newman's conversion to Rome, and the re-establishment of the Catholic hierarchy after three hundred years of persecution. In France, amid continuing anti-clericalism following the revolution, Catholic literature flourished alongside new religious orders and lay spiritual communities. And in America, European immigrants arriving in the nineteenth century were entering a society marked by a long history of anti-Catholicism. They utilized literature to explore a dimension of human thought and experience that was still largely absent from the American imagination.

The Catholic Literary Revival is exemplified by the work of Hilaire Belloc, Robert Hugh Benson, Georges Bernanos, Léon Bloy, G. K. Chesterton, Graham Greene, Gerard Manley Hopkins, Jacques Maritan, Thomas Merton, Charles Péguy, Walker Percy, J. R. R. Tolkien, and Evelyn Waugh. The works of all of these writers have been consistently in print, in modern editions, throughout the last century and up to the present day. The Revival's most numerous members, however, were women, and although some of these women remain well known—Muriel Spark, Antonia White, Flannery O'Connor, Dorothy Day—many have been almost entirely forgotten. These include Enid Dinnis, Anna

Hanson Dorsey, Alice Thomas Ellis, Eleanor Farjeon, Rumer Godden, Caroline Gordon, Clotilde Graves, Caryll Houselander, Sheila Kaye-Smith, Jane Lane, Marie Belloc Lowndes, Alice Meynell, Kathleen Raine, Pearl Mary Teresa Richards, Edith Sitwell, Gladys Bronwyn Stern, Josephine Ward, and Maisie Ward.

There are various reasons why each of these writers fell out of print. Broadly, we can point to changes in the commercial publishing world after World War II as well as changes within the Church itself and in the English-speaking universities that redefined the literary canon in the last decades of the twentieth century. Yet it remains puzzling that a body of writing so creative, so attuned to its historical moment, and so unique in its perspective on the human condition should have fallen into obscurity for so long.

This series brings together the English-language prose work of Catholic women from the nineteenth and twentieth centuries, work that retains its literary excellence and its accessibility to a broad range of readers. Although the series includes some short stories and nonfiction, it concentrates primarily on the novel. The novel was modernity's chief literary innovation. It grew out of several prose traditions, especially the spiritual autobiography, and yet it has been called both a Protestant and a secular form. The novel usually concentrates on the personal lives of a small cast of characters drawn from a range of social demographics; its demand for psychological realism and the nuances of lives lived in the material world means its vision is usually more earthly than spiritual. The novel is able to contain and explore religious concerns, especially the roles of providence and personal conscience, and many great novels depict elements of religious experience. Yet these novels nonetheless tend to remain worldly, secular, or materialist in structure and vision. This is no surprise, for the novel is ultimately resistant to "the pressures put upon it by many writers to transcend the limits" of the secular world.[1]

---

1. George Levine, *Realism, Ethics and Secularism: Essays on Victorian Literature and Science* (Cambridge: Cambridge University Press, 2011), 210. See also Deirdre

However, many of the writers in this series used the novel as an opportunity to rethink the form and its capacity to express a uniquely Catholic perspective. In doing so, they not only developed and advanced the form itself but also brought an ancient faith to bear on life in the modern world. There is a certain paradox here: Catholic writers effectively helped to push the novel into newer, and therefore more "modern" forms, even though they did so in pursuit of a truth that sometimes required a rejection or questioning of modernity's broader cultural movements.

The novel has often been characterized, especially in its early-eighteenth-century form, as primarily concerned with female experience and the domestic sphere. Although prominent counter-examples to this thesis exist in the work of Fielding and Dickens, the genre nonetheless frequently explores the internal lives of female characters and their negotiation of personal relationships within the more limited geographical settings of a single house, village, or city. But the novel is also a genre well suited to the exploration of social and political change. Unlike drama or epic, it can provide a voice for those who do not possess great social power, who must navigate moral challenges, often on their own and in direct conflict with the culture around them, and who, in doing so, offer criticisms of the society in which they find themselves. In this respect, the novel offered a perfect vehicle for exploring the challenges faced by a Catholic in modern society.

The historical period in which the Catholic Literary Revival emerged witnessed a complex renegotiation of almost all European social institutions, from the aristocracy and the family to party politics and the role of the state. There were Catholic writers among the many voices calling for change as well as among the many questioning its validity. Many of the novels in this series are concerned with distinguishing between stale

---

Shauna Lynch, "Gothic Fiction and 'Belief in Every Kind of Prodigy,'" in *The Routledge Companion to Literature and Religion*, ed. Mark Knight (Oxfordshire: Routledge, 2016), 252–62, p. 252.

social conventions that confine, suppress, or limit human capacities and timeless spiritual traditions that are morally and doctrinally true and authentic. Indeed, Catholic writers of the period drew on their faith to interrogate their society while also exploring how modern Catholics could live faithfully in a rapidly changing world.

The nineteenth and twentieth centuries were religiously tumultuous; they were often defined, even at the time, as an age of both faith and doubt. Writers and artists of every stripe examined the role of institutional religion in public life and the personal consequences of lives lived with faith or without it. The period has been described as the beginning of a modern secular society, but it also witnessed powerful resistance to secularization; writers from Austen to Eliot, Wilde to Waugh, identified religious belief as newly urgent and necessary. A nonreligious or strictly materialist worldview was for many an increasingly dangerous proposition. In 1935, T. S. Eliot criticized writers who failed to resist the drift toward secularism: "The whole of modern literature is corrupted by what I call Secularism. . . . It is simply unaware of, simply cannot understand the meaning of, the primacy of the supernatural over the natural life . . . something which I assume to be our primary concern."[2] Indeed, the period saw many conversions to Catholicism, notably among writers and artists, all of whom helped to shape in new and dynamic ways the "Catholic imagination."

This term can be broadly defined as a vision of the world in which the drama of salvation is played out in the mundane experiences of the everyday, in which the visible and created things of the world, the development of individual character and community identity, and the adventure of human relationships—all these are phenomena through which readers can touch spiritual realities. The Catholic imagination is that state of awareness

---

2. T. S. Eliot, "Religion and Literature," in *Selected Prose*, ed. Frank Kermode (New York: Harcourt Brace Jovanovich, 1975), 97–106, pp. 104–5.

through which the seemingly abstract doctrines of Church teaching are played out in a person's day-to-day experiences and moral actions, to the point that some of the smallest human endeavors become nothing less than matters of life and death. From a technical point of view, the novel was uniquely suited to exploring these varied levels of human experience. Its innovations in voice and point of view, in narrative time and the role of description and world-making in constructing human interiority, predispose it to the dramatization of both earthly and cosmic dimensions and moral or spiritual battles both social and personal.

The neglected female representatives of the Catholic Literary Revival cast a distinct and important light on the Catholic imagination. Typically writing from within more introspective, domestic, and romantic contexts, they often root Catholic experience in the everyday, revealing its relevance in and to the lives of ordinary men and women. This less socio-political touch may be one reason for their fall from the public eye, but it is also what makes them so uniquely relevant to contemporary life. As politico-cultural and religious institutions continue to drift into separate spheres of public influence, Christians today often struggle to grasp how faith should or does inform their day-to-day lives. Through fiction, the authors in this series provide a bridge over the divide between religious belief and everyday experience.

If the women writers involved in the Catholic Literary Revival often wrote from a more domestic or interpersonal angle, they were by no means unaware or uncritical of the social, cultural, political, and ecclesial developments of their time. Indeed, their more marginal role in Anglo-American society often allowed them to adopt a uniquely perceptive outsider's view. For many of the women in this series it was precisely their Catholic faith that empowered them to adopt a prominent voice. Inspired by the rich intellectual tradition of the Church and the prominent female saints throughout history, these writers made important contributions to Catholic thought on human dignity and the sacramental potential of the ordinary.

A large number of writers in this series were converts from Anglicanism or from no religion at all. Their imaginations were therefore shaped by a radical change in perspective. Becoming Catholic meant accepting a place outside of the British and American establishment, but it also meant they could often see their society with clear eyes for the first time. Many of the writers in this series also experienced personal suffering to an inordinate degree. Catholic teaching on the salvific nature of suffering provided them with means by which to understand the role that their loss played in the small drama of their own life as much as the bigger cosmic drama in which we are all players. Caryll Houselander, for example, understood personal suffering to be a means by which Christians could "give birth to Christ" in the lives of others. Like many writers, she understood that the novel is itself a vehicle for understanding suffering. Houselander turned to the novel after decades of writing spiritual prose. She did so because she no longer wanted to "preach" to her fellows; she wanted instead to "take sinners by the hand" and walk in their lives for a time. The wounds experienced by our writers, when combined with the existential awakening of a conversion to faith, shaped their particular view of human experience and divine truth. Faced with the emotional and spiritual reality of deep suffering, convert novelists often saw in Catholicism what they saw in the novel itself: a space able to contain all the mysteries of human experience.

Benedict XVI said that "the only really effective apologia for Christianity comes down to two arguments, namely, the *saints* the Church has produced and the *art* which has grown in her womb."[3] We should not, therefore, underestimate the importance of artists for defending the credibility of the Christian faith. This pertains also to the Catholic women writers of this series. Few of these writers will go on to be canonized; indeed some of

---

3. Joseph Cardinal Ratzinger (with Vittorio Messori), *The Ratzinger Report: An Exclusive Interview on the State of the Church*, trans. Salvator Attanasio and Graham Harrison (San Francisco, CA: Ignatius Press, 1985), 129.

them may not have been particularly saintly, but through their interventions in literary tradition, these women powerfully reshaped the literary and religious landscape.

For the Catholic reader, the writing in this series provides a fictional exploration of the moral and spiritual adventure offered by Catholic life. It also offers a way of holding together themes that have become increasingly partisan in the Church today. Most of the women in this series were writing at a time when the Church was grappling to define its relationship to an increasingly secular world. They were innovators who raised questions that would eventually be posed at the Second Vatican Council, but they were also loyal to many of the traditions and doctrines that disappeared after the Council. Their vision incorporates both a rigorous personal morality and a concern for social justice; an awareness of God's grandeur and an appreciation of his presence in the ordinary; and the importance of both piety and charitable works.

For the non-Catholic reader, the writing in this series offers a crucial but overlooked vision of modernity. It provides insight into a unique form of female experience but also a unique means of understanding how the Catholic faith is played out in the everyday. For those interested in the history of the novel, these writers demonstrate some of the ways in which the genre is able to explore and express the highest and most timeless spiritual realities, often through the application of the most avant-garde novelistic techniques.

Bonnie Lander Johnson and Julia Meszaros

FURTHER READING

Tom Woodman. *Faithful Fictions*. Washington, DC: The Catholic University of America Press, 2022.

James Emmett Ryan. *Faithful Passages*. Madison: University of Wisconsin Press, 2013.

Christopher Dawson. *The Spirit of the Oxford Movement*. Washington, DC: The Catholic University of America Press.

INTRODUCTION

THE AUTHOR

Josephine Mary Hope-Scott Ward was born in 1864, just over a decade after the Catholic hierarchy was reinstated in England. She was a descendent on one side from the Dukes of Norfolk and on the other side from Anglican lawyers and writers. Both her parents died before she was nine, after which she was raised by her grandmother at Arundel Castle, the seat of the Dukes of Norfolk and the heart of Recusant Catholicism. In 1887 Josephine married Wilfrid Ward, son of the Tractarian convert William George, and spent her life in close companionship with the most active minds working in the late nineteenth century to restore the Catholic Church in England to the intellectual, sacramental and theological integrity it had once enjoyed before three hundred years of persecution.

Josephine was the wife and mother of a large family, but in this role she was also a force for change in the Church and her broader society, especially its literary and philosophical movements. Among her companions were Newman and Manning, Tennyson and Huxley, Gladstone, Chesterton and Belloc, the von Hügels, Benson, and Maturin. She wrote numerous novels, theological pamphlets, and articles for the *Dublin Review* and *The Spectator*. She raised five children, one of whom, Maisie Ward, would go on to found the largest and most prolific modern Catholic publishing house (Sheed and Ward), furthering in her own century the work her mother and father had begun in theirs. Josephine Ward is one of Catholicism's greatest literary treasures and a leading contributor to English literary history—except that she has all but completely fallen out of the historical record. As we write this introduction, there is no entry for Josephine Ward in the Dictionary of National Biography, though her father, husband, brother, and daughter have all been granted one. If it were not for Maisie Ward's two-volume biography of her parents, there would be little to which we could turn for knowledge of Josephine's life and work. All of her novels have fallen out of print, despite their once high acclaim in the *fin de siècle* literary world.

The married life of Josephine and Wilfrid Ward was lived in full engagement with the intellectual and sacramental life of the Church. In 1884, the young Wilfrid sent one of his early philosophical treatises to his godmother, the Duchess of Norfolk, who replied that she would certainly read them for him if he would in return bring his "magnificent voice" to Arundel to sing the Holy Week liturgies. He agreed, and there he met Josephine.[1] In the same year, he proposed to her and was refused. At the time, Josephine was writing a story called *In the Way*. She sent it to Burns and Oates who forwarded it anonymously to their reader, Wilfrid Ward. He recommended warmly that it be published. Josephine herself was in later life scornful of her early writing, observing that had she not married and experienced life with Wilfrid and their children, her writing would never have risen above the level of the "pious tale."[2] Her early readers, however, were far from disparaging. John Henry Newman, then aged eighty-seven, wrote to Josephine to tell her that he liked *In the Way* "extremely."[3] Three months later Newman wrote again to congratulate Wilfrid after his offer of engagement to Josephine had finally been accepted. Cardinal Manning also wrote to the young couple to express his happiness. In those early decades of the re-established Church, the Catholic community was so small that Cardinals Newman and Manning were regular visitors at the

---

1. Maisie Ward, *The Wilfrid Wards and the Transition. Vol I. The Nineteenth Century* (London: Sheed and Ward, 1934), 152.
2. Maisie Ward, *The Wilfrid Wards and the Transition. Vol I*, 152.
3. Maisie Ward, *The Wilfrid Wards and the Transition. Vol I*, 152.

houses of the laity, especially lay Catholics of such theological activity as Wilfrid and Josephine. They came as friends, spiritual advisors, and catechists for the children. It is in this setting—of close community, intense literary activity, theological debate—that the married life of Josephine and Wilfrid was lived and in which their children were raised.

Josephine wrote novels, Wilfrid biographies: both were concerned with the question of how to realise the fullness of human character in prose. This question was one they approached not just as a literary skill but as theological inquiry. What is a person? How is character formed? Josephine wrote in the *Dublin Review* that "the greatest drama is the unfolding of the action of the will as it adheres to or thwarts the Divine purpose." She held that fictional characters, if truly drawn, must live beyond the knowledge or skill of their author. If the author is not surprised by the actions of her own characters, then her control of them is too firm and too narrow, leaving no room for the divine to animate the fictional character through the creative capacities of the author, just as the divine, through its own mysterious capacities, animates the human person.

For Wilfrid, the challenge was to bring to life a person who had lived, to reanimate their character in a fullness of dimension that few people would have known while the subject lived. Wilfrid often reflected that a person can only be seen partially by each of those who know him, while the biographer must attempt to see him with a breadth of understanding that in truth only God can apprehend. Where Josephine's work sought to create characters beyond her own writerly control, Wilfrid sought to understand his subjects in their fullest and most intricate human dimensions. Of Wilfrid's approach to his biographies of Newman and Wiseman, Josephine said that he "lived in the person whose life he was writing"—so much that they were present at the table, in the drawing room, on walks.[4] G. K. Chesterton said of the Wards that "in

---

4. Maisie Ward, *The Wilfrid Wards and the Transition. Vol I*, 239–40.

truth there is nothing so authentically creative as the divine act of making another man out of the very substance of oneself. Few of us have vitality enough to live the life of another."⁵

This interest in the person and her formation brought Josephine and Wilfrid regularly into contact with one of the most urgent questions facing the modern Church: how best to educate the young. For centuries, Catholics had been barred from English universities and from the many public roles for which university degrees continued to prepare Protestants. Prior to the re-establishment of the ecclesial hierarchy, Catholic families had mostly retreated into the quiet existence of the country squire. Education was provided at home, often with the help of the religious orders. Wilfrid Ward belonged to the first generation of modern Catholics legally allowed to study at Oxford and Cambridge. However, even after restrictions on Catholics were relaxed, the ecclesial hierarchy itself was divided on whether or not a Protestant university was an appropriate place for a Catholic to be educated. Newman believed that Catholics ought to return to public institutions and planned for an Oratory at Oxford; Manning disagreed. Wilfrid's father, who had himself been Fellow of Balliol before he converted, held firmly that no good could come of sending a Catholic child to Oxford. Instead, Wilfrid spent periods of his education at Catholic institutions, both in England and abroad. And yet, Wilfrid himself later questioned the wisdom of this decision.⁶

Josephine was too old to benefit from the emerging opportunities for women at Newnham and Girton, but what about her daughters? As parents, Wilfrid and Josephine found themselves navigating the same problems their own parents had faced: how to make available to their children the best of public, intellectual, and cultural life without exposing them over-much to the influence of an institution that remained fundamentally opposed to

---

5. Maisie Ward, *The Wilfrid Wards and the Transition. Vol I*, 239.
6. Maisie Ward, *The Wilfrid Wards and the Transition. Vol I*, 75–77.

their religious practice and beliefs. For both sons and daughters, this question was bound up with the possibility of vocation, which Wilfrid himself explored during his brief noviciate. If Oxford and Cambridge had for centuries been the training ground of Protestant clergy, were they suitable places for Catholic children to discern their own vocation? These were some of the concerns that drove the Catholic cardinals, with the help of families like the Wards, to establish a Catholic university in Kensington, where Wilfrid briefly studied. But the institution was short lived; as in the case of the Catholic University of Ireland, which Newman helped establish and of which he was rector for four years, there was disagreement about the nature or function of a Catholic university, and so the question of Catholic higher education rumbled on into the twentieth century.

In the years when Josephine Ward wrote her first novel, *One Poor Scruple*, she was preoccupied with questions of education. While problems of conscience and temptation are the novel's dominant concern, underlying these issues is a reflection on the role education plays in the formation and functioning of conscience. In the final line of the novel's postscript, we are told that it is the children of the next generation who, finally comfortable as Catholics in Oxford, can begin the new century by reconciling the old world of the cloistered Catholic with the modern world of intellectual and aesthetic endeavour. But this new world of full integration is a future possibility only glimpsed by the novel's main characters as they reflect on the decisions they made for themselves, while hoping that their children will carry the Catholic faith into the future.

THE NOVEL

One Poor Scruple is a novel situated precisely in its historical moment: it examines the social reality of English Catholics in and around London in the 1890s. But in doing so the novel also depicts the timeless human struggle for happiness when so often the object of our desire is anathema to our deeper human needs.

One Poor Scruple is a love story that draws on the rich literary materials available after two centuries of the English novel, and yet it uses romance conventions in a way that is distinctly Catholic—a fact that makes the novel almost entirely unique in 1899. Decades before Evelyn Waugh examined in *Brideshead Revisited* the human struggle to distinguish between true and false beauty, Ward's novel examines the challenges of ordering conflicting desires and of living a life that is as truthful and good as it is beautiful.

The romance narrative was already a well-established novelistic pattern in which a protagonist must struggle to discern the motivations of a lover, to select from among a range of influences, and to find love and happiness amid an array of choices, each presenting certain goods but potentially also grave threats. In Protestant novels, this romantic pattern was usually constructed along moral, rather than doctrinal, lines. The distinction between those lovers who were morally superior choices for the protagonist and those who were inferior choices was usually drawn from within the novelist's development of character: Jane Austen's Marianne Dashwood must overcome her more immature attachment to the passionate but fickle Willoughby in order to recognize the goodness of the less immediately attractive Colonel Brandon. Jane Eyre must overcome the easy solution embodied by St John and return to Rochester. For a Catholic novelist like Ward, the romance narrative offered an opportunity to explore the tension between romantic desires and religious truth. Where Protestant protagonists had no absolute moral barriers between them and their love object, a Catholic could not marry a divorcee or, at the time, a Protestant. The heroines of *One Poor Scruple* are confronted with both of these challenging barriers. In this way, the novel takes a familiar narrative strategy and renders from it a new means of exploring the significant degree of personal sacrifice that religious faith may demand.

Ward uses the question of marriage and divorce to show that the Christian God seeks to pull the human person out of herself, out of an easy and complacent fulfilment of desire, and he compels her to imagine herself in relation to a larger and more whole reality, which includes the past, the future (including the possibility of eternal life), and the needs of other people in the here and now. This sensitivity to what is "other"—other than oneself, other than the here and now, other than one's desires—is portrayed as a central element of a functioning Catholic imagination. The novel's attention to the spiritual significance of doctrine (such as the indissolubility of marriage) spoke directly to its historical moment. Among Ward's literary and artistic peers in the late 1800s, Catholicism enjoyed a certain vogue. A significant number of English writers of the Decadent movement chose to become members of the Roman Catholic Church. Yet, influenced by the atmosphere of the British *fin de siècle*, some of these converts were drawn to the Catholic aesthetic, with less regard for the faith's doctrinal dimension. In *One Poor Scruple*, Ward makes the case that doctrine matters—that it shapes who we are and how we relate to the world.

In the novel, three London aristocratic women—Madge, Laura, and Cecilia—enjoy all the glamour of Edwardian society, but of the three women only Madge was raised a Catholic. For Madge, the life of high society ultimately takes place against the backdrop of the promises and demands of God and his Church and, particularly, against that of eternal life. In Sussex, the old recusant family (into which Madge, though now a widow, had once married) lives the cloistered way they came to know throughout the centuries of persecution: avoiding all public office, almost all English institutional life, and spending their days in full observance of the Divine Office as though the family home were a monastery. But two young daughters of the household are on the brink of womanhood and must decide the kind of life they want: Mary, devoted to her family and uninterested in the attractions of London, and her cousin Hilda, bright and hungry for intellectual stimulation. When Hilda arrives in London, she must navigate a world for which her country education could never fully prepare her. Through both Hilda and Madge, the novel asks: How far into the world can a Catholic wander, how many fruits can be enjoyed, before the happiness she pursues becomes separated from good and for this reason poses grave moral danger? How can one distinguish between true and false goods, between apparent and genuine beauty?

THE TRANSCENDENTALS AND MODERNITY

The significance of Catholic doctrine only becomes clear in the context of classical Christianity's metaphysical worldview, which involved the assertion—inherited from ancient Greek philosophy—of the unity among the so-called "transcendentals": the true, the good, and the beautiful. This unity came under attack during the period of early modernity that stretched from the late Middle Ages to the Enlightenment to the extent that, by the late nineteenth century, its earlier Christian form was all but dissolved.[7] Ideas of truth, goodness, and beauty still captivated the imagination; indeed, the nineteenth century was in many ways particularly concerned with them, as in Walter Pater's or John Ruskin's insistence on the spiritual, even revelatory, power of beauty. But the true, the good, and the beautiful were no longer consistently viewed and pursued in unison with one another, as mutually conditioning aspects of one reality. The dissolution of the transcendentals, in itself a philosophical development, poses ongoing sociological ramifications. It underlies modernity's array of seemingly parallel but contradictory movements, such as scientific materialism, puritanical moralism, and decadent aestheticism.[8] It helped facilitate the breakdown of the aristocracy, the

---

7. As Charles Taylor has shown, this is not tantamount to saying that religious thinking or belief had come to an end. See Charles Taylor, *A Secular Age* (Cambridge, MA: Harvard University Press, 2007).

8. For a sketch of the philosophical history from a metaphysical to a materialistic worldview and all its trappings, see David Bentley Hart, *The Experience of God: Being, Consciousness, Bliss* (New Haven, CT: Yale University Press, 2013), part 1.

ascendancy of the bourgeoisie and its functionalist, secular values, as well as the replacement of traditional understandings of religion in terms of dogma with reductive understandings of religion in aesthetic, moralistic, or emotive terms. In *One Poor Scruple*, Josephine Ward depicts these trends through her characters, whom she treats with a compelling combination of sympathy and critique. If the Catholic faith is compared favourably to the various emerging secular worldviews, then it is also made clear that its compelling features result from its rootedness in a transcendent God, who unifies the true, the good, and the beautiful.

This God promises infinitely greater rewards but equally makes greater demands than any secular worldview. Madge Riversdale is the widow of the wayward heir to the aristocratic Catholic Riversdale family. Herself a Catholic of loose observance, the elegant and restless Madge is looking to increase her happiness in the world. She is enamoured of the idea of climbing the ranks of London's high society, and her chances of social success seem certain when it materializes that the coveted Lord Bellasis is interested in marrying her. However, on the brink of untold possibilities of wealth, power, and worldly happiness, Madge nonetheless has "one poor scruple": Bellasis is divorced and his wife, though in obscurity, is still alive. Madge knows that, according to her Catholic faith, he is in fact still married. By "marrying" him, she would commit the mortal sin of adultery and risk the salvation of her soul by placing herself outside the fold of the Church.

Other figures in the novel challenge or reinforce Madge's scruple. Both explicitly and implicitly, the various members of the Riversdale family help sharpen her conscience. Her father-in-law's gentle goodness, Hilda's innocent shock at the very idea of divorce, Mary's unworldly sacrifice, Father Clement's apt and incisive sermon: all of these serve as (unwelcome but persuasive) reminders of Madge's religious roots and of the objectivity of the Christian God and his eternal judgment. By contrast, Madge's London friends (who have reduced religion to aesthetic pleasure or emotional stimulation) dismiss and indeed mock Madge's scruples as pointless obstructions to a deserved worldly happiness. Laura cries out, "Madge, what will your life be if you yield to this superstitious madness?" and, appealing to Madge's vanity and self-pity, "After all you had suffered in the past, you had this year enjoyed your life a little—you had won for yourself a unique social position by your wonderful goodness." Madge herself had earlier tried to rationalize doing what she knew to be wrong and to reduce the faith to a source of comfort, even to use it to validate her sins by suggesting that "People had to live in the world, and behave as the world does." Madge's conscience is disturbed, but she experiences this discomfort as a desire to be soothed: she is for a long time trapped in an immature wish for Catholic ritual to merely provide comfort while allowing her to pursue her worldly aims. "She counted on her sister to make her feel more comfortable and more able to go to confession again and to get spiritual comfort in services when she felt sad. [...] Then she wouldn't be nervous and afraid, as she was now, that she wasn't as good as she might be. . . ."

Ward honestly depicts the attractions—and temptations—of the world. Although for Madge these include primarily the social power, prestige, and wealth embodied by Lord Bellasis, other characters experience their own temptations. Hilda is tempted by the emotional sensibility and intellectual sophistication of Laura's protégé, the writer Mark Fieldes. Lady Cecilia Rupert, Madge's rival in relation to Lord Bellasis, embodies a sensual passion and free-spiritedness that the worldly Bellasis recognizes as tempting but, ultimately, unfulfilling and dangerous. Ward's lively and convincing portrayal of these characters is made possible by the way in which the Wards lived out their conviction that Catholics, now legally emancipated, must actively participate in and contribute to the world and its intellectual life. Welcoming Catholics of all stripes and non-Catholics alike into their home, the Wards were intimately familiar with a wide range of intellectual personalities.

This great affection for people of all backgrounds and dispositions is reflected in Ward's portrayal of Mark Fieldes, a self-made man with exceptional intellectual interest and ability but no religion. Mark's modern intellectualism is clearly a feature lacking in the aristocratic Catholic houses, whose families have retreated from the world for too long. He legitimately complains that the friar's sermon "did smack of the monastery chapel in its entire absence of appeal to the intellect, in its absolute taking for granted of the existence of this supremely beneficent Creator, who could satisfy all needs, fill all the emptiness, if we would only give up our wills to His." For the young and clever Hilda Riversdale, Mark's lively intellect—and intellectual flattery—is inspiring and attractive. Her infatuation with him is misguided but understandable. Cloistered too long in the Catholic countryside, she is hungry for intellectual stimulation and Mark provides this: he is seemingly the first young and educated person to take her intellectual life seriously.

However praiseworthy Mark's regard for the life of the mind, it is compromised—and even debilitated—by his failure to understand the objective truths to which we are all subject. Instead, he is trapped in his intellectual and emotional subjectivity. Limited in this way, his learnedness remains superficial. He is well-read, mentally agile, observant, and articulate, but he is neither wise nor morally steadfast. His apparent "good-heartedness" regularly shrinks away from even basic moral values such as truthfulness, honesty, and loyalty, let alone the selflessness displayed by his rival Marmaduke. And his sense of beauty is changeable and ineffective: Hilda's visual attractiveness is diminished in his eyes when he learns that she is not, in fact, an heiress and, although he regularly claims to see "the divine in the human" (in Mary's face, in Cecilia's dancing, in the figure of the friar, in Hilda's innocence), he remains unable to come to a relationship with the divine. Indeed, it eventually materializes that even his seeming freedom from gender conventions was merely a façade or surface phenomenon: his interest in Hilda was based on her supposed fortune and on her ability to provide him with "the domestic hearth whose light and sweetness would have made a charmed circle, within which these demons of nervous sensation could have been kept at arm's length." Obsessed with his own social advancement, the only "sins" Mark recognizes in himself are his "tactlessness" and "ungentlemanliness," qualities that endanger his social standing.

For all its attractiveness, Mark's intellectual curiosity is impaired. Beauty cannot transport him to the transcendent and remains severed from truth and goodness, with the result that he is, in fact, always teetering on the edge of despair. Mark knows himself to be "clinging to a world about which he had no delusions, clinging to it simply because it was a distraction from his intolerable self-consciousness." Whenever the world fails to distract him, he is confronted with an almost unbearable loneliness—and with the loss of love, the fear that results from his lack of faith:

> "I once met a man who said he would rather be damned than be annihilated," he said to himself with a wan smile. "I don't agree, for that would end it all. But it is awful to be alive and to be alone as I am! If it were true that there were a Judge who really existed, He would approve as well as condemn. Love would grow near to fear. And the human instinct to value life which failed Cecilia would not be part of a great illusion. We should gain in hope as well as in fear."

If the loss of God has thrown Mark Fieldes back on the impressions and sensibilities of his intellect, it has focused his friend Cecilia Rupert on the sensual passion of the body.

Both these reductions are emblems of the modern condition, as much today as in the nineteenth century. Mark and Cecilia are trapped in their subjectivity, which gives rise to a range of modern ironies. Cecilia's self-centredness comes with a constant need for company and affirmation, and yet these distractions never relieve her sense of loneliness. When finally her hopes of happiness are ruined, Cecilia finds that "for almost the first time in her self-centred life she was terrified at being alone." Cecilia appears to be the emancipated modern woman: riding on the bus with the working classes, dressing in risqué and masculine clothes, scheming in unabashed pursuit of her own happiness—and yet she turns out to be more vulnerable and fragile than any of her peers. Her skilful and inspired dancing appears even to her admirer Bellasis as "amusing but boring." Her supposed willingness to confront the hard truths about life coincides with a simultaneous inability to live with them: she cannot bear to confront her aunt's illness, let alone her own physical or emotional suffering. And, finally, her insistence that religious faith is nothing but a false drug that fools swallow to make life bearable is matched by her own failing struggle to make her nihilism bearable: she seeks refuge in drugs, fortune tellers, medical doctors, art, and human love and ultimately finds her tragic end when these do not provide the desired results of worldly happiness and success. Ward leaves little doubt that Cecilia's "anodynes" do not work because they do not originate in truth: where Mary's alleged anodyne of religious faith brings her an other-worldly happiness, Cecilia's distractions result in selfishness and, ultimately, despair.

The figures of Mary Riversdale and indeed of Madge suggest that human happiness is inseparable from a willingness and an ability to suffer. The source of happiness does not necessarily present itself as an attraction ("'It didn't attract me,' said Mary, blushing deeply; 'I couldn't bear it.'"), but possibly, in its purest and most supernatural form, as a deeply challenging but irresistible call. Like many Catholic novels, *One Poor Scruple* highlights the ways in which divine grace providentially uses the people and events of the world for the salvation of an individual soul. Even unhappy and seemingly unrelated developments conspire to move Madge's soul in the direction of truth: the death of her only child leaves her with a hunger for heaven that is reawakened when she receives news of the death of a baby and mother in childbirth. Equally, Mary's awakening to the religious life is juxtaposed to the restlessness and frustrations of Madge's hedonistic London life: once at Skipton, various encounters alert Madge, however unwillingly, to the different forces—Church and world, divine and ecclesial authority and human desire—tugging at her soul. This battle plays itself out, above all, in Madge's conscience. Ward's treatment of conscience clearly manifests her close familiarity with the thought of John Henry Newman.

NEWMAN AND CONSCIENCE

Ward's daughter, Maisie, recalls that Josephine and Wilfrid's life together was "lived under the shadow of Cardinal Newman." Newman had been a regular visitor in both their childhood homes, and he remained a close friend whose writings were read and discussed almost daily.[9] Newman even plays a part in *One Poor Scruple*. Although his role as a character in the novel is minor, his ideas clearly shape Josephine's development of her characters. Newman's main theological interest has been described as "the invisible effects of divine grace in the soul of the Catholic, effecting there a moral transformation." This proposition animates Ward's novel.[10] The novel is also crucially concerned with Newman's views on education, on the importance of a person's interior predisposition, and, above all, on conscience. It could be said that Ward's interest in Newman's thinking on conscience began early in her girlhood. Newman's famous 1875 letter on conscience was addressed to the Duke of Norfolk and was written shortly after Ward came to live at Arundel Castle.

Newman famously viewed human conscience as one of providence's central tools in the salvation of the human soul, describing it as nothing less than "the voice of God in the nature and heart of man" and as "the internal witness of both the existence

---

9. Maisie Ward, *The Wilfrid Wards and the Transition*, Vol. I, 239.
10. Stanley L. Jaki, *Apologetics as Meant by Newman* (Port Huron, MI: Real View Books, 2005), 323.

and the law of God."[11] This elevated understanding of conscience is based on the observation that there inheres in us a "moral sense" which "declares that sin is sin" even against our attempts "to prove virtue vice and vice virtue."[12] That this sense comes from outside of us is suggested by the fact that it implies a judgment which we cannot silence or ignore without being haunted by it. Human conscience thus has both a "a moral sense, and a sense of duty; a judgment of the reason and a magisterial dictate."[13] It tells us what is right and what is wrong but also exhorts us to act according to this knowledge and, though it might be malleable by continuous violation, it is not malleable by reason. According to Newman, just as it is reasonable to infer from our persistent sense impressions the real existence of a cause (the material world), so it is reasonable to infer from our persistent internal impression the real existence of a cause (a divine spirit).

Madge's conflict is clearly a conflict of conscience, which has been reawakened by her confrontation with the Catholic faith of her childhood on the one hand and Lord Bellasis's proposal of marriage on the other. The vehemence of this conflict between divine truth and human desire is illustrated in Madge's actions: she travels to Skipton despite abhorring the place, wants to make her confession but keeps putting it off, tries to rationalize her behaviour against her better instincts. Such a Pauline notion of the "divided self" (cf. Rom 7:15–20) is not specific to Madge, however, but regularly appears in other characters too. This notion clearly represents the ordinary human sinner who has come in contact with divine truth but struggles both to recognize

---

11. John Henry Newman, *Certain Difficulties Felt by Anglicans in Catholic Teaching*, vol. 2, *A Letter Addressed to the Duke of Norfolk on Occasion of Mr. Gladstone's Recent Expostulation* (London: Longmans, Green, 1900), 247–48.

12. John Henry Newman, *Sermons 1824–1843*, vol. 2, *Sermons on Biblical History, Sin and Justification, the Christian Way of Life, and Biblical Theology*, ed. Vincent Ferrer Blehl (Oxford: Oxford University Press, 1994), 377.

13. John Henry Newman, *An Essay in Aid of a Grammar of Assent* (London: Longmans, Green, 1903), 105.

it and to live by it. Ward lets the reader see each character's struggles both with divine and with human eyes: the reader equally despairs, sympathizes, and identifies with Madge. Madge's struggles exemplify Newman's observations about the equal inconvenience and tenacity of the voice of conscience. She tries to fight her conscience, first by making excuses and blaming others for her faults: "must, must go to confession and I can't, I can't, I can't. Everybody is unkind to me, everybody that's good I mean, and I am quite alone, and, oh, so miserable, and I must amuse myself, and I mustn't feel." Eventually Madge tries violently to rid herself of her faith by destroying everything that reminds her of it. And yet she fails. Madge's conscience will not be silenced, and any happiness she gains is feeble and momentary. The "dull weight that had appeared to oppress her" since her engagement to Bellasis is only lifted once she follows her conscience by breaking off her engagement. This does not bring Madge immediate worldly happiness, but it clears the ground for happiness to become a possibility. That the world—in Madge's case London high society—should not comprehend the gravity of one's scruple is something Newman himself experienced most forcefully.[14]

Newman was one of the English Church's foremost advocates of the idea that Catholics must acquire an education and participate in the intellectual life. This is evidenced not only in his

---

14. Newman recollects that he and many of his fellows in the Oxford Movement could not remain where they were (i.e., in the Church of England) "without scruple" (*Difficulties Felt by Anglicans*, 1, 99). In Newman's own novel *Loss and Gain*, Charles's flirtation with Catholicisism and refusal to sign the Thirty-Nine Articles is thought to be a "scruple; troublesome, certainly, but, of course, temporary." *Loss and Gain* (London: Longmans, Green, 1906), 340. According to Newman, the anti-Catholic polemicist Blanco White takes issue with Catholicism because it "gave rise to nervousness, scruples, and melancholy." *Present Position of Catholics in England* (London: Longmans, Green, 1908), 171. It is the work of divine grace that offers a serene confidence to the convert in his new communion; "They have no fears, no anxieties, no difficulties, no scruples." *Discourses to Mixed Congregations* (London: Longmans, Green, 1906), 179–180). In this context, Madge's scruples can be interpreted as instrumental to her path towards conversion.

writings but also in his various practical initiatives, including the organization of evening lectures open to the public (women included) and his efforts to create a Catholic university in Ireland. At the same time, Newman was not under the illusion that being well-read and having an academic education would necessarily bring any moral or spiritual gain. Influenced by Froude, who argued that "a man who is morally good, will have a right faith," because "many of our opinions are the result of our character,"[15] Newman argued that it is our moral character which affects our ability to recognize truth and hence acquire right knowledge more than the other way round. That our moral character is thus shaped by living in accordance with our conscience explains why Newman considers following one's conscience to be a more sure way of growing in virtue than acquiring intellectual knowledge.[16] Together with revelation, the voice of conscience facilitates divine moral governance, Newman argues, which explains why he also calls conscience the "Vicar of Christ."[17] Indeed, Newman has been described as putting forward "one living principle" of revelation, revelation promised and initiated in conscience, and brought to completion in the doctrine of Christ.[18]

Ward's novel echoes these insights. The intellectual life is celebrated as a valuable human pursuit, expressive of the human quest for truth and meaning and a vehicle for genuine and vital human community. Yet, as shown in the figures of Mark and Hilda, it has no automatic moral benefit. It can bear fruit only where it is rooted in transcendent, or objective, truth, which in

---

15. Richard Hurrell Froude, *Remains of the Late Reverend Richard Hurrell Froude*, vol. 1, ed. John Keble and John Henry Newman. (London: J. G. & F. Rivington, 1838), 114, 116, quoted in Geertjan Zuijdwegt and Terrence Merrigan, "Conscience" in Frederick D. Aquino and Benjamin J. King, *The Oxford Handbook of John Henry Newman* (Oxford: Oxford University Press, 2018), 439.

16. Zuijdwegt and Merrigan, "Conscience," 449.

17. Newman, *Difficulties Felt by Anglicans*, 2, 248–49.

18. Erich Przywara, "Newman: Moeglicher Heiliger und Kirchenlehrer der neuen Zeit?" *Internationale Cardinal-Newman-Studien* 3 (1957): 28–36, quoted in Zuijwegt and Merrigan, "Conscience," 452.

turn can be found through a functioning and obedient conscience and above all through God's revelation. It is on account of their truthfulness, and ultimately their faith, that Mary and Marmaduke are the moral touchstones of the story despite their limited education or intellectual curiosity.

Like Newman, Ward is sympathetic to those for whom temperament or upbringing make the spiritual submission and moral intensity described by the novel's priest figure, Father Clement, impossible. She notes the tragedy implied in the fact that, although Mark claims that Father Clement's sermon "awoke feelings in his nature that were never entirely lost," these feelings never produce any real gain. Ward's instinct here can also be seen in the work of a much later Catholic author, Muriel Spark, who rejected literary appeals to the emotions as morally dangerous insofar as they can produce in people the sense that their "moral responsibilities [have been] sufficiently fulfilled by the emotions they have been induced to feel."[19] And yet, according to Newman, certain, perhaps cool and stable emotions do play a role in the religious or moral life. As illustrated in Madge's character, conscience makes itself known through "self-approval and hope, or compunction and fear."[20] Conversely, a well-formed conscience is also acknowledged to allow a person to overcome inherited limitations of temperament. As Bellasis purportedly says of Madge, for instance, "She is so easily impressed, yet so hard to force."

The novel's critique of popular Christianity's anti-dogmatic turn and its consequent reduction to aesthetic externals or fleeting emotional sentiments also reflects Newman's thought on liberalism's advancement into the religious sphere. Mark Fieldes says of Laura, "She loves the highest aspirations and emotions of religion, only not the fetters of dogma." Mark recalls Laura's view

---

19. Muriel Spark, "Desegregation of Art," in *Critical Essays on Muriel Spark*, ed. Joseph Hynes, Critical Essays on British Literature Ser. (New York: Maxwell Macmillan International, 1992), 33–37.

20. Newman, *Grammar of Assent*, 105.

that we humans must "shroud our heads and bend them low, 'pour ne rien dire de limité en face de l'infini.'" According to this viewpoint which, in the Catholic context, gave rise to the Modernist crisis, any attempts to convey the divine in human terms are flawed and ought to be discarded. Thus separated from truth (as captured in dogma), religion is reduced to a vague spirituality, and morality becomes a social function driven by either self-interest or majority opinion. Laura, who "doesn't care if her religious emotions correspond to a reality or not," is charitable towards an individual precisely until the moment when her friends rule against her.

Ward is also attuned to the way in which the critique of dogma as unduly limiting God effectively casts God into oblivion by making it impossible to speak of Him. The result has largely been a shift from spiritual to material concerns, which are met with the same religious fervor. The medical doctor functions as the priest ("the great magnate, the revealer of hidden things, who gave hope or fear to all, and healing to a possible few") who enjoys "the position of a sage and of a confessor to many." As in the religion of old, medicine's adherents are called upon to alter their ways (Cecilia is to lead a quiet life, even though she is "not quiet"), yet here they are given neither the motivation, nor the tools, example, or promise needed to achieve such conversion. What has become lost is above all the ability to suffer—an ability Ward, like other authors in this series, recognizes to be central to the attainment of human happiness.

One Poor Scruple retains remarkable contemporary relevance. In no small measure, this is the result of its quintessentially Catholic portrayal of the human condition as one that is restless, even treacherous, but never without hope of salvation. With equal degrees of sympathy and honesty, Ward shows that moral and spiritual growth is difficult but possible. Far from being automatic, salvation comes at a price but where the human soul is willing to pay that price, divine grace can prevail even against the odds. The soul's salvation happens in community, involving all with whom we associate and especially the saints: "we are linked by chains about the feet of God, and the history of Madge's future was not to be independent of another soul in conflict."

When Josephine Ward sat at her table to talk with other Catholics of her generation—Wilfrid, Newman, Manning—she knew the gravity of their corporate responsibility: to keep alive a faith in peril but also to serve each other in the way that all Catholics must ultimately serve each other. *One Poor Scruple* was itself precisely an act of such service to a generation of Catholic readers who had few written literary or theological materials with which to navigate a world that continued to be at best fascinated by their faith, at worst hostile to it. The novel dwells in and finds pleasure in the human desire for love and beauty. It reminds Catholics not to be afraid of the world. But it also reminds us that scruples have a vital function. They do not merely inhibit the soul as it ventures into the world. Understood fully, scruples can guide the soul to true happiness.

Part I

CHAPTER I

HALF-MOURNING

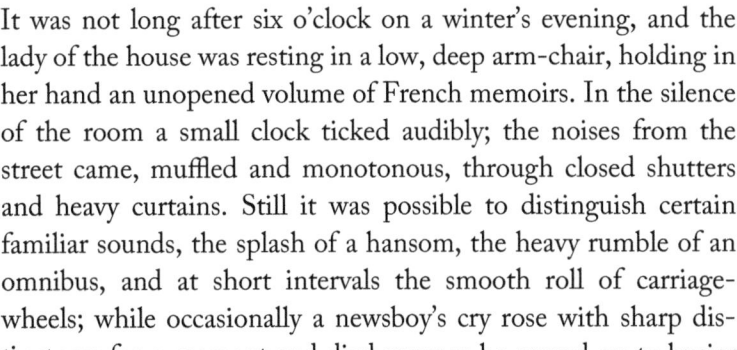

It was not long after six o'clock on a winter's evening, and the lady of the house was resting in a low, deep arm-chair, holding in her hand an unopened volume of French memoirs. In the silence of the room a small clock ticked audibly; the noises from the street came, muffled and monotonous, through closed shutters and heavy curtains. Still it was possible to distinguish certain familiar sounds, the splash of a hansom, the heavy rumble of an omnibus, and at short intervals the smooth roll of carriage-wheels; while occasionally a newsboy's cry rose with sharp distinctness for a moment and died away as he passed on to busier thoroughfares.

The lady of this house did not love the country in winter. She was fond of London, even of the sounds in the streets. They kept off the feeling of solitude which made the country so dreary in January and February. She was fond of her house, and of the drawing-room she was sitting in. It was long, low and narrow, rather too full of furniture and pretty things;—a heterogeneous collection which pointed to much travelling, sufficient money and some originality.

Yet, at first sight there was nothing original or artistic or markedly individual in the very correctly dressed woman in the arm-chair. Mrs. Hurstmonceaux was no longer young, no longer handsome,—if indeed she had ever been so,—no longer capable of being very natural or impulsive or thoughtless. She had not sunk into reverie in her solitude, and she was not unconscious of the ringing of the door bell, soon followed by the appearance of the footman and the announcement of "Ms. George Riversdale."

"Madge! How delightful!"

There was a gentle earnestness in the manner of the hostess. An inaudible greeting from the visitor followed; and then she flung her tiny person into the arm-chair which Mrs. Hurstmonceaux had just quitted.

"I am dead tired, Laura," she spoke with a quick uneven intonation; "I have had an odious afternoon."

"And so you have come here to be rested. How charming! That is treating a friend as a friend should be treated. But what have you been doing?"

"Going into mourning,—only half-mourning; but I had to get the things tried on to-day," said the little lady, closing her eyes.

"But for whom?" Laura threw into her manner a touch of prospective sympathy.

"My husband," said Madge, opening her eyes and sitting up abruptly.

"Your husband! But, my dear Madge!"

"Yes, I know, of course I went out of mourning long ago; and you have seen me in all the colours of the rainbow since; and a year and a bit was long enough, *considering*—" She paused and Laura echoed "considering," with the added emphasis of her impressive low tones.

"Considering," said Madge, taking up her word as though her friend had had no right to appropriate it," that I had not seen him for two years before that. All the same, just two years after his death I have been getting some exquisite half-mourning—fawns and violets are much better understood now than they used to be."

"And if *you* choose them," murmured the listener, "of course—"

"Clothes are my only talent, so you need not be jealous," Madge went on. "But it isn't every day that one finds people relapsing into mourning without fresh cause. I wonder you don't want to know the reason why."

"But I do," said Laura in a tone of delicate reserve.

"It is only because I am going to stay with his people, and I haven't the moral courage to go like this," and she looked down at her geranium cloth skirt and smiled.

A change almost too subtle to be described passed over her companion's face. It was only a slight contraction of delicate lines about the long narrow eyes, denoting an increase of interest and alertness at this announcement. She was sitting on a low chair, nearer to the fire than her visitor. She now turned towards her, as if expecting to hear more. But Madge was not inclined to say anything. She moved restlessly as Laura waited, first trying one arm of the chair and then the other to lean upon.

"You are really going to Skipton-le-Grange?" Laura asked at length.

"Yes, isn't it a bore? But I can't get out of it this time."

"Can't you?" Laura spoke thoughtfully, and turned her gaze to the fire. "Just now when all your friends are coming up and—"

Madge interrupted her quickly.

"I must go to Skipton; there are business things, money matters. I must see George's father—then it doesn't quite do to seem to have broken with them. They are letting the house in Portman Square to pay George's debts. I don't believe it is at all necessary, but that's not my affair. Any how the F—s are thinking of taking it, only the furniture is so old-fashioned. Lady F—told me there was nothing you could lie down upon. Imagine poor Lady F— sitting bolt upright for months like my mother-in-law. I told Lord F— I would see what could be done about the furniture. It would seem odd to them and to lots of people if they found out that I never see the Riversdales."

"My dear, that is very good and sweet of you, but you know everybody quite understands the state of the case. After the way your husband treated you, nobody—"

"Oh, my dear Laura, do let us leave all that alone. I don't mean to rake up skeletons this evening just because I am going to Skipton. It was far pleasanter to have George absent than George present, I assure you."

Madge gave a hard little laugh.

"But, Laura, tell me of some amusing novels to take to Skipton—something a little exciting will help me to pull through the time. Only the oldest housemaid is allowed to dust my French books, for fear of corruption. That reminds me. I have forgotten the candles. My candles used to be on an allowance of so many a week when we lived there. I must tell Celestine to take down a few pounds of candles and some scented soap."

Madge pulled a minute note-book out of her pocket and made notes in it, talking without intermission. Laura leaned back, wondering when she should be allowed to speak.

"I think I shall leave this book out for old Mother Riversdale's benefit: 'List of provisions for a visit to Skipton-le-Grange: soap, candles, cigarettes, *marrons glacés.*' *Le baiser de Juliette,* and a little more French fiction will give her shivers of righteous wrath all down her spine. Then she suffers agonies because of my maids. She is convinced that the worst quarters of Paris are ransacked to find me attendants of the lowest principles. I must take some claret for Celestine. It will be proof positive of her vicious propensities that she can't drink beer."

Laura had laughed noiselessly, but with polite appreciation, several times; she now tried again to speak.

"But besides this economical lady—"

Madge stopped her with a little shriek of derision.

"Economical! It is the most extravagant house in England. I could save two thousand a year in that house and make them twice as comfortable. The only thing that is properly managed is the stables, and now they are selling some of the hunters. It is such nonsense. If they would send away a few of the men who are eating their heads off in the house, and make the others work properly!—but half of them are too old to do anything, and the others are raw boys from the village. I believe the whole of that village lives upon Skipton in one way or another. Then the arrangements are made entirely to suit the housemaids and kitchenmaids. They must have time for Mass and for prayers and for Benediction, and for their own mending. No wonder it takes a round dozen of them to clean the house when their time is as full up as if they lived in a convent."

"But, Madge, who is there besides housemaids? Will you be alone with Mr. and Mrs. Riversdale? I thought people of that sort always had enormous families."

"I believe there were several children who died; she would manage them all herself, and she said the great thing was to harden them. Anyhow it was dreadfully muddled, and George, the eldest, and Mary, the youngest, were the only two who grew up under the Riversdale system of rearing."

Madge's face darkened as she spoke, and she went on in an angry tone.

"The Riversdales have no constitutions. I believe the race is worn out. They have grazed on at Skipton since the twelfth century, and the dulness of it has got into their bones. Elizabeth gave them a little excitement by hanging one at Tyburn and putting his son into the Tower for life. But since then, except for hunting, they've done nothing, nothing, nothing. There are two of George's uncles alive, but they are both priests. Mary is heir to the whole thing, as," her voice became more metallic, "as my baby girl died."

Laura looked a sympathy which was not accepted. Madge jumped up suddenly and walked to the fireplace.

"Yes, there will be Mary and one girl cousin; they are both to come out at the hunt ball. My mother-in-law is evidently afraid that I have accepted for next week, so as to go with them to the dance. But I've passed the days when I used to enjoy those balls. She has always had a grudge against me on the subject since the first ball in the county after I married. Oh, dear, how funny it was! First of all she was in a great fidget when we started, because she thought my dress too *décolletée*. Then she kept giving me hints that in really aristocratic circles it was not the custom for a bride to dance except with her husband. But as George had refused to come with us, she couldn't make much of that. When we got there," Madge's eyes sparkled with pleasure now and she laughed merrily, "Mrs. Riversdale began solemnly presenting me to the great ladies of the neighbourhood, very kindly, but just letting them see that she only wished I was somebody else with more connections to talk about. Well, in the midst of this delightful way of enjoying the ball, who should arrive but the B—s, and royalty with them. Of course I got among their party in a moment, and had a real good time. I could die of laughing now when I think of Mrs. Riversdale's face as she sat by old Lady Archibourne while I waltzed by with Prince A. to whom she had not even been presented."

Laura smiled indulgently, but she had had enough of this chatter.

"And why do you choose next week?" she asked. Her tone was firm and decided; she would get an answer.

"I told you," said Madge weakly.

Laura shrugged her shoulders incredulously—then she went on:—

"There are quite a number of nice things next week, the tableaux at Little Goreham House and the P—'s ball. It is just the time when London is at its nicest *I* think. By the way, I heard from a friend of yours to-day who is coming up on Monday; he says—"

Laura turned to a carved bureau behind her and opened a drawer. A quick colour came and went in Madge's face, but she did not speak.

"I can't find it, I must have left it downstairs," which was mendacious, if necessary, as she had never intended to show the letter that lay before her.

"You mean Lord Bellasis?" said Madge. She was warming her feet at the fire and her back was turned to Laura. "I know he is coming up on Monday; I was asked to meet him at dinner next week at the Duchess of A.'s, but I said I should be at Skipton."

Laura's face for a moment betrayed her surprise.

What did it mean? Had she been mistaken in thinking that Madge—but no, Madge had frankly owned how much she wished Lord Bellasis would come to London. Perhaps she had been too frank, perhaps after all—

But it was very tiresome that Madge should be such a fool, after this letter from Lord Bellasis too; it was really exceedingly provoking.

"I must be off," said Madge, moving a few steps away from the fireplace.

"Oh, no, my dear Madge, it is quite early. We have not half done our talk, you must stay."

"I must go, on the contrary," said Madge. "I have got a splitting headache. I went to that funeral this afternoon."

"Then I don't wonder. How very foolish! My dear, why did you go? You didn't know her well, and she was not even of your religion. I thought you Roman Catholics didn't go to services in other churches unless it was necessary."

"Oh, yes, we go to weddings and funerals. I was at her wedding a year ago. Isn't life short, Laura? You grow up and you marry and you die."

"Well, I haven't died yet," said Laura, "and we shouldn't like to say how long it is since our wedding day. This death was a sad accident, and you and other young women make yourselves quite nervous over it. You should read a few statistics, that would cheer you up."

Madge was standing in front of Laura, holding her sable muff up to her chin with both hands, her attitude betraying complete inattention to what was said. The grey eyes, with long lashes, the eyebrows perhaps artificially darkened, looked more thoughtful and a little softer than usual.

"The baby was buried with her," she said in a dreamy voice, "and I think she was a good little woman. She will have the baby back directly she has done her Purgatory. Was the baby baptised?"

The last question was an abrupt addition and was really addressed to Laura.

"I haven't the faintest notion. My dear Madge, do not for heaven's sake become morbid. I am sure you are not well, and if you go down to that horrid place you won't be fit to speak to afterwards."

Madge laughed, and suddenly straightened herself. She shook her head.

"On the contrary I shall be so thankful to get away, and oh, Laura, I nearly forgot the books. You always know the best ones. Give me something, do."

"Well, here is a new one of Gyp's. I've not read it yet. And here's something by a man I never heard of before. You are sure to like it. It is so fine, penetrating, delicate—not over moral perhaps, but tenderly treated, nothing to shock or startle."

"Thank you, dear, that will do beautifully. Come and look me up to-morrow. I go on Monday. Good-night."

Madge gave Laura half a kiss and walked to the door, then turned round and said: "Will Cecilia Rupert be up next week?"

"Yes." Laura spoke eagerly. "Lord Bellasis tells me that he has heard from her. She will be back in London on Monday."

"Oh," Madge hesitated. "Oh, well, I forget what I was going to say. How absurd! Good night, Laura."

After the door was closed, Laura moved impatiently back to her chair. She was too consciously dignified to let herself appear "fussed" or "flurried," but those conditions were really hers.

"I did think she had more sense. I can't think what she is up to. I don't know what nonsense or notion of making herself interesting that sort of silly little woman gets into her head."

Laura lay back for some minutes, but her thinking soon ceased to be explicit. Her instincts were at play round the question she wanted to solve. At last she looked up with a little glow upon her face. She had got the *mot de l'énigme* that she was seeking for, and although it was not a satisfactory solution, she preferred it to the humiliation of feeling puzzled.

"It is religious—I am sure it is religious. That little Mrs. Wakefield's death upset her. She has got a fright as to her own thin little soul. She is going down to Skipton to give it a sort of spring cleaning, to put it in order and to make it comfortable. I really don't know that it much matters. I will ask Lord Bellasis to come and have a talk. Perhaps he will dine with me on Monday—that would be easier, on the whole, than writing a letter to explain things."

CHAPTER II

UNRIPE YEARS

Another widow of the house of Riversdale, but of the previous generation, was much occupied with preparations for the hunt ball of which Madge had spoken. Mrs. Arthur Riversdale was not going to stay at Skipton-le-Grange herself, but she was sending thither her daughter Hilda, who was to come out at the hunt ball with Mary, the squire's daughter. The two first cousins, the only Riversdales of their generation, were to make their appearance together; and whatever was felt about the matter at Skipton-le-Grange, there was no doubt that excitement prevailed at Brierley Cottage, the little Sussex home of the widow and her daughter.

Mrs. Arthur Riversdale was at this time verging upon middle age. She was nervous, delicate and emotional, and these characteristics were clearly discernible in her thin dark face. The high, well-constructed forehead pointed to an intellectual descent; but a certain indecision in the lines of the mouth indicated that physical strength had probably been lacking to full mental development.

Janet Riversdale was the daughter of James Harding, a critic and essayist of considerable repute, who had lived amongst men greater than himself, and had helped not a little to make them known and understood. At Cambridge he had belonged to a set many members of which had attained in later years to eminence in politics and letters. And his college associates had remained life-long friends.

James Harding's father, the dean of a southern cathedral, had educated him in Broad Church principles, of the Rugby stamp; and James had gradually widened into the degree of tolerance and the kindly indifference to all forms of creed that marked so many of the disciples of Dr. Arnold. He encouraged his daughter Janet and her sister to contemplate all that was good and beautiful in any religion, nor was he much distressed when the outcome of such liberty was, in Janet's case, the passing through a course of Newman's writings to submission to the Church of Rome. At the time when this change took place, Janet's mother had been dead for some years, and her father was living, in a house in Eaton Square, a liberal, hospitable existence, without pretension, but with the full enjoyment of the society of many friends of intellectual and artistic tastes. At the studio of a Roman Catholic artist, with whom her change of religion naturally made her intimate, Janet met Arthur Riversdale, the specimen of a type entirely new to her. To her father's intense astonishment, she fell in love with the tall, large limbed, sunny-faced young man, with whom he himself had not two ideas in common. He supposed, and probably in part rightly, that Janet's enthusiasm for all and everything Catholic had thrown a halo round the youth, who was undoubtedly fervent in his religion.

But, even without this link to draw them together, there was nothing in the attachment that ought to have surprised those who looked on.

"Arthur Riversdale is a proper man, a well-built man, has a fine open face, and, although he is simple, he has the manners of a man of very good stock. What are you wondering at, James Harding?"

Such had been the comment of a great authority among them, as he blew clouds of smoke from his pipe in the long library in Eaton Square.

If Janet had some reason to complain of want of sympathy over her engagememt, Arthur had far more coldness to put up with in his own family. He was the youngest. His parents were dead, and his brothers and sisters were all settled in life. Two of his brothers had become priests, three sisters were nuns, and two had married. His eldest brother, George, had been in possession of the very large family property for some years, and lived with his young wife—who belonged to another Catholic family, the Lemarchants of Lancashire—at Skipton-le-Grange. Arthur had never felt the want of a home. He had always been welcome to come and go as he chose at Skipton. He was devoted to George, and he was amused by his pretty sister-in-law, who ruled and mothered him in a tiresome but kindly way. Then, too, he had been drawn to her by her unsparing devotion to another brother, who had died of a painful and lingering illness, following on an accident in the hunting-field.

To the squire, and to his wife, through him, Arthur wrote in the joy of his heart to announce his engagement to Miss Harding, and the news was received with consternation. The squire told his wife at breakfast, and she could not restrain her wrath; in fact her speech flowed on in such an agitated way that her husband could hardly get in a word of explanation.

"Arthur engaged, and nobody had heard a word about it! Hardings! Who had ever heard of the Hardings? Who were they?"

Helen wished her husband would read the letter more quickly. She was sure she didn't know of any Catholic Hardings. Good heavens! Was it possible that this girl was not a Catholic? No, a convert! A convert!

"Oh, my dear, a new convert, just made a Catholic! Of course she has done it to marry Arthur. How shocking!"

What could be done? George must go up to London and break the engagement off at once; it could not be allowed. What dreadful news at breakfast, and just that morning when she had been so worried. Baby was not so well, and the new housemaid had arrived with a fringe, and had tried to hide it under her cap before she came to Mass—*so* deceitful. And now George would go on reading the letter to himself and would not tell her who these designing Hardings were. A granddaughter of Dean Harding—and a dean, wasn't that a kind of Protestant clergyman? How could Arthur have got among such people? And her father wrote books. Good gracious! And what sort of books? "Essays on Criticism." How shocking and unbelieving they must be! This was worse and worse. And poor Arthur really wanted to marry this girl? etc., etc., till the pretty little face behind the great silver hot-water urn puckered into tears, and the big tender-hearted squire had to leave his coffee at the other end of the table, to avert with unfailing tact and some assertion of authority, a crying fit which might lead to serious consequences.

Although the squire himself was almost as much annoyed at this engagement as was his wife, he insisted on their concealing their feelings in their letters to Arthur. However, quite enough was betrayed in the studied words in which "good wishes" were far more prominent than congratulations, for Janet to read a good deal between the lines. Still there was nothing wanting in either outward civility or munificent presents; and in those days it seemed quite natural that the squire should not bring his wife up to the wedding. It was not until they had been married over six months that Arthur and Janet paid their first visit to Skipton.

Janet arrived in a mood not to be trifled with, and Arthur thought her unreasonable to be dissatisfied with a reception that to the masculine mind was cordiality itself. But Janet's perceptions were quicker, and, in spite of the kindness to Arthur's wife, she was by no means satisfied with the attitude taken up towards her father's daughter. Then, too, she was constantly lectured by her sister-in-law on her duties as a Catholic.

One little scene will suffice to show what soon became the relations between the sisters-in-law in those early days.

Unfortunately one wet afternoon they were left to themselves, and the hostess thought it a good opportunity to say a few things which were in her mind, to Arthur's wife. The difficulty was how to begin with tact.

Had Janet, she asked, seen this week's *Tablet?* There was something in it about a book Janet had got upstairs, *Adam Bede.* Wouldn't Janet like to see what was said about it? Of course Janet could have no idea how wicked it was. Would she look at the notice, and then she was sure she would agree that they had better fetch the book and burn it?

To this Janet replied that she had seen the review and that it was very narrow and unfair.

Helen, bending a little flushed over her needlework, was sure Janet would forgive her for saying that of course she didn't know that it was a mortal sin to read a book like that.

Janet, leaning back and lolling in a way that was intolerable to her companion, got a little flushed also, but remained silent.

Of course, Helen explained, converts couldn't be taught everything at once, and now that they were alone she was sure Janet would let her observe that it was much better to make her morning meditation in the chapel before Mass—nobody could do it quite so well after breakfast.

Janet still remaining silent, Helen hoped she wouldn't mind her telling her about indulgences. Of course Janet didn't know—converts never did know—how many indulgences you could get in the year if you did things on the right days.

But here Janet looked up from her book and interrupted Helen. She didn't think Helen knew that she had a director who was quite satisfied on these points, and she would rather leave the matter to him.

"But then Arthur says you go to confession to Father Newman, and if you don't mind, Janet, my saying so, you know he was a Protestant clergyman, and he can't quite know."

"But I do mind very much," said Janet, rising and holding her tall, thin figure to its full height, "and now, as I am very tired, I am going upstairs to lie down and finish *Adam Bede.*"

"My husband never allows me to read any novels," murmured the indignant Helen, "and I shall speak to him and ask him to speak to Arthur."

At this threat Janet smiled in an aggravating manner and left the room.

Hilda was born in that year, and she has grown since then to be eighteen years old, and she is to go to Skipton as a grown-up young lady. How little look the trifles of disagreement, of annoyance, now, as her mother glances backward through the mist of years; how great and engulfing the sorrows that brought her to a deeper, fuller heart.

If the Riversdales had thought Janet an unequal match for Arthur—if they had shown some worldly contempt and some sectarian prejudices—who else had so truly mourned with Janet his early death? Who else had been so generous in coming to her help when James Harding died, and it was found that his large careless way of living had left his daughters, not only without the considerable fortune that had been expected, but with next to nothing to live upon? Janet, too, on her side had found room in a broken heart for the sorrows of the Riversdales. She had grieved with them over the strange, persistent visiting of the angel of death in the nursery at Skipton. She had shared those terrible and sacred sorrows which had faded Helen's young beauty so quickly, and drawn lines of pathetic resignation round the squire's strong mouth and large blue eyes.

Less easy, less simple to sympathise with, was the greatest trouble of all. For those little children were gone for a very short time, and it often seemed to both the parents that they had not gone far away. In moments after communion, moments when they knelt together alone before the Blessed Sacrament, they felt that those four boys and girls and one tiny baby were about them still. Under the chapel in the vault below lay those short coffins, and our Blessed Lady kept the spotless souls ever in her sight. The simple parents had been willing to bear with Janet's sympathy, and were grateful for kind thoughts, kind words, and best of all for faithful prayers for the father and mother on the anniversaries of the children's death. But when George, the only son, grew up to be a source of incessant anxiety and miserable perplexity, and at last became an open shame, what sympathy could be delicate enough to be offered them?

The story of young George Riversdale was a family tragedy never to be forgotten. Much had been hoped from his possible marriage with some girl of high principle and strong character. Such hopes were disappointed, and he had taken to himself a wife from a far country—morally speaking at least.

During a visit to Scotland—six years before the commencement of this narrative—George had made friends with a family which was notable for its great wealth, due to successful commerce in Liverpool. The O'Reillys were of Irish extraction, and consequently traditional Roman Catholics, though practically and personally their creed was chiefly concerned with Mammon. Their second daughter, Madge, or Midget, as she was sometimes called from her minute proportions, had received her education in a foreign convent of the first rank. There the beauty and refinement of her outward woman had been duly developed. Her French education and her Celtic descent combined to perfection, and produced a strange variation in the Liverpool merchant's family. Yet there was enough to excuse the Riversdales for their dislike to the connection; and George pleaded in vain that the O'Reillys had of late associated with some of the best families in Scotland. Neither this undeniable fact, nor the bride's large fortune, consoled his parents. In their eyes the girl was not only without antecedents, but was weak and frivolous. Her ways and standards were those of a section of the modern world which was unknown to them, and were ascribed by them entirely to her birth and her character. She was no good wife for a son whom they already unwillingly recognised as himself so unstable in character and so much in need of guidance. But seeing that the marriage was inevitable, they behaved in what they thought the most cordial manner. Mrs. Riversdale determined that this unfortunate little O'Reilly girl should live with them so soon as she became Mrs. George, and then she could teach her new daughter-in-law how to be a fervent Catholic and a lady. The results of such a family arrangement may be imagined; but the episode of Madge's early married life at Skipton is for our purposes prehistoric, and need not be further dwelt upon here.

The arrangement had not lasted, and George's subsequent ill conduct and ultimate desertion of his wife, his death in scandalous surroundings, without a priest, and with no message of sorrow left for his widow, had added bitterness on all sides to the memories associated with the union between George Riversdale and Madge O'Reilly.

None had felt more deeply for his parents than Janet. But what could be said to give them comfort? What words could be framed which would not rather keep the wound open?

A little silence then had grown up between Skipton-le-Grange and Brierly Cottage in the time of mourning for George; and both sides were glad when an opportunity arose which made it natural to renew the family intercourse. Such an opportunity was the revival of social meetings at the family house, and the assembling of a party there for the hunt ball.

After thirteen years of seclusion, of a life spent partly in a round of religious duties, partly in a dream world, not much tried by the smallness of her fortune (for her wants were few), Mrs. Arthur was attempting to face the fact that she had a grown-up daughter, a tall, and in her eyes, a beautiful girl, "a maid whom there were few to know, and very few to love," in the quiet Sussex neighbourhood.

On the Saturday afternoon before the Monday on which Hilda was to start for Skipton, her mother went to lie down on the sofa in her bedroom, being under the impression that by so doing she could materially assist in the preparations for Hilda's journey.

It was the largest and most attractive room in the house, and one of the two big windows, reaching almost from floor to ceiling, afforded a wide view of the downs. Within, the room had a charm of its own not easily to be described. The colouring was subdued and not specially artistic. The dimity curtains were clean but not beautiful. The furniture was old-fashioned and stiff. The tables were littered with books, papers and vases of flowers in a careless medley. Yet there was about it an atmosphere of sentiment, of reminiscence, of mental refinement. And it had its treasures. A water-colour by Richmond of Arthur Riversdale in his red coat; a sketch of James Harding reading aloud, by Thackeray; amateur photographs that could only have come from one camera; little scraps in water-colour by no unskilled hands; there "a sunset touch," here "a fancy from a flower bell,—" who has not known and loved such a room, where nothing is a mere ornament, and everything that catches the eye is a living relic of love and happiness?

After she had lain for a few moments on the big, chintz-covered, square-limbed sofa, Janet noticed that an unfinished letter to her sister lay on the table by her side. She called to the maid who was packing Hilda's things in the next room, and sent her to fetch her writing board from the drawing-room. The letter had been begun a week before, and had been forgotten till now. She lay back and wrote as follows:—

> So it is all decided at last, and I am very thankful. It is far best for Hilda to come out at her father's home and at the same time with Mary. I think it is quite generous of the Riversdales to suggest this, for although Mary is a great heiress, and Hilda no heiress at all, there can be no comparison in appearance, still less in mind. But I suspect you may smile at this bit of maternal vanity, so I won't enlarge upon it. I know you think I ought to go with her, but indeed I cannot do it, Elaine. For me to go to a ball party, and now, when so few people keep their weeds, would appear quite singular. Later on it may be necessary for me to do something. I might take Hilda to Rome, or there might be a few weeks in London, if we could afford it. But then whom should we see? All papa's friends are scattered now, and, you know, except the H—s there were no Catholics among them.
>
> Though it is so painful to us to part, and the child is most anxious that I should go with her, I can't but think it is a good thing to have a short separation. Our *tête-à-tête* life has its drawbacks, although we are everything in the world to each other. If we are not always inclined to say all that is in our minds, we appear to be reserved, and then a little feeling grows up which is not good. The child is changing, she cannot help it; she is beginning to feel her feet, to want to walk by herself, and she does not quite know why or how to

do it. Although she still grumbles a little at my not allowing her to go to Newnham, I think she is hankering after more frivolous things than she will acknowledge. The fact is she doesn't know what she wants, or what to be at just now, and she resents being watched or analysed. Do you remember Adonis' half-angry cry to Venus?

Fair Lady, if that any love you owe me Measure my strangeness by my unripe years, Before I know myself, seek not to know me.

But don't think she is less loving and careful of me than she ever was. She is thinking now of all sorts of little plans to keep me amused while she is away. Only I want you to understand why it seems better to let the duckling get a swim by itself, and where could it be safer than at Skipton?

Thank you for telling me of that stupid rumour as to Hilda's supposed expectations. I could wish for the child's sake that it had become generally known how completely all our father's fortune had melted. I suppose people don't know that he only had a life interest in what his uncle left him. All the rest of his income came from the *Times* and his books. As you went abroad and nobody saw me after his death, the error is not surprising.

Here the letter was suddenly interrupted, again to be put on one side and forgotten. A little rustle was heard at the door, a hasty knock, and then a tall girl walked into the room, dressed in a white tulle ball gown, followed by a little, wrinkled, elderly woman, who held up the skirt with one hand and raised the other in indignant protest.

"Now, Miss Hilda, if you would but move quietly; you nearly caught it on the door; it won't be fit to be seen."

Hilda, with her little head erect, her eyes sparkling, and her dark rosy colouring flushed with excitement, paid no heed to these remonstrances.

"Do you approve of me, mother? Brown, do let go and let me curtsy. I want to show mother how the tulle swells out all round me. There, I don't do it badly." Then moving to the glass: "Really I stand a white frock in the daytime better than I expected."

Mrs. Riversdale gazed at her anxiously but proudly.

"Dear child, do stand still," but though the words were repressive, the eyes shone with sympathy. She saw a little shyness, a little pride in Hilda's face, a little wonder at her own excitement, which gave a touch of distinction to the bearing of the tall young figure.

The child seemed half ashamed of showing herself off even here, and she blushed as the parlourmaid brought in the letters which had come by the afternoon post. But Mrs. Arthur could by no means give any attention to the letters at this crisis. Sitting upright on the sofa, she was wondering, fearing, that perhaps one bow of white ribbon was too large.

"I am almost afraid that it's a little—in fact I think—it is—not quite—"

Brown, the old maid, and general referee, waited for further light to be vouchsafed her, and Hilda gave a little wriggle. The short wintry daylight would soon be gone; the sun was setting behind the great ridge of the down, and sending its pure, rosy light through the west window of the bedroom. The radiance gave a touch of colour to the transparent white material of the ball-gown. It lay caressingly for a moment on Hilda's long arms and beautifully moulded neck. It lit up her small irregular features, and was reflected in the depths of the large brown eyes. No wonder if the mother was silent for a moment as she looked at her, and kept them waiting for an explanation of her doubts. Leaning back at length, as though she had come to a final decision—

"I really think that sash is a little exaggerated," she said firmly. "I wish they had not sent the gown down so late."

"But, oh, mother," cried Hilda, suddenly stepping forward so as really to endanger the white folds about her feet, "look at the letters. It is Skipton-le-Grange note-paper; I do hope nothing has gone wrong."

Her mother turned to the parlourmaid who was forming her own opinion of the ball-gown, and took the letter from the salver.

"It is from Skipton; it must be something about your train," she said.

After the first glance Janet's face changed. She read the letter to the end, and then turned to her daughter with a troubled countenance.

"You had better take the frock off now, my child, and leave me for a little while."

"Mother, do just tell me, is it anything about the ball?"

Mrs. Arthur hesitated.

"I am so sorry, darling, but Lord Archibourne is dead and there is to be no hunt ball."

Hilda bit her lip and pressed her long fingers together. There was a moment's silence.

"What a bore; but never mind, mother, you know I was dreadfully shy about it. But what a pity to have got such an expensive dress," and the voice rose plaintively; "it will be quite old-fashioned by next year."

"Oh, my dear, I hope you will use it long before next year. Run and take it off now, and, darling, give me one kiss. I am so very sorry."

Hilda bent over her mother for one quick kiss and was glad to get away without having to speak in too broken a voice.

"Though where mother supposes I shall dance before next year I can't imagine," she thought. "Poor mother, she minds it more than I do. I don't really so very much care."

She pulled the frock off a little roughly, and when Brown remonstrated, asked her what it could matter now, and began to rub cheeks, already suspiciously wet, with a cold sponge, regardless of future effects on her complexion.

Having replaced the glories of the fresh white tulle by workaday, plainly made, blue serge, she ran down the short flight of stairs two steps at a time, crossed the little hall into the drawing-room and threw herself into an arm-chair by the fireplace.

"Oh dear, oh dear. It *is* a bore," she cried, "and if there is to be no ball, I suppose it will be only the regular Skipton lot. Aunt

Helen will take me to the school," she was half crying, half laughing as she spoke, "and Mary will let me help her to arrange the sacristy. I don't think I shall enjoy it half as much now as I did going with mother to visit her great poet last autumn. I am quite sure that, with the exception of papa, the Riversdales are the dullest family in England. I know it's quite true, as mother says, one ought to admire them—their pluck and their faith and all that—but then they've got all that in the blood. I wonder if I've got it in the blood too. Oh dear," she got up, heaved a deep sigh, and looked up at a portrait in oils of her father which hung over the mantelpiece, "I wonder if it's heresy to think that perhaps one's own father was a little dull. Of course mother was in love with him, and so she thought he was perfection. But I don't know what there is to prove that he was unlike all the other Riversdales.

"I don't think mother's right about the sash," she went on. "I suspect it is exactly the fashion—though," with a sharp sigh, "that doesn't much matter now. A plain white satin sash cannot manage to be vulgar—or 'not quite'. I wonder if Valerie is *quite* as good a dressmaker as she was when mother was in London fifteen years ago. Those Freemantle girls, who came in to tea the other day, seemed very smart, but they had not even heard of her. They said they weren't sure that they knew of all the good dressmakers in London, however. One does want to be well dressed at Skipton. Though Aunt Helen dresses Mary so badly, she is very critical about other people. But after all, mother's taste is very good, though it may not be fashionable. She is dreadfully disappointed at my not getting to the ball, but I wonder why she told me to leave her alone. I hope there is nothing else wrong in the letter. Oh dear, such is life!"

More than half an hour passed after Hilda left her mother's room, and during that time the widow was leaning back almost motionless—re-reading the letter between long pauses of reflection.

It was written in a small, flowing, and yet precise handwriting, and was to the following effect:—

My dear Janet,

I have to tell you of a blow for our young people as well as a sorrow for ourselves. Lord Archibourne has died of the results of his accident in the hunting-field, and we shall miss him as a good, upright neighbour, although, poor man, a Protestant. It would hardly seem right to have a hunt ball so soon after this, and so it is given up. I am afraid this will be a disappointment to Hilda—but I hope she will come and stay with us all the same.

Of course for myself it is a relief, as I had dreaded going into the world again. But as it is two years since our beloved son died, I do not think it right to keep Mary, now that she is nineteen, shut up any longer;—not that she, poor child, has any wish for gaiety. Anyhow the ball is put off, and the question settled for us, so we have also given up our house party. Another trial, however, cannot be avoided, and I think it right to tell you of this before you send your girl to us. Mr. Riversdale again desired me to invite dearest George's widow to come to Skipton, and she has chosen this very week. I cannot think that she can wish to see us, but it is possible that, though she thought so little of the baby's death at the time, she may wish to visit the vault where it lies. For the first time I do not regret that George is not buried here. But I must not dwell on my feelings, and we must hope that her coming is a sign of grace. I am trying to get Father Clement to meet her, as he used to do her so much good.

Now you see it will not be very amusing for Hilda, but besides Madge, there will be my nephew, Marmaduke Lemarchant, who is a dear good fellow as you know. His father and his mother have seen the mistake of sending him into the army, which is not at all a safe career for any young man, but they have at last persuaded him to live at home, which is the proper place for the eldest son. I don't want to say anything unkind about Madge, and I daresay it wouldn't do any harm if she and Hilda did make friends. We shall expect Hilda to arrive at Skipton by the four o'clock train, unless you write to the contrary, and remember she must change at Crowby.

Your affectionate sister-in-law,
HELEN RIVERSDALE.

If Madge could have known that her mother-in-law thought it necessary to warn Mrs. Arthur of her corrupting presence at Skipton, how amused yet how angry she would have been. And yet Mrs. Arthur did, in fact, take it so seriously that it was touch and go during that half-hour of reflection whether Hilda was or was not to be allowed to go to Skipton. As there would be no ball this week and Mrs. George would be there, might it not be better to put off the visit until a little later in the year?

Now, neither of these good ladies held a bad opinion of what the world would call Madge's character. They would both have been shocked if any scandalous interpretation had been put on their disapproval of her ways and her manners; and Mrs. Arthur at least had soon become sincerely compassionate towards the poor little woman, for she had no maternal delusions on the subject of George's domestic life. Still, abstract sympathy was one thing; to throw Hilda, who had always had a girlish fancy for Madge, into her society, at a time when she was most open to influence, was another. Janet would of all things have disliked her girl to adopt the standards of a set in which she, in her old-fashioned way, considered social "smartness" to be combined with moral vulgarity.

The long mental colloquy ended however in the decision that Hilda was to go to Skipton to join the diminished party which was to meet there on Monday.

The last evening before Janet and Hilda were to part for a whole week was fraught with specially complicated sentiments and tender suffering on the mother's part. Hilda herself was half surprised at the degree to which she "minded" the prospect of parting, and tried to conceal this after a youthful and unnecessary fashion. Janet had planned last words, little bits of advice, a general effort at breaking through her own reserve. For one great mistake in her method of education had of late been growing clear to her. While she had not maintained any intellectual reserve with Hilda, and their sense of humour had run in the same channels and enjoyed the same contrasts, she had been strictly reticent concerning her own feelings, the deeper sources of her life, the real consolations of her widowhood and the depth of the wound in her heart. She had intended to speak of Arthur this evening, and twice, with a beating heart, she had almost said:—"How much your father would have enjoyed taking you to come out at Skipton, darling;" and twice Hilda had prevented her, once by some little joke about Brown's view of the visit, and once by a sharp sigh of regret for the ball, and a sudden suggestion that she should not go at all. Skipton would be too deadly dull, and Aunt Helen would expect her to sit bolt upright with some plain needlework when she wasn't in the chapel. The collapse of the ball made it harder for Mrs. Arthur to invest the last evening with due dignity —it was spoiled as an event, a crisis in life, and she could not raise those final hours above the trivial.

But when Hilda had at last gone to bed, Janet knelt down on the *prie dieu* by her bedside, and prayed with a fervour perhaps as great as if she had actually known that the child was leaving her for many weeks instead of a few days, and was to see a good deal more of life in those weeks than her mother had done in as many years. On the wall above her head, and just below a large crucifix, there hung a little letter in a black frame. It had been written to congratulate Hilda's parents on her birth, which had taken place on the Feast of the Transfiguration, and it held in a few words all that Janet prayed for, for her only child.

"I earnestly pray," wrote Father Newman, "that the festival on which she was born may overshadow her all through her life, and that she may find it 'good to be here,' till that time of blessed transfiguration when she will find from experience that it is better to be in heaven."

CHAPTER III

MEETING AT A JUNCTION

On the same Monday—a bright February morning—on which Hilda started for Skipton, Marmaduke Lemarchant was leaning back in a smoking carriage of a train going south from Carlisle. His deeply sunburnt, regular features had a military look. His whole bearing produced an effect of strength, both moral and physical. He saw with great satisfaction that, as he got nearer to Crowby Junction, he was leaving behind the frozen snow that had covered the country round his Lancashire home. Some good days with the hounds at Skipton, which lay in one of the best hunting districts in England, was a fascinating prospect after seven winters in India. His jolliest recollections of winters in the past had been the hunting days spent with Uncle George Riversdale.

When the train reached Crowby, the sleepy little country junction was almost empty, and a porter hurried up as if glad of occupation. He recognised Marmaduke and said that he supposed he must be for the Skipton line.

"Hullo, Timmins," said Marmaduke, "how are you? I thought I didn't see you at Skipton when I passed through in the summer. Will you take out my things? I'm bringing two horses and a groom by the next train." And as a few minutes later they met again on the farther platform, Marmaduke inquired how the old man had come there. "I suppose you've left Skipton Station for promotion?"

"Yes," answered Timmins modestly, "but I don't know as I'm particularly satisfied. I miss the old friends, I do, sir. I miss seeing Miss Mary and the squire riding by or coming back by train after the hunting. It's a mistake that going away from home. We are glad to hear, sir, if I may make bold to mention it, that you've given up the army, sir. Mrs. Riversdale, she told my missis, that you was settling down now. She didn't hold with young men going into the army. She says no one in the family had done it before. They used to bide at home. Why, I can recollect meself," here Timmins paused a moment and waved his hand in a general way at the surrounding country, "I can recollect soon after the squire married—there weren't no line to Skipton then—he was out hunting about here on a Friday, and three of his brothers with him, and six of his brothers-in-law, Squire Lemarchant, your father, at the head of them. Only two of 'em all was under six foot. A finer set of men you could hardly see, and not one of 'em had more than a couple of hard-boiled eggs in his pocket, and jolly? why," the old man chuckled hilariously, "I could hear them singing down the lanes a couple of miles off. There was no need for them to be agoing into the army. Much better stay at home and keep quiet, sir, and get married."

Marmaduke smiled a little sadly.

"Do you ever run over to Skipton Station now, Timmins?"

"Why, I was over there only yesterday, I was, and who should I see riding along but the squire. He holds himself wonderful for his years."

Timmins paused to take breath and then rambled on:—

"Wonderful upright surely; he was riding that big brown mare of his that the grooms are afraid of. You know her, sir?"

"Queen Bess?" suggested Marmaduke.

"Aye, that's the one, I'd almost forgotten that joke, When they told the squire that that mare gave more trouble than all the horses put together, 'Call her Queen Bess,' says he, 'she did more mischief than any other woman in England.' He will have his joke, will the squire. But, as I thought to myself yesterday, somehow he isn't the same since Mr. George's death. Though he called out hearty and asked for my missis, when I looked up at him he didn't look hearty in the eyes one bit. We all must have our troubles, mustn't we, sir? Now in spite of all Mrs. Timmins and I did for our sons, we had our black sheep—you'd remember Bob, sir. Well he got into bad company down the line, but we felt his death all the same. But I must be off to the other side. I'll be back for the Skipton train."

And he shuffled off, muttering uneasy apologies in his beard, for his too plain speaking on family matters.

The half smile in Marmaduke's dark eyes died away as the old man left him.

"I'm afraid he is right. They can't forget that scamp George. It will spoil even the hunting season to his father."

He sighed impatiently, and proceeded to light a cigarette.

"No time for a cigar," he thought, "only two minutes before Madge's train is due."

He turned to stroll along the ash footpath at the end of the platform.

"And so Timmins kindly reports the approbation of Skipton and its opinion of my future," he mused. "I am to be quiet and settle down and keep to the old ways. Hunt whenever I can, say my prayers, fast and abstain, and keep as good and as jolly as my uncles and great-uncles before me. They were good enough, and jolly enough, but as to serving their country or being of use in the world,—good Lord! Dear old chaps, it never entered their heads. A man might be called to be a priest or he had duties if he had a property or a wife and family, but to go and look for something to do was entirely superfluous as well as rather *infra dig.* for a man of birth."

He sighed and went on:—

"So now I am quite the good boy, giving up the army and its sinful ways, and Timmins pats me on the back. While, hang it all, what wouldn't I give to be with the regiment again. But it is no use. 'Dooty, dooty,' as Sergeant Macalister told me, when he couldn't walk straight, 'takes one man one way and another t'other way.' But at one thing I draw the line. I cannot marry to please Timmins or anybody else. I am pretty sure that Aunt Helen meant me for some young lady who was to have been at

Skipton for the ball. We have escaped each other this time. One must make the best of life, and there's no doubt the frost here has broken. Be hanged to old Timmins and all the stupid things he has made me think of."

Before Marmaduke had finished his cigarette and before he had thrown off the fit of musing which Timmins had induced, some bustle on a farther platform announced the train from the South. He went on with his walk without distraction, until he perceived that a tall young lady with a maid had crossed over to the Skipton side of the station, and was also walking up and down, under cover. As he came to the end of the pathway, she reached the end of the stone flags and their eyes met for a second before they turned their backs on each other.

"Pretty," he reflected, "though not smart."

Yet he quickened his step until, at the end of the path, he might turn round naturally. She also had turned, and was now standing at the little book-stall, too far off for him to see her properly; but the effect was good at a distance. She was tall, and when she moved on he noticed that she walked well. She wore a long red cloak and a high black hat of gipsy shape; her hair blew in short curls about her face; there seemed to him something familiar in the irregular features. As he drew nearer, recognition was unmistakable in her dark brown eyes—but eyes not so dark as his own, for they had a golden light in them. She held out her hand.

"Don't you know me, Cousin Marmaduke?" she asked hesitatingly.

"Hilda, of course," he cried.

But it was a little disappointing. Here was no interesting stranger, but only one of the family, whom he had known as a child. There was nothing to carry for her but two books. He took these, and walked along the ash path by her side.

"What heavy books!" he exclaimed. "What are they? Good heavens, Jevon's *Logic* and Hutton's *Essays on Literature*. If this is your idea of reading on a journey, what must your lessons be?"

"Oh, I'm not in the schoolroom," said Hilda hastily, and with a little air of dignity; "but I want to do the Cambridge Local. Of course I can't go to Newnham because of mother, but it is horrid not to have a profession, isn't it?"

Hilda's tongue was set working by shyness, not by self-possession, but she spoke out of the fulness of her heart.

Marmaduke laughed. This seemed to him like a parody of his own feelings. Hilda looked offended.

"Hilda," he said, "you must allow that to have seen you last in a brown holland pinafore, with sticky fingers, and then to meet you grown up, travelling with your maid, as if you were accustomed to knocking about Europe, and to be told that you want a profession, might fairly produce a smile."

Hilda laughed as though she had suddenly discovered a good joke.

"It was an odd greeting," she said, "after eight years. But the sticky fingers are a base calumny."

After that they asked and answered various questions about their respective families. Presently Hilda said:—

"I suppose you are coming to Skipton."

"Yes, and Mrs. George too, and Mark Fieldes. Our party has dwindled down to that."

"Mark Fieldes, the author?" cried Hilda; "what fun. That's what I'm really pining for, to meet out-of-the-way clever men like Mark Fieldes. You know mother used to know all the clever men in London, and I've never seen more than one alive."

"Have you seen many dead?" inquired Marmaduke.

"No, but that I can't complain of. And I've seen more than one buried in Westminster Abbey. I have read the *Phantasmagoria of Phidias*" she went on quickly, "and I have often wished to meet Mr. Fieldes, but I never imagined it would be at Skipton-le-Grange. How do they know him?"

"It seems that George, not long before he died, met Mr. Fieldes at Homburg, and gave him a vague invitation to Skipton, a fact which he has somehow made known to them, and he is to arrive to-day."

"I wonder how he will acclimatise himself."

Marmaduke glanced with amusement at Hilda's sarcastic little mouth, but she did not pursue the subject. Her mind wandered to the coming Madge, the widow of George Riversdale.

"Have you seen Madge lately? We haven't met her for ages. I used to think her so fascinating, she was quite my romance, but I feel very shy about meeting her now. You know," she hesitated, "I have not seen her since George died. I suppose she will be dreadfully changed. Have you seen her?"

"Yes, we met in the Highlands soon after I got home."

"Was it very dreadful? I mean did she seem to be broken-hearted—as—as mother was?"

Hilda stopped speaking, and blushed a little as she looked into his face.

"I don't quite know," said Marmaduke evasively; "Madge is not much changed outwardly—but, see, the train from London is in, and I ought to meet her now."

"I wonder if anybody besides Hilda can expect poor little Madge to be a broken-hearted widow," he muttered, as he hurried forward, "Still it is to be hoped that she will come here in mourning, as she will be staying with his people."

But before Marmaduke could get across to the London train, a small figure, in a wonderful greatcoat of fawn-coloured cloth, with a sable cloak over one arm, had reached the luggage van, and was giving directions in the softest of voices to an attentive porter.

"No, thank you, Mr. Fieldes, I always see to my own boxes, my maid is far too stupid. Yes, the Skipton platform," and the porter hurried away with the enormous trunks. "Can I help with your luggage, Mr. Fieldes?" in a still meeker voice. "Ah, Marmaduke, how d'ye do? Let us come, we cross over, don't we? So that is Hilda, so grown up and so badly dressed. Dear Hilda!" She hurried forward and shook Hilda's long fingers in a direct masculine way. "Mr. Fieldes has so very many cases for his purple and fine linen that he ought to bring a servant, but *we* won't miss the train, will we, Hilda?" and with an air of sisterly *camaraderie* Madge hurried Hilda along. It was not until they were seated in the carriage of the Skipton-bound train that they were joined by Mr. Fieldes, somewhat out of breath.

He was tall, taller than Marmaduke, but with a figure not well put together, and stooping, rounded shoulders. His dress was elaborate, but not well put on, and he was known to be the despair of a very excellent tailor.

Madge had instantly settled herself, with all possible regard to comfort, muffled in her large sable cloak, in a corner of the carriage, and was now silently puffing delicate smoke-wreaths from a cigarette, while she looked Hilda comprehensively over. A moment later she said aloud, in a tone of mild surprise:—

"No cigarette, Hilda? Then I must amuse you in other ways. Mr. Fieldes, there you are at last, you and my cousin Miss Riversdale are to know and respect each other. Remarkable minds, I believe, both; at least you have written most things, and Hilda has read all the others."

"This is a trying introduction, and if acquaintance prospers on it we shall not have to thank Mrs. Riversdale," said Fieldes, with a half-melancholy, half-humorous smile at Hilda.

Mark Fieldes could not be called a striking figure of a man; but his head, if far from beautiful, was not devoid of interest. The forehead was broad and low, and rather too large for the rest of the face. The eyes varied constantly from a torpid state of reflection to a twinkling eager gaze. The interest of the face lay not so much in its structure (the lower part being weak and too wide) as in its problematic character. It could, for a few seconds, be positively impressive: it could be vulgar. The eyes might look impertinent or awestruck, reverential or shallow, almost at the same moment. Poor Fieldes, it showed him too plainly to the unfriendly. He was too sensitive to all the influences about him; there was little that he did not see or feel. But it is a complicated world, and no compound of earthly clay is capable of recording an infinite number of impressions.

The present was a comparatively simple moment in his mental history. He was feeling his own clumsiness with regard to his luggage; he was envying Madge's quick business-like ways; he was annoyed by her amusement at his little distress; he was anxiously, half-jealously scanning the handsome, active Marmaduke; he was admiring Hilda, idealising her as the home girl, innocent, natural, but in her whole self eminently aristocratic; he was wondering if she had any money; he was gazing with a sense of quiet refreshment at the cold chaste beauty of the wintry sunset; he was thinking that his own coat was of a better cut than Marmaduke's; and last and almost most vivid in the medley, were his wonder and interest in a figure he had espied on the platform.

"Did you see the monk?" he exclaimed immediately, "What a face! and the dress all completely white. Could renunciation wear a more exquisite appearance? What a glorious habit, yet what a hideous life."

Hilda looked amused, but Madge was irritated by this enthusiasm.

"I know who he is," she said, "and he is a great bore. I do hope he is not coming to Skipton. As for the glory of the habit, it isn't over fresh when you are close to it. He is most tiresome. Do you remember, Hilda, how he scolded me about my maid waiting up for me that time at your mother's house? It was most impertinent."

"And he rebuked me for want of humility because I would not play to him. But don't you think, Madge, there is something striking about him in his whole—"

"Personality?" suggested Fieldes; "but the personality of the unwashed is easier to appreciate from a distance—at least, Mrs. Riversdale thinks so. Still he certainly was picturesque, sitting on a 'returned empty' in the midst of the bustle, reading his Office, with his white hood half over his face, and his white beard reaching his leather belt. There was an aloofness, an unconsciousness about him in the midst of you all; it was as if a Fra Angelico had been hung in the Salon. He made me quite forget the shape of my portmanteaus."

"I only wish he would stay on his empty, and not come to be petted and fed up at Skipton. I would never have come if I had thought there was a chance of his being there. My mother-in-law is intolerable with a pet monk."

Madge was evidently out of temper; and as she was the ruling influence of the moment they all became as silent as Marmaduke, who had been reading his evening paper the while. Presently he offered Madge the paper.

"Is there anything in it?" she asked.

"More trouble with the Boers—oh, and there's the account of Lord V—'s wedding."

"It was to be very gorgeous," said Mark. "They said the roses from Cannes almost hid the chancel."

"The garlands measured more than a mile," said Madge, "and Miss B— had them picked to pieces four times. They had to wire to all the flower shops in London to make up the ones they spoilt. I had a letter from Cecilia about the preparations. She was to be a bridesmaid, you know."

"The jewels were simply gorgeous," added Mark.

"Yes, but all that has been exaggerated," said Madge in a tone of superior information; "I don't believe the pearls are anything like the size the papers make out. Cecilia says he gave her a bunch of orchids and a box of bon-bons every morning during their engagement," continued Madge in a tone of admiration.

"And I suppose she will pay the bill for them afterwards," observed Mark.

"Yes," said Madge, "but she won't notice it. She could pay for anything, happy girl. When I first met her it was very different. I remember I was bored at being introduced. Isn't it strange, to think that that little pale thing we used to see about, whom nobody thought anything of, is to have all the happiness this world can give?" Madge sighed meditatively.

"Is she much in love with him?" came in Hilda's shy voice.

Mark looked at her approvingly.

"Oh, of course," said Madge, "who wouldn't be? And the place is so beautiful, it only wants her money to do it up."

"Did you see that the whole of the wedding breakfast was cooked in Paris and sent over hot?"

"Yes," said Madge, "it was all perfectly done, of course—she is the luckiest woman I know."

"There is only one other marriage that could beat it in England," said Mark, "and in the case I mean the man will be able to give jewels, orchids and all himself."

"You mean Bellasis," said Madge quickly, and she flushed a little.

"Yes," said Mark in a knowing voice; "I wonder if anybody whispered to Miss Cecilia Rupert at the wedding 'Happy bridesmaid make a happy bride'!"

"Why should they say that to Cecilia?" asked Madge in a cold distant voice, looking away from Mark.

Mark answered eagerly.

"Why, surely you must have heard, must have noticed—I never saw anything so obvious as the flirtation between Lord Bellasis and Cecilia Rupert."

"I hear a good many foolish things," said Madge, "but I don't notice them. I was at Bellasis Castle with her, and I am sure nobody could have supposed he meant anything at all. Nobody there thought so, and where have you been lately? Anybody in London would have told you that he has quite changed since then, and has not shown her any more attentions at all."

Madge's voice was so cross that Mark did not venture to point out the Celtic want of logic in her last speech. There was an awkward silence. Hilda broke it, observing in a thoughtful tone to Mark:—

"I wonder if people who have orchids and bon-bons every day get very tired of life."

"Of course they do," said Mark, turning towards her with quick sympathy, "it is those who have had the best of life who generally loathe it most, or say they do; but," speaking to Madge, "I sometimes doubt the extent of that loathing."

He had not in the least understood what Hilda meant this time, and she was still more sorry she had expressed her little feeling when Madge remarked in a cross voice:—

"Of course it is all nonsense when they say that—but people like to think they believe them. It makes the grapes seem really sour."

After this, conversation lapsed, and Madge threw away the end of her cigarette, leaned her head back against the sable cloak and let her eyelids close. Hilda fancied that she looked sad and tired.

Madge's dress, a most successful harmony of grey, white, fawn and black, quite satisfied Mark that she was still in half-mourning. Hilda had expected the full romance of weeds, and this most becoming stage of a young widow's appearance (in the twilight tints open to many interpretations) appeared to her no mourning at all. It had been a severe shock.

CHAPTER IV

THE HOME OF THE PERSECUTED

The same clear wintry sunshine which shone upon Crowby Junction also lighted up the windows of Skipton-le-Grange. The house was big, ugly and prosperous in appearance. It presented large surfaces of flat walls, covered with stucco, and many sash windows that neither intruded nor receded, but kept as closely as possible to the wall surface. But in a fit of remorse, or else in the spirit of adding insult to his unfortunate creation, the architect had placed classical vases of stone at the corners of the square building. There was nothing remarkable in the house itself; but it stood boldly out in the midst of an exquisitely timbered park, the home of a race that had dwelt there for 400 years. And in those years the Riversdales had been among the victims of a system of proscriptive legislation so severe as to appear to us now hardly credible.

In the sixteenth century one Riversdale had been hanged, drawn and quartered, and a second imprisoned for life in a jail where life could only be of the shortest, for the criminal offences of harbouring priests and having Mass celebrated at Skipton-le-Grange. In the seventeenth century the family had gone through all the ups and downs, all the hopes and disappointments that befel Catholics in England. They had fought loyally for King Charles; and had hoped not only that the king should enjoy his own again, but that his restoration would bring a general toleration. Such dreams were dissipated by the success of Puritanism. In the early years of Charles II hope rose for a moment still higher, and was not finally extinguished until James II, the greatest enemy of his own religion in the event, came to the throne.

Then after James had sunk from the eminence which proved so disastrous to those he wished to help, the darkness thickened; and the Riversdales and many other Catholic families with them, became as those who have no hope in this world.

In the "Catholic Committee," whose strenuous efforts at last won for English Catholics a measure of partial relief in 1778, there had been a Riversdale, who died soon after the Relief Act was passed, and was succeeded by his son, the builder of the present house at Skipton. This Riversdale built the new house as a young man, before the final repeal of the penal laws in 1791. The old house which he pulled down had dated back to the first days of Henry VIII. During the centuries that followed Catholics did not build family mansions, and the beauties of Elizabethan and Jacobean architecture were not for the persecuted.

So when William Riversdale built him a house which should take its place in size and importance with the houses of the county magnates, he had fallen upon a bad moment in the history of English architecture. He was not dissatisfied with it himself. The bigness of it, the boldness of its windows, the classical ornaments, the wide sweep of its carriage-drive, preserved no trace of the old house, with its loophole windows, its secret chapel, its hiding-places, its high hedges that came close up to the walls. But William Riversdale had no love for such reminders of former thraldom. The Relief Act of 1778 had marked a distinct growth of the tolerant disposition of Englishmen towards Catholics. A naturally high-spirited young man, he had not only been educated, like other Catholics, in France, but after his father's death, when he was only fifteen, he had passed his holidays with a connection of the family—a French archbishop, who was his godfather. As a young man of nineteen he had been received at court by Louis XVI. and had mixed with the best French society. When he came to England in 1784 he little realised the social proscription or the penal legislation which still had so practical an effect on the life of his co-religionists. Fully conscious of the family history and position he meant to take his place as a county magnate. He confidently reckoned on the opportunities which would soon be afforded by the further repeal of the penal laws. He was too sanguine, and a reaction followed. The remains of the old chains soon made themselves felt, and they galled him. Events did not move fast enough; every year brought some rough reminder of the social and legal disabilities under which as a Catholic he necessarily laboured. The first time he attended quarter sessions he was startled at hearing the officer announce that he had "made diligent search for Papists." At a dinner party the lord-lieutenant of the county, a bigoted Protestant, had nearly left the company on finding a Papist to be present, and Riversdale had been deeply hurt at hearing his host apologise in a low tone, and promise that such a thing should not happen again. Such events soon induced a sullen and proud resentment; and before his real opportunity arrived, he had retired into his shell and settled down in the groove in which his father had lived before him.

The turning point came in 1788. His county neighbours were beginning to see that Riversdale meant to take up a position at which his father had never aimed, and some of them did not like it. He had a quarrel with an acquaintance in the hunting-field, and the man was mean enough to remind him that the splendid animal he rode was only his on sufferance, as the law still obliged a Catholic to give his horse to anybody who offered him £5 in exchange. Riversdale had blustered, and the man had actually at last insisted on proving his rights, to the great disgust of the hunting-field it is true. Mr. Riversdale had walked home and never hunted again.[1]

Such were the memories in which his grandson, the present owner of Skipton, had been educated. Things had changed much, needless to say, in the lifetime of the two generations. Catholics had, to a great extent, won their position socially and in the professions, and were on good terms with their immediate neighbours.

---

1. An incident almost identical with that described in the text happened to the grandfather of the late Lord Arundell of Wardour.

Their traditions and their way of life, however, bore many traces of their past history. The persecuted had come, in many cases, to idealise the enforced seclusion and inaction of penal days. Politics were too dangerous, and the army and navy soul-imperilling professions—in which moreover Catholics were long debarred from the higher grades. A curious, hardly expressed tradition regarded idleness even in the younger sons as both virtuous and aristocratic. This was partly due no doubt to the fact that in the last century trade, which was then looked upon as a shop-keeping sort of occupation, was almost the only way in which a Catholic could expect to make a fortune.

It was a cause of surprise to such converts as Mrs. Arthur Riversdale to find the Catholic families so secluded and so inactive; and still more to find them satisfied and self-contented in their seclusion. That many admirable Catholic country squires and upright land-agents and men of business were still produced by the old *régime,* and that there was a remarkably high standard of piety and purity of manners among their women, all this was only to be expected as the fruit of Catholicism. But surely, the converts argued, it was no compliment to the strengthening power of their religion that its adherents should be afraid of contact with the national life, in which others took their part without injury. This however is happily a controversy that need not now be dwelt upon;—the generation of Marmaduke Lemarchant having decided it (with a few exceptions) for themselves.

Nobody could be a day at Skipton without understanding something of the character of its master. The tall, upright, broad-chested, well-dressed old squire had a charm that was almost hard upon his wife. Mrs. Riversdale might have shone as the wife of an ill-tempered, exacting man, for she was really a good woman. But there was such a pervading sweetness in the personality of the Squire of Skipton that, unconsciously to himself, he became the centre on which all things turned. Not that the mind that ruled the house was an active one. He had accepted views as well as acres as a heritage from his forefathers, and from them he had received one tendency of a persecuted race, the inclination to live and let live in peace.

He was the sort of man who helps to perpetuate a bad or useless system of education by his very excellence of character and manner of life. Men would say that he was a type produced by the good old days. It would be argued among his connections that an education in no sense national, in private schools and without university advantages, had made such men as old George Riversdale, and what could you wish for more?

He was a strong man, strong in will, large in affections, just in personal judgments; a fox-hunter who made an hour's meditation every morning, and a powerful landlord who carried soup to bedridden old women. It was an illustration of the squire's character that to forgive the man who had shot a fox cost him a struggle which could only be successful when it was necessary to prepare for confession, and it was felt in the family to be a serious matter if a fox had been shot near one of the eight great feast days.

Eight times a year Mr. Riversdale went to the sacraments. No one ever supposed that it meant want of piety—all knew that it was rather intensity of reverence—which prevented him from going more often to communion. Moreover, such had been the custom of his father.

The squire and his daughter were returning from the hunting-field in the afternoon on which they were expecting Madge and their other guests. They had had a good though a short day with the hounds. They walked their horses slowly through Skipton Park between the great oaks, sun and shadow playing on the two figures and the mud-sprinkled horses.

Mary was not very tall, but her figure was well proportioned, and she never looked better than when in the saddle. The small amount of feminine vanity in her composition was chiefly expended on her hunting attire. It seemed as necessary to be smart and well groomed herself, as it was necessary to have her mare at its best also. Whether Mary was to be well groomed in order to show off the animal, or the animal be well groomed to show off

Mary, it would be difficult to say, but probably the former. It was still the fashion to wear tall hats and tight-fitting habits, and happily no loose coat hid the outlines of Mary's well-defined figure.

They had been discussing the events of the day in the field, and the girl's clear, rather loud laugh had rung out joyously. The old squire had been enjoying a joke, and his handsome features were lit with a sunny smile. The man's tall broad-shouldered figure was thrown back a little, as he turned to catch her appreciation of the story. At that moment the clock struck four, and the squire unconsciously brought his horse to a stand.

"Four o'clock," he said, and mechanically pulled out his large hunting watch; "Madge will be here in a few minutes now."

A cloud came over his face, and he stooped a little as though some weight had descended upon him.

Mary's sensitive observation of the loved face had told her in the morning that her father was suffering from gloomy thoughts. She had rejoiced to see that he had thrown them off almost as soon as he had mounted his horse. But now they were not even at home again; they had not half finished the discussion of the day's sport, and yet the cloud had reappeared.

She gave a little impatient sigh. Were their brightest days always to be clouded now? It was very "young" to feel this sort of surprise in pain; it pointed to the record of a happy youth. A little superstitious feeling grew upon her in the silence that followed, an ominous ill-defined sensation of the uncertainty of the brightness of the moment before. She gathered herself together; this was absurd.

Other suns would shine, and there would be other days out hunting with her father. Father would not always be thinking about George; and surely, although George was dead, it was right to be happy sometimes. But a deep sigh of self-reproach interrupted this line of thought, and she glanced up in sympathy at the face above her.

For a moment Mr. Riversdale met her eyes with a look of inquiry, as though he wondered whether her sigh answered with understanding to his melancholy. The relations between the two were very simple; and it was with great difficulty that the father refrained from saying anything that was in his thoughts to the daughter. Happily the old man's mind was so full of things simple, holy and of good repute, that nothing in this freedom of intercourse was dangerous for Mary. He was about to speak now, when something checked him. The impulse to confide in her and the difficulty of expressing what he had to say, struggled in him. He remained silent, and Mary was surprised to see him turn from her with an actual blush heightening the deep colour on the weather-hardened face—a thing she had never seen there before.

Mr. Riversdale had intended to tell her gently something of George's past. He had thought it his duty to win her sympathy for George's widow. He feared that he should receive little help from his wife in his efforts at kindness to his daughter-in-law during her visit to Skipton. He felt himself that, as George's parents, they owed reparation to Madge. George's life had been an insult to her. He had been cruel to her even before he left her. Then, too, Mr. Riversdale knew that her character was weak, and he feared the danger of worldly and irreligious companionship among her London friends. For every reason he wished to make Skipton pleasant and attractive to her.

But to Mrs. Riversdale Madge was a reminder of facts in the life of the dead son whom she had idolised—facts which she angrily refused to face. For her George's widow was the undying witness to the family tragedy. How then could Madge be anything but odious to Mrs. Riversdale? The squire wished to convey to Mary something of the true state of the case. But when he tried to frame the words that might tell her something of the last years of George's life, he found it impossible. To see that fair, sensitive, childlike face lose its homely peacefulness and serenity would be unbearable.

Very slowly did they walk their horses as the sunshine faded and they drew nearer to the house. They presently came to the carriage-drive, and absorbed in their own thoughts hardly saw a man walking very near to them.

Mark Fieldes had felt the necessity for exercise, and he had asked Madge to put him down at the lodge gates. He had walked round the park by mistake, instead of across it, and had at last found himself at the lodge on the opposite side. After that he had prudently kept to the road. He had not gone far before the two riders emerged upon it from between the trees. He looked up at them with quick appreciation.

Any stranger might have been struck by the picture they presented. Mr. Riversdale was perhaps more handsome than his daughter, but there was something very winning in the fair face that was looking up at her father's. There was perfect horsemanship in her attitude, and in the way she guided the mare across some rough ground by the roadside. Fieldes saw a picture of prosperity in the bright-coated squire and his daughter on their beautiful horses, but he saw too the cloud on the man's face and its sympathetic shadow on the girl's.

The road in front of them led straight to Skipton-le-Grange, and on this side of the house stood out the chapel in all its barn-like ugliness. It might have been taken for a Methodist chapel but for two things, the cross that was raised over a tiny belfry, and the gleam of the sanctuary lamp with its peculiar still radiance shining through the coloured glass of the window.

Either from habit or from the sense of sadness that was oppressing her, Mary looked with a longing expression at that faint light. Fieldes thought that her lips moved. It did not occur to him until afterwards that she was praying. But he saw a look on the face which came back to him in later years, a look full of the "light that never was on sea or land"; a something of spiritual intensity, which stayed with him through life connected with the image of Mary Riversdale. This he always said was the face that had brought to him the clearest glimpse of the "divine in the human."

How much the walk in the crisp air, the spurt to the imagination given by a country that had not been seen before, his artistic pleasure in the two figures, the youth and fairness of the girl, had their share in the impression it is difficult to say. But even when only a few days later the look on the girl's face became to him difficult to understand, when the light seemed deadened, and the fine sensitiveness to have turned to an oppressed and puzzled suffering, Fieldes never felt that that first impression had been weakened. Long after he said to a friend in London:—

"I believe in angels. I once saw one, so how can I doubt them? She appeared to me in a riding habit, wearing a tall hat."

Fieldes felt very awkward, even while he looked at the two figures in front of him—so awkward that he actually took to flight, turned round and hid himself behind a large tree. This was not well managed, and Mary's horse started, as Fieldes made a rustling among the dead branches.

"Father, I thought I saw a man and now he is gone."

"It must have been fancy," said Riversdale, rousing himself. "If we go slowly we shall just have time to finish the rosary. I don't hear the carriage-wheels yet."

He pulled out a string of beads and he and Mary began to recite prayers in rapid low tones.

When the squire and Mary had trotted up to the front door and dismounted, they were told that Mrs. George and Miss Hilda Riversdale were in the drawing-room. The squire hastened across the hall closely followed by Mary.

It would be difficult to exaggerate the moral discomfort of the group they found awaiting them. Fieldes, as we know, had not yet reached the house. Marmaduke had not come in the carriage. There was nobody but Hilda, who was still regarded as a child by them both, to break the awkwardness of the meeting between George's adoring mother and the widow who had not even kept the externals of mourning for two short years. They had kissed with studious politeness, had "inquired after each other's good health and exchanged the weather," when Mrs. Riversdale proceeded to ask if they had driven Father Clement to the priest's house before coming on to the hall.

"Father Clement!" exclaimed Madge with surprise. "Are you expecting him?"

Hilda gave a little start.

"Surely you saw him, he was to come by this train; I have never known him miss a train, or alter his plans without necessity."

The older lady's voice betrayed suspicion.

"Perhaps he has come after all," said Madge, who was standing with her back to the fire. "Do you remember, Hilda, Mr. Fieldes' excitement about some monk at Crowby Junction?"

Hilda did remember, but she recollected also that she had seen him again at the Skipton Station, and had asked Madge a little nervously if they ought not to suggest to him to come in the carriage. She had received no answer, but it now appeared that Madge had not heard her speak.

"It was a pity we did not know he was coming," Madge said, after a moment's pause, in a voice betraying an indication of temper, hitherto studiously veiled by politeness.

"Then," said Mrs. Riversdale, sitting if possible a little more upright than usual in her large hard tapestried chair, "then he will come in the cart with your maid and the luggage."

Her voice spoke volumes of indignation. She had been prepared, under protest, to endure with Christian courtesy Madge's presence in the house, though convinced that she had been the undoing of George; but temper can bear crimes better than trifles.

When Mr. Riversdale came into the room, he broke the silence that had followed this remark. He glanced hurriedly across the large space, with its stiff groups of furniture, to the ample person of his wife. There was something almost amusing in the simplicity of the anxiety with which he looked from one woman to the other, from the large and now stern face of the stately hostess, in her ample garniture of rich silk and heavy crape trimmings, to the tiny figure on the hearthrug, in its tight-fitting tailor-made costume of black and white check; the hands, sparkling with rings, held out to the warmth behind her, the smartly shod little feet planted firmly somewhat apart. The small face was expressive of temper. He hardly saw Hilda, who was sitting away from the other two, flushed and uncomfortable.

As Madge moved forward to meet her father-in-law, with a heightened colour, the look of ill-temper was lost in some different but still embarrassing emotion.

Mr. Riversdale went straight to her, put his big arm about her, stooped down and kissed her. If she had wanted to resist, it would have been impossible, but apparently this was not what she wanted. No sooner had he raised his head than she made a bird-like spring in his direction, and imprinted a little kiss on the ruddy cheek.

"Well," he said with resolute cordiality to his wife, "so here she is—well, well," and he sighed as he turned round to look for Hilda.

Meantime Mary had welcomed Madge with a shy kiss, which seemed almost unnoticed by its recipient.

"Had a good day?" asked Madge.

Mary was about to recount the features of the day, a very safe subject, when the squire, after welcoming Hilda, and adding due inquiries for her mother, repeated his wife's question—Where was Father Clement? Had he gone at once to the priest's house, where he was expected to make some days' stay? Mr. Riversdale supposed he had refused to come in to tea.

"He is coming up with the maids and the boxes," began Mrs. Riversdale.

"We did not see him at the station," said Madge hurriedly, raising innocent grey eyes to the squire's face. "I *am* so sorry."

It was not Mr. Riversdale's habit to dwell on trifles.

"Dear, that's tiresome, but what's done can't be undone. But where's Marmaduke and where's Mr. What's-his-Name?"

At the same moment the butler supplied the name and Fieldes followed him into the room.

Mark Fieldes was received with the dignified cordiality which was never wanting in the welcome of a visitor to Skipton. Certainly during the tea-drinking that followed he could not complain of neglect. His host, his hostess and Mrs. George all seemed to wish to talk to him, and he once caught Hilda's large eyes furtively examining the distinguished author. Only Mary seemed to be entirely occupied in the matter of tea and eatables.

Marmaduke did not appear until after the guests had been shown to their rooms, as he had been kept at the station waiting for the arrival of his two hunters by the next train. He was able to console his aunt by the information that he had found a fly, which had conveyed Father Clement to the priest's house with sufficient dignity.

"What a boon you are in the domestic circle," said Madge gratefully, when she was next alone with Mark Fieldes. "But where on earth did you learn to talk about poor schools and religious orders? And may I ask how many convents you have haunted? Here indeed is new light upon your character."

The dinner was somewhat dull. The squire made great efforts to talk to Madge, but the efforts were too apparent. No topic seemed to last long, and he generally passed to some remark addressed to the rest of the company. Marmaduke was not very talkative and Hilda was shy. Fieldes would under ordinary circumstances have saved any dinner-table from dulness; but his words were addressed mainly to Mrs. Riversdale, whom he took in to dinner, and were unusually unproductive. "Certainly these people are not brilliant members of society," he thought to himself. He had come prepared with subjects which he thought well suited to his company. But his stories and theories fell flat. Only once did Mrs. Riversdale respond with any animation. He was telling of a friend of his—a Catholic whom Mrs. Riversdale had known as a child and lost sight of. It was a touching love story—the girl's father had for ten years refused to sanction her marriage with the man she loved. At last it was all made up. The father relented and sent for the lover, who arrived at what proved to be the girl's deathbed. "They little knew it at the time," he said, "the doctors thought her only chance lay in not knowing the worst. She talked happily of the future. Death came suddenly and quite peacefully a few days later."

"I think it very wrong," said Mrs. Riversdale with emphatic alertness, "for doctors to behave in that way. The poor girl dies without any proper preparation for death, without the last sacraments, without a priest, simply to give her some slight chance of recovery. It is just what the Protestant doctor did who attended my niece Annie Burchall. He owned to it afterwards. They would never send for him again."

Fieldes soon found that the best chance of conversation was to leave it to his host and hostess to choose their own topics. But even this was a slow process. He exchanged glances more than once with Mrs. George Riversdale, in the course of the long pauses, when Mr. or Mrs. Riversdale seemed to be meaning to say something shortly. The remarks generally came at last in the form of isolated facts notified, or brief comments.

"How much aged Father Clement is looking—I'm sure you'll think so, Madge, when you see him." "The meet on Friday is at Crowby, Marmaduke." "I have told Harrison to-day to cut down that old oak in the long avenue—we tried to save it, but it had to go at last." "Charlie tells me Lord Archibourne is to be buried in Scotland." "You have had a long journey, Mr. Fieldes; I fear you must be tired. Railway travelling is very tiring." "Marmaduke, I want to show you how the firs you planted before you went to India have grown up." "Mary, you *must* pay a visit to the new schoolmistress to-morrow." "The man is coming to tune the organ to-morrow morning—do you care for music, Mr. Fieldes?" "The Crowby line is quite incorrigible; none of the trains are good." "Our local trains can't pretend to rival the Scotch expresses." "I heard from Agatha to-day—the convent is going to keep her silver jubilee; you remember Agatha, Madge, don't you?" "Teresa and Bob talk of coming to us next week." These were some of the remarks which a casual listener would have heard when silence was broken.

After dinner Mark talked to the squire. He spoke of the policy of Cardinals Wiseman and Manning and of the Oxford conversions. He was hopeful at first that he had struck a fruitful vein; for the squire remarked at once:—

"My father used to say that Dr. Wiseman was rather a rash young man."

Fieldes took up his supposed rashness, argued that it was far-sightedness, contrasted Wiseman with Manning and both with Newman, and paused for a reply. But Mr. Riversdale, who had listened patiently, said nothing for some moments. Then he remarked:—

"I don't know the present archbishop; but my father used to say that Dr. Wiseman was a rash man."

There was some music after dinner; and soon after ten o'clock the squire disappeared and Fieldes learnt that he had gone to say prayers for the household.

"Mass at half-past eight as usual," remarked Mrs. Riversdale as the family separated to go to bed and she gave Madge her candle.

Mr. Riversdale reappeared only for a moment to say good-night. Fieldes smoked a cigar in Marmaduke's company and was soon glad, after his journey, to part from a not very sympathetic companion, and go early to bed.

CHAPTER V

AN INDISCREET PHOTOGRAPH

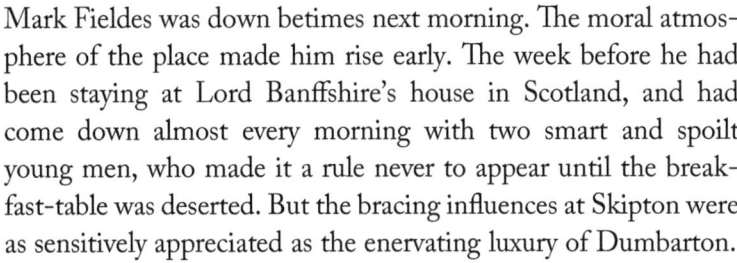

Mark Fieldes was down betimes next morning. The moral atmosphere of the place made him rise early. The week before he had been staying at Lord Banffshire's house in Scotland, and had come down almost every morning with two smart and spoilt young men, who made it a rule never to appear until the breakfast-table was deserted. But the bracing influences at Skipton were as sensitively appreciated as the enervating luxury of Dumbarton.

As he descended the first flight of stairs—his room was on the second floor—he saw Mary with a black veil on her head, walking rather rapidly along a narrow passage, and as she opened a door at the end, and paused for a moment before shutting it to see if any one was following her, Fieldes could perceive that she was entering the tribune of the chapel in the house. It was just half-past eight and no doubt Mass was going to begin. Fieldes hesitated as to whether he should follow her. But he was not sure if their sacred mysteries were open to the heretic. He went downstairs therefore and took a walk in the park. As he returned—some forty minutes later—he heard the breakfast gong and betook himself to the dining-room.

The family gradually assembled, and Fieldes devoted himself to Mrs. Riversdale and talked of the convent, and the school in the village. "Where is Madge?" asked the squire. "She is not coming down to breakfast," Hilda replied—

Hilda had already been to Madge's room for a minute after Mass.

"Ah. No doubt she is tired after her journey. I hope she has had some breakfast taken upstairs," and Mr. Riversdale looked at his wife.

Mrs. Riversdale's face was not sympathetic.

"Oh, yes. Her maid took up a cup of tea and some eggs half an hour ago," she replied.

And a little later the hostess was talking to Mark Fieldes of the self-indulgence of modern days, and of the very different standards of her own youth. And Mark, strong in the consciousness of his early walk, was not only a sympathetic listener but waxed positively eloquent on the subject. Mrs. Riversdale did not quite follow his allusion to a recent visit he had paid to the Grande Chartreuse, and did not see what connection the subject had with her own remarks—except that the Carthusians got up early. But she was quite satisfied with Mark's attitude, and felt that he was on the side of the monks and of herself.

Hilda had found her speech this morning, and when Mrs. Riversdale left the breakfast-table she stayed for quite twenty minutes talking to Mark Fieldes.

"I had no idea it was so late!" she exclaimed, as she looked at her watch and hurried up to fulfil her promise of paying Madge a visit in her bedroom after breakfast. She found Madge in by no means a good humour, and the reason was not far to seek. For she had had nothing but a cup of lukewarm tea and a boiled egg sent her for breakfast, and the efforts of her French maid Celestine to get this supplemented had only produced, after much delay, a little cold ham in addition. It was not that Madge wanted more than this, but it was the old story. If you did not appear for breakfast at Skipton, your morning was made as uncomfortable as possible. Then, too, Celestine had met Mrs. Riversdale who had asked why she was not at Mass and told her that it was the rule of the house that all the visitors' servants should go to Mass. "I told her that Madame had need of me; but Madame Riversdale did not seem to hear me."

However, Madge wished to talk to Hilda about other things, and she had only half-finished superintending the unpacking of her trunks, so after the first moments of wrath, her irritation was set aside.

While the unpacking proceeded, with occasional interjectory remarks from Madge, Hilda had leisure to study George's widow and her surroundings.

She was amused to see how quickly Madge had changed the aspect of the heavily furnished bedroom. Madge had the faculty of impressing herself on the material things surrounding her, and as she demanded of them luxury, ease, and beauty, with a certain power of will, they yielded these habitually. If Hilda had pushed chairs and sofas about, or even put evergreens in a bowl, she would have done it with effort, and with doubts as to her own success, and that is not the spirit in which to deal with matter. Madge treated furniture, flowers and clothes imperiously, and they fell into the right positions, caught the right lights and harmonised or contrasted their colours to the best of their capacity.

Madge herself was dressed in a morning wrapper, an artistic arrangement of chiffon that suited her particularly well. On the sofa behind her lay the sable cloak that was noted for envy among her friends; and on a stiff glazed screen—one was provided in each spare room at Skipton—was flung a most beautiful curtain of Chinese embroidery. Cushions and pieces of silk lay about, and countless photographs, some in solid silver frames, covered the tables. A silver basin, full of violets, and some tall roses in long-stemmed glasses, stood among them.

Hilda no longer wondered at the enormous size of the trunks she had seen piled on the Skipton luggage cart the day before. Madge went on talking to her maid, while Hilda amused herself in looking at the innumerable gilt objects on the dressing-table. Six candlesticks were fastened on to the looking glass, of which the six facets reflected its fair owner's head from various points of view. Needless to say that the glass and appurtenances provided by Mrs. Riversdale had been put away in the dressing-room.

"Oh, thank you so much," Madge had said in her most polite tones to her mother-in-law, "it is all so nice and so comfortable and so kind, and Celestine can rearrange things easily."

Celestine was now standing with an air of great chagrin and repentance before her little mistress, who was explaining to her in French how exceedingly badly she had packed one of her new bodices.

"Isn't it too bad, Hilda?" said Madge, "it is all *chiffonée*, tumbled, messed about," and she pointed impatiently at the exquisitely coloured object the French girl was holding de-precatingly towards her.

"But madame will see that it is not spoiled in the least. Will madame permit that I take it to my room?"

"No, no, you will only make matters worse, and it cost ten guineas, and I must get another, and you know how hard up I am already. It is intolerable."

"Madame has two other new ones," said Celestine meekly.

"Put it in the drawer and go away," said her mistress quickly.

"The fact is," said Madge,—and Hilda was afraid the retreating maid must hear her, she spoke so loud,—"that it pays them to spoil one's clothes. But she shan't have that dress, I can tell her! It is too aggravating!"

Madge lit a cigarette and sank back on the sofa.

"Take some violets," she said a moment later to Hilda; "no, a good bunch. They come by post from Cannes. Aren't they delicious? Do you think I've improved the room? I knew I couldn't exist at Skipton if I did not bring some colour with me, but that stupid woman forgot my rose quilt. It would have been invaluable. I declare, I believe I could have pulled through the time here without losing my temper, if I had had that quilt to look at."

She laughed with self-appreciation, but the laugh was surprised and overcome by a sharp sigh.

"Come here, Hilda," Madge got up and walked towards a long pier glass at the other end of the room. "I want to explain to you about your frock, and what's wrong, and let me look at that hat," for Hilda had been told to bring with her the large feathered hat she had worn the day before.

They made a pretty contrast reflected in the long glass; Madge minute, delicately coloured, highly finished; Hilda tall, picturesque, with the grace and perhaps a touch of the awkwardness of a healthy, vigorous girl of eighteen.

"I don't know about the hat," Madge said, twirling it round and giving it sundry violent pokes and pushes that looked destructive, but in reality improved it wonderfully. "It is dowdy when it is off, but it suits you, and that matters most. There!" She stretched herself up to her full height and put the hat on Hilda's head, and then looked critically in the glass. "Have you ever been told that you are like a family picture by Sir Joshua? and after all," with a kind of good-natured contemptuousness, "it doesn't matter so much for a girl to be smart."

Hilda looked sadly into her own deep eyes in the glass: she liked the family picture idea, but she did not appreciate the last observation. If it were right to be smart, why she wanted to be smart too. There was something irritating in these remarks, showing standards of judgment to which she was not accustomed—she who had been so much petted at home. It had been implied if not expressed, that she was both pretty and clever, but Madge evidently thought nothing of the cleverness, and seemed to consider it a personal defect, to be treated with kindly pity, that her skirts hung badly and that her hat was out of fashion. She shook her red skirts which had looked so nice before Madge pointed out that dreadful fault in the hanging, and sighed again. But she was not going to show her feelings to Madge. The latter—tired of thinking of somebody else—had crossed over to the arm-chair, and flung herself into it. But she wanted to keep Hilda, as she did not wish either to leave her room or to be alone; so it was necessary to make some slight exertion to entertain her.

Lunch at Skipton was at two o'clock; and Madge had decreed that Mr. Fieldes should read poetry aloud at one. Before that Hilda went to her room to write to her mother, and found that, though to Madge Skipton might appear stale and tiresome, yet it supplied her with ample materials for a home letter.

BELOVED MOTHER,

I am going to write you a long letter of first impressions which are sure to be mostly wrong, but it will be amusing to compare them with the final ones when I get home. I do hope you are pretty well to-day and that you don't miss Brown. She is very grand and stiff, and bent on my supporting the honour of the younger branch of the house. Happily she is satisfied that I am better dressed than Mary, which is not difficult except in the matter of her riding habit. Mary was out hunting yesterday and you would realise the improvement in her appearance during the past two years if you could see her in her Busvine habit. Uncle Riversdale was beaming with pride in her, and he was looking as well as he always does in his red coat; they made quite a picture. Marmaduke says that it is pretty to see how devoted all the people here are to those two.

Mary and I get on pretty well so far, but we got rather cross this morning before breakfast upon the university question. I was only arguing in favour of Catholic young men going to Oxford and she said that her father thought it would never do, and she repeated a pompous sentence about Catholic atmosphere. I suppose I ought to have given in at once but I didn't, and she was as much shocked as if I had contradicted the Pope. Mr. Fieldes looked so amused while we were talking. I haven't told you a word yet about Mr. Fieldes. Isn't it interesting to meet him after my excitement over the *Phantasmagoria*. I don't quite know whether I like him or not, although he is very pleasant to talk to. That everybody says; and it is rather quaint to hear Aunt Helen talk to him about all her poor people and about poor George and Mary when they were babies. At this moment she has trotted him off to see the schools. Marmaduke told me last night that he had never seen a man who suited himself so much to the person he was talking to as Mr. Fieldes. 'If Aunt Helen,' he said, 'could have heard him tell good stories in the smoking-room at B— (where we met in the summer) I think her hair would have turned grey.' Marmaduke evidently doesn't like him and is somehow a little jealous.

You know Marmaduke's voice, and his style of singing, and I remember you said once to him that he reminded you of Santley. Mr. Fieldes has a small voice but with something very pathetic about it. He sings pretty little modern things, Blake's words set by some new man. Last night after dinner Madge told them both to sing and both refused and were pressed and refused again. At last Marmaduke moved, whereupon Mr. Fieldes somehow jumped from the other end of the room on to the piano-stool and sang all the evening, and I don't believe we shall hear a note from Marmaduke this time. I like Marmaduke, but he doesn't like me at all; he thinks me unamiable and critical and a prig; and he looked so bored after breakfast this morning when I talked books with Mr. Fieldes. I think it was stupid of me to talk about the *Grammar of Assent*, and I won't do it again. I wonder when I shall learn what not to do in society. Madge says it doesn't matter while I'm quite fresh, but I must listen to other people talking and see how they say things. She says you may talk of almost anything when you know how.

I must stop now, for Mr. Fieldes is going to read to us, but I will go on this evening.

This is how the letter was finished that evening after tea:—

Beloved mother, what are you doing by yourself this evening, and do you miss me a little bit? Will you see that somebody gives Father Jones my school story-books, as they will be wanted for my class. There is little to relate since this morning, and Madge finds life here terribly dull, but it seems to me rather amusing. However, I have had only twenty-four hours, but it feels as if it had been much longer. I have just come from the old school-room. It is a dear untidy old place, just as you remember it, but it might be made lovely. We have been trying to persuade Mary to do it up, but she was a little cross at our suggestions, and said it wasn't worth while to take the trouble. I am afraid there were old things of George's that she did not want to touch, and that we ought to have remembered. It is odd that she has been a little touchy sometimes to-day, and I used to think it was impossible to put her out of temper. She left us to do something in the sacristy, and Marmaduke and I amused ourselves by looking at the old lesson-books and talking of education. We had such an argument first about modern education, and I said I should never get over your not allowing me to have a regular Girton governess, who could have taught me Latin and Greek, and a little science to make me accurate. He says it is all stuff, and prevents women being half as sharp as they are by nature. He said all the insulting things about our instincts being the best part of us and that education interferes with them and makes us reason more slowly than men and miss the right point in the end. I got rather cross; which delighted him, and he said: 'Now here's a proof; you have read heaps of things, and you can talk capitally of things that you don't understand, but I would much rather have Mary's judgment of character than yours. You see all sorts of little things about people which makes you critical and censorious and yet you would be taken in by the first comer. Mary isn't half so clever, but you are much more likely to get into a scrape than she is. She has got instincts and you have got what you are pleased to call your reason.' I protested angrily at this impertinence, which only made him worse. 'Then Mary is much more useful than you are; she works beautifully and she can decorate furniture, while you make pencil studies of single leaves for their own sake, as I heard you telling Fieldes, just as he makes sketches of great houses for their own sakes. If I were your mother I'd teach you "to hem and to sew." Then Mary is far better tempered.' 'What on earth has Mary got to do with it?' I said crossly, for really, mother, he is a little annoying, because I can see he means what he says. He was sitting in a deep chair all the time, hardly looking at me, while he perpetrated these impertinent remarks. At last I said I would stand it no longer, and I walked out of the room.

I must just tell you about Mr. Fieldes' reading. I did enjoy it so. It was all poetry, bits from different people, mostly beautiful, but some of those Madge chose made me rather shy. He reads very well and the timbre of his voice suits pathetic things.

Marmaduke came in towards the end and listened. Mr. Fieldes was just reading those exquisite lines of Matthew Arnold's 'A Farewell.' He read it most beautifully and without any affectation, and he left the room directly afterwards. Madge soon followed. I was left alone with Marmaduke who was sitting near me.

'Do you like that sort of thing, Hilda?' he asked. 'Immensely,' I said, 'don't *you*?' 'I see it is fine,' he answered; 'but there is something in it I don't like. Fieldes would express it for me. Something of weakness, a want of backbone somewhere. It is to me the poetry of a nation that is going down hill.' I said something rather stupid, and without paying much attention to it he exclaimed sharply: 'I say, Hilda, who asked him to read? Who was he reading to?' 'We both asked him,' I said. At that moment Aunt Helen came in, and Marmaduke, who had had lunch, went out with Uncle Riversdale. Aunt Helen talked to me then about your health and other things. Do you know, I am sure she means very kindly! She says that she hopes I shall come again for the county ball and she told me how she used to enjoy it herself. I think she was a little hurt at our not coming here last year, she evidently didn't believe it was fear of the scarlet fever in the village; they all ignore infection and scout drains. Considering her health and her fat, isn't she wonderfully plucky? Always kneeling up straight through Mass, and Mary says she has never seen her lie on a sofa in her life, or read a novel. How Madge does dislike her, but I won't talk much of Madge, because you don't care for her, but she is very fascinating. Now I must stop.

I will write *constantly*, and then it will make a sort of diary of my first time away from you.

Do you remember how we used to play at seeing how we liked each other in new places? Well, I like you better than ever while I am at Skipton.

Your lovingest daughter,
HILDA.

"Is it true, as Madge says, that Skipton and all the property will belong to Mary now that George is dead? Madge said that the odd thing is that it hasn't changed Mary a bit, and that she really doesn't believe she thinks about it—she thinks it is a sort of stupidity, but I don't believe Mary is stupid, do you?"

Mrs. Riversdale had stayed talking to Hilda until the gong sounded for luncheon.

Luncheon at Skipton had always been a long ceremony, but it seemed to Madge now that the old butler and his many subordinates had grown slower than ever. Even after they had finished handing round three or four varieties of sweets, there was still much to be done with cheese and butter, and the ceremonies attending on cake and fruit and wine appeared interminable.

When all was over, Mrs. Riversdale showed no signs of moving, and the others sitting idly round the table waited impatiently for their release. The master of the house and Marmaduke Lemarchant had gone for a long farming walk, so that on Mr. Fieldes devolved the duties of the only gentleman in the company. He had been doing his best to maintain the flagging conversation between the ladies, but had again found it rather a hard task.

Mrs. Riversdale sat at the head of the table, enveloped in her black silk, which was even more covered with crape than the gown she had worn the day before, and weighed down with chains of jet and a large miniature of the late George set in pearls. She looked, in spite of a certain stateliness in her bearing, oppressed by herself and her surroundings. Madge's delicate,

Dresden-china, little figure was now elaborately dressed in a masculine style, just so far in advance of the general fashion of the moment as to appear a little surprising even to Mark Fieldes, as well as to appal Mrs. Riversdale, quite apart from the fact of its being worn by a widow. To Hilda, who had recovered from the shock of the day before, and had dismissed from her mind the ideal broken heart, the dress was extremely interesting, and not unworthy of imitation. She was just wondering how the belt was arranged in that peculiar way, when at last, with the dignity begotten of difficulty, Mrs. Riversdale rose and led the way to the adjoining drawing-room.

All the rooms at Skipton were large, high, well-lighted and well-proportioned, but entirely unpicturesque. It would have needed nothing short of artistic genius, and genius with a large command of materials, to have made that room beautiful. Madge would certainly have begun the work in a spirit of revolution. How often had she longed to have the hanging of the old family pictures—now arranged entirely with a view to their shape and size in a large pattern on each of the four walls. And how often she had had to restrain a mad longing to lay violent hands on the stiff, lonely islands of furniture, whose severance seemed ruled by the inexorable floral designs of the carpet. A magnificent carving by Gibbons and a few bits of historic china on the mantelshelf in the corner where Mrs. Riversdale passed the greater part of her day made one pleasant spot for the eye to rest on, and was a contrast to the general stiffness; though the various efforts of her own and Mary's needles, in the form of banner screens, cushions, etc., were not highly artistic.

Mrs. Riversdale had been a little worried as to the plans for the afternoon. She herself could not go out, as she was suffering from an attack of bronchitis; and she had arranged that Mary should drive Father Clement to visit some of the poor in the neighbourhood. It resulted from this arrangement that Madge and Hilda were left to their own devices, in company with Mr. Fieldes. This was exactly what their hostess had wished to prevent, but she had been too full of Father Clement and the poor that morning to remember Hilda. She apologised to Madge for leaving her to herself, and offered her the landau, but Madge preferred to walk. A moment afterwards the tall, white figure of the monk was seen coming along the laurel walk in the garden. His cowl was thrown back, and showed the shaven head, the narrow dome-shaped forehead, the thin regular features, and the long white beard. The head was held erect, a little thrown back, as if he were scenting the wintry air with pleasure. His step was alert and vigorous, but rather slow. His whole movement seemed in measure to some rhythm, "the rhythm," as Fieldes himself once expressed it, "of freedom willingly in bondage."

Mark Fieldes was rooted to the spot at the sight of him, and it needed an imperious gesture from Madge, who was vanishing through a side door, before he would follow.

"Let us go to the billiard-room!" she exclaimed, as the door shut behind them, and she almost ran down the passage. "It is the only bearable room," Madge cried as they entered. "I arranged it myself, and they had these splendid old sofas in the house already." She flung herself down on a long deep sofa by the fireplace. "I will say for my mother-in-law that the fires are big enough, but, oh, how one pines for coffee. Have you matches?"

Mr. Fieldes had matches, and Madge, cigarette in mouth, mounted on a footstool and leant towards him, balancing herself with her two white hands behind her back. Mr. Fieldes thought that she looked a picture of grace and elegance in the style of a Parisian water-colour sketch, and he hastened to strike a lucifer and light her cigarette; but he was too eager, and he dropped it only an inch from her foot in its open-work stocking. Madge leant forward and pretended to box his ears as he stooped to pick it up, but at this same moment she looked out of the window and saw the monk, who had stopped to speak to the gardener before passing on to the hall. He bowed to her with old-fashioned grace, and walked on. Madge turned red with anger, and flung her cigarette into the grate.

"It is intolerable," she said quite fiercely, "having that man prowling about. It is bad enough to have to go to the chapel twice a day, but to have him prowling round, and sticking his long beard in at the windows, is insufferable."

Mr. Fieldes watched her curiously; he was puzzled at the amount of temper she showed with regard to Father Clement, and he wished to understand why there was this personal feeling. He thought he knew Mrs. George Riversdale fairly well. He had spent three weeks at different times in her company during the year, and had grown almost intimate with her; he appreciated her many little ways of charming and of exciting interest and even something warmer; but he fancied that she was rather different at Skipton-le-Grange to what she had been elsewhere. She was excited, theatrical, and a little nervous, overdoing her good manners with Mrs. Riversdale, and feverish in her girlish friendship with Hilda.

After he had succeeded in lighting her cigarette, Madge flung herself wearily on the sofa which presented the best background of drapery and cushions, and was overshadowed by a spiky palm tree.

Fieldes leant his tall, stooping shoulders against the mantelshelf, and looked down on her while she talked.

"Did I ever tell you that we had to live here when we first married?" she said. "Did you ever hear of such a stupid plan? It was—I can't tell you what it was. You can see what the house is now. Well, it was always full of priests and cousins and old fogies, never empty, and the visitors were always bores. George could hunt and shoot, but I wasn't allowed to, and I wonder I didn't go silly. Of course I was in love with George then, or I should never have been such an idiot as to agree to it. After a year I managed to get a house in London, and there I could breathe, I *could* exist, and after that we came only on state visits."

Fieldes found that facial sympathy was enough, and Madge flowed on, eagerly explaining all the hardships of her past lot; looking very pretty, and at moments very pathetic. He could not but be touched and interested in her confidences, though a little thrown back by the touches of temper she could hardly suppress.

"As I said to Laura Hurstmonceaux," she concluded, after a long tirade against her mother-in-law, "the wonder is that one kept straight at all—she came in between me and George at every turn, and made him interfere with me, and one of the plans was to get this Father Clement to do me good. You cannot think how funny it was to see her little plots to leave us together, and now I bet you anything you like she and he are groaning over me at this moment, and saying that I am going hopelessly to the bad. Heigho," and she sighed deeply.

A few moments' silence followed.

"Tell me about Miss Hilda Riversdale," asked Fieldes abruptly, "she seems quite different from the rest of the clan."

"Oh, yes," answered Madge, "her widow mother—who brought her up—is not one of the old Catholic lot at all. She was a Miss Harding—a convert; and Hilda is her only child and has lived entirely with her."

"A granddaughter of James Harding who had that large house in Eaton Square?" asked Mark.

Madge nodded.

"Then she must be his only grandchild, for the eldest Miss Harding never married," said Fieldes musingly.

He took up a book from the table and there was another pause in the conversation. It was Madge who now spoke first.

"What book have you got there?"

"A stupid thing of Octave Feuillet; it is Feuillet at his feeblest."

He half opened the paper volume as he spoke and then shut it quickly.

"There was a photograph of a lady inside," said Madge, with a little malice.

"And a man," said Mark. "It is only a photograph I took last year with my instantaneous camera."

"Let me see it."

"I'd rather not; in fact," mysteriously, "I really can't; that is, not unless you swear by all that is sacred never to allude to it, never to mention it to a living human being."

As he spoke he withheld the book in a tantalising manner.

"Sworn, sworn a thousand times," cried Madge, delighted to have her curiosity aroused.

"Most solemnly?" said Mark.

"Most solemnly," echoed Madge.

He handed her the book, but she did not perceive the intense curiosity betrayed in his attitude, the mere wish for information mingling with an artistic delight in the study of human nature.

It was some moments before Madge could make out the dim figures. Suspicion and surprise alternated in her face as she looked at it, and a momentary indignation appeared, but was suppressed. The likeness showed two figures, a woman standing and a man kneeling on one knee—the woman was in fancy dress, of antique classical make, the man's large muscular form was in ordinary evening dress. The woman's hand was raised to his lips.

"How did you do this?"

There was a slight touch of scorn in Madge's manner.

"Oh, it was at the Duchess of A's. Cecilia Rupert had been dancing divinely—but *divinely*, it was simply inspired movement. You know what she can be and do. It is genius; there is no other word for it. Well, I saw Lord Bellasis creep quietly out of his place in the audience, and he passed close to me, so that he touched me. I was in the front row, at the end, and as he slipped past the screen close to me I moved one step after him, and saw what you see a dim reflection of now. It was taken in a flash of light from a tableau as he stood in the side screen. I hardly knew what I should find when I developed the reflection. And seriously"—something in her face made his tone more apologetic—"I didn't mean to steal a march upon him, I was resolved never to show it to mortal man, much less mortal woman, but you were so severe on me yesterday when I spoke of Bellasis showing Miss Rupert attention that I could not resist letting you see it."

"You have done it very cleverly," said Madge, keeping a firm hold of the little limp paper, and ignoring Mark's outstretched hand. "When was this?"

"Oh, it was in the spring, at Whitsuntide. You won't tell anybody, will you?"

"Oh, no," said Madge very slowly, "I shall not mention it."

At that moment the old butler came in with a salver load of letters.

"What a heap for you, Mr. Fieldes," said Madge with admiration, hastily slipping the limp photograph, which was half hidden in her hand, under the sofa cushion by her side.

Mr. Fieldes took his letters to one of the windows, and began to look quickly through various notes and invitations, for Parliament was sitting and London was beginning to fill. Presently he raised his head to make an observation on the odious handwriting of that charming Madame de B—, the ambassadress, when his speech was stopped in the utterance by his surprise at what he saw. Madge was holding something down in the fire with the poker, and with such an expression of gnome-like mischief and cruel exultation in her small face and figure, that Fieldes half expected to see that she was burning some living thing in the hot coals; but as he looked apprehensively into the fire, the thing which writhed under the poker curled up in process of burning, and he saw the two dim figures of Lord Bellasis and Cecilia Rupert intensified in expression, as it seemed, by the flame that, a moment afterwards, extinguished them. It was the affair of a second, and Fieldes had only time to look hastily back at his letters, and was so confused as to open and read intently an evident bill, before Madge began to talk again in a much calmer voice than before.

"By the way, Mr. Fieldes, what has become of that photograph you showed me, I want to look at it again, please."

This sort of remark was easily responded to. Fieldes said quite naturally:—

"Isn't it among your letters on the chimneypiece?"

Madge searched, shook her gown and looked about.

"You are sure it is not among yours?"

Fieldes turned them over demonstratively.

"Dear, how tiresome," said Madge, "I'm afraid I must have dropped it into the fire with a heap of envelopes. I am so sorry; but I must get ready, or it will be dark before we get out."

Madge tripped away, trilling as she went in a wilfully irritating way, in her pretty little soprano, "My heart is like an apple tree."

Fieldes was annoyed with her for destroying his property, yet in his heart he knew that she had acted rightly. He had hardly shown it to her before he was repenting of his indiscretion. Why had he been such an ass as to show her the photograph? What fit of tactlessness had made him give it to one of Lord Bellasis' most intimate friends? A thing that he had meant never to reveal, an action he had known to be ungentlemanly. He had seen the curl of contempt on Madge's little mouth. He had done for himself, perhaps, with a whole circle of people should Madge be indiscreet. He would be described to her friends as ungentlemanly, prying and very idiotic. It was characteristic of him that he would in this instance agree quite candidly with their verdict—he—whose ambition it was to be a supreme social success through delicacy and tact founded on his knowledge of human nature. Happily for him Madge had more inducements to hold her tongue than arose from any mere regard for the promise she had given him.

CHAPTER VI

A LETTER FROM LONDON

Madge, after leaving the billiard-room, went on with her singing until she had shut her bedroom door behind her. She had hardly done so before Hilda knocked.

"Don't come in," said Madge quickly.

"Then we will wait in the hall," Hilda answered.

"No, no," said Madge, springing up, "don't wait. I can't come out, I have got so many letters by this post to answer. Take Mr. Fieldes for a walk, and I shall go for a turn later."

"Oh," Hilda's voice sounded dissatisfied. Madge heard her move away and come back.

"But, Madge."

"Well?" rather impatiently.

"Oh, nothing," said Hilda, and she went off again. She had meant to ask Madge if she need go out alone with Mr. Fieldes, but her courage failed. She knew that Madge would divine the shyness that was her only objection, and would be merciless in her laughter.

As Hilda's footsteps could be heard retreating down the passage, Madge said to herself:—

"I don't know why I said I should go out with them, for I never meant to. I've got too much to do."

She was standing by the writing-table and she absently opened a silver box and took from it a *marron glacé*. The soothing sensation of this particular bonbon on her palate was pleasant, she sat down to enjoy it. Presently her thoughts became again explicit.

"Yes, I have got a great deal to do, chiefly of course I must prepare for confession. I was right in thinking I should be quiet enough here, at last, to think things over. And it is a good long time to think about,—since Easter."

The *marron glacé* was dissolved entirely by now. Madge felt the need of another sensation, she drew a vase of violets nearer to her and inhaled a long deep breath. Then she took up her cigarette case and lit a cigarette. A moment more and she had ensconced herself on the sofa and pummelled the cushion behind her into a right state of submission.

"I cannot stand seeing Father Clement; I wonder I wanted to go to confession to him. Now that I see him his face maddens me. It is intolerable of my mother-in-law to have brought him here to convert me. Oh, dear, I wish she knew what a saint my own friends think me. How little she knows," Madge smiled bitterly, "what I went through, she—who had such a husband and two children to care for. I suppose good women will be well punished for their horrid harsh judgments. Now if I had been Mrs. Riversdale—but," and she laughed more naturally, "to tell the truth if I *had*, really I should have died from absolute dulness."

Puff, puff, a little dreaminess.

"I think it would be much easier to go to one of the Servites in London who know nothing about me; only I've too much to do in London, and—and somehow I thought it would be easier down here. I was so extraordinarily good in those old dull days here when I first began to be unhappy, and Father Clement used to . . . I almost wish I had not been quite so rude to him. Well, I suppose I had better rouse myself and go to the chapel if I am going to prepare. Nine months, and I used to go every fortnight."

Madge rose, walked to the table and touched a prayer book near her, but did not raise it. Instead she lifted a photograph and looked at it. It showed a group of about fifteen people, standing about the doorway of a magnificent structure, one of the greatest of English historic fortresses. One or two of the group were on horseback; the others, men and women, had most of them just dismounted. Two or three ladies only were not in their habits, and among these was Madge.

"Oh, dear," she thought, "and only two months ago! What fun it was. There is no place in this world like Bellasis, and it will be quite, quite spoilt for us all if he makes a fool of himself and marries Cecilia. It was mean and low to take that photograph. No gentleman would have done it. I am glad I burnt it. It might have been of use to Cecilia. By the way I wonder if he has kept the film, or if he took other proofs."

"After all," she said presently, "these months haven't been so very bad. I have not worried very much, and I have had some very good times. Let me see, there was the season; although I was in mourning, it was pleasant. Then the shooting party at Mr. Z.'s, and the other visits in the Highlands, then the Duchess of A.'s, and best of all Bellasis Castle. And I haven't done anything wrong, I mean not very wrong, all the time, which is a comfort. But it is so tiring going to confession, and raking up all one's feelings, when far the best I can do is to get rid of feeling altogether. Yet I quite made up my mind I would go to the sacraments down here, and in fact I *must*, and in fact I *will*. Father Clement was to hear confessions after his drive with Mary. I will go to the chapel now, if nobody is about, and I will prepare there. I shall just have time."

At that moment there was a knock at the door.

"Who is it?"

"C'est moi, madame."

"Entrez donc."

Celestine came in. She did not notice the nervous start of relief that Madge gave at this interruption, but she was surprised at the graciousness of her reception. She had just finished repairing the crushed bodice which had brought upon her a scolding that morning. Madge praised her work, tried it on, needlessly, and ordered some alterations which quite puzzled Celestine.

"Did you meet anybody in the passage?" she said a little mysteriously.

"Non, madame."

"Oh, never mind," said Madge irrelevantly, "you can go now." Then turning sharply round: "Go, Celestine, didn't you hear me speak?"

"But, madame, je voudrais remplacer—"

"Oh, go," cried Madge nervously.

Celestine dropped the bodice on the bed with a little gesture of protest. Madge, the moment she was gone, knelt down by the sofa and burst into tears.

"Oh, what a miserable unhappy woman I am. I must, must go to confession and I can't, I can't, I can't. Everybody is unkind to me, everybody that's good I mean, and I am quite alone, and, oh, so miserable, and I must amuse myself, and I mustn't feel. I knew how it would be if I came to this horrid, horrid place. It frightens me. The chapel frightens me, it makes me so dreadfully, terribly afraid of dying. I remember when I was ill in this room, and I thought about going to heaven, and how I should get the love there I couldn't get from George. But now I can't think of those things, but I am frightened because, as Cecilia says, life is a mortal illness."

She sat up now on the sofa: the tears had relieved her.

"I wish I hadn't got into this state," she went on, "I must try to get calm before I can think properly. After all Father Clement will be in the confessional again after Benediction to-night, and to-morrow is a feast. I can easily slip away after tea and begin my preparation then. I am too confused and tired for it to be of any use to examine myself now."

Then she remembered that she had not even opened her letters. She might as well do that, as her own thinking was only waste of time. The first letter that she read was from Mrs. Hurstmonceaux.

My dear Madge,

I wonder how you are pulling through the time down there! I picture you to myself with the priests and the cousins and the old fogies—or better still arranging the flowers for the chapel, or teaching the Sunday school. It presented so many sweet pictures to my mind—as Lord Bellasis said to me to-night, 'How delicious she must look when she is praying.' But seriously, Madge, is this wise? You gave admirable business reasons for your plan, but I have my suspicions of you, all the same.

You said you were going down to Skipton to arrange your money matters with your husband's family. That sounds well, but, Madge, I think it is my knowledge of your character that makes me have my suspicions of this visit. What is it in a woman's nature that makes her love to try experiments? I am half afraid you have gone to see what it feels like at Skipton. I have known people get themselves complicated in absurd religious emotions and scruples who only began with this sort of curiosity, with a wish to experiment on their own emotions. I am half afraid you have gone to try Skipton, to make sure you can throw over your past life. However, though I give you this warning, I am not much alarmed. There is this advantage in your impressionableness, your sensitiveness to influence, in your artistic temperament, that you are easily repelled by what is unattractive. I think the experiment may have a bracing effect. All the narrowness, the prosaic dulness, the superstitious, unreal bigotry, must be repulsive to your nature. As Lord Bellasis said last night, 'She is so easily impressed, yet so hard to force.' This is the second time I have quoted that friend of yours, so I will tell you how we passed this evening together. I asked him to dine at eight, but he said he would rather come at half-past. My dear, whoever has to take that man in hand will have a time of it—and yet one can hardly blame him for being spoilt. I suppose nobody in England has had more of the spoiling process applied to him. And there is something so graceful (if such a huge thing can be graceful) and simple in him all the time. Where I do blame him a little is in his flirtation with Cecilia. Surely he has had enough of more delicate, more subtle overtures from far more beautiful women to resist Cecilia's unblushing siege? Perhaps it is the appearance of extreme openness that he likes. Anyhow she manages to amuse him. Much as I dislike her, I own there is a touch of genius. I never saw anybody so carried away by what excites her emotions. To see her listening to music, above all—to see her dance. I fancy it is partly a touch of hysteria that gives that peculiar light in her eyes; she seems to work herself up into a sort of frenzy of excitement—of pleasure touched by pain. It is the untrammelled, unconventional, almost fierce nature asserting itself. Last night there was a pathos, a melancholy in her dancing that was curiously original. Bellasis and I fell into a sort of reverie, the spirit of old Rome seemed to come out of it. She said before she began, 'Let us play that we are away from it all, all the dulness, the stupidity, the Methodist chapels, the dons, the goody-goody sickening old England; let us play at Rome. Come to the smoking-room.' Well, we put away everything but the low sofas and the cushions and we hid the newspapers, and we lit the lamps my husband brought from Naples, and then we took the carpets away off the marble floor. And in the low light, I played, and she danced, and the splendid pagan creature seemed to take us into the one rhythm that is in all music, the rhythm that our souls have caught from nature and have concentrated in art.

Now, as I am dropping with sleep, I must stop this long-winded letter, dearest Madge, hoping that the fatigue of reading it has not added to the tedium of your present surroundings.

A vous (very much),
LAURA.
Monday night, 1 A.M.

Madge's face had changed several times during the reading of this letter. A sense of satisfaction and consolation had come from the insinuated and repeated compliments of the first pages. Then Laura was quite right; Skipton was simply painful and sympathy was soothing. Laura was quite wrong, however, in supposing that she was in any danger of turning into a *dévote*.

But sympathy and compliments were forgotten as the letter passed to Cecilia's dancing. Madge's face darkened, her hand was clenched. She read each word slowly and carefully, then turned back and scanned them still more closely. Was this in reality, this absurd, high-flown account of Cecilia's dancing, a practical warning? That would be exactly like Laura, and yet what could Laura know or divine that could make her take up such an attitude? Or rather what could she imagine, for there was nothing for Laura to know?

"Nothing at all," she muttered to herself, as she read and re-read the flowing, pointed writing.

So occupied was Madge that it was not until she was startled by the great clock in the chapel tower striking half-past five that she roused herself and hurriedly joined the others round the tea-table. She was not surprised to hear that there was no Benediction that evening; she could not think now what had made her suppose there would be.

CHAPTER VII

A RETROSPECT

If Madge had not seen Mark's stolen photograph that afternoon, Laura's account of Cecilia's dancing would not have given her so much food for thought. Cecilia was evidently becoming a more serious element in affairs of importance than Madge had ever expected her to be. Mark's evidence for his gossip of the day before had impressed itself painfully on her mind. Though this photograph was burnt, she was not sure there might not be another copy; and the incident had actually happened, and must be fresh in Bellasis' memory,—the memory of a man of honour. Then she could not really doubt that there was a definite intention in Laura's absurdly poetical description of Cecilia's dancing in a badly lighted back smoking-room in a dull London house.

A little explanation is needed to show why Madge felt so deeply as to the possibility of a marriage between Lord Bellasis and Miss Rupert, and why Mark Fieldes appealed to her as an authority on the subject, and why Laura wrote to her in detail of the evening which the two had spent together in her house.

The ways and manners of any set in society may differ endlessly, but they have one thing generally in common. Each clique has as a rule its hero or heroine, and delights, by an exaggerated mannerism, in talking of his or her wonderful gifts or peculiarities. They choose an individual who is a specimen of their ideas and their way of living, and who represents them to the rest of the world. They know that they are regarded as So-and-so's "lot," or "set," or "friends."

Lord Bellasis was a marked instance of a man who was the centre of a clique; and he had all the necessary qualifications. He was unmarried, not too young, enormously rich. His home was a very fine old castle, and his yacht was perfection. To an acute eye there were however signs of a possible want of permanence in his usefulness as a centre. He had only recently lived the sort of life and done the sort of actions that showed that he appreciated the good things of the world. His youth had been spent in travel. It was said that he had had wonderful adventures in dim regions, in South Africa, or perhaps South America, and that his command of languages "which nobody can understand" was marvellous. But he had no strong political interests, and his philanthropic enterprises inclined to hobbyism. Since his reappearance on the social scene, which he had abandoned in the early stages of his dancing days, he had talked of political life and political interests half cynically, but with complete information. He preferred as his friends people who had such interests, and they were for the present taking for granted that he had come back to English life to do great things.

Of course there was another side to the fashion of holding him in such immense esteem; he was unmarried, and practical people thought that possibly he "was looking round" (as an American friend suggested in speaking to himself) for a mistress of Bellasis Castle. This notion gave additional importance to the women—and charming women they were—who had grouped themselves about him. So charming were they in every sense, so rarefied was their mental atmosphere and so exclusive, that it was really surprising that Madge had obtained her admission amongst them. Before she had met Lord Bellasis she had not done badly with the sporting, money-spending friends to whom George had introduced her. Now the very thought of such people was distasteful as a faded scent to her nostrils. The change had come rapidly. There had been a beautiful, a delightful week, replete with surprises. It had been in the house of a Lady K., who had taken a fancy to her and who had included her in a large shooting party in January. Madge had not been half an hour in the house before she discovered that the party consisted of Lord Bellasis and his friends, and that she was almost the only one among them who was not of them in any way. Madge's half-terrified soul took fire with ambition. She swore, as she sat in a chilly back bedroom, that she would conquer or die; and her wishes for success were almost prayers. She bore a mortally dull evening with absolute unconsciousness and infectious good humour. Lady Campion, the old aunt of Lord Bellasis, a woman of strong and unaccountable likes and dislikes, became in the course of a few days quite devoted to her. Before the end of the visit she had won her way, for she had captured the very heart of the citadel. She was breathless with unbetrayed excitement when after one breakfast by her side Lord Bellasis chose the vacant seat by her at luncheon. At another breakfast and another luncheon he did the same. Other attentions too numerous to be related followed.

In a less-refined atmosphere Madge might have been betrayed into vainglory, and the ladies of the party might have only resisted her the more. But these people were real ladies, and Madge instinctively adopted their spirit. They told each other, and they told Lord Bellasis, that she was quite charming, in fact they adopted her on the spot *pro tem*. In their rooms at night they told each other how her hands and her feet betrayed the vulgarity of her origin, and that if Lord Bellasis persisted in his new fancy she must be taught a great many things, but that she might eventually become presentable.

Amongst them at that time Cecilia Rupert was held to be the reigning favourite, and she was made to be popular. She was a daughter of the late Lord Rupert, one of Mr. Gladstone's peers. She was good natured and her rampant egotism was on a large artistic scale. She had few small meannesses or petty spites. She and Madge struck up an alliance.

No more details of that eventful week need here be given. Lord Bellasis and Madge had made great friends. He spoke with honest admiration of her goodness and of her gowns, and used strong expressions with regard to the departed George Riversdale, who, it appeared, had not appreciated his own happiness.

All this had happened at a fortunate moment. Lord Bellasis wished to have a friend young enough to be amusing, a shrewd and practical woman, to help his only near relation, his aunt, Lady Campion (who was old and infirm) to entertain his guests at Bellasis Castle when he reopened it for shooting in the following autumn. Before speaking of the matter to Lady Campion he had talked it over with Cecilia. Cecilia made the common mistake of preferring the unknown danger to the known. There was not one among them all into whose hands she would willingly give the conduct of those vitally, terribly, important gatherings at Bellasis. She emphatically vetoed one or two names Bellasis suggested. She rose to the idea of Madge—whom he mentioned as perhaps hardly to be thought of. She thought that this little woman would do very nicely what was wanted, and being on her promotion would be only too glad to take her cue from Cecilia herself. The fact that his aunt—who was so hard to please—already liked Madge, was an argument which Cecilia could urge strongly on Bellasis in her favour.

The thing was decided upon in a consultation as they came home from shooting. That conversation remained deeply graven on Cecilia's mind in the months that followed. It was almost the last of those intimate talks on which her soul had lived and thriven. As she sat on the gate, gun in hand (Cecilia was an excellent shot) with a bright sun lighting up the wooded landscape, Bellasis had talked to her long and confidentially of one after another of his lady friends. As she felt his eyes rest on her, during intervals of silence, in half-amused admiration at her wonderful shooting costume, she had murmured to herself, "O Temps, suspends ton vol." She had longed that the joy of those moments might remain with her for ever. The decision about Madge had seemed a mere episode—a way out of acquiescing in any more dangerous arrangement.

"The little woman is a Roman Catholic, is she not?" Bellasis had asked.

"Yes, Madge Riversdale is of Irish blood and French education," she had replied.

"A bonne fille du couvent?" he had inquired.

"Yes, but not oppressively strict. Her diet includes a good many gnats. But she would not look at a camel."

"There are women for whom camels have no attraction."

"That may account for it," Cecilia had answered indifferently. And that was all that was said of Madge.

Lord Bellasis was enchanted with what proved to be the immense success of Cecilia's notion. Madge had done perfectly; she had hit upon the exact medium between the real hostess and the mere visitor. She had relieved Lady Campion of all bores. She had saved her from the confidences of unavoidable mothers. She had carried through school feasts, Primrose League *fêtes*, harvest homes, with the least possible amount of boredom and the greatest possible amount of credit to the lord of the castle. Then her practical talents had been invaluable. Nothing could have been smarter, better ordered, better chosen than all the details she suggested. And yet Madge had not seemed to interfere; and certainly she and Lady Campion were the warmest of allies. Everybody found what they wanted everywhere without asking; and of information Madge had an unlimited, never-failing supply. She knew where the best cigars and cigarettes were to be got, and Bellasis Castle, although Bellasis himself was no smoker, after her suggestions overflowed with them. She knew when all the trains left; and all the junctions that confused other people were plain sailing to her. She had won the heart of the old Scotch gardener, and more flowers were allowed to come up to the castle, and they were more often changed, than they had ever been before. She was most thoroughly happy and good-humoured. "She had let the dead past bury its dead." She was living *de jour au jour* exactly her ideal life. It was even more delightful, this life in the grand old castle, than she had imagined. Luxury here was more dignified than elsewhere—it seemed part of the air you breathed. Life had nothing little in this historic atmosphere; and the least of the occupations and duties—school feasts or country neighbours to be entertained at lunch—were invested with the halo of great traditions. What then was her pleasure when she felt that it was *her* tact and carefulness, *her* thought and readiness that had helped to bring about the success of house-parties which included some of the greatest men and most interesting women of the day! No wonder that Madge enjoyed herself.

As Lord Bellasis became more and more pleased with his new friend, Cecilia became less and less so. And as Madge's tact grew and developed in the warm, pleasant air she was living in, Cecilia seemed to become less discreet, less sweet-tempered, less urbane in almost the same proportion. A thousand times a day she cursed her own folly in her choice of Madge for the hostess at Bellasis.

"Lady M. must have gone home part of the time," she muttered; "Mrs. D. would have been too fussy and annoyed Bellasis; Louie Harcourt has begun to bore him; Ella would have tried to marry him to somebody and failed; Dottie, or one of the other married ones, might have flirted with him herself—but what would that have mattered? Lady Lena would have spent half the day in her room. This intolerable little thing never goes away and never bores him or makes a mistake; and she isn't straightforward I am sure. She really settled the ball week the moment she knew that I was engaged to the Percys, and then pretended to be miserable."

It was not one piece of successful diplomacy which appeared to Cecilia's distorted vision to have come between her and her host, but a thousand obstacles, and in every instance she thought she could detect Madge's influence.

There were altogether five parties at Bellasis; two for grouse in August and September; one in October; one for Christmas; and the last for a county ball at the beginning of January. Madge had been at Bellasis through September and October with only a week's interlude; then she had paid a number of visits between October and Christmas, and from Christmas until the ball she had again helped Lady Campion. After the ball she had seen that a return to her house in London was inevitable.

Madge was in low spirits when she reached London. The interval of perfect enjoyment was over, and she had a natural misgiving that so unlikely an arrangement as that of the last few months would hardly be repeated. With all her care she had probably, she thought in this gloomy mood, made some enemies. One enemy she knew she had made.

"But then with Cecilia I had no choice, or rather I was obliged to choose between helping or hindering something serious."

Her house, though exquisitely furnished and in perfect order, looked gloomy enough to the little widow on her home-coming. She shivered as she crossed the threshold.

Old thoughts and feelings seemed to have come down upon her, as though a heavy cloak had been put on her shoulders in the hall. There was nothing to find fault with, nothing but a very big heap of bills to distract her now. Also a note from the priest of her parish, whom she hardly knew, asking her if she wished to keep her seat in the church during the New Year.

She was sitting over the fire as she read it before going up to bed.

"Why should he suppose that I wanted to give it up?" she had cried, with unreasonable irritation at the usual formal circular.

She was feeling sad, lonely and deserted this evening. Her excitements were over; and really at Bellasis latterly she had not had quite the same sort of intense enjoyment as in September.

"All things wear out in this dull world," she thought, "I am aweary, aweary of it all."

And the weariness of that first home-coming, for which nobody had cared, had deepened during the days that followed. She went to the theatre, and the plays were slow; she went to concerts, and she came to the conclusion that she was not really musical, which anybody else could have told her long ago. She went to the picture galleries, and though she could not say that she was not artistic, she could find the fatigue intolerable. She was in a mood in which a woman educated in a less vivid faith would have played with religion. On that subject Madge was uncomfortable, thoroughly uncomfortable. The diet of gnats, of which Cecilia had spoken, had given her some sort of moral indigestion.

It occurred to her to ask her married sister to come from Scotland to stay with her, and she thought she would talk over some of the "gnats" with her. She felt sure that she would consider half of them scruples and tell her not to fuss.

People had to live in the world, and behave as the world does. She counted on her sister to make her feel more comfortable and more able to go to confession again and to get spiritual comfort in services when she felt sad. And then she would not be nervous and afraid, as she was now, that she wasn't as good as she might be; and that it would be a bad look out if she should die of anything sudden or of an accident as people sometimes do.

She had not seen this sister, who was a few years older than herself, for several years, and not since the elder one had married a man of good family, a quiet, out-of-the world, Scotch squire. Her sister, delighted, came up to stay with Madge, and found it very convenient to be there for her dentist, for visits to the stores, for seeing the pictures and for many things. She was full to overflowing with her own life and her own plans, and worst of all her own children and her husband's children by his first marriage. She advised Madge in matters of economy because she was saving her own fortune for her children. She told her how much more particular she had grown as to religion, because a mother must give a good example. She was kind and sisterly in manner, and thought she was cheering Madge out of the exuberance of her own full life. But she could be of no real use. She wore the wrong clothes, she said the wrong things, she was inclined to take scandal, in fact the only good part about her was her anxiety to get home again as soon as she had stayed long enough to buy everything she wanted, from a perambulator to a carpet.

"Happily," thought Madge, "I have few friends in London just now." But they were beginning to come soon after the unpresentable sister had left. Madge was delighted to find that a good many people were coming up for the opening of Parliament; she hoped now to have enough going on to cure her of this tiresome sort of depression. And perhaps the lonely time she had been spending had made her morbid, for she was not satisfied with the many invitations and attentions she received. For, in spite of far better things than she had ever had before, and a certain acknowledged position which she had specially desired to win, she was disappointed. Her special goddesses, the little group of women who had been more than cordial to her at Bellasis, made her feel a subtle difference in London. Whether, as she soon came to believe, Cecilia was poisoning the wells, and an effort was being made to keep her out in the cold, or whether it was merely their natural habit to allow some people to come just so far and no farther in their intimacy, was uncertain. Anyhow she felt that her hope of having become one of that most exclusive group of charming and influential women was yet unattained. Once really *of* them, her lonely life would have been brightened in a thousand ways, and the element of struggle to advance, or to retain, which seemed to her necessary in her single-handed existence, would have been over.

At this time came the invitation to Skipton, and Madge decided to go there. This was the culminating moment of her low spirits. It was a day on which she had been startled and upset. Hearing of the *accouchement* of a young woman, a recent acquaintance, one of the "nicest" and "smartest" people she knew, Madge had driven to inquire for her and her baby. As she sat waiting for her footman to bring the butler's message, Laura Hurstmonceaux came out of the house.

"Well," said Madge, with the forced cheerfulness with which she habitually alluded to babies; "is it a nice little girl?"

"Oh," said Laura quietly, "then you have not heard; it is dying, it can only live a few hours."

"Has she seen it? Does she know?"

"Yes, she saw it, but she heard the doctor say that it could not live, and she became unconscious. They were already alarmed about her. There seems now to be little hope for her. Where are you off to, Madge?"

Laura's tone had been sufficiently, but not overpoweringly, sympathetic with the tragedy in the house she had just left. She was surprised at the amount of emotion on Madge's face. Laura begged her to come back to tea with her. Madge would not. She said she had had a splitting headache all day, and they parted rather abruptly.

The picture of what had passed in that house was too vivid to her. It had taken possession of her completely. She knew it all so well, the darkened room, the cautious tread, the white bundle that had been put by the mother's side, the revelation and the loss of hope.

"And if I had died like that! and if I had died like that!" she went on repeating to herself as she drove home.

And that evening came the annual invitation to Skipton, which she had now twice refused, and she at once sat down and accepted it. Madge, after this, was several times on the point of making some excuse, of getting some plea for avoiding the visit. She would have been surprised if she had known how truly, according to her lights, Laura Hurstmonceaux had understood her behaviour. Laura had spoken freely to Lord Bellasis on the subject on the Monday night when he had dined with her.

When Cecilia left them—after the little scene described in Laura's letter to Madge—Laura and Lord Bellasis stood for a moment in the hall in silence. Then he smiled and said:—

"May I stay?"

But when they were settled quietly by the drawing-room fire, he apparently had nothing special to say.

"You were rash to let me get into this perfect arm-chair," he remarked in a dreamy voice; "I shall soon be asleep."

"Then I can go to bed," returned Laura, smiling.

"I was bored at finding Cecilia here to-night, but she has been amusing as usual."

Laura did not speak, she meant him to take his own time. To be the confidante of Lord Bellasis was a *rôle* worthy of the discretion on which she prided herself. How many of the ladies who hardly acknowledged Mrs. Hurstmonceaux as more than a mere acquaintance would have envied her the intimate relations with him that had been opened by his last letter!

A close observer might have seen that Lord Bellasis was affecting an ease he did not feel. Laura noticed that one of the feet in the old evening pumps—Lord Bellasis was always wearing things that were half worn out—gave a nervous quick movement which was unusual with him.

He was a big man, large featured with heavy eyelids. He had had unusual physical powers, which he had, as a younger man, exposed to every strain. Perhaps he had overdone it, for he looked more than his forty years, and his friends observed in him at times a certain inertness that might be the result of reckless abuse of strength in his twenties.

Laura had a few moments in which to wonder what this man's character was really like, before he spoke again.

"Were you surprised at anything in my letter from Bellasis last week?"

"Yes and no," said the lady.

"Deign to interpret," answered Bellasis, a little amused at the diplomacy betrayed in this answer.

"No, because," with a little glow of fervour, "no admiration or warmer feeling for Madge could surprise me; yes, because I had no notion of the state of your mind when I was at Bellasis those two days in October."

"Nor had I," answered Bellasis with a short laugh. "The case is a simple one. I found it out when she left Bellasis after that last party. I can't live there without her. You cannot think how stale and unprofitable it all became. Every room lacked her presence; every meal with the others, without that sweet cheerfulness, that delicate tact and kindliness, was a penance. I went away to a country house party, and it was fun. Cecilia was there. But it only proved to me that I could not go on through another month without Madge. So you see why I wrote to you."

Laura bent forward and with a bright smile, answered:—

"No I don't in the very least."

"No, how should you?" he said, with a deep sigh. "For if all were plain sailing I should not have asked your help. I have got to bore you by talking of myself before you can understand. May I?"

Laura's subtle face looked unutterable sympathy from the glance of the narrow eyes and the curve of her thin lips, even to the pose of the finely shaped chin. Bellasis seemed to full of gloomy thoughts to be quite conscious of her presence.

"I was once a young man—what an idiotic beginning—I mean I was once a younger son. My brother Bellasis and I were the only children. Our parents both died before I was eighteen and he was nineteen. We were old enough to go pretty much our own way. We both had a craze for travelling. His was more for the sake of climbing, mine for knowing all sorts and tribes of men. He was killed on a peak in Switzerland. Poor fellow, he was only twenty-two. But perhaps my mania brought a worse punishment. I fell in love with a Mexican beauty at a theatre in Florida. I married her; I divorced her after three years of untold misery; and she is still alive."

"What you must have suffered!" came in eloquent tones from the thrilled listener.

Lord Bellasis waved his hand; a little characteristic gesture, expressive of the fact that the listener was not expected to dwell on the personal element in the narrative.

"The man with whom she went away would not marry her. He said that she drank; which was true. I provided for her in a convent, where they are wonderfully good to her. But they will persist in writing of her as my wife. It is part of their narrow creed. Well, I have put the matter aside for fifteen years; except that I always pay the allowance myself and make conventional inquiries to satisfy the nuns. But now it has come up again. For I feel bound to let Mrs. Riversdale know that I am what is kindly called 'an innocent divorcee.' As a Roman Catholic she cannot marry me. Of course I might propose first and tell her afterwards, but I don't think that would be fair."

He hesitated for a moment. Then looking at Laura, he said firmly:—

"Now do you think I must give up all hope? for she would have to abandon her religious prejudices for my sake."

"Oh, no, don't say that," came in soft tones from Laura, "surely, surely, something might be arranged. The priests—"

"Impossible, my dear lady," answered Bellasis, "they can't do it. History would have been different if they could."

Laura was most anxious to avoid anything so unpleasing and crude as the situation Bellasis was preparing. Besides if he spoke to Madge in that way, how could she accept him? It would be so undignified and put her in quite a wrong position. The thing could be worked far better than that.

"In these days, Lord Bellasis, I assure you it is all so different. The priests are so much wider than they used to be. You must not judge by those narrow Spanish nuns. Besides, Catholics always say more than they mean. They are taught to do it, to preserve their oral traditions."

Bellasis looked mystified. But he perceived that he had not treated the situation with tact. And he was ready to give her her lead.

"Well," he said, "if you can manage it all the better. Personally I don't want to destroy her religious belief if we can avoid it. Her quaint, mediaeval sort of view of things is part of her attraction, and gives one the confidence one can't but feel in her."

He paused, and Laura was also silent. Then he went on, a little impatience being betrayed in his voice:—

"What do you suppose has taken her down to Skipton just now? Couldn't you have prevented it?"

"I did try to stop it, and if I had known what you have just told me, I would have tried still harder. But I am not sure that I much regret my failure to do so."

"I don't understand," said Lord Bellasis irritably.

"It is an experiment, I own. But, my friend, events that we have dreaded most, often prove to have worked better for us than we could have worked for ourselves."

"In this case I cannot see how a *rapprochement* with those old-world Roman Catholics can be—well," with a short laugh, "of use, to say the least of it."

"Don't you see," said Laura, speaking earnestly, "that if, as I expect, the visit is a great failure, it will really help her to finish that chapter of her past more completely than if she had never been there. She has had a hankering after the place, an uneasy feeling about it. She told me once, in a fit of the dumps, that the old squire there was her truest friend in the world, if not the only one. Then you know," Laura lowered her voice, "she had a baby and, though she has never told me, I am sure that it must be buried there."

"Then I consider this visit to be absolutely fatal," cried Lord Bellasis.

"How unreasonable you are," said Laura quietly, "and," with a smile, "how rude to interrupt me!"

She busied herself smoothing the lace of her fan as she spoke and relapsed into silence.

"I beg a million pardons. I am all penitence. You talk like a book, and a very subtle book. But you know I belong to everyday life."

Bellasis took a low stool, and sat himself not ungracefully almost at her feet. Laura went on:—

"All this would have left a halo about Skipton as long as distance lent enchantment to the view. I shrewdly suspect that by this time to-morrow she will be disillusioned."

Laura looked up at the clock as she spoke. "You see, my dear sir, she has travelled miles and miles away from them in these two years. She has become a member of the habitable globe we live in. She can't go back and be as if she had never known the world at all. It will be the evaporation of a little sentiment, and that will be wholesome."

"Let us hope so; but what do you suppose was the immediate cause of her going there?"

"I think it was the death of Mrs. Wakefield and her baby. The logic is not clear, but Madge is not logical. She was crying the day on which the baby died, and Mrs. Wakefield had not been an intimate friend of hers. Oh, it was a *serrement de coeur,* a little burst of the religious and the maternal sentiment. The deaths supplied a sort of meditation. It was *la morale en action* to a woman who had been brought up in a convent. I think she intended to *make her soul* to some priest down at Skipton. Let her do it quietly, and come back to life and enjoyment. She can't go on mourning for the baby, and she will have had a surfeit of piety."

"Now," said Bellasis, rising restlessly,—and moving towards the chimneypiece he leant one hand upon it,—"we come to the point. I've not told you this simply because you are the only woman I know who can keep a secret, but because I want you to do something for me."

Laura was quietly attentive, and in a moment he continued:—

"I want you to tell my story to Mrs. Riversdale for me."

"But, my dear Lord Bellasis—" Laura looked troubled.

"Is it too much to ask?" He flushed a little.

"No indeed," cried Laura, "I would do far more for my friends than that. Only how can you think that that is the way to persuade her? Won't you tell her yourself—use your own influence with her?"

"That is just what I don't wish to do. I might not command myself. I should go too far. I think she ought to know, she ought to have time to think of it quietly before—" he hesitated.

Laura felt in his tone the self-will and obstinacy of a man who was rarely contradicted. She was sure that he was making a mistake. She would far rather have thrown them together for a few weeks while she prepared Madge's mind by a general treatment, and then left him to do the real work. If Madge heard the story in cold blood and from another woman, it was much more likely to fail. However, to satisfy Lord Bellasis, and to have the full and practical advantage of his friendship, was really the important point. And so the colloquy ended in Laura accepting the *rôle* of ambassador.

After he had said "good-night" and left the room, Laura stood by the fire and began to think over the situation, when he suddenly reappeared, his dark sunburnt complexion having turned to a deeper red, his manner hesitating, and yet not undignified.

"Do you think," he said, "that she at all thinks of me—in short, could be in love with me?"

"I can't tell," said Laura, "she is without doubt deeply interested in you and—"

"And what?"

"She can't endure the idea of your caring for anybody else."

"Thank you, thank you. It is such a mercy that I know she would not marry me unless she could really care, isn't it?"

"Yes, indeed!" cried the astonished Laura, and he again left her, this time not to return.

"Does he think that Bellasis Castle, and all that it involves, has no charms for our dear Madge?" thought Laura, and she broke into a heartier and more natural laugh than she had enjoyed for many a long day. It struck her as a touch of true comedy.

She ruminated for a few minutes and then wrote the letter which we saw Madge read at Skipton.

CHAPTER VIII

DAME MARY RIVERSDALE'S PORTRAIT

Mark Fieldes, when he left the billiard-room after his talk with Madge, sauntered down the passage into the hall. The hall was by far the most striking part of the house. It was wainscotted in oak, and decorated with the heads and horns of various animals, and portraits of their murderers. These last, though of varying merit as to art, all presented fine, large figures of active, well-made men, with something of marked nobility and distinction in their physique. Few of them had been specially prominent before the world, in days when nearly all public careers had been closed to Catholics, but among them there had been men of blameless honour, of warm affections, unworldly, God-fearing, country-loving Englishmen, albeit under the ban of that country's direst proscriptive laws.

Mary was sitting on a low oak chest playing with a very fine collie, who was struggling to lick her face while his paws rested on her knees. She was laughing heartily, a clear laugh, rather too loud perhaps, but joyous; and Fieldes smiled at her in a paternal manner.

"Are you waiting for Father Clement?" he inquired.

"Yes," she said, "and he and mother are having such a long talk that we shall not have time for him to do half as many cottages as he hopes."

"He does not look like a great talker," observed Fieldes, sitting down on a low bench opposite her.

"No, but he is a good listener," said Mary without intended sarcasm, "though I think his silence is sometimes very alarming.

He does not consider it at all necessary to talk. I have known him sit in the drawing-room half an hour without saying a word."

"After all," said Fieldes, "it is quite a European notion that silence is rude."

"Once," continued Mary, who was drawn to talk to Fieldes as were all children and unselfconscious beings, "he did not speak for an hour and a half. He had had a telegram to say that his father was dying, and he came into the drawing-room after breakfast and told mother that he must go away by the 11.30 train, and then he stood on the hearthrug and did not speak again till the carriage came round. No one spoke for more than an hour, and Father Clement stood looking in front of him as if there were no one there; yet I think he understood how sorry we were."

"What a striking picture. It reminds me of St. Louis and St. Francis. Do you know how St. Louis went to see St. Francis? If not, let me tell you the story."

"Oh, do, please!" said Mary.

Fieldes smiled and began. He liked telling this fair fresh country girl a story as if she were quite a little child.

"Once upon a time Louis the king went to see Francis the friar," and so he went on to the end of the episode, almost in Ruskin's words—words so marvellously adapted for conveying the spirit of the "Fioretti" of St. Francis. He told how the king journeyed many miles to see the friar, and how when the two saints met neither spoke one word to the other.

"Both," said Mark, with a little tremor in his voice, "were lost in God. Their souls met and mingled together in a communion so close that earthly speech would have been only an interruption. Then they parted without words, but full of joy, and never met again."

He was silent for a moment after that, suppressing an allusion to the Buddhist Nirvana which had risen to his lips.

"What a pretty story," said Mary, chiefly because she didn't know what else to say. She was puzzled by a strange, "Protestant, very clever man" (everybody who was not a Catholic was a

Protestant in Mary's eyes), talking about the saints in this way. Then the facility with which he spoke of the Holiest tried the reserve which comes with the deepest reverence.

"After all," said Fieldes, "there is something in it. 'Keep ye on earth your lips from over speech.'"

"Is that from the Bible?" Mary inquired.

A low laugh, and a voice such as he had never heard before, made Fieldes look up.

"Swinburne, is it not?" said the monk walking across the hall. It is difficult to describe the quality given to a voice by habitual disuse. It has a kind of peculiar distinctness which is not disagreeable, though it conveys some sense of effort.

Mary introduced Mr. Fieldes, and Father Clement turned and spoke again.

"I have read your books with interest," he said. "You see much that is true, but you don't look it in the face. I was sorry for Phidias in your novel, but then so were you. I believe in dogma which is strangely old-fashioned, but that is too wide a topic at this moment. Will you come and talk to me at the priest's house?"

The smile which lit up the wintry face and deep brown eyes was like the sunshine that was lingering on the snowy ground without. It won Fieldes, while the quaint bluntness of the speech amused him. He responded warmly, but Father Clement seemed to have no more to say. There was a silence of half a minute; then he and Mary got into the pony carriage. Mary took the reins, and they drove off.

A moment later Hilda appeared, and Mark was not sorry to find that she was to be his only companion in their afternoon walk. Their *tête-à-tête* seemed all too short when Hilda brought him in for tea at five. Mark remained in the drawing-room until Madge had finished her own rather late tea. He thought she seemed absent as she talked to him. After she had left the room he once more wandered through the house, looking at pictures and trophies. An interesting though not a large collection of old books, quite half of them belonging to the sixteenth and seventeenth centuries, and printed at Douay or Antwerp, occupied a good deal of his time. *The Disposition and Garnishment of the Soule* (date 1596) kept him for some time. He read with wistful sympathy the wail of the Catholic writer over the extinction of the tapers in all the churches of his native land, symbolic of the extinction of the light of the faith; the account of England, frost-bound with the chill of heresy. Then from the picture of Dr. Riversdale, the friend of Cardinal Allen, and the picture of his brother, Riversdale of Skipton, the Elizabethan martyr, from the old letters preserved in the Museum, written by Edgar Riversdale, the faithful follower of Charles I, from his picture and that of William Riversdale, the builder of the present house, he constructed for himself with great imaginative pleasure the romantic story of the race. He had spent several hours before coming to Skipton in reading Dod's history and other records of the chequered career of the Old Catholics, and these pictures and documents in a moment gave actuality to the story and made it concrete. And then he turned back to the modern pictures in the hall of Riversdales and Lemarchants mounted on well-bred horses and clad in red coats, and looked again at the three brushes which Madge had shown him—the trophies of Mary's success in the hunting field during the past two years.

"Yes; that is the aspect given in Macaulay's account of the Catholic squires," he reflected. "An interesting blend. Heroic devotion to the cause of their faith, and yet the qualities most obvious are not those of the mystic, but of the manly out-of-doors sportsman, who may seem to be nothing more than a bluff Englishman who rides to hounds and does his ordinary duties. Yet one of these red-coated cavaliers would, I haven't the least doubt, if occasion called for it, show himself capable of the very highest heroism. Men of action, I should say, and not of reflection. And that charming girl whom I first saw in the riding habit—though *her* face might be that of a mystic—she is like the rest, simple, open-hearted, riding to hounds with the pluck of her uncles, and ready no doubt any day to be martyred for the faith, and to regard it as the performance of simple duty, and nothing to boast of. A race I should say of few words, but of brave deeds. The priests ready to die for the Church, the cavaliers for the king."

On the first floor there was a picture gallery with more family pictures—chiefly of the ladies of the family. Here was the Dame Riversdale who had sheltered Charles II after Worcester (where her own husband had just fallen), and had contrived his escape in disguise while Cromwell's soldiers were actually in the house. Here was Mistress Riversdale who died in exile in attendance on the queen of James II.

Mark was still standing in the long narrow gallery, when Mary came upon him, a little out of breath from running upstairs two steps at a time. She had been for a gallop after her drive with Father Clement and was in her habit and holding her hat and whip in one hand. Her hair was tumbled about her face by the wind, and one long fair plait fell over her shoulder. She seemed singularly full of health and strength, and her golden hair had brought back some sunshine into the darkening house. She was as usual a little shy.

"I have been looking at the pictures," said Mark, "but it is getting too dark to see much."

"Have you looked at that one?" she asked, pointing with her whip to a portrait Mark had not noticed. "I believe it was painted by a Flemish artist."

The information was given in a voice that sounded a little weary of necessary civility to a guest. Even in the dim light Mark saw that the picture was artistically of far nobler origin than its companions. Yet they were of silk-robed and jewelled dames, and this was of a sober-hued nun. It was far more characteristic of the family history, this picture, than the others. What there was common to nearly all, the nun included, was a strong likeness to the young girl in her riding habit who was now pointing to the Flemish portrait. They nearly all, Mary included, had the high, narrow, purely white foreheads, the open fearless eyes, the wide simple mouths, the well set neck and shoulders. But the expression on the nun's face was more complex. The Flemish artist had been a true genius; he had painted her probably for his own satisfaction, had (may be) asked as a favour in return for his charities to the convent to paint the high-bred elderly lady from over seas. The face he had depicted was worn and wrinkled, and the light that he had put into the great blue open eyes was almost contradicted by the struggle in the mouth.

Mary Riversdale waited in polite silence while he looked at it. "How like you, and yet how utterly unlike you," were the words he suppressed, as he turned from the great-great-great-great-aunt to the niece, in her buoyant youth and strength.

"What was her story?" he asked.

"It is told," she answered, "among the 'death-bills' of the Benedictine nuns. Dame Mary Riversdale was filled with the wish to save souls, so she fled over seas to the convent in Flanders to offer up her life to pray for England. There she fell ill and was not able to keep the rule and work with the other nuns. So she prayed that she might have some suffering greater than the penance she could not keep on account of her health. And the next day, so says the death-bill, she fainted, and it was found that she had a mortal illness, with terrible pain, which she bore bravely for three years, and then died in repute of great sanctity."

So far the informant in a dull monotony of voice. The increasing darkness almost hid the suffering face in the rich mellow colouring of the background of the Flemish picture, while the face of the girl, with its vigour and brilliant colouring, became almost equally indiscernible. Mark heard an impatient sigh.

"I ought not to bore you with so many questions," he said. "But what a strange sad story of spiritual patriotism."

"It was specially for a near relation of her own who had conformed to the Protestant religion that she offered her life—for her brother. It doesn't bore me, Mr. Fieldes; but do you know, ever since I was a little child and used to come down the passage to mother's room, I have disliked that picture. I used to wish that I had never been called Mary."

"And now?" he said, venturing a little too far in the tone of greater intimacy.

"Oh, I don't know," Mary answered almost brusquely, and walked away, leaving him to try and decipher the dim glance of that strange heroine, who had prayed for physical suffering and who was of the same root and stock as Mary Riversdale.

"Wonderful survival," thought Mark, as his thoughts passed from aunt to niece. "Instinct with the health and life of this world and of to-day; and yet beyond doubt sealed with the stamp of mediaeval sanctity and other worldliness. She could devote herself as absolutely as the nun of the picture. Yet she would hunt, her whole soul intent on the fences and gates and hounds, until the moment for suffering arrived. She belongs less to this world than her cousin, though the cousin has more mind, and less capacity for dealing with matter. Both of them are heiresses—and likely to be run after—but this one seems hardly made for human love."

CHAPTER IX

MADGE VISITS THE VAULT

Marmaduke waited for some time in his uncle's study, to catch him for a few moments' private talk, on Wednesday morning. It was a large south room, and the sun seemed to have reduced everything in it to a neutral tint. A general impression of colourless leather prevailed;—large oak writing-tables, with tops of faded morocco, arm-chairs not too luxurious in shape of the same hue, queer old water-colour caricatures of absurd incidents in the hunting field, hanging between maps of the county; bookcases filled with large worn volumes on law and sport, reference books that had once been red; and dull but imperishable Turkey carpets. All was in perfect order; even the walking-sticks and fishing-rods in one corner did not look untidy. There was nothing to distinguish it from the business room of any other large landlord and active English magistrate except the ivory crucifix upon his own writing-table and the silver holy water stoup hanging by the door.

The squire when he came into the room did not see that Marmaduke was sitting in a distant window reading the *Times*. It struck his nephew afresh, as he watched him cross the room and sit down heavily on the chair by the writing-table, how rapidly his uncle had aged during the years of his absence. A sharp sigh and a few words muttered to himself showed that he thought he was alone.

"Thy Will . . . on earth as—" Marmaduke caught the broken sounds and rustled the *Times* in his hand. Mr. Riversdale raised his head and looked round. Unconsciously he began to speak in the same words he had used when he first saw Marmaduke in London after his return from India.

"Glad to be back in the old country, eh, Marmaduke? Going to settle down, I hope. You'll have plenty to do, you know—they tell me you'll have a time of it with the small farmers round you. Just fancy what I saw the other day, and near here too; they must think I am getting old. We were after a fine fox, had a splendid run all through the Cartchester country—the fox was creeping up a thick hedge, hounds scenting the field below and just going to follow him up. I could see it all from the other side of the dell—when a brute of a farmer came through a gate and shot the poor creature dead. So cruel, so cruel! well I daresay I've told it you before, but you see it does make a man angry."

Mr. Riversdale paused, then began again:—

"Yes, you will have plenty to do—you know that agent of your father's isn't up to the mark—not up to the mark. If he were more like Smith now—but you couldn't find many like Smith I'll own."

"I met Smith last week," said Marmaduke. "If you don't mind I will just tell you what he said to me."

"Yes, yes, go on," answered Mr. Riversdale.

Marmaduke made an effort to begin. He was standing now in a window near the table looking out on the carriage sweep.

"There was one thing Smith spoke of—it seems that Smith has not yet paid a bill of three years ago, from Druce, of £1200 for drawing-room furniture which must clearly be Madge's own affair. He wants to send it to her and to represent to her what sacrifices the family have already made to prevent her being applied to."

For a moment Mr. Riversdale was silent. Then he spoke in a voice that reminded Marmaduke of the days of his boyhood, when he had been greatly in awe of Uncle George's mighty tones when angry.

"Tell Smith that that is a subject not to be reopened. He can let the shooting in Lancashire or we can sell near here. For what was spent during my son's lifetime I am responsible. As to what she has done since then, she must see to it herself."

He took up his pen as if to conclude the subject, and Marmaduke moved away, wishing to leave the room, when his uncle stopped him.

"He was right to tell you and you were right to tell me, my boy. Now, stop a moment—after all," and the last words seemed to be addressed to himself, "we can't wash our hands of it that way."

Marmaduke sat down and waited.

"You've seen more of her this year than we have, met her in the Highlands, didn't you?"

"Yes, and in the south also, and in London," said Marmaduke.

"And you are friends I can see. Well, now tell me: she is not in a right way, is she? Is it a very fast set she is in or why does she wear those clothes and smoke and read French novels? But it isn't one thing or another; it is more the way she does them, and the whole look of the woman. I can't say I'm happy about her."

"I think she did get into a bad set at first," answered Marmaduke, "the set they saw something of before George's death. But the people she meets at Bellasis are better—though of course they are worldly."

"Well, I don't understand these things, but you'd hardly say that she lives as a Catholic young woman should, would you?"

There was the humility of age admitting that the younger man knew more of the world of to-day; and there was also in the speech the full confidence he felt in appealing to Marmaduke's judgment.

"No," admitted Marmaduke unwillingly, "she doesn't look easy in her mind."

His uncle went on:—

"Do you think she wants to marry a Protestant?"

"I haven't any idea of anything of that kind," answered Marmaduke. "Of course she does live entirely among Protestants now, but I've got the impression that she does not want to marry again."

"Mary has got a notion into her head that there is some immediate danger. She had it out with Father Clement yesterday. Poor child, she was disappointed because he would not try to meet Madge. He didn't give Mary any help about it. Perhaps he is hurt. I don't know," with a sigh, "perhaps he is right,—no use forcing things. He says he has got very little faith in external applications; best to leave it alone. He never had much tact, and he might put her back up." He paused, and then went on, half to himself: "Only a guess of Mary's after all. One doesn't quite see what it can be just now—unless it is to marry a Protestant who won't give the conditions." Then speaking more distinctly to Marmaduke: "Anyhow Madge isn't safe leading that life. She is not like an English girl of our sort. She might have been different perhaps," his voice faltered, "if she had had a strong hand to guide her. We shall hear of her getting into some scrape." He stopped again and then went on: "Are you to be in London now? Well, then, see something of her, keep an eye on her. I am glad she is here and I don't suppose she will stay less than a week. I want to make it nice for her. I want her to come again."

"Couldn't you talk to her a little, Uncle George?" said Marmaduke, getting up; "she is really fond of you."

"I'll try, but I doubt how she will take it. She used to be very much taken up with Father Clement, but she was quite rude to him yesterday. Poor child! Poor child! She did better in the first days of her trials. It is not for any one who knows the past in this house to throw a stone at her."

Marmaduke, on leaving his uncle, went to have a talk with the farm bailiff. He wished to make friends with the functionary in question—a new importation since his former visits to Skipton. He then returned to the house and had been standing for a moment at the drawing-room window when his attention was drawn to three figures on the lawn which stretched along the side of the house and was divided by a ha-ha from the park beyond. Madge and Hilda and Mr. Fieldes had come out together and dawdled along the path chatting not very briskly; Madge was not talking and, from time to time, glanced at the windows. Then she left the other two and walked away to the shrubbery of evergreens that spread out beyond the farther side of the house.

Marmaduke stood for quite twenty minutes, with a newspaper in his hand, but his eyes fixed on Fieldes and Hilda as they paced up and down the path. Hilda was listening eagerly, excitedly turning her eyes, lit up with thought, to Fieldes, who was talking with evident enjoyment and looked more of a man than when he gossiped with Madge. Marmaduke felt excessively annoyed.

"What things girls are," he thought; "Hilda, so well brought up and kept out of vulgar nonsense, flings herself at the head of the first man she meets, just because he can talk. She knows nothing of his character, and if she had eyes in her head she would see that he is a snob. They oughtn't to have that sort of unbelieving writing man here at all. Well, what are they going to do next, putting their heads together over some manuscript, consulting about what he writes. I shouldn't mind anything so much if he weren't such a d—d humbug. What's his object in jawing away about nuns and the Grande Chartreuse, and going to the schools? If Hilda had any money I should understand it; if she had Mary's fortune for instance."

But at last he felt rather foolish standing at the window, doing nothing, and he went back into the room, where he wrote several letters with a melancholy countenance. They were addressed to a Catholic army chaplain, to a former brother officer, to several privates, and were chiefly concerned with various charitable undertakings, schemes for helping soldiers' wives, temperance leagues, etc., for he had thrown himself heartily into all that very large work which is carried on by her Majesty's officers of all denominations. Marmaduke had been found particularly useful in dealing with his Irish and English co-religionists, and it was a part of his trial in giving up the army that he had to bid farewell to many friendly fellow-workers. He had just finished a letter to a sergeant (in answer to a magnificent effusion he had received from him that morning, stating in grandiloquent language his own remarkable perseverance in the virtue of temperance) when Fieldes came into the room to fetch a book. Marmaduke thereupon walked out on to the lawn where, as he expected, he found Hilda pacing up and down. She was reading some printers' proofs with great absorption.

"What have you got there? Are you going to bring out a novel?" said Marmaduke, trying not to look cross.

"No," answered Hilda; "it is an essay by Mr. Fieldes," and she looked down again at the proofs in her hand. It was evident to Marmaduke that she did not want to be disturbed by him, perceiving which did not tend to sweeten his temper. He walked by her side for a moment, in silence, reflecting that she looked distractingly pretty, with her head bent over those wretched proofs.

"Have you read all the other things Fieldes has written?" he inquired presently.

"Oh, yes," said Hilda abstractedly. Then she added with condescension: "He writes exquisitely, why don't you read them?"

"Because I don't care for attacks on the faith and *risqué* stories," said Marmaduke hotly.

Hilda stopped short in her walk and turned round upon him with flashing eyes and heightened colour.

"How can you say anything so unfair, so untrue, so odious!" Then with a grand air of indifference she turned back to her reading.

"Well, then," said Marmaduke, "let me see it."

"Certainly not," she answered with less dignity and more temper. "It is an unpublished work that has been confided to me by the author."

"And do you suppose he would mind my seeing what he has confided to you? Then he must feel guilty indeed."

This was an ingenious turn to give to the argument and Hilda felt half inclined to let him glance at the essay, knowing that he would not read it; but the title "Faith in its Decline," and the opening, an eloquent lament over the impossibility of belief in these latter days, might startle him. How could one explain to an ordinary young man like Marmaduke how thoroughly Fieldes appreciated the beauties of the Catholic Church and yearned to be able to believe in it. Her confusion was evident and he pressed his advantage.

"I don't think it is honourable for a man like that to stay here and to play with your faith with his infidel notions."

"Infidel!" said Hilda with fine scorn, "he is an Agnostic! I suppose *you* will call him a modern Voltaire."

"Well I don't know much about 'Hagnostics,' as my friend the learned sergeant calls them, but it seems to me they come to much the same conclusion practically. However, pray tell me what an Agnostic is."

Hilda sighed and put the proofs under her arm with an air of exemplary patience.

"An Agnostic," she began; but then she hesitated and flushed and tried to think how she could explain enough for Marmaduke to understand. She did not venture on the derivation of the word because as to the dead languages Marmaduke knew more than she did. It was tiresome to find it so difficult to explain. This evident difficulty delighted Marmaduke so much that it nearly restored his good temper. "An Agnostic," she said at length, "is a man who knows nothing."

"I see," said Marmaduke, "a complete ignoramus; poor Fieldes, that is rather too hard!"

"You really are too aggravating!" exclaimed Hilda, "I wish you would—" but turning round she saw such handsome laughing eyes and such good-humoured teasing in their expression, that her priggish mood vanished and she laughed heartily.

"Now," said Marmaduke gaily, "instead of 'proofing' your affection for Mr. Fieldes come and let us have a row on the pond."

No lecture could have done as much as that very poor pun. "'Affection' for Mr. Fieldes indeed!" Hilda tossed her head magnificently. Then it was a fine day; and she loved rowing; and she was fond of dirty ponds and Marmaduke would think her selfish if she refused. So they walked off across the lawn. Marmaduke jumped down the ha-ha and held out his hand to Hilda. She jumped airily down; but what were the feelings of Mr. Fieldes who was watching them from his bedroom window and who did not know that the ha-ha was dry, to see many white sheets fluttering in disorder to the ground as she jumped! She had quite forgotten that the proofs were under her arm. He watched them pick up the pages and saw that Hilda, who had looked distressed at first, was soon laughing. The young man was evidently making a comic show of apprehension and pretending to hide under the ha-ha. "Really," thought Fieldes, "he is an absurd sort of person! quite intolerable. And what a silly school-girl he makes her look!" Marmaduke then bounded up the ha-ha and went into the house with the proofs. A moment later he had rejoined Hilda, and they were walking off to the pond.

What had become of Madge when she left Fieldes and Hilda on the lawn?

Madge had said to herself only yesterday that she had so many things to do at Skipton that she could not spare time to go out with Mark and Hilda. Yet, as so often happens in the best planned afternoons, nothing had been done, unless indeed account be taken of the smoking of a cigarette, the absorption of a *marron glacé*, the shedding of a few tears, and the reading of a gossiping letter. These were not the actions that Madge had intended to do at Skipton, and so there was evidently still much to be done. Why then dawdle away half Wednesday morning talking to Hilda and Mr. Fieldes, and why now stroll listlessly into the shrubbery?

Madge looked back at the big, square building behind her. She looked at it earnestly, as if her mind were dwelling on what was going on within it. It was so; but her thoughts did not dwell on any part of the house that has yet been spoken of. Nor did she think of the housekeeper's room, where that dignified functionary was explaining some detail of the list of the linen in the endless length of cupboards before them to Mrs. Riversdale, who ought by rights to have been still in bed, and whose unnecessary victory over that weakness of the flesh bronchitis, had not added sweetness to her temper. Yet if she had seen into the room in question, she would have gained some information which she wanted. She would have seen Mary go into the room and stand waiting while Mrs. Riversdale was saying:—

"Yes, Thomson, of course the linen is old, but if it only had proper work put into it,—this," taking up a fine towel and pointing scornfully to a patch, "this is not darning at all; this is—" words failed.

"Yet I've taught and taught those girls till I'm sick of it," said Thomson with only partially suppressed irritation. "I'll just fetch you what was done in the housemaid's room yesterday, ma'am, and you shall judge of it, for its no use *my* speaking."

She left the room and Mary seized her opportunity.

"Mother, may I have the key of the vault?"

"The vault?" said Mrs. Riversdale in surprise. "Why do you want to go to the vault?"

"I should like to have the key," said Mary evasively.

"Why?" asked her mother.

She spoke with authority, and Mary, with slightly puckered mouth, answered:—

"I think Madge would like to go into the vault, and she will be shy of asking for the key, and she is out walking now, and if I might just leave the door open she could slip in and—" she hesitated.

Mrs. Riversdale turned away.

"Madge will ask me for the key if she wants it," she said, not very graciously.

Mary came up to her.

"Mother, dear, do let me have it, only to please me, mother."

The loving face that still held for her mother the baby's look, produced its inevitable effect, and Mary went off with the key before Thomson came back.

Mrs. Riversdale sighed deeply. It was a great effort to part with the key: it seemed as if she were letting in an irreverent glare upon her sacred places.

Mary meanwhile walked quickly and nervously along the great brick tiled passage into which the servants' offices opened.

It was no unusual sight to see her there on some quest of food or help of some kind for man, horse or dog. But the butler, as he paused in eloquent condemnation of a footman who had been caught playing a concertina in the morning, and the stillroom-maid, who hoped that Miss Mary had not heard exactly what she had been saying to the girl who had broken the milk-jug, and the cook, who was concluding a bargain as to her private supply of spirits with the local grocer, all these, and others, watched the fair girl go down the broad passage in the changing light and shadow as she passed the doorway of pantry, stillroom and kitchen, and all wondered kindly what had come over Miss Mary's pretty face.

Mary felt a nervous excitement, and a sense almost of guilt, in the daring of having made a plot which she had wished to conceal even from her mother. She walked very quietly, as if she were afraid of being heard, till she reached the great whitewashed, heavily weighted doors at the end of the passage. She pulled one back with an effort, and passed through, and it banged to behind her.

In front of her was the large open yard which was hidden by the shrubbery from the rest of the grounds. Mary walked in among the bushes; each ilex, each box-tree, each laurel had that intense familiarity that the shrubberies of our childhood have for each of us. In that laurel she had hidden in defiance of her governess; she had gone to cry among those stunted box-trees on the rare occasions of blame from her father, and there she had also spent moments of morbid self-consciousness inevitable in the course of growing up, though in her case they had been very few indeed.

Mary passed hastily among the bushes now, until she had turned the corner of the house, and was pressing her way between the overgrown laurels and the chapel wall. Soon she came to an open space, through which a curving gravel walk led from the garden and ended in a flight of steps to a low underground door in the wall of the chapel.

Mary ran down, unlocked the door and left the key in it. She was springing up the steps again when a thought struck her. She stepped quickly back, opened the door which grated on some fine gravel, and knelt down beside it and covered her face with her hands.

"O little baby!" she whispered, "you only saw your mother for those few minutes, but you are safe up in heaven. Little baby, we can't help her, and so you must."

Then she got up quickly, stifling a sob, and went away as she had come, but soothed, comforted and hopeful.

Meanwhile the baby's mother was walking in the shrubbery and thinking to herself how little Laura knew that it was a tiny coffin that had brought her to Skipton-le-Grange.

Madge more than once had turned into the path that led to the door of the vault, and had followed it until she was close upon the chapel; and then she had abruptly left it and walked away through a green path that wound towards a gate in the park palings. The third time that she made this circuit she hesitated.

"I wonder if by any chance the door might be open. I will not ask Mrs. Riversdale, she might have the sense to leave it open. I know she will think it an unnatural crime if I don't go there, which is enough to keep one away. Oh, those old plots to make me good and meek and submissive! She would have liked me to sit with my front door ajar waiting for George to condescend to come back. And now he is dead why can't she leave my poor soul alone? She wants to soften me. I know she does, she thinks—oh, I don't know what she thinks—but why can't I be allowed to have my little baby to myself?"

At the tender words the vision she had successfully banished so often came back to her—the one look of the tiny drawn face, so wise, so full of meaning. They come with that look into the world, as if a little tired with their own knowledge, and very conscious of the intense personality which is theirs. They lose it soon; they are soon reduced by swathings and baths and nonsense and bottles, indigestion and temper, to the merely undeveloped, helpless human infant we all know. Only those who meet them first feel the mystery, and are hushed into awe at its sacredness. To the mother the mystery has a difference, for her it is a sacred deposit given into her keeping, a great secret, clothed in her own flesh.

Madge had felt, if dimly, this revelation, as the tiny thing in its white robes was laid beside her. She had looked on her child's face with an immense surprise. This was not a baby such as her friends had had; this was a human being. This was her best friend, this wise soul in its tiny coverings. She had touched the fingers and asked if they were not too blue.

"Oh, she's just out of the bath," the nurse had said soothingly, "now she must come away."

Madge had hardly known when the little girl was moved away. She never saw it again. She had no longing to see the dead body; for it was the mighty spirit, the individual mystery that she had seen, and that was gone. It was for that that her mourning had been very bitter. Only she implored the nurse, amidst her sobbing, not to let anybody else see the baby. By 'anybody' she meant Mrs. Riversdale, and the nurse had understood her. Mrs. Riversdale was away, but was to return that day. George thought it wise of the nurse to wish to close the coffin, the better part of him had been roused at the time by his loss. It was best for Madge to know that it was closed.

That was little more than five years ago, and it was frightfully vivid to Madge as she walked in the shrubbery. At length, as she came round among the bushes again, she moved deliberately towards the chapel. When she came in sight of the door she heaved a sigh of relief; it was open, not wide open, but just enough to make it evident from a distance that it was not shut up. She drew nearer and listened. Not a sound anywhere. She hoped that nobody was there. She came close to the top of the steps that led down to the heavy oak door. Then unfortunately she looked up. The sacristy window was the only one from which that side of the chapel could be seen, and in the sacristy, looking out of the window, half-concealed behind the open door of the vestment press, was Mrs. Riversdale, waiting doubtless to see if she would go to the vault. One glance was enough for Madge; she did not move forward or go away. She put her hand in her pocket, drew out her cigarette-case, and felt for a match-box in the pocket of her coat. She tried to strike a match, and failed. She threw it down. Then she raised her foot on to the green stone kerb above the steps and struck again, lit her cigarette, threw away the second match blindly, and it fell down the steps. She walked slowly,—very slowly,—away, puffing delicate wreaths of smoke in front of her. A moment later, she had made the tour of the shrubbery and had walked with the same slow, deliberate step through the front hall, and up the first flight of the big staircase. She passed through a baize door that opened from the landing, and hurrying into her own room, let the door slam behind her.

That afternoon, Madge, Hilda and Mark Fieldes took a long drive—Fieldes was to be shown an old country house in the neighbourhood, with a priest's hiding-hole and a secret chapel. When they got back Madge complained of cold feet and said she would go for a turn in the shrubbery. It was getting dark, and the sacristy blind was down. Madge walked quickly along, till she came to the steps. Then she raised her veil, and looked about as if for something she had lost. It was getting dark. Madge knelt down and felt with her hand along the moss-grown steps. No, the matches were not there.

"She sent to fetch them away. I am sure she did," thought Madge. "I suppose she told King that Mrs. George had been smoking near the chapel. How hateful."

Poor old Mrs. Riversdale, sitting in the stiff, high-backed chair, gazing into the fire, knew that the additional touch of wheeziness she was feeling had been her punishment for a hasty descent from the sacristy to gather up the desecrating matches. She would not for the world have spoken to anyone on the subject. For herself, she felt that no such revelation had been needed to show her what sort of girl poor George had married. The sadness, the dull ache, the profound unselfish pain of the poor old heart, which was a deep if a narrow one, found some relief in thinking what a different man George would have been under other influences.

CHAPTER X

BENEDICTION

There could be no question as to the charms of the billiard-room at Skipton that Wednesday evening. It was a perfect room, with its huge fireplace and its big sofas, and its shaded lamps, in which to lounge away the time between tea and dinner. Madge was half lying on a sofa, and near her sat Marmaduke, reading aloud scraps of information from the *Morning Post*. Hilda was leaning over the billiard-table playing with the balls. She was still shy enough while talking to strangers to find her hands difficult to dispose of. Mark Fieldes was standing near her, and they had progressed rapidly as usual through the walks of modern literature (interrupted by exclamations as to her own bad shots with the billiard balls) to quasi-religious questions. Murmurs in which the names of St. Francis, of Rossetti, of St. Paul and of Matthew Arnold were audible came to Marmaduke's ear, and did not make his reading more smooth or intelligible.

"Really, Marmaduke, you are absurd," said Madge, who had been too absent-minded to notice before how very confused was the information she was receiving from the columns of the *Morning Post*. Besides trying to hear Hilda's conversation with Mark he was making vain attempts to get a good view of her without appearing to do so, from behind his newspaper, as she moved her head backwards and forwards, catching at one moment the full light of the lamps over the table on her eager face and large shining eyes, and at the next receding into the darkness beyond. "What an extraordinary collection of people you are putting together."

"Oh, I beg your pardon," said Marmaduke, looking over his paper with a would-be humorous expression. "I see now one paragraph was about a party at your friend the Duchess of A.'s, and the other was only the discovery of a gambling hell in Paris."

"You'll produce a scandal before you've done," said Madge wearily.

At that moment a bell rang noisily through the house. Madge sat up abruptly.

"It is the chapel bell!" she cried; "and I thought we were going to have a little peace!"

"What does the service consist of?" asked Mark.

"Oh, first there are endless dull prayers—I shan't come till Benediction, Hilda."

Hilda was sorry to be interrupted, but knowing that Mark was watching, she moved briskly.

"May I come too?" he inquired, following her.

Hilda was all graciousness, and they left the room together.

Marmaduke had half risen before Fieldes spoke. Then he settled down again into the deep chair.

"I shall wait for Benediction," he said, "and come with you."

Mark, having waited in the hall while Hilda went to fetch a shawl of black lace, which she threw not ungracefully over her head, followed her up a winding staircase until, turning to the left, she led him along a passage. There she paused opposite to a red baize-covered door, on which hung a small stoup for holy water. It was the door by which Fieldes had seen Mary and Hilda enter the chapel the previous morning.

"We go into the gallery, which is organ loft and family pew in one. Nobody from outside the house comes up there, except one or two boys who sing in the choir. It is rather dark, and there are two steps which one can tumble over. Aunt Helen likes visitors to kneel in front of the gallery."

Fieldes saw that Hilda was a little eager and pleased at his having asked to come to Benediction, and was evidently anxious that nothing untoward should occur to mar the effect of the service.

The extreme plainness of the interior of the chapel was now happily veiled by the "dim religious light," and it took some moments before Fieldes realised its ugliness. The upper part of the walls was bare, and shiny yellow blinds hid the long oblong windows. The only decoration he could see consisted of a number of small devotional pictures hung at equal distances and all framed alike. For the chancel or sanctuary were reserved greater artistic efforts, and for the two small altars that flanked it. The chancel was small and square. Its corners were fitted with pilasters of imitation marble, and the door that opened from it into the sacristy had heavy supports and cross beams of the same salmon and green-tinted material. This was carefully matched by a false door to satisfy the eye on the other side.

The Roman altar was of yellow marble, and on it stood tall gold candlesticks, of that kind of Parisian Gothic so common in French churches. Above the altar was an apse, filled by an enormous transparency, representing the resurrection, and in the space between that and the real window of the building, a cunningly disguised gas jet, now lighted, showed up the singularly unfortunate colours of this representation. On either side were raised two huge figures of St. Peter and St. Paul, which seemed to Mr. Fieldes to have been cut short at the knees, and so placed on their gilded renaissance brackets. He was half fascinated by the curious hideousness of the whole effect, which did not prevent a certain sense of its being a consecrated atmosphere into which he had been admitted. To whatever this atmosphere was to be attributed, he had always recognised it in Catholic churches.

While Fieldes was examining the little building, as far as the dusky light allowed, people had been coming in below and passing under the gallery to their places. The chapel still served, as in the days of persecution, as the parish church for the Catholics of the neighbourhood; and the services were generally attended by a certain number of villagers as well as the household. The organ soon began to discourse, and really to discourse sweet music. It was a beautiful instrument and it was well played. The moment he heard the firm touch upon the keys, Fieldes turned round and saw that Mary was the organist. A few moments later the music ceased as the monk emerged from the sacristy door and announced a hymn which was sung by the small congregation in rather a perfunctory manner. When it came to an end Fieldes expected to hear the prayers of which Madge had spoken, instead of which to his surprise Father Clement mounted the altar steps and turned round with the evident intention of preaching. He folded his arms under their enormous flowing sleeves, making a magnificent series of curves with each movement, and he threw his head back in the same way that Fieldes had noticed when he seemed to be scenting the air in the garden. He broke the silence in a low clear voice:—

"Commit thy way unto the Lord and He will bring it to pass."

His sermon will not be given here; but it cannot be passed by without some brief description, because it was believed to have had a considerable influence on the lives of two of those that heard it. Mark Fieldes many years afterwards owned to having introduced it in that novel of his, which was not very successful, called *Phidias Redux*. In the following passage from *Phidias Redux* he gives a brief account of the sermon heard by Phidias in a Catholic chapel.

"It was very simple in style, it was sunny and yet stern. It was as if the preacher were surrounded, pervaded, by the serene unearthly atmosphere of one of Fra Angelico's pictures—the magnificent monkish figure doubtless aiding the impression. It was remote from the atmosphere of daily life, yet it touched the listeners' most intimate moral experiences. While he could hardly breathe the air in which throve this ideal of asceticism and renunciation, Phidias yet recognised that it was a human claim that was urged by one who in his nature, in the stuff he was made of, was the same as himself. It was a very simple homily on sacrificing the created will to the will of the Creator, on the fitness, the profitableness, nay, the dire necessity of this surrender; for 'to whom else should we go?' In one thing it was very unlike such discourses as we suppose are often heard in monasteries, that was in its subtle analysis of human motives and delusions. It was on no man of straw who 'haunted the antechambers of the great' or who loved gold like a miser that the monk called for renunciation. His summons would apply to any self-wearied human being, clinging to a world about which he had no delusions, clinging to it simply because it was a distraction from his intolerable self-consciousness.

"But it did smack of the monastery chapel in its entire absence of appeal to the intellect, in its absolute taking for granted of the existence of this supremely beneficent Creator, who could satisfy all needs, fill all the emptiness, if we would only give up our wills to His. Yet so electric is sympathy that Phidias felt at the moment, that coming from this son of the early ages, whose life was a fulfilment of the sternest traditions of Christian self-denial, it had a reality in the note of confidence and of triumph to which it soon passed, of a sure experience that all things good and true and joyous were indeed added to those who seek the Lord. It seemed as if the long fast, the midnight penance, the hideous bareness and discomfort of his own life had but enhanced in this son of the desert the actual enjoyment of some overmastering vision. Nothing in it was more pathetic, more touching, than its suggestion of the entire satisfaction of the affections by a personal intercourse with the Unseen.

"Bringing all his hearers into his companionship he seemed to take for granted that the golden atmosphere of his ideal was in and about them also; and that they could congratulate each other on the deeper meaning of the text, that our own hunger for joy could be satisfied, our own imperious wills tamed through the process of self-denial and self-rejection. All that can be said is 'Amen, So be it' to those to whom it is possible. To Phidias it was not possible: and so for him the sermon could win no lasting conviction. Yet for this experience he was always thankful. Though to him the mental submission and the moral intensity described by the old monk were equally impossible, the sermon enriched his spiritual experiences. It awoke feelings in his nature that were never entirely lost. It widened his sympathies to see that a sublime spiritual union is not only believed in but is found satisfying by a human heart like unto our own."

In the midst of the short and simple discourse of which we have borrowed his description, Fieldes had been irritated by the sound of an opening door, and looking round saw Madge hastily enter the gallery followed by Marmaduke. There was a little rustle before they were settled. He felt amused in spite of his annoyance at the interruption, at the thought of Madge's feelings on being obliged to listen to a sermon unexpectedly. However, he was too much interested in the monk to be distracted for more than a moment. But when, having given his blessing, Father Clement turned to leave the altar, Mark looked round and noticed that Madge was already on her knees, her face buried in her hands, and something of emotion was discernible in her attitude which he had never observed before.

Madge had knelt down hastily on the *prie-dieu* in front of her as the sermon ended. Her black lace veil fell over her shoulders on to the sleeves of her tea-gown. It was rare for her to be seen in absolute simplicity of pose of gesture. Now she was very still. She felt soothed and at rest. At rest in the chapel she had avoided, at peace after a sermon from the monk. She had felt repulsion to Father Clement in ordinary social meeting, yet she was intensely soothed by him now. This was what she had dreaded, this chapel and that voice. And now both had brought peace. She was still the Madge who, as a child, had taken her childish troubles to the Convent Chapel, there to weep them away.

Yes, she found to her own surprise that she was at peace. She was very tired, and there was no need to struggle here. How much she took in of the sermon it is difficult to say. It sounded to her touching and very kind. It was not to her distinct enough to be more than soothing. It was reminiscent of the days when Father Clement had made her wish to be very good indeed, the days of her unhappy marriage before the baby came, when she had dwelt peacefully, though tearfully, on the thought of heaven. The influence she had dreaded had come, but with a difference. It had come as a wave of emotion with tender thoughts of her past self and of her baby. It had come as a reaction from her fit of temper that morning; and here in the chapel she was not very far from the little coffin in the vault. She knelt by it in spirit as she prayed, and so stayed in a holy joy and quiet till the service was ended.

But we are linked by chains about the feet of God, and the history of Madge's future was not to be independent of another soul conflict, that had begun also, or rather had become conscious, during that short homily.

It needs the skilled hand of a psychologist to describe the phenomena of a great discovery in our own consciousness. We grow silently, unconsciously, in some given direction, and we are suddenly startled by finding where we are. Take the commonest form of this, the one of which novelists give us scores of descriptions, the discovery of being in love with one known perhaps for years, and supposed to be an object of indifference—or take that marvellous account of Jouffroy of the moment at which he discovered that the old faith was gone from him. So, too, there came a flash of another kind to Mary, which illuminated a whole range of unconscious thought and moral action in the past.

Sitting on the narrow organist's bench, with her back to the organ, with her legs crossed and her small white hands folded upon her knee, her head erect, still in her riding habit, but with a little veil thrown over her head, which did not cover her face, Mary listened to the sermon. Her blue eyes were bright, her cheeks flushed, her chestnut curls were tumbled round her high, white, narrow forehead. No one in the chapel, half filled by people who loved her in varying degrees, could see the changes on her face. She who was loved so dearly by the people of Skipton, to whom all that was about them was to belong in due course, whom they would have done all they could to shelter from pain, she was to suffer in a strange loneliness.

"In the beginning of creation," said Father Clement in one passage of the sermon, "the Master and Maker of us all commented on His work, and each day He saw and pronounced that it was good, until He came to the making of man. Then having made Adam He did not say that this work was good. But He did say, 'It is not good for man to be alone'. It was as if in man only there were a flaw that God wished to remedy. God provided for him a companion; but human companionship has ever been but a partial and temporary supply of this, man's deepest need. Has not man been alone ever since? And have not the greatest of men been the most alone? The heights of all mountains are lonely, all great thought moves alone, all true poetry is sung alone. Why, Lord, are the best and the purest and thehighest of Thy creatures, the most open to Thy criticism in the beginning? Why, Lord, do they go in such awful solitude, if it is not good for them to be alone?

"My brethren, why, having seen that we need companionship, did the Creator leave us all in such a large measure of solitude? Why did He so leave us that words hide our meanings, that looks are a dim and obscure revelation and seem only to tell us that there is a secret behind them that they cannot convey? that the acutest pain is borne alone before helpless onlookers, and that death comes as a passage even more lonely than the solitude of life? Why does He not give us companions who can fully understand us and whom we can understand? Because," Father Clement glanced upwards and then with a strange smile looked round at his listeners, "because, children, only He who made the soul can really fill its need. His chosen ones He calls absolutely to have no companions but Himself."

Here it was that Mary's mind became distracted and worried. A certain tension in her listening was relaxed. She moved her feet, uncrossed her knees, tried to reach a footstool and could not, tried to keep still and could not. Why did these words give her such restless thoughts, why did the text seem painful, as it kept constantly returning, "Commit thy way unto the Lord"? From a little child Mary had committed her way to the Lord, so why should she be troubled? What,—anybody might have wondered,—could trouble her? She was happy: she felt strongly and healthily even now, in despite of her grief for George, the pleasures of her daily life. Now what had there been, she asked herself as the sermon went forward, that had of late made her restless as to her own employments. Trivial incidents came to her mind. Why had she told her mother with a sigh that it would not be worth while to carry out her scheme of painting her bedroom with Japanese designs? Why had she felt so little pleasure when Mrs. Riversdale had insisted on her having a new riding habit? She became conscious that there had been lately symptoms of some change working under the surface; symptoms which came back upon her in petty detail and teased her now. Her mind seemed to be going back upon itself in trembling bewilderment, clinging to such things as her horse, her dog, as if she were trying to keep awake, to keep away from some state of being that would otherwise suck her in. Yet she hardly said more to herself than that she ought to pay attention to the rest of the sermon, and that she was not doing so.

"I must not be distracted," were words that kept rising to her lips, as she tried to listen to the monk speaking of the different ways in which souls were led, and how all were called to some form of renunciation but in differing degrees. That each act of renunciation was to forego union with and dependence on the creature, and advance one step in union with the Creator; to accept loneliness and then to find it transformed into the joy of intercourse, higher, purer, than had yet been known. Then Mary, looking at the tabernacle, drew her mind to submit to her will with an effort, and whispered her favourite ejaculation, the word of another Mary, "Rabboni." It was to her the formula of a complete submission. But, as in a flash of lightning, there seemed to come the answer, "Sell all that thou hast and follow Me." This was the discovery; this was what for months, nay, years, she had been growing to; this was the manner in which "her way" was to be "committed." To Madge, in the mood of the moment, it might seem that the way of the Lord would be easy; but to Mary had come the hard saying, and with all her woman's sensitive complex consciousness she felt that it lit up her past with lurid distinctness. She shrank piteously before it. Why was it such a blow? Why had she not seen it long before? Why had she been allowed to grow up loving that home, those parents so intensely, if she had been intended all along to leave them and go forth?

"Rabboni, Rabboni," she repeated to herself, clinging to the good will that had always brought her peace, but which seemed now to be leading her into deep waters, where no man could follow her, where she would for ever from henceforth be alone.

Mary did not cover her face with her hands. She was motionless now. Her suffering was inarticulate; it was past thought. The monk's concluding sentences seemed dull and meaningless, though in reality even the most ordinary words of the sermon were being graven on her memory. It was a relief when he stopped speaking, a relief to be obliged to play the hymn. During the Benediction service which followed, she was still occupied with the organ; still appeared to herself to be cold and indifferent and half asleep. More people sang during Benediction, and Fieldes was surprised by the improved quality and harmony of the voices. The litany seemed to grow in a special intensity as it went on. But was it that the alternate verses were sung by a young contralto voice ringing with a strange pathos, a singular purity of note that might have befitted a disembodied spirit? There was something in the solo that surprised and infected the congregation, who felt that they had never before appreciated the power of Mary's singing.

A few moments more and the short service was finished, and the lights were being slowly extinguished. Mary half mechanically lighted a votive candle before the picture of "Our Lady of Perpetual Succour" in the tribune. She had intended, after Benediction was over, to go to the sacristy and speak to Father Clement about a poor woman in trouble, but she shrank from seeing him. She was oppressed; she was suffering; she wanted to escape; and, with only a hasty genuflexion, she left the chapel. Directly she had closed the door, she ran along the passage, and mounting the back stairs, two steps at a time, reached the old schoolroom, which was now her sitting-room.

There Carlos, the collie, was lying in front of the fire, and he rose and went to meet her, his brown eyes looking love and wisdom. Mary knelt down by him, put her head down to his face, and burst into a passion of soothing, free-flowing tears. God's dumb, wise, loving creature seemed to be a piece of homely, earthly being with whom she could find refuge from the supernatural.

CHAPTER XI

MADGE LEAVES SKIPTON

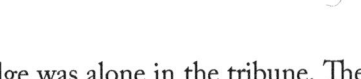

Madge was alone in the tribune. The lights on the altar had been extinguished, and the little flame of the sanctuary lamp was the only relief in the darkness of the chapel below. It shone faintly, but the brass door of the tabernacle could be distinguished in the circle of dim red light, as well as the ivory figure of the crucifix on the throne above. A few worshippers had lingered after the Benediction service, but they were now gone; only an occasional sound from the sacristy showed that somebody was still there. Madge sat on, soothed by the stillness, tranquillised by the atmosphere of peace and adoration; that indescribable atmosphere made up of the traditions of ages, of the recollections of childhood, the experience of life, that clusters round the belief in the Divine Presence. But Madge had yet to find that peace could not last for her if she stayed on before the tabernacle. It must be for her the "Yea" or "Nay" of a moral struggle. To Mark Fieldes it had been an evening of agreeable emotions; to Madge it must be more or less.

Presently the sacristy door opened, and the tall white figure of the monk passed across the sanctuary. He genuflected just under the lamp, and turned towards the chapel, which he supposed to be empty. The votive candle, which Mary had lit before the Madonna in the tribune, shed too dim a light to show him the little white face, the shining eyes which strained to see him in the darkness. For a moment Madge saw him clearly, and the sadness, the tenderness, and the peace of the old face seemed legible to her. He turned into the bench, and knelt down and sighed deeply. As Madge looked at him she said to herself, "Yes, I will go to confession and tell him all," and Madge moved close to the picture of the Madonna, that she might be able by the light of its candle, to read her prayer-book, and opened it at the page headed: "Preparation for Confession." All the rebelliousness of that morning seemed gone—the irritation at Mrs. Riversdale, the repulsion to Father Clement. The smell of the fragrant incense, the figure of the kneeling monk, the lamp that burned before the sanctuary, the remembrance still fresh of the words of the sermon and of the Holy Presence at Benediction, blended together, and she was collecting her thoughts and going through the stages of preparation, so familiar to little Madge O'Reilly at the Convent of the Sacré Cœur ten years ago, when every Saturday took her to confession to M. L'Abbé. She had come to Skipton to make her confession and now she felt that she could do it. The peace on her face, usually so restless, which had struck Mark Fieldes as he left the tribune, looked still deeper now, and she began to pray.

The minutes passed by. The monk was still praying. The chapel was silent. It struck a quarter to seven. Madge did not move. Seven o'clock struck and a quarter past, and she was still kneeling. Had Fieldes returned now he would have seen that the expression of peace was no longer on her face. She read her book, and put it down and read it again.

"Call to mind the occasions of past sin, and firmly resolve to avoid them in future," she read. "Consider what persons and places have been a source of temptation in the past, and resolve never to go near to them henceforth. He that loves the danger shall perish therein."

What was it in these words that brought back to Madge's face the old restlessness? Was not confession a simple affair now—now that the angry feelings of the morning had passed away? Why did she not turn over the page and read the words "having now firmly resolved to avoid all sin and its occasions, make the act of contrition"?

"Surely," she said to herself, "it is no real temptation— it may never be a temptation."

But she looked at the same page again, and did not turn over the leaf. The clock struck half-past seven.

"I must go to Father Clement at once or I shall be late," she thought. "I will tell him I had not time to prepare properly."

She started to her feet. She had gone two steps down the stairs that led from the tribune to the chapel, as quietly as a thief, when a bell rang loudly in the house. It was the dressing bell. Madge sprang up the steps again and bounded across the tribune.

"I can't," she cried to herself, "I can't. I shall be late for dinner." She sobbed as she ran, tears fell down her face. Her handkerchief was held up to her eyes.

She reached her bedroom. There was Celestine just as usual, the spirit lamp lit, the curling tongs in her hand.

"Madame ne m'a pas dit quelle robe elle allait mettre ce soir."

Madge paused: this was always an interesting question.

"Ma 'tea-gown' réséda—non, non, la demi-toilette blene. Ah, que mes cheveux sont en désordre! Vite, Celestine!"

She sat down, seized the tongs and began to curl her fringe violently. "Ah, maintenant je suis brulée, malheur." She looked tenderly at a tiny scar on her forehead, then suddenly she turned round upon the impassive little foreigner.

"Ah, comme ça serait triste d'être vraiment bonne, n'est-ce pas? On est bon ici, on est même saint. Et moi, cela m'étouffe. Je partirai demain matin. Il faut emballer tout cela pendant que nous sommes à diner, mais n'en dites rien à personne—vous comprenez, à *personne?*"

While she spoke Madge was dressing hastily: she seized the gown off the bed.

"Mais madame a dit la demi-toilette blene, et maintenant elle met la 'tea-gown' réséda!"

Celestine was astonished and excited. She had never known madame uncertain, *égarée*, as to her toilettes before—it was far more surprising than tears or changes of plan.

The evening passed off well, for Mrs. Riversdale had gone to bed with a fresh touch of bronchitis.—Madge talked gaily and prettily to her father-in-law. Mary, too, was quite bright and chatty, occasionally almost passing to a giggle, which was so unlike her as to surprise even the preoccupied Madge. After dinner, led by Madge, they all sang Mr. Riversdale's favourite hunting glees, and Madge gave him some Scotch songs of which he was fond. It was the brightest evening they had had during the visit—and they planned the practising of some fresh glees on the morrow. Madge's soprano, Mary's contralto, and the two men's voices, all well trained, were wonderfully successful; and Hilda's little mezzo-soprano was quite harmless.

The merriment was brought somewhat abruptly to a close by Madge, who suddenly announced that she had had enough. She left the piano and went to sit down on a low stool by her father-in-law. She put a hand on his chair. The others were still round the piano and could not see them. The old man put his large brown hand over the white one with its many rings. They sat thus for a moment when Hilda called out to Madge to play one more song.

"No, no," cried Madge, "I've had enough," then she suddenly bent down and kissed the old man's hand.

The squire looked a little surprised.

"Child, child," he said tenderly, "let nothing divide us, eh?"

He bent forward and tried to see her eyes, but she had sprung up and in her usual voice bade him good-night, and waving her hand to the others ran out of the room.

At seven next morning Madge crept down to the dining-room through the lamp-lit passages. The house felt very cold and she picked up her fur cloak in the hall and put it over her shoulders. It had been Celestine's opinion that it would excite less attention to put the tray in the dining-room than to take it upstairs. The fire was just lit and the figure of a housemaid flitted away through a farther door as Madge entered. The lamp on the table lit up the brown teapot and dish of bacon intended for the servants' breakfast—of all breakfasts in Madge's eyes the most unpalatable. She sat down and drank some tea. She could not eat, it was too early. She looked at the clock, she wished the fly would come before anybody was about. It was nearly a quarter past seven; if it were punctual she might be off in a few minutes now.

It was Mr. Riversdale's habit to go to the chapel at seven o'clock, and he was kneeling there with a hand-candle to read his meditation, when he heard the sound of wheels, unusual at that hour, stopping at the front door. He rose, and looking out of the tribune window saw a fly; and after a moment, the flyman—more astonishing still—disappeared into the house and came out again carrying a lady's trunks, evidently Madge's, helped by the steward's room boy. The old man hurried out of the tribune and almost ran downstairs. He saw that there was a light in the dining-room and he went thither. Madge was standing in front of the fire, her fur cloak lying at her feet, dressed in a smart tailor-made travelling gown. An impression of something he disliked in the effect of the little figure, caught there on the dark winter's morning, going away on the sly, revived after she had gone some recollections of the one French novel he had read many years before. With the greatest difficulty he restrained his anger as he came hastily forward.

"What's the meaning of all this?" he cried. "Why didn't they tell me you were going? And a fly too," he rang the bell impatiently, and an astonished butler in most untidy morning *déshabille* hurried up from some avocations in a distant pantry,

"The brougham to come round at once for Mrs. George—did not Miss Mary order it last night? I am sorry, Madge; it was very stupid of her."

The old man spoke with dignity and Madge felt ashamed. The bad taste of her method of departure struck her forcibly for the first time. But she was desperately anxious to catch that train.

"Oh, it doesn't matter," she said lamely, "the brougham can't possibly be in time."

"Then you can go by the next train, an hour later," said Mr. Riversdale, "but why are you going at all?"

He had seen with supreme disgust the earthenware teapot and the dish of large slices of bacon, but these he ignored.

"Going?" said Madge and she seemed unable to speak another syllable. "Going, oh, because I must see the dentist, I've been in agonies all night, and yesterday at Benediction I was crying with the pain. I haven't slept at all, so I thought I would get off by the eight o'clock train and get to London at twelve, and catch my dentist."

"It is curious how this place gives you the toothache," said Mr. Riversdale a little hastily; he could not quite keep his temper with prevarication. But he recollected himself, for he always felt that he owed Madge all the reparation it was in his power to make for his dead son's neglect and selfishness. At that moment too there fell a tear on the polished steel grate, and Madge took out her pocket handkerchief.

"I am a brute," said Mr. Riversdale; "but, Madge, what have I done that you can't trust me, eh, child? If you would but be open with me, I believe I could be of use to you. It is distressing me and my wife beyond measure."

Madge had looked up at him as he spoke, but her face hardened when he alluded to Mrs. Riversdale. She turned to the clock,—would the brougham never come? Mr. Riversdale felt the weak point of his words. His wife had always sided against Madge. But he made one more effort.

"Madge," he said, "don't go now; don't leave us like this. What have I done to deserve such treatment?"

There was a touch of dignity and pathos in these words hard to resist. To Madge it was intolerable; she was as fond of George's father as she could be of anybody, but she had made up her mind now. She hated scenes, and she wanted to get away. She made a diversion.

"Thank you," she said, "I know you are good to me, but I must make my own life now. But, father, do tell me, what is the matter with Mary?"

Mr. Riversdale started. "The matter with Mary!" he exclaimed. "Why, what makes you say that?"

Madge could not tell what had made her say it, and yet now that it was said it seemed to have a good deal of meaning. It had come without intention or reflection, yet neither of them could let it pass, though Mr. Riversdale was as earnestly bent on other topics, and Madge had no wish, in her anxiety to avoid her own affairs, to plunge into any question of intimate importance to the Riversdales.

"I don't know," said Madge in a slow puzzled tone, "but she is not like herself, not like what she used to be somehow."

Mr. Riversdale was not responsive to the matter-of-course tone that Madge tried to adopt.

"We can none of us be the same as usual," he said very sadly, looking earnestly at her; but he was partly thinking of Mary and he let her go on.

"She does not look well, she seems nervous and her eyes are often red: and she doesn't really care much about anything except her horse and Carlos."

Madge was surprised to find how much she had to say, and how true her observations seemed to herself though they had been made quite unconsciously. She had left the fireplace and seated herself in a deep morocco arm-chair. Her voice was eager and she spoke rapidly, but her eyes were fixed on the door, and her ears strained to hear the noise of carriage-wheels. The inward indifference to Mary was betrayed, and jarred upon the listener.

He forced himself to think only of Madge, but what could he say? Were there words that George's father could use to her? The precious moments were passing and he was silent. Then all thought of George, all sense of personal embarrassment left him. He moved nearer to her and his soul seemed to force him to speak to hers.

"Oh, my child," he said, "believe me nothing is worth it. Perhaps I have stood aside from life, perhaps I can't tell what yours is, what lies before you, what the world holds for you. It may be as charming as it is dangerous. But don't blink the truth. Wherever you go, whomever you trust, be very sure that you don't deceive yourself. We don't want to keep you here against your will. But if you choose a life for yourself, make very sure that it is a safe one. If you won't listen to me go to somebody better, stronger, than I am, but, little Madge," he stepped to the side of the chair and put his big hand softly on her shoulder, "don't go to the world, mind that, child, mind that."

"There could be nobody better than you," cried Madge—she jumped up to kiss him, she had heard the carriage drive up. It was the lightest kiss. She moved to the door. He did not follow her. She turned and looked at him. Was it perhaps the last time that she was to see the tall figure, the large regular features? His outline was distinct as he stood there,—his head bent a little in a way that was growing upon him; the blue eyes whose tenderness she knew well she could not see. For a moment she longed to run back to him, to cry freely on his shoulder, to tell him that he should be her shelter. But it was too heavy a price she would have to pay for an old man's peace and affection. He did not move, she lightly kissed her hand in his direction and went away.

A moment later she was driving through the park and expressing an almost hysterical amount of temper towards her maid. "Whoever heard of anything so stupid as the idea of having her breakfast in the dining-room that morning, it was *bête, bête, bête!*"

CHAPTER XII

MARK SINGS A HYMN

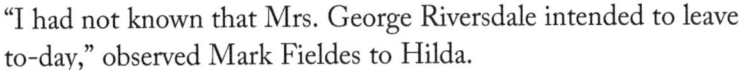

"I had not known that Mrs. George Riversdale intended to leave to-day," observed Mark Fieldes to Hilda.

"No, nor did I, nor did anybody, I think," said Hilda in a puzzled voice. "At least Marmaduke seemed very much surprised."

"Yes," said Fieldes, "Lemarchant did not conceal his annoyance."

The two were alone in the drawing-room. Mrs. Riversdale was unusually late, owing to her bronchitis, and had not yet left her room. Mary had gone out in the waggonette to execute some commissions for her mother, and to send off a small box which Madge's maid had forgotten in the confusion of her hurried departure. There had grown to be an intimacy between Mr. Fieldes and Hilda, and he had ventured on showing before her alone certain indications of a respectful amusement at some of the ideas and ways of Skipton. But Hilda had no intention of discussing with him this mystery of Madge's departure, for she could see that there was something of a mystery about it. She stiffened a little when he made this remark about Marmaduke, and Fieldes hastened to give it a different complexion.

"What a fine fellow he is!" he exclaimed, "one of the most popular men I know, and so straight."

He watched Hilda as she answered eagerly:—

"Yes, isn't he. And you know it was so funny; they were all so frightened at his going into the army, except Father Clement. And yet I think they all own now that he has turned out pretty well."

"He is so plucky," Fieldes continued, "once I saw him do a plucky thing. A man told a story—*un peu trop fort*, as even I thought,—in the smoking-room at a country house party, and

Lemarchant got up and walked straight out of the room; and everybody liked him the better for it, even the man who told the story."

That the *raconteur* in question was himself, Fieldes did not think it necessary to mention, but Hilda had an uncomfortable recollection of Marmaduke's saying that Mrs. Riversdale would have had a fit if she could have heard some of Fieldes' stories.

Mark did not know whether to be annoyed or pleased at Hilda's apparent indifference to this anecdote about Lemarchant. It might mean anything.

"You say that there are strong objections held by Catholics against the army," he went on. "Do you know, that fits in with one of the few objections I have always felt against Catholic education; I think it is too timorous, more inclined to keep men out of temptation than to prepare them for it."

"I like that," cried Hilda, "from a son of the persecutors to a daughter of the persecuted. And pray who has kept us out of the national life for centuries? Who shut us out from the schools and colleges of our country? Who forced us into these habits of concealment, of fear, and these traditions of do nothingness I should like to know?" and Hilda turned upon Fieldes with an air of righteous wrath and laughing eyes.

Fieldes laughed. "How long was your cousin in India?" he inquired.

"About five years, I think," answered Hilda. "His parents were very anxious that he should leave the army when the regiment went out, and settle down at home, but he would not."

"Rumour said that he wanted heart healing. It was curious that he and your other cousin should have been rivals."

"What other cousin?" said Hilda, too much interested to show her dignity to this retailer of gossip.

"Mr. George Riversdale," observed Fieldes.

"And was George refused by the same lady?" asked Hilda, "I mean did gossip say so?"

"No, he was accepted."

Light dawned upon Hilda. He meant that Marmaduke had been in love with Madge. She blushed furiously and was furious with herself for blushing. A thousand little things came to her mind to confirm the idea. She knew that Marmaduke had had a disappointment. She had once heard Marmaduke and George called rivals. Then it struck her that this idea tallied so well with Marmaduke's attitude towards Madge now; he was so immensely interested in her. There was a chivalrous respectfulness, a willingness to serve, a total absence of any touch of flirtation; just such an attitude as an ideally good man might hold towards a woman whom he loved, and whose recent widowhood demanded reverence and reserve.

But the notion, though so easily planted in her mind, was anything but pleasing, nay, it seemed almost revolting. The sting of it made her cheeks fiery. There was only a moment's silence during which Fieldes was watching her closely. It was so probable that his guess was true. It evidently tallied with information of Hilda's own, or it would not have been so easily received; he was quite sure now that he had spoken the truth and a very convenient truth it was. Hilda's sensations were soon overwhelmed by annoyance at Mr. Fieldes being the witness of her blushes and confusion. She was determined to cover her momentary disadvantage.

"Yes," she said in distinct staccato tones. "I heard some story long ago, but I was too young to be told much; and of course people outside the family would never speak to me on the subject."

Hilda drew up her long neck with a touch of hauteur which added to her attractions in Mark's eyes. He thought that the blood of all her father's ancestors was shown in her at such moments. He plunged hastily into another subject. Hilda, though still hot and angry, was afraid that her snub might have been rude. Her pride was easily roused; but any action it led to, she speedily had her doubts of. "I live in a state of remorse," she had once said to her mother, and she was quickly remorseful now. So she readily responded to Mr. Fieldes' wish to talk of something less embarrassing.

"I had a most interesting letter from a very remarkable woman, a great friend of mine, this morning," he began. "May I read you a few words from it?"

"'Your picture of a great old Catholic family has pleased me extremely. The lord of the manor riding to hounds with his fair daughter; the white-robed monk; the village children; the intelligence of a younger generation, perceiving, understanding, yet reverencing them all. I once met and was much struck by Mrs. Arthur Riversdale, a woman of such delicate, such fine feelings, animating a mind that might otherwise have been almost too keen and logical for a woman. It was a personality not to be forgotten!'"

Fieldes read these few lines with a ring of appreciation in his voice. It would not have surprised him in the least if he had known that the writer could not remember with certainty if she had ever seen Mrs. Arthur Riversdale. He had frequently found himself that if he could recollect nothing about a person it was safest to talk of his or her "personality." Hilda was delighted. Nothing could have pleased her better than this admiration of her mother. It had occasionally occurred to her that logic was not her mother's strongest point; but she had always dismissed the idea. Mr. Fieldes had been quick to perceive that what Hilda loved most and was most proud of, with an almost resentful pride, was her mother's family, not the long line of her father's with its feudal antiquity.

He had won Hilda partly by his unspoken sympathy on this point, and he seemed to her to be an echo of the opinion of a bigger world in which James Harding was still quoted and admired.

"Who wrote the letter?" she inquired eagerly.

"Mrs. Hurstmonceaux."

"The Laura Hurstmonceaux whom Madge quotes so often?" inquired Hilda.

The lady to whom the great author had been evidently writing about herself, was, she knew, of particular importance in Madge's eyes. That she was meant by the "intelligence of the younger generation" Hilda had perceived with delight. Though maternal love had given her a fairly good idea of herself, it had been rather a matter taken for granted than expressed, that Hilda was a clever attractive girl, and she was quite new to out-spoken compliment; but it is an easily acquired taste. Madge might be contemptuous because her gowns hung wrongly, but there were other people in the big world besides Madge who might think differently. About that big world she longed to know more.

"Tell me about her," she said, lounging back in the deep armchair, in which she had sat up so stiffly a few minutes before.

This was much pleasanter than talking about Marmaduke.

"What is she like?"

Mr. Fieldes was sitting at an old-fashioned big round table, of the kind that was considered an exciting innovation when Emma persuaded Mr. Woodhouse to allow her to introduce it at Hartfield. He was turning over the leaves of a big book by Louis Veuillot, profusely illustrated, and not too mundane for Mrs. Riversdale.

"How am I to convey Mrs. Hurstmonceaux to you?" he exclaimed, with knitted brows and rising and walking towards the fireplace. "Ask me questions and I will see how I can answer. It is so difficult to describe her off-hand like this."

"Is she handsome?"

"Oh, no."

"Is she graceful?"

"No again."

"Does she dress well?"

"No, yet again."

"Is she wonderfully witty?"

"She can say witty things, but she doesn't do so often. There is something in her talk better than wit. I think she feels the sadness of the age too much to be witty. You want faith to be witty, Miss Riversdale. 'A tender expression of spiritual sympathy,' she once said to me, 'is more effective now than the most sprightly jest of Sydney Smith's ever was.' I think the secret of her success is that she understands the spirit of the day."

"You are getting on now without questioning: but I will ask another. To what religion does she belong?"

"I don't think she belongs to any in particular. But don't look horrified. I think she is one of the most religious people I know. She loves the highest aspirations and emotions of religion, only not the fetters of dogma. She quoted to me once those wonderful words of Renan. 'Let us,' she said, 'shroud our heads and bend them low, "pour ne rien dire de limité en face de l'infini."'"

"But is dogma a limit, or a suggestion of the infinite?" said Hilda in a puzzled tone. "But that is beyond me; and, Mr. Fieldes, I don't think your friend is getting clearer to me at all. She is plain?"

"Oh, no," cried Fieldes.

"Awkward?"

"Oh dear no."

"Dresses badly?"

"Good gracious! no."

"Then she is too mediocre to be called anything."

"Horrors!" cried Fieldes; "I see that I must never try to describe anybody again. She is emphatically original and yet there is nothing obtrusive about her. She can say the most daring things without being unconventional."

"Do you know, Mr. Fieldes, I think she must be a good listener."

"Admirable!" cried Fieldes, laughing, "she listens to perfection. But I must get her clearer to you. She *never gossips*. Mrs. Hurstmonceaux never knows the news on the Rialto. She is deaf and blind to scandal." And he added fervently: "Her infinite delicacy and tact prevent her ever blundering. She never believes anything against anybody till every one else agrees about it. Then," Fieldes was expressively dropping a note into the fire as he spoke, "then, when the reputation is hopelessly gone, she says what she thinks! I don't think I have ever known a woman so completely charitable before! That fellow Hobbes, you know, all through that scandal you met him at the Hurstmonceaux's—she evidently knew nothing about it; but when it was clear that everybody else had given him up—then he vanished."

Hilda looked thoroughly puzzled by this bit of praise. It sounded to her like kicking a dog when everybody else had finished kicking. But she reflected that she knew very little about it, and she did not wish to say anything too innocent to Mr. Fieldes, or to show that she had never heard of Hobbes.

"Shall I tell you," she said, "what kind of person you have conveyed to me, in all honesty, as if she were no friend of yours?"

"Yes, do."

"Well then, I think she is plain, but that she makes you forget her plainness; that she is not graceful but too well trained to be called awkward; that she is so frivolous that she doesn't care if her religious emotions correspond to a reality or not, but that she has immense strength of will. If you told me that she were enormously ambitious and trying to exert great influence of some kind I should understand it better. But I don't see now-a-days what kind of career a woman has. Does she try to have political influence?"

"No, I don't think so," said Fieldes. "I suppose her ambition is social."

"How very uninteresting!" said Hilda, with a little *moue* of contempt.

Fieldes laughed. "I am not sure that I agree with you," he said; "anything that needs skill and tact, and secures power over your fellow-creatures must be interesting. Then in this case she is triumphing over special difficulties. She was quite unknown in London herself, and her husband's people though of very good family are very old-fashioned. Well, I've made a failure of my description, but it is better than describing too well. More than once when I have wished to make two people whom I admired know and like each other I have made the mistake of praising them too much and of course they were disappointed. But one great mistake you have made—she is certainly not frivolous. She is if anything almost too much in earnest."

At that moment Marmaduke came into the room.

"I am going to walk across the park to meet Mary. There is something wrong with the skating rink. The ground under the asphalte is giving, and she wants me to look at it."

"I should like to come too," said Hilda, which was just what he had hoped.

"And so should I," added Fieldes, which was just what he had feared. At this, Hilda ran to get her things on.

As Fieldes was waiting for her reappearance, Mrs. Riversdale came into the drawing-room. All Mary's efforts had failed to keep her mother in her room. She was too much upset, too restless to be quiet. Fieldes saw that she was perturbed. The falling crape collar, which formed the background to the miniature of her son, was tumbled; the folds of the rich silk gown rustled in an agitated manner. Mrs. Riversdale was on the defensive. She knew that her husband thought that if she had made her more welcome Madge would have stayed longer, and in Marmaduke and Mary's worried looks she saw criticism. She was aggrieved, and her conscience was not perfectly easy; she was a very good woman, and capable of generosity, though naturally narrow; but her idolatry of her son had been her ruling passion from the moment when the old nurse had laid a red-faced white-robed object beside her, saying in a voice of triumph:—

"A son and a heir, the beauty."

She was up in arms for his memory now, and indignantly refused to listen to vulgar gossip. It had been all Madge's fault anyhow; and then her own husband actually said that she ought to have been warmer to Madge—to Madge, who had not even had the decency to come to Skipton in mourning. Had she not done her best? Had she ever been more courteous to anybody? Mr. Fieldes, attentive and deferential, just suited her this morning. And besides, she had somehow grown to imagine that he had been an intimate friend of her son's. She settled herself in her large armchair, and turning to him said graciously:—

"Are you fond of miniatures, Mr. Fieldes? because, if so, this one of my son at eight years old is worth your attention. It is by one of our best artists."

She opened a case, and showed an exquisite picture of a fair-haired boy, playing with a dog. There was the touch of real genius in the work, its exquisite minuteness giving no effect of littleness. It was suggestive down to the slightest touch. A child's individuality is hard to catch but it was caught here. The wilful pride and eagerness in the exquisite little face only enhanced its beauty.

The night before, Mrs. Riversdale had wept a torrent of tears over that picture. "Was it for this," she cried in the truthfulness of the night, "that I bore and bred you, my beautiful son, for a wasted sinful youth and the breaking of your father's heart?" Now she was showing it proudly to Mr. Fieldes.

"It shows the manly straightforward character of the child," she said. "Yet he was always to be led by affection, by good influences. It was a character that needed good influences, and as long as he was under our control he never had any other. We never agreed with Marmaduke's parents about education. We kept him away from the world. At sixteen he was as innocent as any girl."

Before Mr. Fieldes could speak, she had shut the miniature case and put it down with a certain dignity.

"I don't know if you agree with me, Mr. Fieldes, but I sometimes think that the foreign way of arranging marriage has its advantages."

"Undoubtedly," said Fieldes with respectful sympathy. But any further discussion on foreign matrimonial customs was prevented by the appearance of Hilda, who summoned Mr. Fieldes and told him that Marmaduke was in the hall.

It was rather a silent trio that took their way across the park and along the two miles of high-road that lay between the south lodge and the station. A flickering political discussion went on between Fieldes and Marmaduke as to the effect of a Gladstonian Government in India, in which Hilda tried mildly to maintain the position of the "intelligence of the younger generation." If Marmaduke had been less absent-minded and worried that morning, he might have teased her for her answers, more sharp than well-informed, to his observations on the condition of

India. As they came near to the little country station they wondered at not having met Mary.

"She said she would be at the lodge by 11:30, and now it is nearly 12 o'clock," observed Marmaduke.

A little curve in the road brought the station in full view. The waggonette was standing in the road, with quite a small crowd of porters and labourers and women round it.

"It looks as if something were wrong!" exclaimed Marmaduke. At that moment the group opened to let a footman with what looked like a stretcher pass into the station; and they could recognise the Skipton livery.

"Stay here, Hilda," Marmaduke said in a tone of command, and he ran swiftly forward. Fieldes was quite willing to stay also. He was no lover of horrors, and he felt no strong sense of his own capacity to help.

"I had better stay with you," he observed to Hilda in a protecting voice.

"Oh no," she cried, "do go and see what it is. But I do hope it is nothing. Please go and find out."

Fieldes hesitated. Perhaps it was unfair to him,—for it was certainly no situation of danger that he was avoiding, nor was it likely that he could be of any particular use,—but the contrast between the two men, both in appearance and manner, struck Hilda forcibly at that moment;—Marmaduke with well-knit active figure, swiftly approaching the station; Fieldes standing irresolute without any sense of readiness for action, of quickness to help, perceptible in his face. But Hilda was too terrified as to the nature of the confusion at the station to do more than receive an impression of which she was hardly conscious at the time. She was pale with terror. What was it? Had anything happened to Mary? Horrible visions of mangled corpses left by trains in their ghastly wake, crowded before her mental vision.

"Oh, do go!" she cried almost fiercely, turning upon Fieldes.

"I am not going to leave you alone," said Fieldes a little pettishly. "I shall stay here."

Horrible visions had made him pale also.

A moment afterwards Marmaduke had disappeared in the little crowd, and then a boy came running towards them. On seeing this Fieldes started to meet him, running in a curiously shuffling way, his long legs interfering with each other. The little boy delivered his message to Fieldes, full of self-importance, and began running back to the station at once as if he felt he could not be spared.

Fieldes began the same curious movements towards Hilda.

"They are all safe!" he paused to shout; but evidently Hilda couldn't hear. She ran, swiftly, gracefully, to meet him.

"She is all safe!" he shouted again.

"Hurrah!" cried Hilda joyously.

They slackened as they drew nearer, and Fieldes was very much out of breath.

"What has happened then?" she inquired.

"No man or woman hurt," he said; "but it is very horrid, very nasty. I'm glad Lemarchant made us stay here. It is the dog, your cousin's dog."

"Carlos, Mary's beautiful Carlos?"

"Yes, it was killed by the train. Miss Riversdale had crossed over to speak to the station-master, and the dog bounded across to her just as the train was starting, and was smashed."

Their first sense of relief was lost in the horror of it. The beautiful Carlos with his golden brown shagginess, his magnificent human eyes, his intense devotion to his mistress. They walked on to the station in silent sympathy, both dreading the meeting with Mary. They had not gone far when they met the waggonette. Mary and Marmaduke were seated in it. Mary was very white, and there was a pathetic look of misery in her blue eyes; but only the suspicion of tears. The little sensitive marks at the corners of her large full lips were quivering. They stopped, and Hilda and Fieldes seated themselves on the empty side of the waggonette. They drove home in unbroken silence except that Marmaduke told Hilda that she ought to put on a cloak, and Hilda obeyed, assisted by efforts from Mr. Fieldes. Not one of the four saw anything of the wintry landscape. They all had one picture in their minds; the beautiful eyes of the great collie, as he jumped lovingly to meet his mistress.

When they got to the lodge Mary said in a low voice to Marmaduke:—

"I should like to walk across the park;" and they all knew that she wished to go alone, so they let her get down.

When Mary was out of ear-shot Marmaduke leaned across to Hilda.

"You had a fright," he said tenderly, for a moment forgetful of Fieldes.

"I was afraid it was Mary," said Hilda, answering his look and turning pale at the thought. Then she turned a little abruptly to Mr. Fieldes who was sitting by her.

"The stretcher added to our horrors, didn't it?"

"Was it to take Carlos away?" inquired Fieldes.

"Yes," Marmaduke answered. "The very moment the train had passed they threw sacking over him before Mary could see. She wanted to bring him home, and the station-master didn't like to refuse, though he knew it wasn't possible. He was greatly relieved to see me. He asked me to take her away. He was quite upset himself. It is extraordinary what feeling everybody here has for Mary. One thing they all said was that they wished 'the poor brute had been som' 'un else's'! I think she is the most popular character in the country round."

The rest of the day passed heavily at Skipton, and things seemed to Hilda to be going contrariwise. Fieldes was absorbed for a long time in conversation with Father Clement, who lunched at the house; and when the monk left, the old squire devoted himself to his guest, to whom he feared he had been not attentive enough so far. Marmaduke had been asked by his uncle to attend a horse show at the county town.

Mary was busy with her mother, who had been persuaded by the doctor, much against her own wishes, to go to her despised bed, and Hilda found time pass very slowly. At tea-time Mr. Fieldes thought himself in luck at last, for he found Hilda alone with the tea-pot and cakes.

"Have you seen Miss Riversdale since the accident?" he inquired, taking his tea from Hilda's hands, which, though they could not be called "small or fair," being rather large and brown, were well-shaped, with long tapering fingers.

"No," said Hilda. "She must have had lunch after we left, and gone up to her mother's room afterwards. I am so dreadfully sorry for her. She was so devoted to the dog." Hilda held out a plate of hot buttered tea-cake.

"Wait a moment," said Fieldes, "I want to show you something before my fingers touch that."

He drew out of his pocket a little leather case. It contained an exquisitely bound and illuminated copy of *The Following of Christ*. "I had it painted for myself at Oulton Abbey by the Benedictines. Is it not exquisite? See, each capital is a separate design, nearly all quite original. The others are taken from old MSS."

Hilda turned it over delicately and admired it with enthusiasm. Fieldes drew his chair near to hers to show her some special letters.

"What a book it is!" he cried. "Think of its being granted to one man to give expression to the aspirations that haunt men in all ages. I suppose Father Clement lives upon that book as his gospel of renunciation!" As he spoke Fieldes looked more at Hilda than at the book. He liked to see the graceful head bent, the rapt attitude, and he thought he had never noticed before the beauty of the shape of her little ear.

Presently Hilda turned to the end.

"What is this hymn, painted by somebody else surely, but very pretty too?"

"Yes, that was painted by me; a wretched insertion after the rest. But I am so fond of that hymn and it seems to me to be such a fit ending to the book. Let me sing it to you—but after tea. Now let me put the book away and turn to creature consolations!"

Marmaduke here broke in on the *tête-à-tête*, and thought the effect was not artistic. The man was lanky and clumsy, and Hilda always looked excited when she was talking to Mr. Fieldes. Hilda gave Marmaduke his tea and inquired about the horse.

"Was it a good one?" she said.

Marmaduke laughed. "Well it had good points and bad points, but you wouldn't understand either if I tried to explain."

"But Mary would, I suppose?" said Hilda. "Oh yes, Mary is a capital judge *for* a woman."

There was something distinctly masculine about Marmaduke. He seemed to be always reminding Hilda that she was an inferior kind of person, whereas Fieldes exalted her in her own eyes.

"Do you know," said Fieldes in his shrill voice, "that while we were doing our spiritual reading, my tea has got cold. Will you give me some more?"

"What was the spiritual reading?" asked the other.

"The *Imitation*," said Fieldes. "And by the way, Miss Riversdale, remind me to show you a passage of Renan's, a few most exquisite lines on the subject."

Marmaduke was disgusted. Hilda reading the *Imitation* and Renan with Mark Fieldes! He did not know which seemed to him the most irreverent. Hilda was cross. She did not like the expression on Marmaduke's face.

"If spiritual reading always consisted of admiring illuminations, I don't think I should miss mine so often." She was annoyed at herself for giving explanations to Marmaduke. What business had he to look like that? What was the harm if she had read the Gospel itself with Mr. Fieldes? He was perfectly reverent. Only somehow she always did give in when Marmaduke looked like that, and she was sure Mr. Fieldes understood. He always understood everything, which made it more annoying.

As soon as Mr. Fieldes' tea was disposed of, he went to the piano and began playing softly. Marmaduke had drawn nearer to Hilda, to see the illuminated *Following of Christ*. Fieldes played on, but as nobody spoke, he said in a quick sharp tone:—

"Do you want to hear the hymn, Miss Riversdale?"

"Oh, yes," cried Hilda, "please sing it. Do you need the words?"

"No," said Mark, "I know it by heart."

Mark sang the hymn well. It always roused his emotions. He glanced upwards from time to time as he sang. When the religious sentiment was strong in Mr. Fieldes, he always glanced upwards; it was a relief.

> Art thou weary, art thou languid,
>   Art thou sore distrest?
> 'Come to Me,' saith One, 'and coming,
>   Be at rest.'
>
> Hath He marks to lead me to Him,
>   If He be my guide?
> In His Feet and Hands are wound-prints
>   And His Side.

Mark was the only one who saw that Mary had come in at the other end of the room. She was standing with her hand on the door listening. Her face was very pale, and her eyes had a set, tired look in them. Something there was about her which checked his inclination to stop the music and speak to her. He went on with the hymn.

> Hath He diadem as monarch
>   That His brow adorns?
> Yea, a crown in very surety,
>   But of thorns.
>
> If I find Him, if I follow,
>   What His guerdon here? Many a sorrow,
> many a labour,
>   Many a tear.

Fieldes glanced down the room. Mary's face was very sad, but he saw that she was listening intently. The childish expression had left the blue eyes, and the very fairness of the colouring seemed to reveal little lines of pain round the mouth.

"Was she in love?" thought Fieldes, "did she care for the dark-haired soldier too?"

It was a new view of the circumstances; but he instantly dismissed it. His power of vision was too true. He had sung half the next verse while this thought came and went.

> If I still hold closely to Him,
>   What hath He at last?
> Sorrow vanquished, labour ended,
>   Jordan past.
>
> If I ask Him to receive me,
>   Will He say me nay?
> Not till earth and not till Heaven
>   Pass away.
>
> Finding, following, keeping, struggling,
>   Is He sure to bless?
> Angels, martyrs, prophets, virgins,
>   Answer Yes.
>   Amen.

The *timbre* of Fieldes' voice seemed to vibrate with the great question in the last verse; but it was hardly equal to the concluding line.

There was a moment's silence. Fieldes had looked at the others. Then he turned towards Mary, but she was gone.

For some moments he became *distrait*. He hardly heard what they said. There was some mystery about Mary, some moral condition which he could not even guess at. She puzzled him. "We needs must love the highest when we see it," had long been his favourite quotation. After the first day at Skipton he had ranked Mary as the highest nature there. Yet he thought he did not love Mary, and he was very nearly in love with Hilda.

It was not simply that Hilda was, he believed, an heiress, for Mary was far the greater heiress of the two; but that Mary seemed to belong to another sphere, a sphere which he honestly told himself was out of his own reach. He had hitherto believed that sphere to be a happy one. He had thought that the children of the saints had at least the consolation which gave them the heaven they hoped for in their own breasts. However rarefied and exhausting that heaven might appear to others, he had supposed that it meant joy to them. But if this were so, where, in Mary's case, was this joy,—the light of faith and serenity that illuminates prophets, virgins, saints and martyrs, in their testimony? What was it that obscured the radiance with which Mary "Answered yes"?

That evening he gave her his beautiful copy of the *Imitation* as a parting gift. She was very simple, sweet and courteous in accepting it; but he found it lying neglected on the hall table next morning when he took his departure from Skipton-le-Grange.

Part II

CHAPTER I

LAURA'S EMBASSY

Thursday morning was dark in London, and by the afternoon a yellow fog had settled down over the West End. Mrs. Hurstmonceaux gave up a projected round of calls as the weather had become impossible. She thought she would not go out. About four o'clock however a telegram was brought in, and she instantly changed her mind and said that the brougham was to come round at once.

Laura's eyes sparkled as she read the telegram again and again:—

Have got away. Can you come to me?—MADGE.

"Already!" she cried joyfully, "and she went down on Monday. She has only been able to endure it for two days."

"Have got away." The three words conveyed all that Laura wanted to know. If the visit had been anything but a complete failure Madge would not have sent such a telegram.

"I must make sure of her state of mind before I speak," she thought; "but I am inclined to think that boldness will be the safest policy. I don't see anything to be gained by delay."

A quarter of an hour later and Laura, muffled in black velvet and sables, was driving, slowly on account of the darkness, in her faultless brougham across the park, a little elated and excited, and not quite in her usual conventional attitude.

She came into Madge's drawing-room eagerly, stretching out both hands. Then she paused and looked at her with a dramatic intensity of sympathy.

"Dear friend, how have you borne it?"

Madge rose briskly, pushed aside a little pile of notes, and almost ran up to her.

"Ah," she cried, seizing her by both hands, "the comfort of having you again, Laura." But her tone soon changed. She pushed the tall stately figure of her friend gently into a chair, and taking up her cigarette, puffed a moment in silence.

Then she cried: "Ah, Laura, what it was! The boredom of it! Mrs. Riversdale and her monk! The whole family wanting to convert me!"

"Yet it was right that you should go there, so right," said Laura earnestly, and her pale face was lit up with a stern sense of duty.

"Well," said Madge, "it is over now, so let us be merry. *Ohimé!* what's been going on?"

"What is going on?" said Laura cheerfully. "Well, there was a charming party last night at Lady F.'s. She has discovered a dear little singing bird of a woman with the most lovely blue eyes, an innocent child, but with the *timbre* of every passion in her voice."

"Ah," answered Madge, "was it as crowded as usual?"

Madge did not know Lady F. Laura did very slightly.

"Oh, no, only a few *friends*, nothing formal."

"I see," said Madge, looking down at her notes, "that the Duchess of A. is going to give a ball already."

Laura did not know the Duchess of A. Madge did.

"Then," Mrs. Hurstmonceaux continued, "I went yesterday to the meeting of the Society for Protecting Circus Girls. Oh, my dear, the things they told me. But why make your heart ache too? You have been through enough trouble already. But tell me," she added suddenly, "more of the visit to Skipton. The family seems to be not without its attractions. Mr. Mark Fieldes tells me in a letter to-day that they are all charming, particularly the fair girl who rides, and the monk who preaches. I think he was also impressed by the number of the male retinue and the amount of silver plate."

"Oh! I've done with it," said Madge, "I've been back for the last time. The whole life there stifles me. It is a huge relief to have done with it. I might have imagined that it had an influence over me, that I could not break with it. I am very sensitive to local impressions, to houses, to—" she hesitated. "Now that it is over, I feel a little tired, and I want to be amused. I want to see my friends."

"And your friends want you," said Laura with solemn emotion, and there followed another pause. Laura rose. "The fact is, Madge, I had better be straightforward, as I don't know how to be diplomatic. I have something to tell you, and I hardly know how to do it."

Madge started, but Laura saw very little surprise in the nervous tremor, only a good deal of anxiety.

"Cecilia?" cried Madge.

"Nothing whatever to do with poor Cecilia," said Laura in a voice charged with meaning. Madge looked relieved. "But what it has to do with is harder to explain. I must do the old old thing. I must tell you a story. I must sit here, as I don't wish to see your face. I feel unequal to my *rôle* of ambassador, as I have to treat with the princess herself."

Every word she spoke, in spite of the playful flattering tone, was excruciating to Madge's nerves. She was so intensely anxious as to what was coming that all her energies were forced into the one effort at physical self-control. She did not speak.

"I have a friend," began Laura, but a slight movement of Madge's shoulders made her add,—"if I may venture to call him so,—who is very honourable, very chivalrous. He has set his heart upon a great wish; and although other people can hardly believe that his wishes could not be gratified, he has many doubts himself. However, of those I need not speak. Briefly, Madge, this man has suffered very much because, although he has been flattered, he has not been loved. He married"—Madge sank back in the arm-chair—"he married somebody who loved him even as savages love and no deeper. It seemed to him an idyll in the wilderness. Nobody knew of this marriage in his own land. It was the love of a summer's day, brief as it was fiery. Then came disillusion, disloyalty, a low story. It was to have been another Lord of Burleigh and his lady; it was in fact merely a prairie episode, love, drink, madness—even I believe some attempt at assassination. He was very young at the time, very rash, but he was magnanimous. He made every arrangement for the unfortunate girl after her lover had deserted her. He was, according to the laws of the country, easily set free. Madge, a man who dares not trust himself to speak to you, who longs to make perpetual the brief sunshine of your presence at Bellasis, has a scruple. He wishes me to tell you of the existence of this poor half-mad girl in a convent in some obscure South American State."

Madge rose at these last words and stood facing Laura, but with no speculation any longer in her grey eyes, which were stretched to their fullest extent. Laura looked at her as freely as she would have looked at a somnambulist. There was no sort of risk that Madge should observe her expression.

"Dear child, do not say anything to me. Do not let me intrude further into this sacred privacy. I have most unwillingly brought my message. Now let the messenger be discarded," and she rose as she spoke.

Madge turned away as Laura finished speaking; she clutched at the chimneypiece as if to save herself from falling. There was a moment of complete silence. Madge seemed to have a difficulty in speaking; then, in a low voice, she said huskily:—

"But doesn't he—don't you know that I am a Catholic?"

"Oh, yes, but he wouldn't mind that in the least," said Laura cheerfully.

"But, then," said Madge, almost in a whisper, "don't you even know what Catholics call such a marriage?"

Laura flushed red with anger.

"Madge, this is absurd. Is this your answer to his sensitive chivalry?" she said coldly.

"But, but—" said Madge again.

"No, don't go on," said Laura with cold decision, "don't say things that you will regret. If you wish to take a line of that kind, if you wish to air views of that rarefied description, choose your audience, my dear. Remember my cousin, Mrs. Amherst, for one, who is good enough to be my friend, who married John Amherst, an innocent divorcee and a most upright man. No, no, go back to Skipton and say all that to them. We are not good enough for you in London."

There was temper in this, and temper well managed may look very much like surprise. Madge only took in part of what was said to her. She was half terrified and half stupefied at suddenly hearing transformed into substantial fact a dream which had seemed to her almost beyond possibility, and being brought close to a temptation which had appeared for weeks as distant as the dream had been improbable. Bellasis did love her. The ideal vision which had haunted her could be realised. And she was, in an instant, brought face to face with the cost which must be counted.

Laura was still standing, and she drew on her gloves. Her action roused Madge, and she put out her hand to detain her.

"Don't go."

Laura sat down and waited for what would be said next. The idea of suggesting a consultation with wide-minded priests had not left her mind, but she began to think, as she watched Madge, that it certainly would not do to allude to it just now.

"No, no," Madge whispered, clutching her hands together and speaking to herself; "no, no, I never could have meant that, I never saw it, indeed I never did. When I left the chapel, when I couldn't go to confession, surely, surely I never meant that. Don't Laura," and now she looked at her more directly; "no, don't speak. From your point of view I know what it would be. Position, life, glorious life, freedom from the past,—but I can't, no, indeed I can't. Oh," Madge sank down on the high cushioned fender, and seemed to shrink together into a very small figure indeed, "oh, Laura, if I didn't believe too much, if I hadn't been brought up by those nuns, if they weren't praying for me now, what a glorious life I could have." A sparkle shone in the dullness of her eyes. "Oh, isn't it hard?" she held out her hands towards the warmth, and turned herself away from Laura.

Laura, seeing that she was too unstrung to be suspicious, tried a bold shot.

"Then you had no notion of this mad episode in his youth? It is indeed a blow for you."

"Yes, I knew," said Madge faintly.

"You knew?" cried Laura in astonishment, "and yet with your views—" she sank speechless on the nearest chair.

"At least I knew there was enough to prevent a Catholic marrying him." Madge was too completely absorbed by her own emotions to notice Laura.

"Poor man!" cried Laura, "certainly there is a law of compensation that deals hardly by the great. How he has been misled!"

The word was well chosen to bring Madge to her senses.

"Misled!" she cried. "What do you mean?" and she drew her tiny figure to its full height.

"I think I never in my life heard of such a muddle!" said Laura; "what could have made you stay all those months at Bellasis?"

"Months?—I was never there for a month at a time."

"Don't you see how you have treated him?"

"No, I do not," cried Madge hysterically; "I knew I could not marry him and I knew that he knew it."

"How did you know?"

"Cecilia told me."

"Cecilia! Then Cecilia knows the whole story. They must be very intimate. My poor Madge, I beg your pardon." She paused. "I see it all now. I ought never to have come. He ought not to have put me in such a position. How difficult it is to understand men, to follow their moods! You must own that it looks on the face of it as if you had treated him very badly. But he will understand some day if he cannot understand now. Some day," her look and voice became dreamy, "Cecilia will no doubt tell him all about it, and they may respect you the more for scruples that seem to me and to the civilised world absurd."

The ambiguity of Laura's mysterious sentences, the kind of fog under which she apparently wished to retire, puzzled the now irritated Madge. She was the kind of woman whose emotions naturally effervesce in wrath, but she did not dare lose her hold upon herself just now. That she was being insulted she was certain, and that she must bear it for the moment was clear. After all, the game was in her own hands; after all, Bellasis had spoken what he could not retract. How easy it would be some day to put Laura in her proper place if, if,—and even in that moment of confusion, a castle in the air rose before her in the crudely concrete form of Lady Bellasis refusing a tenth, nay a twentieth invitation to dine at the Hurstmonceaux'. She pulled herself up at the puerile trick of imagination, and she shivered.

Laura was standing again. She had said her say and she wanted to go. She had fired her last shot, her allusion to Cecilia. Madge had made absolutely no answer. She was so angry that if other motives had not been too strong for her she would have quarrelled with Laura on the spot. But, as Laura knew well, that was impossible. She let Laura say her good-bye, and received her kiss coldly, but instantly reflecting on her folly pursued her on to the landing with a peace-offering of value to them both.

Laura had gone half-way down the stairs. Madge could just see her bonnet.

"Laura," she called out, "if you have nothing better to do on Thursday, this day week, do come in to luncheon. Miss Armitage, the author of *Lily-white*, who I hope is coming, will amuse you. The Duchess of A. wants to meet her."

A smiling countenance became visible through the banisters.

"Certainly, dear," answered Laura; "I do so want to meet Miss Armitage."

They parted, and Madge went back into the drawing-room alone. She walked up to the fireplace and looked into the fire for a moment. She caught sight of her face in the glass above it and was startled at its whiteness. "Well, that is settled," she said in a whisper. "I suppose she will tell Bellasis to-night. Now I must not stop to think. I'll write those notes and then dress for dinner." She sat down and wrote two notes hastily but not less neatly than usual. One was to Miss Armitage, the other to the Duchess of A. Then she heaved a deep sigh before she began a third. "One thing is clear," she said aloud, "whatever may be the end of this, there will come a time when I shan't endure Laura Hurstmonceaux."

The third note was to the said Laura.

DEAREST FRIEND (she wrote), forgive me if, in my pain and sorrow to-night, I failed in lovingness to you.

You will not utter a single syllable of our conversation to any living human being? not even to Lord Bellasis? I must take my own way of telling him the truth. I cannot bear he should think the sacrifice less than that of my whole life. Only leave me a little quiet, a little peace just now.

Ever yours, with much love,
MADGE.

CHAPTER II

HILDA IN LONDON

The Duchess of A. was among those who had stayed at Bellasis Castle in the autumn and had rather liked Madge; so she lunched with her on the meagre excuse of meeting Miss Armitage. It was a pleasant meal. Besides Mrs. Hurstmonceaux there were two friends of the duchess, a diplomatist who had published a book of really good poetry, and a distinguished Irish *littérateur* who wrote eloquent articles on contemporary foreign politics. They were the most proper circle that could be imagined; and they analysed from the highest standpoint two plays then being acted in Paris, and decided what points must be left out so as to fit one of them, an excellent story in itself, for the English stage.

"The teeth must be drawn of course, before the British public will look at it," agreed the diplomat.

"But then how will it bite?" came in the shy voice of Miss Armitage, whose remarks were very civilly treated throughout.

When they adjourned to the drawing-room, the duchess remembered that this insignificant looking little person had written *Lily-white*; so being really a very lady-like woman she talked to her about it with the greatest good humour, plainly showing that she had not read the book, and adding that she thought it quite a charming story. After she had done her duty in this way for a few minutes, the duchess left and her two friends followed in her wake. Miss Armitage shyly removed herself also, wondering if what had passed would be of any use in her next story, slight as it had all been.

Madge and Mrs. Hurstmonceaux were in high good humour.

"My dear Madge, I had no idea what a remarkable woman the duchess was before. If we had more women like that in London!

I don't mean so much her beauty or her wits alone, it is the something in her personality, the fine individuality in everything she says and does."

"Yes," answered Madge eagerly, "I really feel that she has been to me a liberal education, as some one once said of somebody else."

Then they passed to Miss Armitage. The same good humour and brightness underlay their talk: and when Mr. Fieldes called about half an hour afterwards, he met with a gracious welcome.

Now when Fieldes had called a few days earlier, on his return from Skipton, he had been very differently received, and it had been plainly conveyed to him that two other friends who were present had made very good company before he came in. Some men would at least have let Madge alone for a while after that; but from a certain incapacity for dealing with human beings Fieldes never could leave things alone. The result of this kind of complaisance was that he got a good deal bullied by his friends. Madge was not a person of very great consequence, but she had a good many friends that were, and she was of quite sufficient importance among them to fulfil Fieldes' notion of what his lady friends should be. For some days he had been worrying his head as to what he could do to please Madge, and he had now brought with him a little book which she had once expressed a wish to read. Fieldes was therefore much relieved at his reception, the cordiality of which may have been partly due to the fact that she had heard the Duchess of A. say that the duke was immensely pleased by an article on the bill for "making it easier for people to get rid of their property, you know," in the current number of the *Bi-monthly*. It was written by a Mr. Mark Fieldes who must be wonderfully clever.

So genial was the atmosphere that Fieldes saw that his little book would be a superfluous offering, and decided to suppress it.

Presently Mrs. Hurstmonceaux, who had gone to the window to judge of the weather, exclaimed:—

"Who is your visitor, Madge? A lady's trunks and a maid paying the cabman."

"Oh, it is Hilda, I had quite forgotten all about her!"

Just in time to hear these words Hilda appeared in her gipsy red travelling cloak and her high black feather hat. A journey is seldom beautifying, and the first effect was not good. Fieldes felt disconcerted. He had told Mrs. Hurstmonceaux that Hilda though rather countrified was distinguished looking. But in these surroundings, with Madge and Laura in exquisite clothing, she looked dusty and untidy. And it was annoying too that his friend should see her receive so slight a welcome from her hostess. But Mrs. Hurstmonceaux, who was the leading spirit at the moment, created a diversion. She beamed upon Hilda and after a dramatic aside to Madge, "What glorious eyes!" asked to be introduced.

"I have so often heard of you from Madge," she said immediately, with more readiness than strict regard to facts.

"May I take my things upstairs, Madge?" Hilda inquired after a few moments, and Madge rang and sent her to her room. When she came down again she found that Mrs. Hurstmonceaux had gone, but that two other visitors had come in. Madge had hardly given Hilda credit for the *savoir faire* which had made her carry her train-begrimed clothes into retirement so quickly; and really the black net frock which she had saved from last summer had not at all a bad effect. As she came forward, a young man rose from behind a screen near the fireplace and came to meet her. It was Marmaduke. He said, "How d'ye do, Hilda?" in an almost solemn voice, and having shaken hands with her went back to his seat.

Hilda had greeted him with a quick nervous movement; and she was not sorry to sit down near Mr. Fieldes, who beamed upon her and seemed unobservant of any embarrassment on her part. Her attention was soon attracted to a lady who stood near Marmaduke with her back towards the rest of the company. This was a girl in a rough tweed cloak, and a very short frieze skirt of the kind that is sold for "charitable purposes" in the big shops. One foot she had extended on to the kerb of the fireplace, in an elaborate high-heeled shoe which displayed a good deal of ankle in an open-worked stocking splashed with mud. Her hat was a coquettish toque very neatly veiled. Her right hand, on which shone some splendid rings, was holding on to the chimneypiece. The effect produced by this medley was like the disguise of a countess preparing to elope in an extravaganza.

"Are you ready for tea, Cecilia?" Madge inquired; and in a voice even softer than her own, Cecilia Rupert answered.

"Directly I have dried this foot, my dear," and she held that delicate object nearer to the fire.

"Where did you get into such a puddle?"

"In Regent Circus," she answered. "I had missed so many 'busses all the afternoon at different corners that I grew desperate, and I made a great jump at one which landed me in a puddle. But a charming young painter pulled me up. I hope he has not painted me, has he?" and she turned herself round appealing to Marmaduke to look.

"I don't detect any paint anywhere," he answered laughing.

Cecilia continued, her tone being that of languid recitative.

"He told me that he and his father are employed by the Board of Works, but he don't think much of them it seems. I told him my father was dead, and he asked me if he had been in the shoemaking line while he was alive; but he was rather shy of me, though I let him know that we had been in the cattle-breeding business."

"You astonish Marmaduke," said Madge, "you know he has been some years in India,"

"In India?" said Cecilia, turning her large light eyes on him in a caressing manner, which might have been flattering to an oppressive degree, only that just as it seemed to become personal an absent look came into her orbs as if she were puzzling to make out what it was she was looking at. "In India?" and she seemed to remember that it was a man's head that was before her. "Ah, I wonder I never met you; but we may have been there at different times, and there is a good deal of space in India."

"But I want to know where you went this afternoon?" interrupted Madge.

"I went to the city," said the young lady, resuming her recitation. "I went to see if I could get a sealskin coat cheap there. I got one," she concluded sadly, "for seventy pounds. It was a bet that seventy pounds. Now it is quite dry, isn't it?" and she kicked her shoe off in the direction of Marmaduke who carefully felt the sole and pronounced it to be quite dry.

"Thank you," answered Cecilia, and without holding on to anything or stooping she stood on one foot and pulled the shoe on to the other with her hand.

"It takes a great deal of practice to do that with grace," she said to nobody in particular. "*Now* I want tea, Madge, my beloved," and she sank into a chair near the tea-table.

"A bet! What about?"

"It was a game of leap-frog. They thought I couldn't play, but I could you know—there was Sydney Lightfoot and Lord Rankin and Lord Bellasis. The bet was with Bellasis."

A moment was spent in sipping her tea. "Mark!" was her next observation. "Mark, I've been reading your article in the *Bi-monthly*. Everybody is talking of it. It is exactly what I have always thought on the subject, only I've never found time to write it, and I shouldn't know how to spell the words you use."

"I wish you would help me now," observed Fieldes, "in an article I am just going to begin on 'Signs of the Revolution.' I am going to mention the new craze for mixing with the lower classes. Your going in busses for instance. Do you think the people will put up with you any better because you jostle among them? The only chance we have is to be idealised or feared from a distance."

"Thank you," said Cecilia, bowing with mock politeness. "I will try to remember that I ought only to be seen from a distance."

"'On nearer view a vision yet a woman too,'" quoted Fieldes. "But mind my words," he continued in a mock Cassandra tone; "if you let these people see you saving pennies for your own ends you are done for. I don't know which will be more fatal to the present *régime,* its frank avowal of its fierce wish to save money, or its determination to spend hundreds on jackets!"

"I think your remark is hardly logical," said Madge. "Fatal to be seen saving pennies and fatal to spend hundreds on jackets!"

"It is because you save the pennies to buy the jackets," said Cecilia in a cross voice, "or at least I do, it appears. Mr. Fieldes takes life so very literally, but his remarks are, I will say for him, generally more crude than illogical. Mr. Marmaduke, for I think that is what they call you, will you ring the bell? For the sake of the present *régime*, though I don't think it deserves much, I will go home in a hansom."

Cecilia was standing about while she waited for the cab when Madge spoke next.

"By the way, Cecilia, what are you doing to-morrow?"

"I?" said Cecilia; "I hardly know—oh, yes, I intend to hurry the country on to socialism by going with a lot of girls to the pit at the Haymarket. We shall be quite a'bus load from Grosvenor Place," she pirouetted on her toes as she spoke and whistled the "Marseillaise." "By the way, Madge, could you extend to me the light of your chaperonage at the Doncaster's to-night? I never go anywhere without one or two chaperons," she concluded. After the most delicate kiss bestowed on Madge's forehead she went on, escorted to the door by Marmaduke.

"I think I am getting just a little tired of Cecilia," observed Madge, as soon as she had vanished.

"She is very fatiguing," said Fieldes with feeling. "You should have seen her at Duntrevor when the duchess told us that Bellasis was going to be married. She acted the wildest spirits; but she looked hideously sad at moments, till Tom Duffin purposely sang a verse of 'Punchinello,' to tease her,—'he never danced or sang so madly as that night, the people said.'"

"What did she do?" inquired Madge.

"She gave him a box on the ear and told him not to sing out of tune. She was in a rage. We were all laughing." Evidently Fieldes gloated over this little incident.

"What a horrid shame to treat a girl like that!" cried Hilda indignantly.

"Oh!" said Madge, "you don't know her; she is quite up to taking care of herself."

"And no one," said Fieldes almost tenderly, "no one would treat a nice quiet girl like that; but these young women must give and take."

"I quite agree with Hilda," exclaimed Marmaduke, who had returned and had been listening to what passed, and who would have contradicted Fieldes on any topic. "It is a shame to treat a girl like that. She has her feelings though she may be a little wild!"

This eager defence was hardly pleasing to Hilda.

"You see, Miss Riversdale," struck in Fieldes, "the prim good girl is quite out of fashion. Motley's all the wear; you must learn to do likewise."

"You couldn't if you tried," said Marmaduke.

"You think I am not clever enough," Hilda said, looking at him rather crossly.

"Not in that kind of cleverness," he rejoined.

Madge turned to Fieldes.

"Tell us," she said, "of something rational to do. I am not up to Hilda's heights of intellect. What are you doing just now?"

"I am frivolling chiefly. By the way, shall we meet at Lady Doncaster's to-night?"

"I am dining there," said Madge, with a touch of evident satisfaction.

"So am I," said Fieldes nonchalantly.

Madge's manner warmed to him at once. To dine at Lady Doncaster's was an event to herself.

Hilda had at once turned to Marmaduke while Madge spoke to Fieldes.

"I don't see," she said, "that it wants so much cleverness to be like that Cecilia—by the way, what is her surname?"

"Miss Rupert, Lord Rupert's sister."

"But I do think it wants a great deal of prettiness and gracefulness. I think she is charming to watch."

"For heaven's sake don't take her for a model!"

"No," answered Hilda still crossly. Some sudden whim made her anxious to extract a compliment from Marmaduke. "I haven't the grace, the beauty, the wherewithal, I know."

"Do you mean to be contradicted?" said Marmaduke, looking at her rather eagerly.

"No, I don't," said Hilda sharply.

"If it were Miss Rupert talking of you now, I could manage it."

"Of course," interrupted Hilda.

"But I can't pay compliments," a change in his tone struck her and she kept her eyes fixed on the carpet. "I can't pay compliments where I really care."

Hilda knew that he was looking at her, and after a moment's hesitation began to wish that she could see what he was looking like; but it was a difficult thing to manage. A furtive attempt at glancing upwards through her long eyelashes, after the manner of a naughty child, was beginning, when the sharp quick voice of Mr. Fieldes made her start.

"Should you care to see the Positivist Chapel, Miss Riversdale?"

It was annoying, but it was also an escape from embarrassment.

"Of all things!" she cried. "What is it like?"

"That is just what *I* want to know," said Fieldes. "I want to see the practical *cultus* of Humanity. It is in the city, so that it is within reach of the poor in the east end."

What had become of Marmaduke? He was gone and Madge with him.

"You can't think how to-day changes the atmosphere of London for me," said Fieldes, seizing the moment for a little sentiment.

Hilda looked straight at him without the least embarrassment.

"It is chilly to-night," she said.

"Very," answered Fieldes rather sarcastically. "Ah, Mrs. Riversdale," as Madge reappeared, "I've spent an unconscionable time here. Good-night, or rather *au revoir*." He too was gone and neither he nor Marmaduke had said good-bye to Hilda. She was young enough to be afraid that they were hopelessly offended, and she didn't want to offend Mr. Fieldes.

Madge, directly they were alone, went on with her own thoughts, which turned on Cecilia.

"How do you like Cecilia?" she inquired.

"Very much," said Hilda eagerly; "and there is something so pathetic about her eyes."

"I don't quite see the pathos," said Madge; "of course she looks absurdly old for her age, but that is the way she rackets. It would want the strength of two men to lead her life. There is nothing she doesn't try to do. But it doesn't answer, you know, to play the fool like that. A man like Lord Bellasis will amuse himself with a girl like Cecilia just to pass the time, but he doesn't mean anything by it."

"But he can't be a very nice man to do that, can he?" asked Hilda.

"Yes, he can," answered Madge sharply; "he is one of the most perfect gentlemen I know. And I don't blame her. Any girl would be thankful to get him. Seventy thousand a year, Bellasis Castle, an angelic yacht, and a sublime shooting box, besides the title—older than the deluge, and hardly a relation living nearer than a cousin! I can't say I blame Cecilia, except for not seeing how little he cares for her. Just like him to give her seventy pounds for making a fool of herself."

Yet that seventy pounds had annoyed Madge a good deal.

"Well, I can't think a nice man would play with a girl."

"Don't be absurd, Hilda. Didn't you see that Marmaduke was chaffing her about the paint, though he hadn't even been introduced; and she meant him to do it too."

"I say, Madge," said Hilda with an effort, "is it true that Marmaduke was in love with you—of course before you married, I mean?"

Madge had never heard of such an idea before, but she was perfectly ready to receive it. Of course it was true, and that was why he was so absurdly careful to avoid flirtation now.

"Well, my dear, and if he were?" Madge's smile was a satisfied one; but it had something provoking in it too, and Hilda blushed scarlet to her own great annoyance.

Hilda had a little dinner by herself that evening, but she did not find it dull. Was not there enough to think about on this arrival in London to have filled up a whole week of lonely evenings? Oh that blessed facility of excitement, when one is eighteen, and the drama seems to have been arranged for one's own *rôle* in what one imagines to be a comedy! How could she have hoped for this delightful visit? Did it not seem when Madge spoke of it at Skipton to be the most impossible of events? In fact it had been a combination of circumstances that had overcome Mrs. Arthur Riversdale's doubts as to Madge's fitness as a chaperon. First, the openly stated reason had been the scarlet fever which had attacked the young housemaid, and made it dangerous for Hilda to go home from Skipton. Secondly, and chiefly, there was the unmentioned attraction of Marmaduke's presence in London. That Marmaduke was most anxious that Hilda should accept Madge's invitation, and that he evidently had other motives than the alleged one of Madge's good, had been conveyed to Mrs. Arthur Riversdale by the squire. The squire was anxious for the visit, not only from a benevolent wish that Hilda and Marmaduke should meet again, but because he wished to keep in touch with Madge, and Hilda's presence would be additional security that Marmaduke would know what she was doing, and would afford a convenient pretext for visits to Madge from other members of the family. He had no scruple, therefore, in persuading his sister-in-law to let Hilda pay this visit, and the unspoken, unacknowledged worldliness that the best of women may feel for their daughters, however completely they have lost it for themselves, made Mrs. Arthur more ready to acknowledge the squire's wisdom and to view Madge as charitably as possible.

After dinner Hilda went upstairs and settled herself in a corner of Madge's big sofa with a *Nineteenth Century*, and prepared herself for a literary evening and the forbidden joys of black coffee. But though she was wide awake, in an excited over-tired state, the clearness of brain was delusive. She shut up her book and tried to return to the day-dreams of London life which had filled her mind during dinner, dreams in which shadowy figures of young statesmen, and geniuses of all kinds and sorts, made vague speeches which she answered herself with singular brilliancy.

But the shadowy figures would not come again; only two substantial realities, to whom she had not spoken either wisely or well that very afternoon, Mr. Mark Fieldes and Marmaduke.

"People never repeat themselves," sighed Hilda; not a bad sentence that, which was soothing. Marmaduke wasn't quite the same as at Skipton, nor was Mr. Fieldes, nor, most annoying of all, did she feel quite the same herself. The fact was that she had experienced an uncomfortable moment when she had seen Marmaduke unexpectedly that day, yet she had been wondering during her journey if she should see him. "I don't care and I won't care what he is doing, or how handsome he looks, or what he cares about," said Hilda, and she gave the cushion at the bottom of the sofa a little vicious kick. "And I'm not at all sure he ought to come here as he once cared for Madge; it is too soon after George's death It is like a bat—I mean a moth—and a candle. And I don't like his manners with Cecilia, and after all I'm not his cousin; and what I do is no business of his; and he oughtn't to look at me—I'm not a king—and if there is a thing I hate it is a virtuous flirt!"

Hilda was tired and she was almost crying, and that would be too absurd.

"I wonder if Mr. Mark Fieldes has ever been in love before? I doubt it. I wonder if I hurt him to-day. I don't want to hurt him—I suspect I am in love with him; the fact is I've got rather a cold nature or I should feel more about it. I want to have him as a friend, and wouldn't it be grand to convert him! And any how I won't be a nasty flirt. I hope I shall have a great deal of talk with Mr. Mark Fieldes."

But then came Brown the maid (venturing into the drawing-room with a deferential softness of tread) who recommended bed; and Hilda was just old enough not to resent the suggestion, so to bed she went.

CHAPTER III

A DINNER-PARTY

Saturday.

Dear Mother,

I was sorry to send you only that hurried line yesterday. To-night I shall have plenty of time, for Madge has gone out to dinner and I have the house to myself.

Perhaps I am inclined to feel dull to-night because last night was so exciting, which proves that I am eminently spoilable. Last night Madge had some people to dinner. There were five visitors, and Marmaduke, who did host. The visitors were Miss Cecilia Rupert, Mr. Fieldes and a Mr. and Mrs. Salvolatile. She is a Jewess and they roll in wealth; she is quite strangely ugly. Madge says he loathes her, but he married her because he was hard up. He is very handsome and she worships him—from a distance, Madge says. He was the son of a great tailor, but he is very smart indeed. Then besides Cecilia Rupert and Marmaduke, there was a Lord James something whom they all called "Tim," and who lives by selling cigars and getting people to insure their dogs. But he told Cecilia that he had serious thoughts of becoming a dressmaker. I don't think the talk at dinner would amuse you much. It was all about people they knew. Mr. Fieldes tried to bring me into it sometimes, and Cecilia tried to amuse Marmaduke, but as soon as the others mentioned some one they knew, these two chimed in at once. Mrs. Salvolatile hardly spoke, but listened intently to her husband, and seemed to be making eyes at him—such little, twinkling eyes, not at all my idea of a Jewess!

The way she went on was so funny, and his kind of snubbing glances, that it seemed almost as though they did it for show! In the middle of dinner Mr. Salvolatile began to abuse the Jews. Lord Tim shut him up and told very funny stories of his own shooting in Africa. There is something very taking and jolly about Lord Tim, although one or two of his stories made me a little shy. After dinner Mrs. Salvolatile began to talk to Madge about shopping. Cecilia joined in and they told each other about the places where you can get lace and old silver and things cheap, and furniture. Mrs. Salvolatile's fat voice got quite excited as she explained an extraordinary bargain she had made of some old china with a poor woman in a village. Yet she seems very charitable, too, and she is working a scheme by which the shop girls can get half an hour in the country in the middle of the day.

Suddenly while they were talking Miss Rupert jumped up and went into the next room to look at some plants. Then she looked back and beckoned to me.

'They are so dull,' she said, yawning behind a splendid feather fan, 'come along and talk to me.'

So far Hilda had let her pen run on easily enough. Now she paused and looked at the paper in front of her. "I don't quite know," she said to herself. What she did not quite know was whether she really felt disposed to give an account to her mother of the talk which followed. It was new to her to have had a talk which did not bear writing down. She flushed a little and fidgeted on her chair. She did not feel sure now that she had quite understood the drift of Cecilia's chatter the night before. Certainly when it began her remarks seemed to have no method in their madness. Hilda went over that talk now, sentence by sentence, and she became more and more uncomfortable as she did so. She thought that Cecilia had looked very handsome, and that her movements were graceful, though abrupt. She had first settled a great cushion behind her as she sat down on the sofa. The regularity of her features was almost classical, and her dress, though, in Hilda's eyes, rather queer, was gorgeous. She wore, even in the evening, short skirts which showed her lovely feet and ankles.

"Aren't my stockings pretty?" she said suddenly. "Lord Tim got them for me in Paris, but they won't interest you, will they?" and she looked at Hilda rather blankly. "So you've come to stay with Madge," she went on abruptly. Then she murmured to herself, "Certainly they are pretty stockings."

"Yes," Hilda said, "there is scarlet fever at home."

"Why, who has got it? there is only your mother, isn't there?"

"Yes, but it is the housemaid."

"Oh, and do you like the housemaid?"

"I hardly know," Hilda said, laughing.

"Silly question, wasn't it? Might as well ask if you like the dustpan. I'll try again. You like your mother, I know, so I won't ask that—well, do you like Madge?"

"Oh, yes, so very much. Isn't she charming?"

"Oh, quite too divinely nice; only too good, you know, too particular. Don't you think so?"

Hilda tried not to look surprised, but she failed. Cecilia looked at her curiously.

"It is a pity to be scrupulous," she went on, "but perhaps you are worse still. Alps beyond Alps of piety and all that. But all you people on the summits of virtue, all your family adore Madge, don't they? Cousin Marmaduke, for instance, doesn't he?"

Hilda blushed crimson and was furious with herself for blushing; but Cecilia's voice seemed to her so odd.

"Oh, not now," she said nervously.

"Not now?" repeated Cecilia, "why, have they quarrelled?"

"Oh no, only that was so long ago, before she married."

"Of course," said Cecilia very gravely, "and Cousin Marmaduke is a very good boy," she went on, "isn't he?" and she kept looking at Hilda in a furtive sidelong way that concealed the twinkle of humour in her eyes.

"Oh, yes, and he is so good-natured and helpful to everybody."

"So helpful to Madge too," observed Cecilia.

"Yes," Hilda said; "he stays in London on purpose."

No sooner was this spoken than she felt conscious it was not a wise thing to say.

"Perhaps he has come up for somebody else," said Cecilia; "he wasn't so very sorry to see you, was he?"

"Oh, no," she answered hotly, "it isn't for me!"

"Only for Madge," said Cecilia in an absent voice. She was arranging the lace in the front of her gown as she spoke, and not looking at her companion.

"Oh, no," Hilda cried in a voice full of trouble; "why do you say it like that? it is not in that sort of way, you know."

"Of course not in that sort of way—my dear child, don't look so scared," Cecilia went into a fit of laughter. "Of course it isn't *that sort of way!* Oh dear!" and she sighed. "There is 'no mirth in idiot laughter only,' and I have heard you laugh to-night. I'd give anything to laugh like you. Madge used to laugh like that, and I'd laugh now if I were she; but for me to laugh—well it leaves a bad taste in my mouth. Ah," she said suddenly, "the joy of living, do you know what it means? It means"—and she sprang up and stood in front of the astonished Hilda—"it means bathing for five minutes and awful cramp afterwards. It means a delicious ice and sour cream in your coffee. It is just nearing its best when it always fails. Last summer I paddled in the sea, in the sunset under the downs. My feet looked white in the red water, but the best waves, those that were biggest, that had most of the sunset in them, that came and kissed my ankles and seemed to swathe me in light, took the sand away from under my feet. Do you know the feeling? All joy and glory for the moment; and then slipping, sliding away—that's life. You don't know yet, you are too young and too good. You've never hugged your own limbs with joy because they are beautiful and alive, and thought at the same moment how foul they will, must, become some day."

Cecilia was looking at Hilda, staring at her with eyes that seemed frightened.

"Do you ever think of diseases," she said, "and lungs that are gone and limbs that must be cut off? Do you ever think of those things in the night?" her voice sank to a whisper, "they are real, quite real, you know. They are all round about us. We have all got something big, bad and dreadful to suffer; and they *can't shoot you, you know*, think of that. They shoot even the dogs to put them out of their pain. Ah! that is the last and worst, that is the hideous, hideous thing—the animal in us won't let us kill ourselves, and religious people hang—yes, they *hang* the men who would save us. Have you ever felt pain?" she went on; "I suppose not. But I oughtn't to talk to you like this, it is selfish."

She stopped. She had been speaking in a hurried low voice, and she appeared haggard to the child before her. "But then you see on your Alps they give you anodynes, don't they?" and her eyes became sarcastic. "Mark and I have written splendid sermons on the vanity of all things. Mine was headed 'Life, a Hospital for Incurables,' and Mark's, 'The World, the Condemned Prisoner's Cell.'"

She laughed. "You can't think how striking they were. They beat Massillon hollow because there were no anodynes. Real unvarnished facts, nothing else. No attempt to cocker you up with ideas of heaven and a future life, and—but I won't name the great anodyne because I don't want to shock you, I've startled you enough already. But you rather like it, your big eyes are stretched quite wide and shiny. I can tell you lots of things about yourself; but first tell me before I forget, why didn't Lord Bellasis come to-night?"

Madge had told Hilda not to say to Cecilia that Lord Bellasis had refused to dine.

"Why should he come?" she said lamely.

"Why? Because he was asked. You really are too clever to say anything so stupid. You see I wasn't asked till he refused, that's flat. But I thought you might know what excuse he gave."

She paused, but Hilda didn't speak.

"Now, for yourself," she said, "you amuse me and you touch me too. Words fail to express how little you understand yourself or anybody else. And yet you are very clever. Mark sees that. But your education has been too intellectual by far. If you just packed up and went home now, you might be saved some suffering and trouble; but you won't. You are of the kind that gets into wrong places, and has to learn things for itself. And after all anything is better than stagnating. Then for you there are the anodynes to fall back upon. Only, you know, remember my text, when the waves go back they will take away the sand you stand on, and you will have nothing except the anodynes. There are some mixed metaphors for you. Come here, Mark, how long you have been, I've had to preach to pass the time, our favourite discourse of course, *Vanitas Vanitatum*. I always feel it strongly after a good dinner. Besides my aunt was worse to-night, suffering horridly. Let us play baccarat. Where's Madge?" And then lowering her voice she went on: "Madge is not in very good spirits, is she?"

So ended the conversation which Hilda found impossible to retail for the maternal benefit. She said in her letter that she had had some odd talk with Cecilia which was too long to be repeated, but that she would now tell her mother all about the event of the evening. This she thought would be an easy subject, and she began glibly to describe how, while the rest of the party were playing baccarat, with the exception of Mrs. Salvolatile who had fallen asleep, and she and Marmaduke were talking, there had come a sudden interruption of an exciting kind.

> Lord Tim talked to me a little while, and I thought he was very funny in his account of the old man from whom he got his cigars in Constantinople. Soon after that came the baccarat tables, and there was some discussion as to how they should play. Madge said at once that I didn't know how to play. Lord Tim offered to teach me, but Madge said I was not to play, which was a comfort to me.
> Mr. Salvolatile, Lord Tim, Madge and Cecilia and Mr. Fieldes played, and Mrs. Salvolatile went to sleep. Marmaduke came and sat by me. Then came the event of the evening.

But here again Hilda paused in her letter. She leaned back in her chair, thought over what she called the event of the evening, and then slowly put her pen through the last line. She passed that little incident in mental review. "How did it happen?" she thought, "and how stupid of Madge to have the pampas grass so near the lights. But I suppose it wouldn't have happened if the Jew woman hadn't gone to sleep, and bent over near the piano; and that pulled the piano draperies which upset the pampas grass on to the candles on the cabinet. What an escape Madge had! her gown was blazing and how white her face was—if it hadn't been for Marmaduke—and he was the farthest off after all. . . ."

She sat looking at the spot. How Marmaduke had put out Madge's burning train nobody had quite understood; and then all the men had pulled down the pampas grass and stamped it out on the carpet, Lord Tim evidently enjoying himself. Marmaduke had looked round once and had said, "Get away, Hilda," very roughly, though she was a long way off. There was a second's silence of relief. It had been "a biggish flare up" as Lord Tim said, breaking the silence. Marmaduke was looking at Madge anxiously. She was looking at her frock, Hilda was looking at his hands, when they were all startled by a noise at the door. It opened and disclosed a small patent fire-pump, with the red perspiring face of Mark Fieldes behind it. They all laughed almost hysterically.

"Is it out?" said Fieldes in a crushed voice.

"How on earth did you get it upstairs?" cried Madge. "That thing is such a weight."

"Oh, no, it was quite easy," said Fieldes rather grandly; but an idea suddenly occurred to him. The pump had been comparatively light because it was empty!

Hilda flushed with annoyance as she recalled the scene although she had laughed at the time. If only she could be sure that Mark Fieldes had not run away while the pampas grass was burning. Perhaps really he had done the wisest thing in going for the fire-pump, but why hadn't he found out that there was no water in it? How everybody had laughed. What funny things Lord Tim had said. But Marmaduke had been very quiet and Hilda had caught him looking at her curiously. Was he trying to see whether she minded the rather rough ridicule that was being administered to Fieldes? No, the story was not worth telling her mother at any length, and so the event of the evening was thus described:—

> The pampas grass somehow got knocked over on to the candles, and there was such a blaze. Nobody was much hurt and the men stamped it out, which looked horribly dangerous but was all right.

Hilda had added "much" after writing "hurt"; and now she looked at it again. It wouldn't do, "nobody much hurt" showed that somebody had been hurt; but she did not want to write an account of Marmaduke's hurting his hands. It had been while she and Madge were drinking seltzer water on the landing just after the visitors had left, and looking at Madge's gown which was badly burnt, that Lord Tim had suddenly reappeared. He had come to ask Madge which was her nearest chemist.

"I want to take Marmaduke there at once," he said, "his hands are rather badly burnt, at least the right one is,—enough to make him swear a bit when we got out, and I know exactly the thing to stop the pain."

Madge had made some fuss about this when they were alone again.

Hilda thought that Madge was rather pleased that Marmaduke had got his hands burnt in her service. "The moth got singed this time," and Hilda tossed her little head, and went to her room angry with everybody. She was angry now, while she was writing to her mother. She was not going to make a story about Marmaduke,—that was just what her mother would like: and she was not disposed to make a fool of Mark Fieldes. She put down her pen and looked at her hands. "It must hurt to burn one's hands," she reflected for about the tenth time that day. Then she took her pen again and hurriedly finished the letter, just alluding to Marmaduke scorching his hands.

After all this care, however, she looked through her letter again, and came to the conclusion that it was hardly one that she would care to send home. She re-read the passages concerning the dinner-party. And this time she tore it into little bits, and threw it into the scrap-basket.

Then she felt cross at having done so.

She took up an essay by Mark Fieldes which she knew well already, and this proved soothing. The noble clearness of style, the insight into character, the wisdom of the heart that breathed through her favourite passages seemed to give her spiritual strength. She turned over the pages, ensconcing herself more deeply in her cushions, and taking comfort as she read. The page was headed "The Ethics of Sacrifice."

"Marmaduke couldn't understand it," thought Hilda with a sigh of satisfaction. There was no tone of assertion of the writer's superiority in it; yet in certain passages he seemed almost oppressed by his own power of vision. To Hilda, although she possessed no very striking talent herself, intellect had an extraordinary attraction. Her mother had brought the girl up to enthusiasm for intellect, and there was much of her grandfather's character in her. Old men, old priests, who were dull fogies to Mary herself, if they were even mildly intelligent, had never bored Hilda. Even Brown, her mother's maid, who had, unfortunately for all concerned, a natural love of intellectual rather than practical matters, and who could quote Newman, but who could not remember that the braids at the bottom of skirts are in constant need of renewal, was a favourite of Hilda's. Her mother had encouraged her to criticise stupid people. Mr. Fieldes was the first man of really superior intellect she had met, and a glow of sympathetic interest came to her with his lightest words. In a certain degree they were akin, and they met among people of a different kind. He conveyed to her at times a strong sense of his intuitive insight, of thought instinct with wisdom, yet fully conscious of its own limitations. There was nothing pompous or pretentious about his mind. While talking with him, Hilda felt that there was a great universe about them, that there was a "before and after," and that for him the story of mankind was a connected, although mysterious whole. But again, in some ways his qualities made her recognise his defects more clearly. She wanted him to be great, and instinctively she knew that he was not great. Her first impulse was to be hard on Mark Fieldes; but her second was to interpret him as favourably as possible. He might have been something very dear to her, so anxious was she concerning him. When the absence of manliness, or the presence of pettiness in him, oppressed her, she was repelled; but she tried to explain either or both away. But why not leave him alone? She could hardly have told why not, except that it would have been the loss of a great interest, of a first companionship with something which singularly stimulated her intellect.

No doubt it was partly her power over him that she did not wish to lose; his flattery that gave her that estimate of herself which she so much desired. Also, strange as it may seem, though she had no worldly ideas respecting Marmaduke's wealth and position, and was angered by the notion that everybody must think she cared for these things, she had worldly ideas about Mark Fieldes. He represented to her the realm of intellect, of social excitement of a refined kind, of the life she most wished to lead. What more dull than life at another Skipton? what more amusing than a small house in London, with hardly any money perhaps, but with the best society? And he was good-hearted, thoroughly good-hearted, and capable of tender sympathies; although these were provokingly indiscriminate.

And here at least she was right. He was full of sympathy for Mary's spiritual struggles, for the tailor whose bill he didn't pay, and who he thought was treated disgracefully by really rich men; for his invalid sister, to whom he wrote almost daily, for Hilda's vanity, for Mrs. Hurstmonceaux's ambition—but naturally he sympathised most of all with Mr. Mark Fieldes.

If Hilda could have known what manner of supper party he had hurried off to the night before, the essay on the "Ethics of Sacrifice" might not have proved so soothing.

CHAPTER IV

AMATEUR DIPLOMACY

The room in which Cecilia was giving Mark Fieldes his tea on Saturday—the day after Madge's dinner-party—was a tiny excrescence jutting out at the back of a house in Charles Street, Berkeley Square. The room had been arranged as a sitting-room for Cecilia; and her friends were often taken to it, so as to avoid her aunt, the elder Miss Rupert, in the drawing-room.

"What have you done to this room since I was here last?" inquired Mark, who was stretched at full length on a kind of divan opposite the fireplace.

Cecilia was sitting in a swing, which was fastened to the ceiling—a special device of her own. She had put down her coffee cup on a stool, and let herself sway backwards and forwards, the soft material of her white tea-gown making a perceptible noise as it swept the matting on the floor. The room was so small, that the fumes of the cigarettes made a faintly clouded atmosphere, slightly laden with opium.

"Oh, I have brought more of my things here, and my writing-table," answered Cecilia, as she pointed with her cigarette to a huge old *marqueterie* escritoire, which blocked up the window and pushed itself against the fireplace. "I am more out of the way here, and I can't see the doctors go up and down. I used to see them, and then I had to ask them things; and it was all horrible. Besides, the nurses used to come in fidgeting me about nothing."

Cecilia's voice was angry, and she kicked the ground with the heel of her shoe and sent herself so far forward that she knocked over a frame which stood on a low table beside Mark's couch. Mark rose and picked it up. It was a large photograph of Madge.

"To dearest Cecilia from Madge," was scrawled half across it. He put it back carefully. Cecilia looked at it with a smile.

"The comfort is that it is not in the least like her," she said.

"No, it is not quite like her," said Mark. "The items, nose, eyes and chin, etc., seem correct enough; but it has missed the special effect. Mrs. Riversdale's charm has something French in it; one can't imagine her ever being anything but perfectly dressed. She is more *élégante* than artistic."

"That was a curious little scene last night when the pampas grass was burning," said Cecilia.

Fieldes flushed and fidgeted a little. "Lemarchant was zealous," he said in a voice full of meaning.

"Yes," answered Cecilia, "and I was amused, because I had just made the girl Hilda say the funniest things. She is delicious. I had asked her if the handsome cousin were not devoted to Madge, and she turned red and said, 'Oh, not like that,' in quite a shocked little voice."

"But why not now when she is a widow?" asked Mark.

"I suppose because the husband has only been dead two years," said Cecilia with a laugh, "or because Miss Hilda somehow does not like the idea."

Mark kept silence. Cecilia lighted another cigarette at the little silver lamp on a Cairo stool beside her.

"He will have a large property, won't he?"

"Yes," answered Mark in a dull voice.

Cecilia settled herself back in her swing and looked up at the ceiling.

"What a wonderfully good-looking man he is!"

"Do you think so?" asked Mark quickly.

"Yes." A pause, and then: "Is there any reason why he shouldn't marry Madge?" Her colour rose as she spoke, and excitement was betrayed in her voice. An idea occurred to Mark.

"How stupid I have been," he thought; then he said aloud: "Not so far as I know. He was in love with her before she married his cousin."

"Well, then, why shouldn't they take it up again now? There is no deceased cousin's widow bill," interjected Cecilia.

"None. But I don't think Mrs. George Riversdale would quite see it. She tried marriage with the eldest son of one great Catholic family. I don't think she will want to be daughter-in-law to another Skipton. Besides," Mark turned and looked straight at his hostess, "besides, I think she will look higher, don't you?"

Cecilia's flush deepened. She was no diplomatist. She turned from him, and with shaking hand knocked the ash off her cigarette. "Though I can't help liking him, he is a cad," she muttered to herself.

"There are so few marriages for Roman Catholics," she observed. "But, joking apart, I don't think this youth now wants to marry Madge. I think it is Hilda he is after, don't you?"

Cecilia in her turn looked straight at her companion. Mark hauled down his colours.

"You have guessed my secret," he said, with a sigh.

"I'm not surprised," said Cecilia, becoming in a moment the cordial *confidante*. "She is awfully pretty and a very good sort. I have taken a great fancy to her and I mean to see something of her."

"I am very hopeless," said the confessed lover.

"That's the correct thing, but I don't see why you should be. Hilda has got the wits to appreciate you, I can see, already. Only—"

"Only?" echoed Mark.

"Only that her family are sure to want her to marry the handsome Roman Catholic Marmaduke, and he likes her, and I'm not sure she doesn't like him. Really, for your sake, that is not a bad idea of mine that he should marry Madge."

"An admirable idea," responded Mark.

"And frankly, Mark, though I am ready to be your friend, I won't pretend to sublime unselfishness. Madge is a bore, you know, and (in confidence) you can see that she isn't quite a lady. I made a mistake I own in taking her up. Several of us took her up, and she has got out of her natural sphere. They all see it now.

We should be glad to have her out of the way in the wilds of Lancashire. You can't think what a bore she became at Bellasis in the autumn. She was so absurdly eager to do everything that I and a few friends of mine did. You can't think how funny she was and how pretentious. And there was something so *nouveau riche* in her absurd extravagance. She had a different gown every quarter of an hour."

"I can see her," said Mark, with a derisive laugh; he enjoyed all this confidence hugely.

"Well, you know, Bellasis became dreadfully bored by her, and he would be delighted if she married this man and went off to Lancashire."

"All so true," sighed Mark, "but how can we make them do it?"

Cecilia sent forth a peal of laughter.

"I haven't the least notion," she admitted.

"Throw them together?" suggested Mark.

"Keep Hilda out of the way?" said Cecilia.

"Throw Miss Hilda into somebody else's society," said Mark, with a shy smile.

"Quite so. Then the handsome cousin may easily be persuaded that he ought to look after Madge—save her from worldliness and all that. That is a certain card to play with these Catholics. I am not sure but that he has the idea already. Then if Hilda is out of the way, propinquity and 'interest in Madge's soul' may do much. Gossip is useful, too; and we can both talk—can't we Mark? little things about his always being with her, about his burning his hands—make out that she always cared for him, that may do something if it gets round to him. Men are all open to that. Let plenty of people know that there has been something between them long ago. Get a thing on the *tapis* somehow, and it often grows of itself. It really would amuse me, Mark, very much if we succeeded."

"She means to let it come round to Bellasis," thought Mark.

"I might," he said, "see what impression Lord Tim got of the pampas grass affair. By the way, is Tim a friend of Lord Bellasis?"

"Yes, I met him at Bellasis. But will you have some more tea? By the way, Hilda is to come to lunch with me to-morrow. Mark, I'll be your friend without any nonsense."

"And I your devoted cavalier," said Mark, laughing. Silence followed for a few moments. Mark was the first to speak.

"How is Miss Rupert?" he asked. "You want two nurses for her now?"

"Heavens, yes," said Cecilia, "two nurses and they are overtired it seems; don't let us talk about it. I can't bear it. I would give anything to leave London now."

"And you can't leave your aunt?" said Fieldes sympathetically.

"It is just because of her that I wish I could go," said Cecilia; and she shivered. "I am no good to her, in fact I am bad for her. She never has me off her mind. *Oh*, it is *too, too* horrible."

Cecilia stopped the swing by putting her feet to the ground and bent forward with distended and frightened eyes that seemed to see something dreadful; her arms came out of her loose sleeves and showed white against the red ropes she was holding.

"Think," she cried, "it is pain, always pain, terrible pain, and she lies there moaning. I could hear her sometimes in the drawing-room; and yet she may take months to die. Nobody thinks of putting her out of her pain. They do everything they can to keep her alive. Of course they give her morphia and those things, but you know it does nothing, nothing really; and one day—conceive how awful!—she wouldn't take the morphia because she was afraid she should die unconscious. She said she would rather suffer. Conceive what her clergymen and her people must have reduced her to before that! They come and see her, a horrid old white man with a beard, and a young horrid black shaven one, and they rejoice over her because she prays so much and gives them money. I believe they dread her dying. And all the time she is talking to them she is being tortured, and she tells them that she thanks the God who tortures her, and that she is glad to suffer because of her sins; she who has been only too horridly good all her life! Fancy, Mark, fancy if one were to be tortured for what one had done after a life like hers—where should you and I be, I wonder?"

Cecilia laughed, a ghastly little laugh.

"But why has she got you on her mind?" asked Fieldes.

"Because unfortunately she is, I'm afraid, fonder of me than of any other living thing. She has got one of those unfortunate natures that have a craze for giving up to other people, and she gave up to me all my life, and now she thinks I am going to the bad, and she has plots to do me good. Isn't it awful? They come to me sometimes, day or night, and say they think she is 'going,' they mean dying; and I have to come whenever they catch me. And then she rambles on about all sorts of things, and I see her face contract with pain. One night, late, late at night—but I don't know why I tell you all this, Mark—"

"No, go on," said Mark gently, "one night—what?"

"One night I had had such a glorious evening. I had been at Laura's and I had danced while she played. And somehow we both seemed to get a little wild, and there was a wonderful rhythm of joy and life in the music, and in my dancing, and I felt as if I were very beautiful and a sort of mistress over life and death; as if all things about me were happy and warm and living. I don't know what possessed us. Bellasis," her voice softened, "was the only audience. I came home and went up to bed, and I was so excited that I almost forgot all the horrors, and just ran up past her door as I had always done when she was well. And I took my things off and rolled myself warmly up in bed, and I lay there almost as happy and peaceful as I used to be years ago. And just then they knocked, and in came one of them. And she said in her horrid voice that my aunt had been asking for me for a long time—all the evening. I asked was she light-headed this evening? and the woman said no; that she had refused to take morphia, although it was a bad night, till she had seen me, because she wanted to speak to me. It was awful, and it came crushing down on me just when I had had a few minutes' happiness. It was a horribly cold night too, and so I said I wouldn't go, and I argued with the woman that my aunt ought to take morphia at once, until she went away. And do you know, Mark, I believe that woman hates me. They all hate me now, and they used to like me. But how can they expect me to stay with her and watch all the tortures; for, Mark, you know it is the family illness and I shall have it some day." The last words rose in a sort of wail of self-defence and self-pity.

Fieldes looked at her, half fascinated, as he might have looked at some beautiful, dangerous animal; and yet there was so much that was human in the terror, the fear, the impulse to confession in order at once to relieve herself and to see how it appeared to him.

"They are not fair to me," she said bitterly. "I don't know what they think I am; but imagine what they did to-day! The servants made a mistake and brought me her luncheon. I didn't know and I didn't care what we were going to eat. The cook settles my aunt's dinner with the nurse and I only say let them spend whatever they like—a little more or less won't make much difference—and don't worry my aunt. Well, to-day I saw there were oysters, and I didn't think anything of it; but I found afterwards they were all that were left of a barrel that had been sent for my aunt, and that she had taken a fancy to them. Do you know I believe the nurse knew it and wouldn't come and tell me. I believe she wanted to make out that I had eaten the poor creature's oysters on purpose. Isn't it disgusting?"

Fieldes was silent; but after a little he said abruptly:—

"Do you know, Cecilia, I think you are becoming hysterical. You will have some sort of nerve collapse at this rate. You must go away and get calmer. Go abroad,—oh, go anywhere!" he urged.

"Go away!" said Cecilia, and a strange light came into her eyes. "How little he knows," she thought, "the strength of what keeps me in London. No," she said, "I shall stay here, and avoid the horrors as much as I can, and talk to Hilda and look after her."

Mark after that left her. He passed through the mews of Farm Street to get to South Street. Outside the Jesuit Church he stopped. There were faint distant lights twinkling before the altar.

"Oh," he cried almost aloud, "cannot any Church keep its power? Must all fail? Must we have many Cecilias? Oh, whatever we lose, whatever we say or do, let us keep the power of the crucifix to save the women!"

CHAPTER V

HILDA'S LETTER TO HER MOTHER

Monday.

DEAREST MOTHER,—

I am glad you understand how difficult it is to find time to write in my present excitements. I've not been out much in the evening so far, but I am to go to a party at the Hurstmonceaux', and Mr. Fieldes is using his influence in the House of Commons to get me into the Ladies' Gallery. He won't be satisfied with anything but a really good night, as he has told one of his friends in the Government. We have had tea in his rooms to-day. It was great fun.

The rooms are just what I thought a bachelor would have, but Madge was disappointed and told him that he ought to make them more artistic. She certainly made herself at home, running about the room looking at things, asking him questions, and even opening drawers and pulling out photographs. 'And what is this?' she asked, taking a framed photograph down from a shelf. 'Ah, that is rather interesting,' said Mr. Fieldes, who was fussing himself and his servant with the tea-things. 'What is it about?' 'Well,' he said, 'it is quite a long story told in pictures in an old *palazzo* in Siena. It is a sort of Faust, only it is a woman who has concluded the bargain with the devil. First you see her, old and shrivelled, with an angry discontented face, coming out of a church hobbling on her stick, and scowling at a grand young woman in a chariot. Won't you have some tea? I think it is just right now.'

But Madge wouldn't come to tea. 'Finish the story first,' she said. 'Well, then,' he went on, while he poured out a cup for me, 'the next picture is the same old woman in a wood followed by Mephistopheles, who is dressed as a cavalier. He is walking behind her whispering, while an exquisitely painted angel, whose white draperies shade off into the blue, is floating over her, pointing to heaven. It is a glorious sky, and the clouds melt away until they seem to suggest that within the wonderful circles of light must be the very throne of God. On a quaint little hillock hard by, a rugged crucifix stands out against the red light on the horizon.' 'But this picture?' said Madge, who had kept staring at it. in an odd way she has sometimes. 'If you would but have your tea,' said Mr. Fieldes quite piteously, 'it is getting cold.' Madge said, 'How you do tease,' half-laughingly, and poured out some tea herself. Mr. Fieldes went on: 'Then in this picture you see she has yielded. She is a beautiful young woman, gorgeously dressed, and with people bowing before her. The curious point is that in all the descriptions of the pictures the lady is supposed to have sold her soul for gold, and jewels and power, not for love. The knight is an incident or necessary appendage, whereas in Faust the man sells himself for youth chiefly for the sake of love. Do you think it is natural, Miss Riversdale?' 'I should have thought it would have been just the other way,' I answered. 'Faust being a man might sell himself for power. The woman would do it for love.'

'I don't agree with you,' he said; 'my experience is that ambition is the one overpowering passion in a woman. Don't you think so, Mrs. Riversdale? As often as not when a woman falls, it is from hope of advancement?' Madge didn't answer. 'But what happens to the woman in the picture?' I asked. 'Well, that is the best part of it, only I couldn't get the photographs. First a monk is preaching to her and her attendants, and she laughs at him. Then she is kneeling by a dead baby, and then, in the next scene, she is in a convent cell, but the devil is seen laughing behind the door (evidently he daren't come in), and holding out a paper which I suppose is her bond. He had promised her fifty years of life, and it ends in her giving up the long life she has purchased from him, and consenting to die before the time, and the devil rages over her dead body, while she flies up with an excited angel through the ceiling of the cell. The last two are the least good of all the series—in design and execution.'

Madge had moved to the fire. 'Usually the devil won his bargain in those stories, didn't he?' she said. 'Not always. In the middle ages the devil was often made a fool of. Then Shakespeare ignored him; but he went up in the world with Milton, and had his own way with Goethe, and he was a striking individual with Byron. He is quite out of fashion now.' 'People sell their souls to the world now,' I said, and I suppose I must have been pompous, for Madge cried: 'Spare us any of your preaching, my dear Hilda.' 'Personally I think he is a loss,' said Mr. Fieldes, 'he was a great convenience. I knew a child who on being asked why she did wrong, said, "I could not help it, the devil tempted me." We were all like that child until they took away our devil.' 'But then mother knew a modern child,' I said, 'who when she was asked why she was so naughty said, "I can't help it, it's a law of nature."' We laughed, and Mark said, 'But the laws of nature can't do half the business. Is it a law of nature for a pretty girl to marry an old man for money? No, the devil waving a box of diamonds was a much more artistic way out.'

Madge walked about the room again looking at his pictures and other things, and then came back to us suddenly and said, 'We must go. I thought you took photographs, but you've no camera or anything about the room.' 'I only take snapshots,' he answered, looking rather awkward I thought. 'And I never keep any: they are not worth it.' 'Why, what's that thing I saw in a drawer?' said Madge. 'Oh, that was done by a friend, I never keep mine.' 'What, *never?*' said Madge. 'Never, dear lady,' answered Mark, and he looked more angry than I've ever seen him before. After that Madge made him fetch her fur cloak, and she said while he put it on: 'Do you think that people who believe in hell would ever sell their souls?' She spoke to nobody in particular. Mark came in front of her and looked hard at her. 'I do believe it—don't you?—if they got a good offer?'

Well, Madge came away in a temper. What can they have meant? I'm sure Madge wanted to find something in his room. I must say it improved Mr. Mark to lose his temper. He looked more of a man. But Madge abused him all the way home, though she had just pressed him to come to lunch whenever he liked. She said he was not a gentleman, and his manners were hateful, and he shouldn't say 'dear lady,' he didn't know how to do it, and that he was too familiar. She had quite got her colour back by the time we reached home. I'm afraid this letter will bore you; the conversation seemed much more interesting before it was written down, and now I must dress for dinner.

Your loving child,
Hilda.

But Mrs. Arthur Riversdale was annoyed as well as bored by her daughter's letter, the first long communication from Hilda since Skipton. It told her nothing about Hilda's self, and gave her an unpleasant impression of her surroundings. Hilda said nothing of Marmaduke, but perhaps that was a good sign. The mother longed for more knowledge of her child; and she had to put up with a would-be clever account of a tea with "that tiresome Mr. Fieldes." Hilda's visit to London was becoming an increasing source of anxiety to her from her knowing so little about it. This was hardly the way in which her mother had intended Hilda to see life. And that night, long after the other inmates of the house were at rest, the widow sat thinking over the question whether she ought to summon Hilda home.

Little did Hilda imagine how evenly the two sides hung in the balance that night, and how nearly she had risked being sent for by writing that letter. Over and over again the musing mother summed up the case; on the one hand Madge as a chaperon, her friends as companions; the child's crude, simple acceptance of it all as simply so much fun, evidently taking all she saw and heard as a matter of course. For her those people would become the ideal of life and society. Surely it was wrong to leave her alone with Madge. This was the first conclusion. But the defence?

Where else could she be? The housemaid with the scarlet fever was better, but not well enough to be removed. And then there was all the disinfecting to be done. She could not have Hilda home, and she could not ask them to have her at Skipton when Mr. Riversdale had been so pleased at this visit to London, and had more than hinted. . . . But there was so little about Marmaduke in the letters. Still, was that altogether a bad sign? Hardly. And then surely Marmaduke must be taking care of her. They could not be such very objectionable people, or he would have warned somebody; he was always to be trusted. And it would be—it certainly would be so very happy if . . . And then she smiled tenderly and sighed and began thinking again, and decided that it was impossible to afford to take Hilda to Brighton or Eastbourne. After all, the disinfecting would not take more than a fortnight, and Hilda could not get much harm in that short time. On the whole, it was best to let things take their natural course.

CHAPTER VI

A DULL WEEK

There is little more of importance to record concerning Hilda's doings and experiences during the rest of the week. Monday in the week following was fixed for the Hurstmonceaux' musical party. Poor Marmaduke had been laid up since the pampas-grass episode, with his injured hands and a touch of fever. Madge went about a good deal and did not often take Hilda with her.

Madge was indeed much preoccupied. Many of her own friends were friends of Lord Bellasis, and again and again before lunching or dining out she had been in a fever of expectancy—she must meet him before long, and what would happen? However, they did not meet. She had asked him to dine, in an impetuous moment, on the previous Friday; and when he wrote briefly that he was engaged, she had been greatly relieved. And on each occasion when a meeting had been half expected by her, if she felt a little disappointed, she felt on the whole more relieved not to find him. Once he was actually in the house when she arrived, but apparently did not see her, and a few minutes later she found that he was gone. Neither did she happen to meet Laura Hurstmonceaux: and this too was a relief. She seemed on the whole to shrink from anything which might lead to further explanations, or bring matters nearer to a definite issue.

Madge remained then during that week *distraite* and absent. She had little mind to give to Hilda. She was glad to find that two of her friends seemed to occupy that young lady's time during the day, in a quiet but sufficiently entertaining manner. And as to the evenings she had warned Hilda not to expect a rush of gaiety.

The two benevolent beings who rapidly developed independent intimacy with the responsive Hilda were Cecilia Rupert and Mrs. Hurstmonceaux. Cecilia's society was exciting to Hilda—full of interest, but not entirely pleasant. She dreaded the *tête-à-tête* she was always seeking, and which always produced the same result—a headache, or a touch of neuralgia, complaints entirely new to her. After one of those talks in which Madge or Marmaduke was sure to be casually introduced, and his disappointed affection of years past brought somehow before her mind, Hilda would go to her own room, blaming herself and everybody else. She found the writing of letters home more and more of an effort, and she dreaded lest her mother should detect the constraint which only ten days' stay with Madge had already produced. Her prayers too seemed constrained in the same way as her letters. She had never before had so much to amuse her, but she had often been far happier. She was not positively unhappy. She would not have echoed Cecilia's condemnation of the world as a "husk of pleasure round a heart of sorrow." But she did not feel good; she dreaded being disloyal; she did not assimilate Cecilia's suggestions without some healthy resistance. She listened, and thought herself wrong to listen, to constant insinuations against Madge. She preferred perhaps to impute to her conscience some sadness of heart which she would not acknowledge.

The kindness shown her by Mrs. Hurstmonceaux on the other hand was nothing but delightful. Several days during that week were spent by Hilda almost entirely with Laura. Mark Fieldes sometimes made a third, in some visits to picture galleries or theatres: and when he was not there, Laura talked of him.

Mrs. Hurstmonceaux had indeed resolved to marry Mark to this supposed heiress. It was not remarkable that she should have taken Mark's account of the girl's wealth without inquiry. Her zeal in his matrimonial interests needs more explanation. Everybody has his or her weakness, and Fieldes was a weakness with Mrs. Hurstmonceaux. She had discovered him at a country house, where the young school inspector had been invited to stay, in order that he might speak at a large political meeting. He had confided to her a work in manuscript which she had warmly pressed him to publish, and she had been justified by its great success with the public. She had naturally exaggerated her own share in the success of the *Phantasmagoria of Phidias,* and she piqued herself on helping the career of her genius. Fieldes also exaggerated the service she had done him; for he was prone to overestimate social and feminine influences. He was not morally strong enough to believe that his own good work could make its way without the help of such women as Laura. It is rash to make general assertions, but it does not seem very risky to assert that society, although it may make and unmake other reputations, does not make or unmake authors, unless it may do the latter work indirectly by helping them to injure their own powers. That society was doing this last evil work to her *protégé* Mrs. Hurstmonceaux was quick to discover.

"You are not writing half so well as you were," she had said to him. "This sort of thing doesn't do for you; you get too anxious over it, and that doesn't suit it."

By "sort of thing" and "it" Mrs. Hurstmonceaux meant "Society" with a big S, but she was too true an artist to say so. "That article in the *Bi-monthly* was a success just because it said what the Duke of A. and a dozen important men wanted said at the moment. But if you once take to that kind of thing as an object it won't do. You will fritter your powers away, and people will see it too. Can't you treat them with a little wholesome indifference? There is something of the bully in all sets of people. For heaven's sake don't go in for that foolish swagger of professing cynically to have low objects. We have not low objects in reality. These are the affectations of people whose place in the world is ready made: yours is not."

So convinced had Laura Hurstmonceaux become that London society was not the proper element for her "genius," that she had been glad to hear that he thought of marrying and of marrying money. He was not so successful as a bachelor that he could lose much by matrimony, and a clever girl might be the making of him. In spending the time with the two she skilfully contrived for them the sort of amusement and occupation in which Mark was to be seen at his best. She had with extreme candour given him some advice. She had told him to suppress the gossipy, small side of his talk.

"Your mind is your attraction, my dear Mark," she would say, "and you can't be pompous! it isn't in you, so don't be afraid of showing a little intellect. I for one always feel crushed at your attempts at gossip. You lose all your sense of humour."

Mark was very happy that week, happier than he had been for years. He really enjoyed this innocent unworldly atmosphere. With Hilda and Mrs. Hurstmonceaux in her present mood he felt almost like a boy. There was no straining after a kind of talk and a state of mind unnatural to him, no fear of bad form, no anxiety lest he should be above or below his company. If some of the women whom he was always trying to propitiate by descending to their level, as he supposed, could have heard him talking with Laura and Hilda, making little silly spontaneous jokes as well as saying deeper things, they would have thought him wonderfully improved. Mrs. Hurstmonceaux liked him better than ever, and Madge said she did the same when Laura asked her; but it was difficult to know how far Madge's mind was present with them at all at that time.

Mrs. Hurstmonceaux was however distinctly bored during a good many of the hours she spent with the two, and she groaned a little when she got home. But she had a strong will; she was determined to marry Hilda to Mark; and she was quite accustomed to being bored by human beings when she wanted to do anything with them. Laura was not sorry that Hilda should have this week of rational enjoyment, with Mark for a guide, but she did not intend her *protégée* to continue to live so quiet a life. She meant the little party at her own house, to which Madge was to bring Hilda, to lead to her young friend going out more.

Laura was in a fair way to being satisfied with her little parties just then. The Hurstmonceaux' received frequently, "a little"; "not many, but often," was their principle, or rather her principle, for her constant use of the pronoun "we" was fictitious, and known to be fictitious. Mr. Hurstmonceaux was an excellent, good fellow, and he had quite as many personal friends as she had; but the ways and doings of the house were ruled by her, as indeed he much preferred that they should be. This was from no height of unselfishness, but from a long-standing conviction that his wife could accomplish more for him than he could accomplish for himself. Coming himself of a good but old-fashioned stock, he marvelled at what seemed to him the wonderful success of his wife, who was of no family worthy of mention. They were not very happy together, but they were not more unhappy than many other couples; and his confidence in her wisdom smoothed away many difficulties. He proved his confidence for instance by allowing her a free hand in their expenditure, and she took full advantage of this liberty. It is difficult to analyse her methods (she never analysed them herself) without being vulgar, and what could be more vulgar than what Cecilia once said of her? The two were certainly antipathic by nature. "Mrs. Hurstmonceaux," she had exclaimed when provoked out of all patience by that lady's manoeuvres, "Mrs. Hurstmonceaux can even manage women; and she never forgets to flatter men as well as she feeds them!"

Yes, she fed them to perfection, and she threw a soft melancholy poetry into her very viands. "We have a sadness about us," she seemed to say (it must be remembered that she never did say anything of the kind). "We want cheering. We can never forget the mystery of the starving multitudes of our great cities. We have a soft melancholy about us. Nothing must be spared in giving us such delicate viands as will best soothe us; no *salon* now could be attempted with tea and bread and butter in an attic; we have less faith than our forefathers. It is a serious loss for our emotions; but so it is. We must cultivate the highest in art—in every art. The dinner-table should be perfect in its way. Mediocrity is now intolerable. And the company must be chosen with infinite care. We live in a democratic age, therefore never was rank so much sought after. We must have it in sufficiency: yet it must not overwhelm talent. Above all, let us not be pretentious. Whoever comes to us, however great or small his rank or talent, must be a real friend."

CHAPTER VII

CECILIA APPEALS TO MARMADUKE

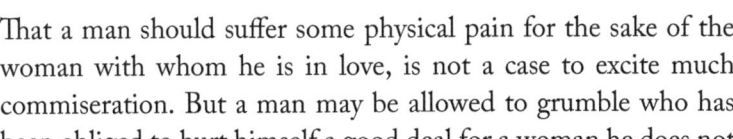

That a man should suffer some physical pain for the sake of the woman with whom he is in love, is not a case to excite much commiseration. But a man may be allowed to grumble who has been obliged to hurt himself a good deal for a woman he does not love, in the presence of another whom he does love.

Marmaduke certainly did grumble when he found that his burns were very considerable, and that the doctor insisted on his staying in his room for several days. On the second day after these orders a touch of the Indian fever, that was always lying in wait for him since a bad illness in India, developed sufficiently to prevent his being able to leave the house. His friends, when they went to see him, did not find him very amusing company. He had no sitting-room—for, without reflecting that he could now afford better ones, he had gone back to the lodgings of his poorer days—therefore he could not ask ladies to tea. There were only two ladies whom he would have invited if he could, namely, Madge and Hilda. Madge was very assiduous in calling to inquire how he was; but he could not find out (as he disdained to ask his servant) whether Hilda came with her, and the only allusion to her in Madge's numerous notes was contained in the "we," for which Hilda's authority was doubtful.

Marmaduke had plenty of time for reflection during these days. He was a good deal surprised at his own state of mind. His love for Hilda had begun in such a quiet, reasonable, willing manner, and seemed so appropriate and fitting, that it had not borne at first the appearance of a *grande passion*. He had been very glad, during those days at Skipton, that he was so much attracted by exactly the girl whom his parents would wish him to marry; and although he had been by no means confident of success—for he felt sure that Hilda had plenty of individuality and will of her own—still there was no reason to be despondent. The incipient flirtation with Mark Fieldes had been annoying, but not very seriously disturbing. Mark did not seem a likely man to win a girl's affections against such odds as were suggested by his want of religion, his belonging in Marmaduke's eyes to another class than hers, his lanky, awkward person and his poverty.

Marmaduke had left Hilda at Skipton, where she had stayed until the following Thursday, and then as we have seen they had met again in London. And there to Marmaduke, as well as to her, all seemed changed between them. It was to him a strangely thrilling recollection, that of Hilda coming quietly into the room, on the afternoon on which she arrived in London, dressed in her black net frock. He had been leaning back in the arm-chair near the fireplace, looking up with amusement at Cecilia, who was evidently taking stock of him as a new acquaintance who excited her curiosity. He did not know that Hilda had arrived; he was not sure on what day she was to come up from Skipton; so that immediately on reaching London, after changing his clothes at his lodgings, he had gone to see Madge and find out when she was expected. Then, before he had asked any questions about her, the door had opened and Hilda had appeared. It seemed to him that it took a long time to get out of his chair and go to meet her. There was a sense of constraint, of bewildered astonishment at the extent of feeling revealed to him by the sight of her. How fascinating, how beautifully shy she had looked coming across the back drawing-room! What a delicious freshness in the raised colour, in the little natural curls about the high forehead. There was in her aspect something so infinitely better, purer and higher than in that of any other girl, and she was, especially, so much above the two other women who were in the room with her now! But into that very moment of passionate feeling there had come a jarring note. She shook hands with him very gravely, and then turned smilingly to Mark Fieldes whom she had evidently seen already since her arrival, and he overheard them laying plans for meeting again. From that moment Marmaduke had begun to take Mark Fieldes seriously. Hilda's manner varied enough to keep him on the stretch—at moments there was that delicious tremor and shyness about her that seemed to be an actual response to his own feelings, and then she would turn deliberately, sometimes almost vehemently, away from him, or seem relieved if somebody else intervened.

These were many sensations to have crowded into the short interval between Hilda's arrival in London and the burning of that pampas grass on which in his solitary hours he vented so many expletives.

But at last the hands were healed and the touch of fever had passed off completely. He wrote to Madge on Thursday to tell her that he might come out to luncheon, and to ask if she would be at home next day, and he observed at the end of his note, "it seems an age since I have seen you."

Madge read the note at breakfast and remarked to Hilda:—

"Poor Marmaduke, what an odious time he has had of it. I shall have to stay at home for luncheon; you will explain to Laura why I can't come, won't you, dear? She really likes having you better than me, and I shall see her at her party. As poor Marmaduke says 'it is an age since he has seen me,' it would really be unkind to go out."

Hilda's first impulse on hearing of Marmaduke's coming had hardly arisen before Madge's final words made her answer quickly:—

"Oh, yes, I will go to Laura. Tell Marmaduke when he comes how glad I am he is all right."

Hilda after that gave her whole attention to a letter from her mother. Madge wondered for a moment what the letter could contain that Hilda's cheeks should be so flushed while she was reading it.

At a few minutes past one Marmaduke followed the servant into the drawing-room. He could not run up as usual without being announced, because he could not open the door with his bandaged hands. Madge was reading the *Morning Post* by the fire. Hilda had her hat and jacket on, and was pulling on her gloves, with her back to the window. Marmaduke was still very weak and walked into the room with uncertain gait. He saw what Hilda's attitude and her gloves meant in a moment, and he turned a shade more pale. Hilda was startled to see from his face how ill he had been. She went forward to him with an instinctive movement of sympathy.

"Oh, how ill you look!" she cried, holding out her hand and then withdrawing it with a pained glance at the sling which held the two scarred hands. The mixture of feelings was almost too much for him,—the joy in the mere sense of her presence, irrational anger at seeing that she was going out when he wanted her to be at home, his keen perception of the pity and feeling in her large eyes.

"I'm not ill, thanks," he said rather gruffly, "only shaky after the touch of fever."

Madge advanced with graceful cousinly bustle, got Marmaduke into a chair, and laughingly held a large bottle of salts at the right distance from his nose. Hilda stood silent for a moment and then said abruptly to Madge:—

"I must be off or I shall be late. I will tell Laura why you can't come."

"When shall you get back?" asked Madge, as Hilda moved towards the door.

Marmaduke was looking wearily at the fire; he did not move, Hilda noticed, or show that he knew what Madge had said.

"Not before five o'clock, I think, as Laura and Mr. Fieldes want to see the pictures thoroughly."

Marmaduke observed that she did not even ask whether she should find him still there when she came back. Yet the look in her face, he thought to himself, had been so intensely kind. And now she was gone; and how was he to pull through two long hours with Madge—while his hands smarted and his head ached.

Why had not the ass of a doctor forbidden him to go out! nobody wanted to see him!

Marmaduke thought himself glad to escape from Madge when the brougham, which the doctor had insisted upon, came to take him away at four o'clock. But as he drove off to his lodgings, the solitude awaiting him seemed intolerable. He would not and he could not go back. At the same moment he remembered that Miss Rupert had told him to come and see her, and that he should pass her house in Charles Street on his way. Marmaduke had been amused and attracted by Cecilia, and was not insensible to the fact that she had taken a great liking for him.

Cecilia was at home, and a few moments later he was comfortably installed in the little back sitting-room. Her pleasure at seeing him was unfeigned. Even if there had been no further reason, if there had been no uneasy hankering to be in touch with Madge's surroundings, Cecilia would have been glad to see him.

"Now that he is pale he is even beautiful," she thought, as she scanned his face with the frank enjoyment of a connoisseur. This was part of the freedom of her nature. "Pagan, I regret to say," to quote the immortal Pecksniff, but involving in her case a certain simplicity. The firelight was bright in the waning of a dull foggy day; it lit up the dark eyes which, as they looked at her, betrayed some bodily pain and a mental state which made her kindly greeting and almost caressing manner a relief. Cecilia and he talked of many things, of India, of pig sticking, of home and hunting; but it was inevitable that they should talk of Madge and Hilda. And in Cecilia's manner there was a struggle of sympathies checked by various motives. She hated Madge; she liked Hilda well enough; but she wanted this man to make love to Madge, and obviously he preferred Hilda. She was, it has been said, a novice in diplomacy, and he had the far more complete simplicity of a man. So the talk was crude and disjointed, Marmaduke, a little disappointed at not being able to speak much of Hilda, Cecilia praising and pitying "little Madge." At last Cecilia stumbled almost unawares on what was needed.

"I suppose Madge is not what you would call a strict Catholic. But people are so different. Some friends of Lord Bellasis made such a fuss about driving, I don't know how far, from Bellasis to go to Mass. Madge had said nothing about it."

Marmaduke looked up quickly at this, and an anxious expression came into his eyes. "Was Madge at Bellasis for several Sundays?"

"Oh, yes, on and off, for eight or nine Sundays at least. And she went to Mass two or three times if the carriage took anybody else, but she would not have it for herself. I think she was quite right. I can't think people need make themselves so tiresome about religion. Then you know how religious people fidget about early church. I have never heard Madge allude to going out early, since I have known her. And besides all that, you know she isn't straitlaced about anything, she is not *difficile* in her ways and her manners."

There was no doubt that Marmaduke was thinking about Madge now. Cecilia went on with a little laugh.

"I know I am a heathen in your eyes, but I think if I had any religion I would do it thoroughly. Madge never makes the "confessions" which other Roman Catholic women I know go in for so often—she certainly never went at Bellasis. It seems so queer to believe in all the sort of things Madge believes in, heaven and hell, and the whole future affair, and all her Church sacraments, and for it to make so little difference to her."

"But don't you believe in more than you act up to? You are an exception if you live up to your theories whatever they are."

"Yes, but then I whittle away the theories when I don't want them."

"That is just what Madge can't do," said Marmaduke, smiling.

"Because she is a Catholic?" asked Cecilia, rising from her chair and standing opposite to him, "and yet—" She looked at him with a mystifying smile and paused.

"And yet what?"

"Well, you see," said Cecilia frankly, "I don't know how much you know about what is going on, so I am rather hampered. Hasn't it struck you that Madge is in a queer state of mind?"

"I don't know," said Marmaduke. The growing anxiety in his pale face was exactly what she wanted to see there.

"Would you all be very much put out if she gave up being a Catholic?"

"Oh, she won't do that," and Marmaduke laughed. "You don't know what it is to do that."

"Well," said Cecilia, "of course it is nothing to me, but I think some of your people had better look after her. She is in a very tight corner."

She paused again, and a servant, bringing in a lamp, prevented her from continuing. Marmaduke saw her face distinctly now, and when they were again alone he said quite simply:—

"What do you mean?"

It was the strain, the passion expressed in her grey eyes that had startled him.

"I can't tell you," she answered and her voice shook, "only—" another pause.

"Only?" repeated Marmaduke, very gently.

"Only, Mr. Marmaduke," in a voice struggling to be calm, "if you wish to save a soul, ah, and to save a heart," she covered her face with her hands, "for pity's sake keep close to Madge, take care of her! You don't know what good you may do." She got up, and her face was disfigured with tears, which had come in an instant. She looked suddenly aged. She tried to laugh. "How melodramatic, wasn't I? But you know I am fond of Madge, and I believe people have hearts, and you believe they have souls. You think souls so precious because of a future life; and I think hearts the only thing worth anything in the earth below, or the heavens above, or in the waters under the earth. It has been bad for you, all this talk while you are ill. I ought not to have done it, but I don't know what time there may be yet before, before—"

"Oh, it won't hurt me," said Marmaduke feebly, "thank you very much. I won't pretend to understand, because I don't; but I will try to help, though what on earth I can do without knowing more I can't imagine. I think I must go now." He had turned a shade paler, and he closed his eyes. Then with an effort he pulled himself together and went away.

Cecilia, unnerved and upset, sank back in her chair.

"Poor little goose of a Hilda. He went out of my room like a knight to the combat, with his moral spear in rest. Marmaduke *à la rescousse.* All for that puny abstraction, Madge's soul! And every word I spoke was true, so awfully true."

CHAPTER VIII

THE EVENING AT THE HURSTMONCEAUX

"Rather a full night," whispered Cecilia to Madge whom she had followed closely into the Hurstmonceaux' long, narrow drawing-room on Monday, the night of the party. She was craning her head about, looking on either side with her peculiar gaze.

At the other end of the room Madge distinctly saw Lord Bellasis. Hilda had been kept back for a moment by her hostess at the door.

"I've heard such a thing said of you to-day, my dear, that I cannot resist the indiscretion of repeating it. Fancy one of our best known authors declaring that you have one of the most remarkable minds he has ever come across. But *il faut me taire.*" At that moment Fieldes appeared in the doorway. Hilda drew back, and he turned instantly to her. Hilda was shy but greatly excited, and indeed what young woman of eighteen with literary tendencies would not have been excited by such a compliment? She felt that she must keep up this reputation for a remarkable mind by plunging into a deep discussion with Mr. Fieldes, but first she wanted to know "who was the handsome lady with the huge diamonds who was speaking to Madge."

"That is a charming woman," observed Fieldes in a low voice, "the Duchess of A."

"And who is Miss Rupert's friend?"

Cecilia was already sitting in a corner talking eagerly to a tall, heavy-featured, muscular son of Britain.

"That man listening to Miss Rupert is Lord Bellasis. Have you not seen him before? You will see plenty of him now that you have begun to go about."

"Why, and how?"

"He is a great admirer of Mrs. George Riversdale's."

Hilda looked shy, which amused Fieldes.

"The funny thing is that though he is the most stiff and particular of mortals, he is such a friend of Miss Rupert's."

Yes, he might be a friend of Cecilia's, but his eyes were constantly directed elsewhere, as Hilda after this hint observed. For some time she and Mark continued to talk, but it must be owned that neither of them gave evidence of their remarkable intellects. Fieldes very much enjoyed doing *cicérone* to the London world, and as there were fresh arrivals or departures, or one group shifted itself into another, he was full of information not badly given. But what puzzled his audience was that the conduct of the people he described did not seem to fit in with what he led her to expect. Lady R., a very great friend of his, a "dear woman," gave Mr. Fieldes a very slight nod; while Mrs. K. whom he "hardly knew," who "lived somewhere in Richmond," seized him by the hand and said, "Remember we didn't finish that talk last Thursday."

At length a very smartly dressed youngish woman, in pale green satin, wearing a striking necklace of black pearls, descended on them and began—

"Ah, Mr. Fieldes, we are all full of the *Bi-monthly* article."

Fieldes responded eagerly; and at that moment to Hilda's surprise Marmaduke appeared by her side.

"You ought not to be here!" she exclaimed. "Isn't it very foolish to come out at night already?"

He was very pale, but the paleness suited him. One arm was in a sling, the left hand was enough healed for him to wear a glove.

"Very foolish, if you think so," he answered, laughing.

Their eyes met with the sense of sympathy which Hilda could not always conquer. For her own sake, as well as his, she wished he had not come. He would spoil her pleasure and do himself harm. She had only met his look for a moment; then she tried to assume the bright air with which she had been speaking to Mark.

"Who is that woman with the lovely eyes and pearls talking to Mr. Fieldes?" she whispered.

"I don't know," said Marmaduke; "I don't know a face here."

To Hilda, full of excitement at her plunge into society, this ignorance of the world was dull and rather contemptible.

"Of course you have been so long in India," she said in a tone of kindly condescension which rather amused Marmaduke.

They were interrupted by the general "hush," which announced that Herr Joachim had just begun to play a Hungarian dance. Hilda listened with rapt attention, and Marmaduke sat down beside her. When the music ceased she turned to him, but they were interrupted by Mrs. Hurstmonceaux, and Marmaduke moved away.

"There is such a nice girl here, who particularly wants to know you. Miss Rupert, Miss Riversdale," and round the corner appeared a fair, rather plain, well-dressed girl of cheerful countenance, whom the hostess had been puzzled how to dispose of.

"I'm not Miss Rupert," she said cheerfully; "I'm only Cecilia's cousin." Her manner implied "I'm a person of no kind of consequence, but I'm really very nice when you know me." "Do you know Cecilia?"

"Oh, yes," cried Hilda, "isn't she fascinating?"

Cecilia's cousin laughed good-humouredly.

"Oh, if you are with Mrs. George Riversdale, you must see plenty of Cecilia; they are bosom friends." Her innocent eyes turned from Cecilia and Lord Bellasis towards Madge, and she gave a little laugh. "They form a trio generally, and they would like to be all together now probably, only that Austrian secretary is so attentive to your cousin."

At that moment Cecilia rose and walked towards Madge, but Lord Bellasis did not follow her. He had turned to a little group of ladies near him.

"And do you like London?" continued the cousin, trying to make talk to Hilda, when a young man whom she knew intervened, and asked her if she would have some supper.

"Me!" she exclaimed, in a voice of surprise. "Do you mean me? Do you know my back is so often taken for Cecilia's!" and with a laugh she disappeared.

An interval, hardly long enough for Hilda to feel that she was alone, followed, before Marmaduke had come back to her. Just as they left the room she noticed the lady with the beautiful pearls presenting Mr. Fieldes to the Duchess of A.

They went down to supper, and ate some delicious sandwiches, like little breakfast-rolls cut up in a hurry. Hilda was enthusiastic about the rolls, about the lemonade (she had resolved not to drink champagne), about everything. It all seemed like a play got up for her amusement, the little snatches of talk she could distinguish, the affectations which she half admired although they amused her. She said to Marmaduke:—

"Isn't this fun? don't you enjoy studying life? I do."

"Do you call this life?" inquired Marmaduke in a dull absent voice.

However, it didn't matter; there was plenty of amusement without his being required to add to it.

"Shall we go?" he asked when she had finished.

"Yes," said Hilda and they made their way to the door. When they got close to it they were brought to a standstill by the crowd, and as they stood there silently Hilda heard some words which she hardly noticed then, but which came back to her afterwards with an almost superstitious sense of their appropriateness to her conduct that evening. A rather affected slightly *passée* woman, with a good figure and an air of conscious youthfulness, was engaged in an argument with an old general, when with mock solemnity he turned from her with the following words: "Too late, my dear lady, too late. You are not the first woman who has thrown away a faithful heart from some motive of pique, and who has lived to repent it."

The crowd in the hall had increased, going and coming from the supper-room, with additional arrivals of late theatregoers. Presently Hilda thought she recognised the face of a well-known actor among them.

"Isn't that S— B—?" she whispered eagerly to Marmaduke.

"I don't know, I have only seen him once," Marmaduke answered abstractedly. "Shall we go this way?" he was leading her across the hall to a small deserted conservatory.

"The German is singing again," observed Hilda, who wanted to go back to the drawing-room. Marmaduke made no answer. The little conservatory was empty; a few Chinese lanterns lit it dimly. It was decidedly dull; there was nothing to see; and the magnificent baritone upstairs was rolling out the "Two Grenadiers," which she had often heard mentioned as his masterpiece.

"It *is* the 'Two Grenadiers,'" said Hilda sadly, but again Marmaduke made no answer.

Suddenly he took hold of her hand with his left one, and she trembled. Alas for them both! it was the worst moment he could have chosen. He was jealous, he was irritable, he was ill and overstrung; and these feelings, though they added intensity to his tones, did but arouse a combative instinct in her. His mind and heart were simple and manly; he was particularly devoid of pettiness, but all the more incapable of dissimulating the kind of irritation which his love experienced from Hilda.

"Hilda," he said abruptly, "I love you: could you," a little break in his voice interrupted him, "could you care for me?"

Startled beyond measure, nervous and frightened at this very new experience, she looked up at the angry eyes (as they seemed to her) that were looking at her, and the spirit of defiance broke out in her. She defied him; and she defied something else, she could not have told what for the world.

"No, I could not," she cried angrily, "and," she went on passionately, "I don't believe it."

Her tone had a bitterness that surprised herself. Oh why, she thought, must she go through this, why did he not see that it was humiliating to her? was his self-deception so complete? This was not an intentional mockery, she felt sure, but it was an utter delusion. She almost said aloud:—

"Can't you see, won't you see, that you still love Madge?"

Poor child, it was hard to bear. Mark's insinuations, Madge's vanity, Cecilia's broader hints, had done their work; and she believed it now. It seemed to her so cruel that she should be asked for love for the first time in this way. Was he trying to save himself from Madge? Perhaps he knew that Madge cared for some one else? Could he be asking for her heart as a refuge? She could not be sure. She was sure he cared for Madge. All else was confusion.

Men have often been angry with the goodness that seems to make women hard. Hilda was crying out against the goodness that could make a man so stupid.

"Oh, thank God, thank God," she thought, "that I don't love him, or this would be unbearable." Her eyes filled with tears. She turned from him abruptly, and began to pull at the leaves of a creeper by her side.

Marmaduke was greatly startled. He had been intensely anxious. In his fear that she had already been attracted by Fieldes, he had only put his fate to the touch lest delay might make things worse. But he had expected to be treated gently. This almost rough, passionate conduct startled and hurt him. His wounded irritability turned into temper, and he lost the chance of making her explain herself. Never had she looked more lovely than when answering him so defiantly. But never had he felt more capable of tearing himself violently from her than he quite suddenly did at this moment.

"You do believe in Mr. Fieldes?" he said in a smothered voice.

"And if I do?" said Hilda angrily.

"It is no business of mine. Thank you, Hilda. Well, though he is an unbelieving snob and though he doesn't care for you—"

"Who said he did care for me?" interrupted Hilda angrily.

"Though he doesn't care for you a tenth part as much as I do, I can hardly wish that he should be treated as I have been treated. And, Hilda, if another man should ever offer you his heart and tell you that he is ready to do anything on this earth to please you, remember that this sort of treatment may send one to the devil."

Hilda gave a little sob, and with her head still averted and her trembling hands pressed against the wall, she cried: "Oh, Marmaduke, how can you, how can you?"

Perhaps, perhaps if he had made her turn round then—but at that moment Madge appeared in the doorway escorted by Mr. Fieldes.

"Come, Hilda," she said, "I'm tired and want to get home."

Madge looked both tired and worried; but Hilda was too much occupied with the control of her own face to notice her chaperon's. The two ladies fetched their cloaks and found Marmaduke and Fieldes waiting for them in the little crowd outside in the hall. Madge immediately began to speak to her cousin in a low voice.

"Marmaduke," she said, "where have you been all the evening? Why didn't you talk to me? Are you too going to leave me alone?"

The sad little face was turned up to him, gentle and pitiful. He looked down at her with a glow of sympathy. He too was hurt. He too was wounded and sore. He smiled at her sadly.

"And I thought it was I who wasn't wanted," he said, as if it were a small joke. Hilda turned away from them to Mr. Fieldes.

"When," she said eagerly, "are you going to the Positivist Chapel?"

"Next Monday, so Mrs. Riversdale has decreed," answered Fieldes.

They were walking across the hall as they spoke. Mrs. Hurstmonceaux was standing on the lowest step of the staircase leaning on the banister. Lord Bellasis was below listening to her, but as Madge came towards them he said good-night to his hostess and vanished. It was the third time that Madge had been close to him, and he had made no attempt to speak to her. Marmaduke had gone to see after the carriage. Mrs. Hurstmonceaux drew Madge towards her and they sat down on a step of the staircase.

"Child," said the older woman in a half-jesting tone, "you mustn't look so tired."

"No," said Madge bitterly, "I know I mustn't. A lonely woman should be as strong as a giant." Madge's eyes looked large and ghostlike and her hair was ruffled. Mrs. Hurstmonceaux did not like bitterness or untidy hair. That very evening she had been talking to the Duchess of A. about Madge, who had been the link between them. Laura had flowed in speaking of her friend's virtues, and the duchess had said it was quite time that she should marry again. Mrs. Hurstmonceaux had answered by a still further eulogium.

"Madge," she said, "always brings to my mind those words, 'blessed are the pure in heart.'"

"Quite so," said the duchess, who had had enough of the subject, "and now, dear Mrs. Hurstmonceaux, find her a husband; she is so pretty, it will not be difficult," and she glanced expressively at Lord Bellasis. But even to a duchess Laura betrayed nothing.

Since that little talk Laura had heard other things about Madge which pleased her less, and she did not quite approve of her as she appeared in the hall in company with Marmaduke. She was going to speak when Madge prevented her.

"Laura," she said in a low hurried tone, "Laura, have you said anything to Lord Bellasis?"

"No," said Mrs. Hurstmonceaux, looking at her keenly; "I think that that little affair had better die a natural death."

Madge looked up quickly.

"Don't let him know that I can't do it,—I mean not at once, you know. But, Laura, why has he avoided me the whole evening?"

"Why, indeed?" said Mrs. Hurstmonceaux in a light tone, as Marmaduke came within earshot.

Hilda and Madge drove home in silence, Madge was generally observant, Hilda not the reverse; but they were both self-occupied, and with a common egotism each supposed herself to be watched by the other. Madge, in order to distract attention from her own tired face, took Hilda into her room when they got home, and talked brightly while her maid was undressing her. Since she had been in trouble Madge had given up any little habits of consideration for her servants she might have had before, and Celestine in particular had had a hard life of it. So Madge and Hilda spoke with eagerness of the party, laughed at the frumps, and admired the beauties with spirit for some few minutes, until the maid had gone. Hilda then rose to go also, but was surprised by Madge's suddenly putting her arms round her neck and kissing her, while she looked at her with dry, burning eyes of apparent affection.

Madge was not at that moment very particularly devoted to Hilda. She was wilfully ignoring the hint she had received that she might help her towards a happy marriage with Marmaduke; in fact, Madge's deluded vanity made her half-consciously inclined to keep him to herself. But that night she wanted something to kiss, something to cling to, some human touch to soothe her, some living thing to caress, and to pet her in return.

Hilda was touched. Madge, a tiny, childlike figure in her silk night-gown, her little feet half showing in her Turkish slippers, for the first time weak and clinging, was very pathetic. Hilda kissed her affectionately.

"Go to bed, little Madge," she said. And Hilda persuaded her to lie down, tucked her into the sheets, and smoothed her hair away from her forehead.

"Don't go, Hilda, stay and talk to me."

But after a very few moments of disjointed talk Madge felt sleepy and said so irritably. Then Hilda gladly escaped to her own room, and when she had torn off her gown—that lovely new gown which Madge would have respected had it been hers, even in the moment of supremest emotion—she knelt down by her bed, buried her face in her hands and sobbed.

Oh why, why was it all so sad? Why had her first party been such a horrid failure? Why was Marmaduke like that? Why, oh why, was she herself such a nasty horrid girl?

She said her prayers with words broken by sobs, then got up and brushed out her great mass of hair, threaded with gold among the brown, and stood looking at herself in the glass. She was thinking the matter over after a favourite manner of hers, as though it were somebody else's affair.

"Such a pity," she thought, looking at the girl who was brushing her hair in the glass, "such a nice Catholic marriage it might have been, such a noble-hearted, good man, so true and strong; and she a remarkably clever girl; it was a pity he didn't really care for her; he had never got over that other affair, you know, and the girl didn't care the very least bit for him. Oh dear, what a stupid world."

CHAPTER IX

MADGE HAS A NEW FEAR

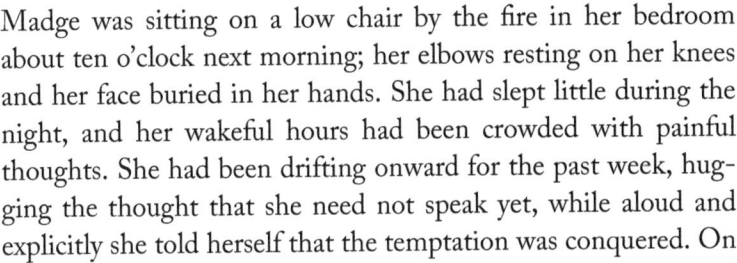

Madge was sitting on a low chair by the fire in her bedroom about ten o'clock next morning; her elbows resting on her knees and her face buried in her hands. She had slept little during the night, and her wakeful hours had been crowded with painful thoughts. She had been drifting onward for the past week, hugging the thought that she need not speak yet, while aloud and explicitly she told herself that the temptation was conquered. On the strength of the fact that she had said "no" to Laura, she had continued to repeat her prayers, and go to Sunday Mass; but that she had not said "no" to Lord Bellasis himself had been the main fact of her present existence.

However, this phase of her mental life had been too misty, too intangible to put into words. In it what was explicit was not true; but it was reiterated loudly enough to allow the underlying current to flow on undisturbed. She had wondered what she was going to do, as though she had been a mere onlooker. And to the onlooker the prospect had brilliant glimpses, special scenes, on yachts, in drawing-rooms at Bellasis Castle, with a little figure admirably dressed as their centre. But she had not looked in the face of that little figure. She dreaded to detect on it a look of shame. For that little figure of Madge, Countess of Bellasis, safely and securely assured by English law of the rights of a Christian wife, would be in her own eyes weighted with dishonour. That in Madge's eyes the woman who married an innocent divorcee was no more than his mistress, was a simple fact which must be realised before her position can be understood. To state this is not controversy; it is a mere matter of psychological accuracy, necessary for the understanding of the rest of her story.

In this state of mind Madge had gone to the party at the Hurstmonceaux', taking with her Cecilia as well as Hilda. She had gone, as she always went into society now, wondering whether Lord Bellasis would be there, and wondering what would be the outcome of the evening if they should meet. They had not, as we have seen, met once since Laura's communication. And the relief she had felt on each occasion when she had expected to see him, had imparted a touch of real thankfulness to her prayers. Somehow, too, she was feeling more kindly towards Skipton. She liked Marmaduke's visits, which were growing more frequent. She had read and re-read a kind letter from the squire about some unimportant matter of business. The very day it arrived she had expected to meet Bellasis at an evening party. Madge had put down the letter with a short sigh before starting. This was the evening on which Bellasis had actually been in the room when she arrived. But he had left a few minutes later, apparently without having seen her come. It was a relief. And when she got home that evening she read the squire's letter again, and the tears stood in her eyes.

At the Hurstmonceaux' party she again expected to meet Lord Bellasis, and she thought she felt more equal to it—less uncertain of the issue.

"It will be our parting," she murmured to herself. But she was not long in the room before a new development of the situation dawned upon her. She began to doubt whether the temptation were still offered to her, if the game were really still in her own hands. The knowledge of power which had blown out the sense of her own consequence to its full extent, received a warning prick. Perhaps, after all, this large bit of the world's best of goods was not lying at her feet.

That evening she spent two hours in the same room with Lord Bellasis and he did not approach her; he all but cut her. It was the first time that he had ever failed to make her a centre for others at an evening party, by his own marked attentions. His presence had in the ordinary course an extraordinary effect on the demeanour of his women friends in her regard. It was to her the breath of life to belong to that set of women, and she had managed so admirably with them all at Bellasis. There had been several of the group at Laura's house, for it was known that Lord Bellasis was to dine there. This was almost the first large party he had gone to since the opening of Parliament, and they were there surrounding their idol, gracefully, without too much insistence, but with an air of belonging to each other and admitting one another into a family party. And some of them when they first came in greeted Madge as quite one of themselves.

But with the marvellous rapidity of their trained perceptions, they had quickly seen that Lord Bellasis was leaving her out in the cold, and was occupying himself with Cecilia. Nor did Cecilia quite keep her head. Her spirits rose too high, and her "good night" had a touch of impertinence towards her hostess as she went away with young Lady Farley, ignoring Madge who had brought her to the party.

And Madge felt that Laura saw it all. She knew that Laura knew that while she appeared to be so happily occupied with the Austrian *attaché*, while she had supper with the often-snubbed but now radiant Mark Fieldes, she was really in torment. And yet if she had but sent him a message, if she had answered when he wanted her to answer, what would have been her position now? Engaged to Lord Bellasis. The scene at that evening party might easily be imagined. The contrast was vividly present to her. If Bellasis had given her the slightest opportunity, Madge would at that moment have offered herself to him instantly and absolutely. Her soul would have been a poor price to pay to be saved from such humiliation. But he had not given her the chance, and in the watches of the night she doubted whether he ever would give her the chance again.

In the morning light, with her still cold hands pressed on her hot forehead, and her untasted breakfast on the tray beside her, she tried to understand better what was passing. An unpleasant light was thrown on the events of the past days. Had Lord Bellasis's frequent failures to appear come from a wish to avoid her? What did he mean? Was he trying to retire, to back out of what he had said? Had he taken her silence as a refusal? Or had Laura said something to put him off or turned it into a refusal? Had he perhaps never meant Laura to be so explicit? Had Laura been playing some game of her own? It was possible that he had only asked Laura to feel her way, and find out what in general would be Madge's view of the marriage of an innocent divorcee. And had Laura made too much of it, and then—Madge rose and walked about the room, the thought was maddening—had Laura for some purpose of her own led Madge on to a refusal before he had proposed?

She became more and more confused, rejecting suspicions and recurring to them again in a circle that always ended in the wish, the determination, to see Lord Bellasis alone, to judge for herself what power she now had over him, and for how long he would stand suspense. "It is not too late, surely it is not too late," she muttered, "and yet—" She heaved a deep sigh; but it was time to dress now.

Before she began the long ceremony which produced the dainty finished effect in which she was remarkably successful, she moved to a corner of the room and knelt down as usual before the little altar.

She concluded her prayers rather abruptly, and walked across to the glass. She saw that her eyes betrayed the weeping, and bathed them in hot water; then she went back to the dressing-table and powdered her face artistically, glancing at the effect with each addition of whiteness.

She then rang for her maid, and soon they were both absorbed in work which took their whole attention, and had a singularly soothing influence on Madge's nerves. The sense of perfect grooming is a wonderful sedative. If—

> Serenely full the epicure may say,
> Fate cannot harm me, I have dined to-day.

so also—

> Serenely fair the *élégante* may say,
> Fate cannot harm me, I'm well dressed to-day.

But with neither can such pleasant feelings be sure of remaining unruffled. As with other sedatives, the effect is passing.

Madge was writing notes in the drawing-room when Hilda came in from a shopping expedition with her maid. Madge was glad to see her. She wanted somebody to talk to, and she began to discuss Hilda's purchases with animation. A hat had to be looked at and some shoes. Madge approved the shoes but condemned the hat.

"I must take you back there this afternoon," she said. "You shouldn't try to buy a hat alone. Where did you go to for it?"

"I saw it in a shop in Oxford Street."

"My dear, how silly," said Madge in a superior voice; "you never can get the right things in the wrong places, unless you've a genius for rearranging them yourself. How could you judge of it from outside; and when you got in I suppose they overpersuaded you? I must take you to a proper place. Valérie had some beauties yesterday. Yes, we will go to Valérie."

And to Valérie Hilda knew they would go, and would buy a hat costing three times as much money as the one Brown had helped her to choose; and her bills were already rather alarming. One of Madge's consolations in the present crisis was to spend a great deal of money; and as she was in an extravagant mood, she was extravagant for Hilda as well as for herself.

"It was a stupid party last night," said Madge suddenly, Hilda blushed scarlet, and Madge thought she was thinking of her.

"I'm not a judge of parties," said Hilda, putting the condemned hat sadly into its box. "I thought there were some very pretty people. Who was the dream of beauty in pale green satin—she wore black pearls?"

"Oh, that is a cousin of Mrs. Hurstmonceaux, Mrs. Amherst, a great friend of the Duchess of A. She is really handsome, though I shouldn't be so ecstatic as you are about her. Her features are too straight and it's a great pity her teeth are not straighter. She married Mr. Amherst two years after he divorced his first wife."

Hilda looked at Madge in horrified amazement.

"Oh, Madge, how shocking!"

Madge gave a loud laugh which jarred on Hilda.

"My dear innocent, even in your sylvan retirement you must have heard of divorce laws."

Madge's face darkened as she spoke.

"Of course I've heard of divorce, but I never, never thought that a good woman would really marry a man like that. But then I suppose my beauty isn't a good woman. Oh dear, how sad!"

Hilda was standing with a bunch of scarlet anemones, which she had just bought, held up to her face, pretending to sniff at their scentless magnificence, but in reality trying to hide the blushes which would come in talking of such a subject. For a moment Madge thought Hilda had been put up to the situation, that she had been prying upon her, and was now preaching. She sprang up, upset the small table that stood by her chair, and rushing across to Hilda caught hold of her two hands roughly.

"What do you mean by saying that; tell me what you mean?"

For a moment Hilda thought that Madge was really mad. She had thought her very very odd before. Sometimes she looked so excited as to appear almost crazy, and now evidently she was becoming violent. What on earth was Hilda to do? The brilliant colour faded from her cheeks and she looked a picture of terror.

"Tell me," repeated Madge, tightening her grasp, "what do you mean? Who has put you up to preaching at me?"

"You?" cried Hilda again, "what on earth have you got to do with it?"

Madge felt that she had made a mistake. She dropped Hilda's hands and tried to recover herself.

"Really, Madge, what *do* you mean?" ventured Hilda, when she saw a more sane expression return into her companion's face.

"What could I have said? You must have misunderstood me. One comfort is that however worldly Catholics are, this is not one of their temptations."

"Thank you, my dear, I'm perfectly aware that I am a Catholic," said Madge in a cold angry voice, "but I don't know why you should think me so worldly."

"You?" cried Hilda, "what *can* you have to do with it?" She coloured violently, but before she could speak again Madge had rushed past her out of the room with streaming eyes. A moment afterwards through the door which Madge had left open Hilda heard her saying in a voice of forced brightness:—

"Good morning, Marmaduke, I've got to see my dressmaker, but I'll be down presently. You will find Hilda in there."

Hilda was new to such agitations. In her quiet life at home there had been no scenes, no sudden necessity for command of countenance when her feelings were excited. Feelings had been deep but placid. It might be almost a want in her education that she hadn't mixed more in the lives of men and women, and come across something of their struggle, pain and passion. Madge's rushing out of the room in tears unnerved Hilda completely; it frightened her with doubts as to how she herself could ever learn how to behave, how to be tactful and discreet and not hurt people's feelings, when they looked half crazy and the slightest word seemed to fire a mine. Hilda was naturally given to generalisations, and she was immensely oppressed by the difficulties of life and her own incapacity for dealing with them. Last night she had been clumsy and rough with Marmaduke; to-day she had made Madge cry. What a world! Making a hasty effort to appear natural she began to unpack the hat again so as to have a look of occupation. Poor new hat, it was not receiving the gentlest treatment. Marmaduke finding her blushing, her hands trembling, and on her eyelids a suspicion of tears which she seemed anxious to hide, felt a sudden uncontrollable hope that she might be softening, might even be sorry for what she had said the night before. He looked at her eagerly.

"Good morning," said Hilda excitedly, "isn't this tiresome, look at this hat, Madge says it won't do, and yet it doesn't suit me badly, does it?"

She put it on as she spoke and Marmaduke felt a sickly feeling creeping over him. Was she really simply a vain self-occupied girl who could coquette with him just after refusing him? He stood back and looked at her very gravely—how beautiful she was to him, how wonderfully beautiful with the great deep eyes with a suspicious dew on them which had not yet reddened the eyelids; the whole face, with its slightly irregular features which seemed to have been made to express emotion, so tell-tale and sensitive were they, and the exquisitely arched forehead;—no, surely, surely she could not be devoid of feeling. Had he been calmer he must have seen that she was not giving a thought to her own appearance at that moment, and he might have seen that a curious look, a half-sad expression, as if she were asking something from himself, had come into her face. Yes, she was thinking whether in such a difficult world a *very* good man who really and truly cared for one very much would not be—well—nearly everything? But after a second she looked across him to the glass that hung opposite.

"Why," she cried, with a little nervous laugh, looking at the hat in the glass, "it is on the wrong way."

She took it off and began to put it back in the box; she wished Marmaduke would speak and not look so horribly angry.

"They ought to send these things in bigger boxes," she said, sitting down with her back to him and forcing the hat into the cardboard box. "Oughtn't they?" she added interrogatively.

"What things?" asked Marmaduke in a stern voice.

"Why hats, of course," said Hilda, and silence followed; but she could not sit with her back to him any longer. She would be bold. She would try an experiment. She faced round on her chair, leaning over the back, and said:—

"Madge was crying, and it was I who made her cry."

The change was instantaneous, the peculiar way of looking at Hilda was gone, for hope had gone too. This then was what had upset her, nothing to do with him. He sat down and said with interest:—

"Crying, what about?"

"Well," said Hilda hesitating, "nothing"; then it occurred to her that he might think their quarrel was about himself, and she must say something more to prevent that.

"It was about a friend of Madge's whom I don't like."

"Who?" persisted Marmaduke.

"Mrs. Amherst."

"Mrs. Amherst, is she a friend of Madge's?"

"Yes, Madge was angry at my thinking she could not be a good woman because she married Mr. Amherst. She said I was preaching at her."

"Yes!" said Marmaduke, but it was a questioning "yes."

Hilda was shy and could not go on. Marmaduke was too anxious to hear about Madge to be considerate even for her, she thought.

"Only it ended in my saying that it was a comfort Catholics were out of some temptations, you know, and Madge said angrily that she quite remembered that she was a Catholic."

Hilda had looked away as she spoke, and was greatly relieved at having said so much. She felt that there was something in the air beyond her comprehension, and Marmaduke above anybody could be trusted. He was looking puzzled and worried.

"Hilda," he said quickly in a low but more natural voice, "perhaps I ought not to worry you by being here after last night. The correct thing would be for me to go away, I know; but you will understand that I must be here," his voice trembled, "for Madge's sake, won't you? There is something up I can't understand, and she has nobody to help her."

"Yes, of course," said Hilda in a voice of disappointing hardness, "of course, let us play as the children do that last night never happened."

A moment's silence and then Mr. Mark Fieldes was announced.

"I came to see if you and Mrs. George Riversdale could come to the Positivist Chapel to-day," he said in his sharp metallic voice. "It is going to be closed for repairs and so it is our last chance."

"Delightful," cried Hilda, "and you will stay to lunch, won't you? I know," she added, "my cousin would wish it."

But in the animated talk that followed there underlay all other thoughts the remembrance of Marmaduke's earnest trembling voice saying to her: "Hilda, you will understand it is for Madge's sake."

CHAPTER X

TWO LOVERS CONFIDE IN LAURA

Mrs. Hurstmonceaux was sitting in her drawing-room on Thursday morning and her only companion was Mr. Fieldes.

"Is she coming here to-day?" he asked in an anxious voice.

"Yes." Mrs. Hurstmonceaux smiled at a splendid *Gloire de Dijon* in her hand.

Fieldes leant upon the mantelpiece. This was a favourite attitude of his, and he thought it particularly suited to an appearance of admiration and yet sufficient self-assertion in looking at a woman. Fieldes had at one time been sentimentally attracted by the elder lady's not immediately apparent but very real charm; and this it was in him that had partly appealed to her, though she knew enough of human nature to recognise that he possessed a very large faculty for being smitten. That this weakness, however, was of no depth was evinced by her helping him to make his way with Hilda.

"Do you think it would be safe to do it now?" As he spoke he pushed his hair off his temples in a nervous manner, and then remembered to smooth a favourite lock back into its right curve on the forehead.

"What are you afraid of?" asked Mrs. Hurstmonceaux mercilessly. "Is it the cousin?"

"No, it isn't only the cousin. This is the danger. She thinks, you know, that she is going to make me a Catholic, and I'm not at all sure that she will have me if she gives up that hope."

"But why should she give up her ridiculous hope? My dear Mark, leave it all very vague, or, if you like, promise to give it your best consideration. Once you are engaged I think she will stick to you; and you won't mind giving her any number of 'the conditions,' as they call them. I believe you would wish her to keep up her religion thoroughly. For myself I must say the Catholics who don't are very unattractive people."

"But hadn't I better wait and make my way with her first? You know I should be horribly upset now if I lost her—she is quite too charming."

"No," said Laura after a moment's thought, "no, emphatically no. There is nothing that need distress your vanity in my opinion that it is now or never. She is interested in you now, excited by your attentions, and, most important of all, she is piqued with her cousin who is not a cousin. Do not be angry if I say so much. Reflect how natural it is that those two should be brought together. Let her see a little more of life, and she will learn the value of his position. Let her leave London, and all home influences are brought to bear in his favour. He is young, good-looking, virtuous, manly, an eldest son and a Catholic. Is it likely that she will resist? And if he is not intellectual—what is so easy to suppress in a girl as the small amount of thought that generally interferes with her instincts?"

"You make it evidently, obviously hopeless," said Fieldes sulkily.

"Not at all; I am still hopeful. I am almost of opinion that the iron is hot, and I own I think it is no small triumph for you."

There was a touch of the feminine love of inflicting mixed sensations in these words, the feminine satisfaction in social tyranny. They brought so vividly to both their minds the fact that Fieldes could not bear comparison with the advantages that had been ascribed to Marmaduke.

"To carry off the heiress, though a Catholic, and a most beautiful heiress too, will be a triumph. You will have done it in a way to be proud of, by your great gifts and your specially great gift of sympathy. And, Mark, you are wonderfully lucky, for it is a most loyal nature. Conscience," cried Laura, with kindling eye, "is her king. You need never fear. Supposing—for we must be frank—that she does deceive herself and that the handsome not-a-cousin has more hold than we suppose, once she is bound to you, you are safe. But you must be going now for fear she should come in, and I don't want her to find you here."

Laura held out her hand with a gracious smile and he had to rise. He hesitated, and fidgeted with his hat. "Do you mean you would really do it at once?"

"At the next good opportunity."

"And how am I to know which is a good opportunity?"

Laura kept her gravity. He needed soothing.

"My dear friend, you have managed admirably so far, why lose nerve now? And now go you must, for it is past eleven and you will certainly meet her if you stay."

Mark after one or two more inarticulate attempts at words got himself away.

Ten minutes later Hilda appeared. She too needed soothing this morning when she succeeded Mark in Laura's drawing-room. This morning had seemed to confirm the effect of all Cecilia's suggestions about Madge and Marmaduke. Madge had been extremely cross and in very low spirits at breakfast. Hilda had been glad to escape to her own room. When she was ready to walk to Laura's she had gone back to the drawing-room and had found Madge in tears talking to Marmaduke.

Marmaduke's dark face was manifestly troubled; he remained silent after one glance as if to remind Madge of Hilda's presence, a glance which seemed plainly to say to Hilda that she was in the way. As she was leaving the room, after telling Madge in a rather high voice that she must hurry off to Laura, Hilda saw the two reflected in the opposite glass. Marmaduke had drawn his low chair a little nearer to Madge's side, and was leaning forward with an expression of distress and sympathy not untouched by tenderness.

Laura's warm greeting and kindly comment on the brightness of her flushed face were very welcome to Hilda after this.

They were soon sitting together on or rather in a deep cushioned sofa, and half an hour's conversation on the great influence she was exercising on Mr. Mark Fieldes brought Hilda into a more peaceful condition.

In the brief rest she took before dressing for dinner that evening, Laura was lying in her boudoir, drowsily thinking, when she was annoyed at being disturbed by the footman.

"Lord Bellasis wishes to see you." It was a quarter past seven, a most inconvenient moment. "They told his lordship that you were resting; but he said he hoped you would be able to come all the same."

Mrs. Hurstmonceaux was in a very handsome dressing-gown, and whatever art was employed to add to those charms which nature had bestowed upon her, it was not of the kind that could be surprised in an unguarded moment. This served her now; for in an instant Lord Bellasis had run upstairs, and was speaking through the door.

"May I come in?"

"Certainly, I only hesitated as to giving you the trouble of coming up."

Laura opened the door as she spoke. A magnificent fur cloak had been thrown over the dressing-gown. The slight untidiness of the hair was an improvement on its usual almost too correct condition. Her dark but rather inanimate eyes seemed to have some light in their dull depths.

"Well," she said, with a slow smile, "to what may I owe this morning call?"

Bellasis had walked across to the fireplace; he did not seem to have discovered that he was not in the drawing-room. He was in evening dress, rather untidy in its details. It did not suit his great muscular form. No man less spoilt than Bellasis would have ventured to be so careless as to appearance as he was; but then perhaps he knew that some women said that he could not look anything but grand and noble, and so what did it matter? Laura was familiar enough with his very sunburnt face to detect some annoyance, though the regular heavy features would have shown nothing to most of his friends. People said that you never knew whether Bellasis was pleased or angry.

"I came to see how you were getting on," he said slowly, and stooping to pick up the poker. "What a wretched fire!"

"Did you reflect upon the fact that it is the usual hour for dressing for dinner?"

"You were going to dine with the Stapletons?"

"I *am* going to dine with the Stapletons."

"No, you are not, because the party has fallen through. The *clairvoyante* could not come; she is ill. I told Lady Stapleton that it was no use dining if the woman could not come, or at least I said something to that effect."

"But why hasn't Lady Stapleton written to me then?" said Laura.

"Because I undertook to tell you, and Cecilia undertook to tell Mrs. George Riversdale, who was coming it seems; and Lady Stapleton sent notes to the others. I think she is rather cross, and thinks we ought to have dined there; but you see you have a better cook."

Laura started. Her face changed.

"But, my dear Lord Bellasis, you can't dine here. The cook won't have time. You will have a horrid dinner, and then you will ruin her reputation."

"I swear to you I won't," said Bellasis earnestly. "I'm sure you can depend upon the woman. Let us see," and he took out his watch, "half-past seven—say we dine at a quarter to nine. Let her make that *tête de veau à la vinaigrette* we had the other night. I assure you I wouldn't worry. These *impromptu* things often do best."

Laura yielded, rang, and ordered whatever the cook could do in the time. "Though I know she will give warning," she added.

"If she does I shall take her," said Bellasis thoughtfully.

"Now," said Laura, softened by this piece of flattery, "suppose you go away. I will dress and then we will go downstairs."

"But this is comfortable, and that cloak suits you wonderfully. Couldn't you dine in it? Though perhaps it would look a little,— what shall we say,—eccentric downstairs. No, I will give you time to dress, though it is a pity you should; but first let us talk."

Laura sat down at a little distance.

"You are the most spoilt man I know," she thought, "and so the only way to manage you is to spoil you even more than you are accustomed to be spoilt; but your wife will have a time of it, for you have a nasty temper too. I am almost afraid of you myself. I wonder what you have come here to say."

Bellasis had apparently become quite absent minded, and seemed to find sufficient occupation in looking at the photographs on the chimneypiece.

"You have never seen this *clairvoyante?* I wish you had been at the B.'s when Cecilia consulted her. I should like to know if you think her a fraud."

"What did she say to Cecilia?"

"Cecilia wouldn't tell, but she came out shaking and very white, and then of course she talked all sorts of nonsense about the magnificent things the woman had promised her; but yesterday when I got her alone she told me that the woman had been very strange. She had told her that she knew her heart was fixed on a great happiness and that she thought she would attain it, but that if she did not—'If you do fail,' she said, 'you will die an early and miserable death.'"

"And Cecilia dared to invent that," thought Laura to herself. But aloud she exclaimed: "What ridiculous nonsense, isn't it?"

"I don't know," said Bellasis, "I talked to the woman myself, and she said exactly the same to me about Cecilia. I know Cecilia is candour itself, but I thought she might have been overstrung and put her own imagination into it. It's queer anyhow. But you must not breathe a word of it. I should not have said so much to you only I know you are as secret as the grave."

"And when did you see the *clairvoyante?*"

"Yesterday, at her own house. I went to tell her that she must be ill to-day and not go to Lady Stapleton; she was thankful to be paid for an evening's rest."

"And why was she not to go to Lady Stapleton's may I ask?"

"Oh, the whole thing was a bore, and I could not get out of it any other way. And—" he paused and turning to look straight at Laura added, "I did not want to meet Madge."

Bellasis was calm; but there were in his face the unmistakable signs of pain.

"Until she has made up her mind to overcome these absurd scruples?" asked Laura in a suggestive tone.

"Scruples!" said Bellasis bitterly. "I am not sure that Madge and scruples go well together."

"Poor child," said Laura feelingly, "the world does not understand such things."

"Am I the world?" said Lord Bellasis, as if the idea were too ridiculous. "No, what an ordinary man can't understand is what she is about. Mind I should not be surprised if she were a devotee, living out of the world, or even of the very strict good sort like some of the religious people. But for Madge—well, we all know Madge." His voice softened, and he breathed a little hard.

"Is it likely that Madge should have this overstrained ridiculous idea which would befit a nun?"

"Well, but if it is forbidden by her religion to marry under the circumstances?"

"If only I could think that were it. But I am beginning to doubt whether it *is* religion. From what I can learn she is not keeping up her religion at all. If she really cared about it, she would be constantly seeing the priests, and she would be quoting Father this and Father that to you all the time. But that is not all. There are other things—very serious things as I can't help seeing. You must I think allow that a young cousin of her husband's is not her best possible companion, as he is in love with her. It appears to be an old story, and she cared for him before she ever married George Riversdale."

Lord Bellasis paused with knit brows, and then continued:—

"The cousin is there incessantly, and takes the host's place when she entertains. That pretty child who lives with her is evidently in love with him and jealous of Madge."

"Stop," cried Laura, "stop; these are too many assertions already for one sentence. For one thing, I can assure you that the pretty child, if you mean Hilda Riversdale, is likely to be Mrs. Mark Fieldes before long—and I certainly never heard that young Lemarchant was at any time in love with Madge. The whole idea is new to me. How did you hear it?"

"It comes from Mark Fieldes for one," said Bellasis.

Laura was for a moment disconcerted—she had felt sure he would say Cecilia.

"And Fieldes told you this?"

A deep flush of red mounted in Bellasis's face, and his grey eyes looked light and angry under his puckered forehead. Laura was a little frightened. Bellasis was silent.

"I beg your pardon, of course I did not mean that; I mean," said Laura hesitating, "how do you know that Mark Fieldes said all this?"

"Tim heard him talking of it at the Reform, and Tim thinks he is right. Tim was dining with Madge one night, and Lemarchant was there as usual. There was something caught fire, and her gown caught. Lemarchant put it out, and Tim says he could see that he was in love with her. He mooned on in the house, though his hands must have been agony. Cecilia said to Tim at the time, 'Did you ever see a man more in love?'"

Mrs. Hurstmonceaux gave a deep sigh full of meaning at Cecilia's name.

"Yes, I know you don't like Cecilia, but no one has ever said she was anything but frank and open."

"Can't you see?" cried Laura impatiently, "that he is in love with Hilda?"

"And so burnt his hands for Madge?" said Bellasis ironically. "Besides is it likely that this girl should refuse him if he is? You say she will marry Fieldes, a man from nowhere, and hardly a man at all, a sort of producer of clever essays, no money, no manners, no looks; and the other, yes," said Bellasis, with a quiet smile, "the other is a goodly young man, handsome and well-groomed," he looked down at himself and shrugged his shoulders, "all that is wanting to many of us, and quite a sufficiency of acres. Cecilia says that this Hilda is thoroughly in love with him and very jealous of Madge, although she is too young and too *ingénue* to understand much. Don't mistake me. Nobody suspects anything in the least wrong; they are both far too good for that," his voice became sarcastic. "Only you know, or you don't know," he looked bitterly at Laura, "that once when I loved a girl,—it was after my matrimonial incident,—I found that she was quite willing to marry me, most willing, but, as it came out, there was an objection, in her eyes of no consequence, that she loved somebody else who provokingly enough did not own Bellasis Castle. I thought I should never recover from that business. Now, as you know, I have recovered. But you must forgive me if I am a little anxious—a little suspicious. Mind I could almost have been happier now if she had told you at once that I was to think no more about her. If she really had this strong religious objection, she would have refused me definitely at once; but she does not. Am I very mean for thinking that possibly these magnificent scruples are a pretext to cover an indecision due to other motives? She wants to give herself time to choose between us,—between love and wealth. It is an old story."

Laura for a moment kept a startled silence. Cecilia's influence had been stronger than she had expected; and she was much puzzled to find that Mark, for whom she was doing so much, was busy making mischief. Bellasis watched her, and saw that she hesitated.

"You own that this state of things is discouraging?" he said.

"Not in the least," said Laura, gathering her forces, "but I gather that the rumours have been more complicated than I supposed. I saw that Hilda Riversdale was being made use of in some way, but I did not know in what way. As I said just now, Mr. Lemarchant is in love with her, and with nobody else. But, after all, Lord Bellasis, it is not for counter-assertions that you have come here. And I do not wish to enter the arena with people who are imagining or repeating foolish stories, any more than you do. You want definite proof of her love for you, and I own that so do I. The time has come for Madge to make up her mind. She has given no sign of life, though quite three weeks have passed since

I put the question plainly before her. She ought to answer, and she must. But if she will not answer me—and I will make one more trial—let there be an end to all this," a faint flush rose to her cheek; "I shall have done a friend's duty, and no more, both to Madge and to you; you must manage the rest for yourselves. No, no, don't thank me, I don't mean that; but I want you to feel that, for both your sakes, it would only be wrong of me to continue to be what is called 'a mutual friend,' if she does not make up her mind."

This was said with quiet dignity, and Bellasis understood in all simplicity that Laura had laid him under obligations as a man and as a gentleman, whether she should be successful or not. Then the approach of the *impromptu* dinner was announced by the dressing-bell, and Bellasis could no longer keep Laura from dressing.

The meal was as successful as he had predicted, but Laura did not enjoy it, although she had never been more agreeable. She was anxious and worried. She foresaw that the same topic, which she had merely staved off for the moment, must come up again, and she hardly knew what line to take. If Madge were going to be a fool, it would be so much better to have done with her at once. If Laura could only keep off the subject for that evening.

CHAPTER XI

OPPORTUNITY

When Mrs. Hurstmonceaux and Lord Bellasis had finished their coffee and he had refused to smoke, they went slowly upstairs, pausing once or twice to look at some of the queer art treasures she had picked up abroad. A holy water stoup of Delia Robbia ware made them linger at the door. While speaking of it they entered the room, without seeing that there was somebody already in it. Suddenly Laura stopped and looked entirely bewildered; at the other end of the long narrow room, leaning back in a low arm-chair behind the screen, lay a little person in white satin. For a second the figure was motionless, then, leaning forward, Madge showed a face intensely white, with frightened eyes.

"Laura," she cried, trying to rise, and sinking back, "I thought you were sure to be alone. I never thought of asking. I was going to the Rivers' squash, and I felt faint: and I was passing here, and I knew you had been stopped going out to dinner so I thought I might come to you."

"Poor child," cried Laura, leaning over her, "you must have something at once."

"Champagne," said Lord Bellasis decidedly. He had stood in an awkward, embarrassed attitude in the middle of the room.

"No, no," said Madge in a weak voice, "but if you have any sal volatile, Laura."

"Of course," said Laura in a business-like way, "I'll fetch it at once; will you have it hot or cold?" and Madge could only murmur "hot" before Laura had vanished.

The embarrassment of Lord Bellasis redoubled. He moved forward, and taking a large crystal bottle of salts from the table offered it to Madge. She took a long breath, and then said in a weak childish voice:—

"I'm sorry."

"What for?" said Bellasis shyly.

"That I've come here—you didn't want to meet me."

"Good heavens," cried the much distressed man, and Madge leant back with her eyes shut. One white hand held the bottle on her knee, the other lay listlessly beside it.

"Why," she cried, opening her eyes, and with a little sob, "why don't you like to see me?"

The big figure beside her writhed with discomfort.

"Why," he said, "did you never answer me?" the words were jerked out harshly.

Madge began to cry. In another moment he was kneeling beside her chair.

"Don't, don't," he cried helplessly.

"How could I send you a message by her?" sobbed Madge; "I thought you would speak to me yourself if—if—"

"If what?" cried Bellasis with intense anxiety.

"If you really cared, and if," she hurried on now, "and if you didn't care—not very much—I didn't know what to say."

She covered her face with her hands, and her whole frame trembled so that he could feel the chair shaking.

"God knows if I care," cried the deep voice passionately.

"But," persisted Madge, still in her child's tone, "then why didn't you speak yourself?"

"Oh, my darling," cried Bellasis, leaning over her, "I meant it well. I thought it more honourable. I couldn't trust myself not to try and overpower you: and since then—but," he cried joyfully, "never mind since then. Can you love me, darling? Love me, though I am a fool."

He seized her cold hand and kissed it passionately. She put it with a touch, as if a caress, on the bearded chin, smiled, and opened her eyes. They fell on the flushed eager face and earnest eyes of the man kneeling by her. But the smile began to fade in an instant; her head dropped on one side. Madge had fainted. Bellasis leant forward, kissed the cold forehead devoutly, sprang up, and rushed to the door. Laura met him carrying the sal volatile.

"Brandy," he cried, "and quickly. That is no use; get something hot for her feet—quick—but, no, let me fetch it; undo her things,—you know what to do," he rushed downstairs and terrified the butler.

When he came back with the brandy, he found Mrs. Hurstmonceaux and her maid placing the unconscious figure on the sofa. They tried to force brandy between the lips, but failed. Bellasis's face expressed intolerable anguish.

"A doctor," he said, "a doctor would be best."

"Yes," said Laura, "I will send."

"Let me go," he cried; and then a little proudly, "I have the right to go."

Laura gave him a look of sympathy as he hurried away.

An hour later, when Madge had been put to bed, and the doctor had relieved them of anxiety, Laura left her with the maid and went down to the drawing-room. Bellasis was standing looking at the chair where Madge had lain.

"There is not the least cause for anxiety," said Laura.

"I caught Dr. Rule as he came down and he told me she was all right," answered Bellasis; then lifting Laura's hand he kissed it with a courtly gesture. "I won't thank you to-night," he said. "Did she—did she say anything?"

"She whispered that I was to give you her love, and to ask you not to tell anybody yet."

"Of course not. But why, why did she faint?"

"She has strong feelings," said Laura, "and it was the relief from a great strain. When I left her she was sleeping like a child."

Laura did not add that Dr. Rule had given a dose of morphia to secure such a complete rest as the patient needed.

It was then decided that Lord Bellasis should breakfast with Mr. Hurstmonceaux next morning. He was obliged, as Laura knew, to go down to Bellasis in the afternoon for some local business. "But that leaves me three hours, if you don't mind," he concluded.

After he had gone, Laura sank down on a chair to give way to her excitement. The engagement had actually taken place in her house. It could not have been done better if she had planned it herself. And the world would give her the credit of having done it. Then her thoughts dwelt on certain centres, on certain individuals hearing the news; on the paragraphs; on the way the Duchess of A. would say, "So after all it did happen at Mrs. Hurstmonceaux'," and sigh a little for her own daughter that there were not more men to be had like Lord Bellasis.

"There's not an engagement in England except a royal one that would excite so much attention," murmured Laura ecstatically, "and it came off at the Hurstmonceaux'."

"Could she have known he was here?" wondered Laura, who unconsciously almost regretted in the interests of art that it should have ended so simply. Still she was not without employment. "One must tide them through the engagement now," she thought. "A little mystery and secrecy will help. If only he can keep it from Cecilia for a time. She might do anything: she might make public the impediment, and how unpleasant that would be. I suppose that is still the cause of Madge's excitement. I should never have thought her scruple would have died so hard. How Romanism clings to these shallow little people! It must be a short engagement. Her agitation looked like enough to love to-night, and yet—" Laura shrugged her shoulders expressively, "strange if the thing he hankered for he should have missed by a shave, almost a chance. If he had not met Madge to-night—who knows? However, a wife who adores a man in that wild way is a doubtful advantage."

Next morning Lord Bellasis and Mr. Hurstmonceaux, after a brief, "Congratulations allowed?" on the one side, and a friendly nod on the other, ate a big breakfast and talked of the political situation. Laura did not appear till nearly eleven. She had sent a little note to the visitor, giving a good account of Madge, but saying that she was still asleep and must not be woke.

"My dear friend," she said, sweeping into the library, "good morning; you don't want me, I know, but you'll have to put up with me for a time."

Laura when she tried to be skittish bored Bellasis; and if Madge wasn't really ill he didn't see why she was not ready to see him by this time. However, there was enough to talk of, and Laura led him on skilfully to speak of himself. She could not but admire how absolutely satisfied and happy he had become; how his fears had vanished; how Marmaduke and Cecilia were completely forgotten. He quite prattled of the future, of what Madge would like, asked anxiously if Laura thought Madge really enjoyed yachting, and consulted her as to where he could have the family diamond tiara reset to fit Madge's tiny head. Still in the end Laura regretted to find that he and Madge would still have an hour to themselves, but it could not be helped. He was fidgeting again and looked indignant, so Laura yielded.

"I will go and put her on the sofa in my boudoir," she said, "and in five minutes you may come up."

But there was nothing for Laura to regret in that hour. Madge was in a mood of elation, of triumph. The blank of unconsciousness, the dulness of the morphia, seemed to have wiped out all that she did not wish to think of. When the big-framed man knelt by her again, she was not afraid or oppressed. She put her hand on his hair, she let him do what he liked with it; she told him that she had always been afraid of him; she teased him and petted him with a light touch of pride and power that fascinated him. It was to her literally the world at her feet at last; she could pet and punish this king of the society whose notice she had been ambitious to possess but a year before. He wanted to give her presents at once, but she would not have them. "Don't be King Cophetua too soon," she said; and that completed the fascination. She was quite definite, however, about plans. He must keep his engagements in the North even though they extended over a fortnight, but when he insisted she said he might come up and meet her at Laura's once in about a week. His voice growled a little over this. A tear trembled in Madge's eye.

"You see," she said in her weak voice, like the last night's a childish one, "I shall be worried and teased by the priests and people when they find you are not a Catholic." She looked away as she spoke.

"Then why not marry at once?" he inquired, "and go for a cruise in the yacht?"

Madge shut her eyes as if in weary protest.

"But you don't want a grand wedding?" he asked rather roughly.

"No, indeed," sighed Madge: then with a little gulp in her voice, "let it be quite private."

"Well, I'll do as you like and go away, but you will marry me in three weeks."

He spoke with such decision that he thought he had overpowered her, but this was exactly what she wanted him to say.

"Then," he went on, "not a soul shall know, and when I come back in a fortnight—I don't count the one evening I must have in the middle—we will say we are engaged, and then as soon as it is known, we will slip off and be married with the Hurstmonceaux' for witnesses. You shan't be worried, little woman."

"It would be kinder not to tell Cecilia," whispered Madge, as he was leaning over to say good-bye.

"Don't bother your little head about Cecilia, she shall know nothing, but she doesn't deserve much kindness at your hands."

CHAPTER XII

"RABBONI"

The great drawing-room at Skipton never varied much in appearance. When the family were alone there were rather fewer nosegays of brilliant flowers in the centres of the big tables, but there were as many oil lamps and as many wax candles for Mr. and Mrs. Riversdale and Mary as for their visitors. Nor were these lights fed on paraffin oil or composition candles—economy was as little known as luxury at Skipton—pure colza and fine wax lit up its large, dignified, unbeautiful apartments. There, nearly a fortnight after Madge's engagement to Lord Bellasis, Mr. Riversdale was sitting with Mary, after his wife and the household had gone to bed, with the exception of the butler who was waiting in the pantry to put out the lights when the master had retired. Mr. Riversdale was sitting in a large armchair near the fire, looking at the burning coals in silence. Mary was on a low seat by his side with one hand resting on the arm of his chair.

There seemed to be a tired absence of thought in the old face; an anxiety that was latent, not active at the moment, was its most marked expression. In these few weeks Mary had grown thinner, her eyes seemed larger, her features more defined. She had something of the appearance of a convalescent; she looked older, as she might have done after a long and dangerous illness; but there was also the suggestion of new life, of new power, of the subtle promise of health and strength that makes the contrast between youth and age greater in convalescence than in times of normal health.

But Mary had not been ill. None of the loving eyes about her had detected any signs of bad health during the winter. She had hunted as much if not more than ever. Indeed her father had seldom been seen anywhere without her; and it had been a joke among his dependants to say that they wondered the squire didn't take Miss Mary with him to the bench. She had been as cheerful and as bright as ever. Her spirits were still called wonderful by many a tired cottage mother or worn old labourer. Yet a change there had been, if it was only in the rapid deepening of familiar lines of character. There was more gentleness in her voice, more tenderness in her face. She was more drawn to the babies now than ever, and would look at them with a surprised awe-struck tenderness in her blue eyes. There was more of reverence in her manner with the aged, the ill or the suffering. One small trouble her mother used to feel with her had passed—she no longer disliked the society that came and went at Skipton. She was no longer shy with young men, nor did she look awkward or bored when she had to undergo her share of teasing from older friends as to a girl's tastes or a girl's prospects. But when her mother spoke of these things to her father with approval, he never assented with any pleasure. He was fretful on the subject of Mary.

"Improved? I don't see what you mean. Her voice softer? I never heard that it was too loud," his own voice rose as he spoke; "gets on so well with visitors?—what does that matter?—nonsense, nonsense. What do you say? That the change came soon after Madge's visit? She was cross while Madge was here I know, but she has just been her old self since, nothing else."

His wife had not seen him so angry for a long time; and she, poor soul, had her own unacknowledged fears, her own trembling over the girl who was growing so rapidly more beautiful, more gentle, more tender, more entirely lovable than ever to the mother's eyes. And Mr. Riversdale was sometimes testy with Mary herself—and in such a new way, for such strange reasons. One day in Lent he noticed that she ate no vegetables or pudding, only the joint or fish at luncheon and dinner—another time it struck him that she was never to be seen now lounging in a comfortable chair. Then he became irritably conscious of her perpetual unselfishness. He could not make sure what it was she enjoyed and what she disliked. If her eyes sparkled and her face was bright at the question of a day's hunting, it seemed almost equally bright when doing any service for her mother, even when asked to tidy the cupboards in the old schoolroom. She had actually become careful enough in her dress to satisfy her mother. Then she prayed so much; though a year ago her father had often had to remind her of some devotion which she would otherwise have forgotten, or to scold her gently for not being up in time for Mass in the morning. Now Mary never forgot her prayers and was never late in the morning.

Two or three times lately, after Mary had been generally supposed to be in bed, the squire had waited about in the cold passage until he had made sure that what he feared was true, that Mary was in the chapel for nearly an hour after the others had gone to bed. He would shrink back into his room and listen while the loved footsteps passed gently along, and Mary found her way in the dark to her room. And always as he came out of his own door he could not help seeing the Flemish picture of his great-great-aunt who had lived and died in the convent beyond the seas. Mr. Riversdale hated that picture. One day to his wife's astonishment she found that he had told the housemaid to hang it in one of the spare rooms. The squire had never been known to give an order to a housemaid before. It was most unconstitutional. Yet the mistress of the house asked for no explanation and did not appear to know that the picture was no longer in sight when she left her bedroom.

At length there had come an outward sign of a change, a step forward which could not be ignored. The ball which had been put off, as we saw at the opening of this story, on account of the death of a local magnate, was now fixed to take place in Easter week. On the morning on which Mrs. Riversdale had received a card for herself and party she had begun to discuss whom she should invite to stay in the house as usual for the event. Mary had joined in the talk so far, but when her mother asked her to come to her room to see if the ball gown which had been prepared in January could be trimmed with spring flowers, Mary had told them in a low voice that she thought she would rather not go to the ball. After that she had flushed deeply and left the room; the father and mother were quite silent. Then Mr. Riversdale spoke hurriedly:—

"She isn't well," he said, "that's what it is; we must take her to London. She mopes in this horrid old place. She must have a season. She must be presented. That's all she wants. Never mind the money, we will take a house in London." He gathered his letters together as he spoke, and his hand shook. She, poor, big, flabby lady with her narrow mind and slow sensations, seemed to be frightened and bewildered only; but she knew far better than he could allow himself to do what was passing in his mind, and what it was that made the incoherent muttering of patent untruths seem almost like a comfort to him.

That day he had to sit on the bench, and the distraction and the business of the town were a relief. He was a power on that bench. Not that he was eloquent: he adhered without knowing it to the famous rule, never to give a reason for his decisions, he could not in fact have explained himself if he had tried. He had a firm line of his own in interpreting justice; and his reverence for the good old laws and customs of rural England did not prevent his modifying the traditions of the bench very considerably. He shrank from innovations. He would not have smiled on the Society for the Prevention of Cruelty to Children. He would have considered heresy against the game laws very dire heresy indeed. But the man who had kicked or starved his children knew that he would get all the punishment Squire Riversdale could give him, even to the stretching of the law; while the gamekeepers thought him almost dangerously lax.

As he was riding home to Skipton after a day's justicing he heard his name called from the other side of a tall hedge and a wide ditch, and saw a young man he knew, walking along the field adjoining the road.

"Holla, Charlie!" answered the squire. "I didn't see you. Having a walk about your fields, eh?"

"Another farm on my hands, Cousin George," said the youth cheerily, "but won't you come across and see mother now you are so near?"

"No, thank you, Charlie, I must be getting home. Mary wants to go and see about some cottage; a nice life she leads the agent, that girl. But won't you come along with me?"

Charlie's face beamed.

"Delighted, Cousin George," he said, and they then began to talk farming, using terms that they would have thought alarmingly scientific on any other subject. Their talk so far had been shouted rather than spoken, but a tall gate and a bridge across the ditch before long became visible. Charlie vaulted lightly over and was soon walking beside Riversdale's horse. He was a tall, well-built youth of open countenance, a distant cousin of the Riversdales, and a favourite with the squire. The chief unspoken bond between the two men was Mary: but there was much besides in common between them—what Miss Austen would have described as a sense of mutual worth; their entire honesty and singleness of purpose; a certain slowness of intellect and a shrinking from public life perhaps completing their sympathy.

It was as they neared the hall that Charlie unconsciously took up the thread of the dreaded subject which was to make that so memorable a day at Skipton.

"So the hunt ball is to be after all," he said. "Are you going to take a party from Skipton?"

"I think so," said the squire.

"Anyhow, Mrs. Riversdale and Mary will come?" said Charlie anxiously, alarmed at the doubt in the squire's voice. There was a few moments' silence.

"Mary does not want to go," said her father, and he looked away and began to whistle. Charlie stopped short in the road, the squire's horse went slowly on. Charlie looked at the old man's shoulders, it struck him for the first time that Mr. Riversdale had begun to look old and shrunken. He did not seem to know that Charlie had fallen behind him, and so they went on slowly in silence. When inside the Skipton gates they met a groom, and the squire dismounting gave him his horse and walked across the park with his cousin.

Not long afterwards they spoke to each other about that silent walk.

"I was only feeling for myself, trying not to see what things meant," the old man said. "It was hard on you."

"I had never had any hope," said the younger man, and he turned his boyish face away to hide the tears. But the squire did not tell him, indeed could not have analysed had he tried to do so, why it was that the company of the fair, tall youth had been especially trying to him that day.

"It was hard," repeated the squire, "but how came you to understand? I did not understand it myself."

"I don't know," said Charlie, "but I must really have been expecting it, though I did not know I was. It came to me suddenly and yet it did not seem new."

That was three days afterwards. But the day on which they walked so silently across the park has still to be finished as it had then to be lived through. Charlie had his tea with Mr. and Mrs. Riversdale and Mary in the drawing-room, and then in the spring twilight went for a pottering walk with the father and daughter. He left them but a short time before dinner, and the family trio were alone again. Dinner was a silent meal, and then came an almost equally silent hour before the bell rang for night prayers at ten o'clock. Then Mr. and Mrs. Riversdale and Mary betook themselves upstairs to the tribune of the chapel and waited there until the servants had filed in below and found their places, the men on one side, the women on the other. Somewhat monotonous, somewhat old fashioned and pompous sound those morning and night prayers of the old *Garden of the Soul* to modern ears, but not one word would the squire have altered. Had he not heard them all his life? had he not wondered in his childhood what his father could mean by longing to be "dissolved" every night? there really seemed to be so little in common between his father and a lump of sugar.

So on this night like every other night the squire's deep voice went monotonously on, until the quantum of vocal prayer for night in the *Garden of the Soul* was finished, and then the little congregation remained for a few moments of silent prayer. At length the servants with the exception of one pious footman had gone quietly away, and Mary and her father and mother were left alone. Ten minutes passed and then Mrs. Riversdale rose and the others followed. It was not yet half-past ten, but Mrs. Riversdale liked to go to bed early, while her husband and Mary always enjoyed nearly an hour of talk and draughts in the drawing-room after night prayers. As usual therefore Mrs. Riversdale kissed Mary and bade her good-night at the top of the front stairs that led down into the hall, but to-night she forgot to give her usual caution not to stay up too late. As the father and daughter walked down the broad shallow steps she stood for a moment watching them, then she went slowly and heavily to her own room. She did not know that she wished it to be otherwise, but as she went slowly along the passage she thought of the baby days when Mary had seemed almost wholly to belong to her, when her husband had been too awkward to hold the rounded little figure, and the baby had laughed triumphantly in its sense of security when it was back in its mother's arms.

Mary and her father had then settled themselves as was seen at the beginning of this chapter, he in his big arm-chair, she on the low seat by his side with one hand on the arm of his chair. They were silent, intensely conscious of each other's presence, dreading what might come. At length Mr. Riversdale laid a trembling hand on Mary's and said in an almost testy voice:—

"Foolish child, why don't you want to go to this ball?"

"Father," Mary's voice did not tremble now, "father, it is because I want to be a Sister of Charity."

There was silence. Mr. Riversdale took his hand away and covered his face; he did not speak or move. Mary slipped down on her knees by his side. "Father, father," she cried, "look at me, kiss me, help me, father dear, help me." She put her face against his shoulder and cried freely.

"You would leave us?" he said slowly, still not moving. "Are you sure you have a vocation? George has gone, and now you go."

"Oh! father—don't, don't," cried Mary. "I can't bear it, oh, father, if you knew the pain it has been."

"Has been!" he repeated, and he took his hands away and looked at her.

"Yes, it was leaving you, leaving mother that made it seem hard then. I was wicked, father, and I tried not to see it. I had hoped all my life that if I were spoken to I should say 'Rabboni,' but I didn't": a look of pain came over her face different from the sorrow of those free flowing tears. "Still, He is so good, He will forgive me and take me all the same."

Her hands were clasped. She was leaning back and her look passed from her father to a crucifix that hung above his head.

"If I am allowed to be a Sister of Charity,"—she paused, her face was lit up with a strange light.

Then he knew that the blow had surely fallen. He looked at her beautiful face, he thought he had never known its full beauty before. The strange pain of the supernatural was upon him, a wild sense of rebellion, of terrible desolation. He seemed almost ready to repel her too. Was this cruel goodness, this selfish self-lessness his own Mary's? He shrank back; the look of brightness left her face; she looked at him longingly, looked at him as she had looked as a child when afraid of his anger. He felt cruel too. *That* added to his pain. Why make it harder for her? Harder! Would to heaven he could make it impossible! His Mary to lead a life of sorrow, of poverty, of labour, of suffering! How did they know that she was fit for it, strong enough for it? Why, it might—it might kill her! But who were the "they"? Whose fault was it? It was not Mary's. No—it was—yes! it was the fault of— Him who called her. He bent his head. Mary was standing now, kissing him, fondling him. She had his arm round her; he too was weeping; and she could hear him whisper in her ear one word—*"Rabboni."*

CHAPTER XIII

SIDE-LIGHTS FROM CELESTINE

Madge had accepted Lord Bellasis without either Marmaduke or Hilda perceiving any change which put them on the road to discover her secret. Yet Marmaduke believed himself to be doing his best to find out the mysterious danger to Madge of which Cecilia had warned him. He came dutifully to the house; he led the talk as near as Madge would let him to the question of religion and to any topics that might break down her reserve. While he spoke or Madge answered he was intensely conscious of every movement of Hilda's; or if she was absent he was wondering how soon she might come in, and his conversation inevitably turned from Madge's interests to some allusion to Hilda or question about her. Not that he found Madge responsive on this topic. She had no thought to spare for Hilda or Marmaduke or Cecilia, beyond her anxiety as to what they knew and what they could mean by the faintest allusion to Lord Bellasis, or what they could suspect as to herself.

Marmaduke in some ways teased her the most. She was worried by his constant visits. She would have liked to be able to tell Bellasis safely that she saw very little of him. For though nobody had hinted to her that he had been used as an unconscious means of exciting Lord Bellasis's suspicions, she had had enough feminine penetration to discover a note of jealousy in her masterful lover's careless tone, when he had alluded to the handsome cousin. And, moreover, now that the die was cast, the Skipton relatives in general were a reminder of the painful wrench which could not long be postponed. Yet she dared not shake Marmaduke off at present. It was much safer to keep him near her and to blind him herself to what was going on, than to let him go away. For who knew where a rumour began? Bellasis was so careless in details. Every day—sometimes twice a day—a large envelope with B. written in the corner was posted by the servants at Bellasis Castle; and although it went straight to Madge's bedroom and was soon under lock and key, who might not notice and report from the other end?

She felt that the merest piece of gossip or a premature paragraph, which Marmaduke would usually be the last man to attend to, would now act as a match on a train of gunpowder. Marmaduke was in fact hovering on the verge of discovery; and if he had been on terms with Mark Fieldes, or less strained in his relations with Hilda, he might have at least found out that Lord Bellasis was the hero of the mystery. But as it was, Madge and Marmaduke, Mark and Hilda, jogged along side by side like so many horses with blinkers, looking onwards in front of them at their own aims, and seeing little or nothing of all besides.

But one person at this time, during the fortnight after the engagement, knew pretty well the state of things. This was Madge's maid Celestine. Celestine during the autumn had been with her mistress at Bellasis Castle, and had there contracted a sort of conditional engagement to the under butler. The under butler was treated with peculiar friendliness by the valet, on account of the latter not being on speaking terms with the butler. Ample, therefore, were Celestine's means of obtaining information; and she had a masterly power of treating details in their due proportions. It was all very well to say that Lord Bellasis had invited her mistress so often simply because she was of use to his aunt, Lady Campion, and that everybody knew he was in love with Miss Rupert. *Tiens!* All that was really very interesting, but then why didn't he marry Miss Rupert? No, no; Celestine said little; she was content to wait. But then had come several weeks in London and no Lord Bellasis, and she was tired of a dingy London house, and madame was *maussade* and *triste,* and in fact intolerable to wait upon.

But worse was to come. The very week when Lord Bellasis was coming up, off they went to that abominable Skipton. What was the meaning of that? and with Miss Rupert in London at the very same time. Well, happily that didn't last long, and back they came to London. But what was the use? Lord Bellasis came not. Madame gave dinners and Lord Bellasis did not come; there was not even a card in the hall. So three weeks passed, and then one day madame had seemed furious after Miss Rupert had been to see her, and had told Celestine that the dinner-party she had been going to was put off. That evening madame went to Madame Hurstmonceaux' and fainted there, and when Celestine was sent for to bring the things for the night she soon learnt what had happened. Celestine was in the seventh heaven. All had come right. No doubt mischief had been made by that bold Miss Rupert; but, ugh! who cared for her now? Celestine's mind became full of happy visions of the future, leading on to the time when the under butler should be the butler, and she herself should rule over the housekeeper's room at Bellasis Castle.

"But *they* can marry *now!*" she concluded with a sigh of envy.

Still, things did not seem to be going as smoothly as the maid had expected. From that time madame's conduct, her air, everything about her, became a positive mystery. The first morning indeed she was excited, triumphant, all that was natural, quite gay. But after that madame began to become odd. Why all this secrecy? Why this fuss about bringing the letters so quickly upstairs? Why all the mystery as to the shopping? Miss Hilda mustn't know there were new tea-gowns. Miss Hilda must not see the yachting costumes. Only Mrs. Hurstmonceaux, *toujours* Mrs. Hurstmonceaux. Why couldn't a great lord like Lord Bellasis announce his marriage like a man? "Enfin c'est tout ce qu'il y a de plus extraordinaire. Nous ne faisons pas comme ça en France heureusement." And Celestine shrugged her shoulders and sniffed suspiciously.

But then it appeared that there was much less mystery at Bellasis Castle. His lordship put his letters in the great china tray in the gallery just as usual, and a valet or an under butler could see the address to Mrs. George Riversdale from two yards off. Then my lord had been fussing about in his mother's boudoir and had had a long talk with the housekeeper, who mentioned to the whole table at dinner in her room that she intended to keep her own counsel, and that changes in her opinion were not always for the best.

So the anxiety for secrecy was not so much on the part of Lord Bellasis as on that of madame. And one little incident about a week later proved this beyond dispute. Madge was in the drawing-room with Marmaduke and Hilda, after an early dinner before going to the play. They were drinking coffee and Hilda was trying, as far as she dared, to get Madge to start, as she did not wish to miss the first act, after Madge's usual habit. The butler came into the room just as Madge was saying rather crossly that she would not be hurried over her coffee, and Hilda had moved away to the fireplace to conceal her impatience.

"A man has called from Garrard's, ma'am, to fit on the tiara by desire—"

Madge leapt up exclaiming:—

"It is some stupid mistake," and ran out of the room, meeting Celestine, who had brought down her opera cloak, at the door.

"Show him into the study downstairs and I will explain the mistake. Come, Celestine," and as she passed into the study she told Celestine to follow her and to lock the door after them.

There stood by the table an elderly man of important and responsible bearing, with one hand reverently guarding a large red morocco case that lay on the writing-table. Madge, with heightened colour and in a hesitating voice began:—

"There is some mistake. I don't know why you wish to see me."

As she spoke her eyes glanced furtively at the old red jewel case with its gilt coronet. The box dated back to the days before George III had created the Lord Bellasis of his day an earl.

The man bowed deferentially, and held out a letter, which placed the matter beyond dispute. In it Lord Bellasis stated that he wished the tiara to be made to fit Mrs. George Riversdale and to have any alteration in the setting that should be ordered by that lady.

To Celestine's relief madame after that made no further comedy of not knowing why the tiara had been brought. And indeed it would have been a thousand pities to lose such a sight. Both mistress and maid gave a little gasp of admiration and turned to each other for a moment in the human need for sympathy in strong emotions. It was a complete *parure* of rubies and diamonds with a coronet rising above the necklaces, bracelets and brooches. The diamonds sparkled and the regal rubies reposed on the mellow old white velvet, and the whole had an intangible effect of having a long history of its own, a history of triumphs and greatness alternating with dignified retirement. For a moment it struck Celestine that Madge was hardly equal to the jewels, nay, with a rapid feminine instinct she thought for the first time that in spite of her beauty and her gift of minute elegance, madame would hardly make the great lady, the superb woman whom Celestine would have chosen for such a position. "Tant pis; mais nous ferons de notre mieux," and the little woman firmly resolved that the lady's maid at least should be found not wanting. Meanwhile she quietly gathered all the candles in the room on the table in front of an old Italian glass that hung on the wall, lighted them, and put a chair for madame. As she moved one of the candlesticks, her sleeve knocked over an old photograph of George Riversdale. Celestine paid no heed to it. "*Sapristi!* what a good thing we have done with all that," and with a contemptuous sweep of her skirts, she pushed the frame under the bureau from which it had fallen.

Madge seated herself at the table, her eyes sparkling with excitement and her hands trembling with eagerness, as she pulled at the string of beautiful pearls round her neck to take them off and make room for the diamonds and rubies. A too impatient pull—too rapid for Celestine's cry of warning—and the string broke and the pearls fell scattered over the table and the floor about her.

Mr. Garrard's gentleman looked shocked, but Madge said magnificently, "Oh, it doesn't matter," and held out her hands for the necklace. Celestine knew that she ought to be picking up the pearls, but she too was intoxicated with the sight of the jewels, and she stood with clasped hands in an *accès* of enthusiasm, while Madge was decking herself with the *parure*.

"The hair," said the important functionary very solemnly to Celestine, "should be raised to hold the tiara"; and he signed to Celestine to come forward without treading on the fallen pearls. Madge held her little head at its full height, craning her neck to see as much of the effect as she could in the glass. It was impossible to fix the tiara—which was shaped like an old-fashioned coronet—on the very small head; though Celestine tried to puff the hair out on each side so as to support it. Failing that, the man held it in its right place with a gesture of reverent admiration. Celestine was satisfied. Madame wore them far better than she had expected; in fact the little figure, the bright eyes, the small head, seemed a wonderfully brilliant picture in the old glass. And if the attitude was a little stiff and the whole face too consciously full of self-satisfaction, these critics were hardly of the kind that would note in all this the absence of some of the moral qualities of a great lady.

A few seconds of the tableau before the glass, and then Hilda's voice called Madge on the staircase, only once and not impatiently, but it broke the spell of enjoyment. To the maid's great annoyance, Madge's face suddenly changed. She became quite pale, and a strange inexplicable look of anxiety—nay of shame—dulled the eyes that had been sparkling with pride and excitement. What on earth was the matter with madame that she should be so *bête*, so odd? Madge quickly divested herself of the jewels; and then standing up and hardly glancing at the gems, as the man packed them with scientific care into the case, she spoke in a hurried low tone.

"It was a mistake, I don't mean you were wrong to bring them, but Lord Bellasis did not quite understand. I did not want them—for family reasons in fact. I may speak to you as a confidential agent of Mr. Garrard's?"

"Certainly, madam."

"Did you mention to my butler that you came by desire of Lord Bellasis?"

"No, madam, certainly not. I said that I came by desire of Mr. Garrard."

"Very good; that is quite right. And for the next week or so it will not be known that the tiara is being altered for me."

"Certainly not."

Madge's courage was reviving and she said with more dignity:—

"The reasons for privacy are temporary, but I wish nothing to be said till Lord Bellasis tells you where the wedding presents will be shown."

The man bowed lower than ever and left the room.

Madge turned to Celestine.

"I have to trust you," she said, "and I shall reward you if you can hold your tongue."

Then gathering her opera cloak round her, she went to join Hilda.

Celestine did not hear Madge's words of explanation when she entered the drawing-room.

Hilda was leaning back on a sofa near the door. Marmaduke was standing by the fireplace holding an evening paper upside down. Madge did not even perceive that there was something wrong between them, or that Hilda had apparently forgotten her anxiety to get to the play. They neither of them were acutely interested when she said with the utmost effort at a natural manner:—

"I have been seeing some rubies. I want to have them in exchange for the emeralds the Riversdales gave me."

Sunday brought further information for the acute little Frenchwoman. She made a discovery that startled and surprised her, and for which she had not been prepared. She had heard Madge say on Saturday night that she should go to ten o'clock

Mass at Farm Street Church on Sunday, and Hilda intended to go to High Mass at the Oratory. Accordingly next morning Celestine dressed her mistress, who was very pale and complained of having had a bad night, in time to start punctually at a quarter to ten. Celestine then flew upstairs to dress herself and follow, and if there was one thing she disliked it was to be hurried in putting on her Sunday bonnet. However, she would have gone with it quite crooked and without a veil, rather than be late for Mass. So with quick walking she got into the Farm Street Mews at three minutes to ten. A good many people were hurrying in the same direction, and several hansoms were jolting over the stones. At the same time a few who had lingered after the last Mass were coming away.

Celestine never passed a *toque* or a bonnet without a deliberate judgment on its merits or defects. Something *élégante* was coming her way. "Mon Dieu," it was the bonnet she had fixed on madame a short quarter of an hour ago; this was madame herself coming away from the church. For a moment she thought madame must be ill, and she was moving to meet her and offer help when an instinct stopped her. There was something in the pale face that frightened the little maid. What was it? What strange thing made madame leave the church like that, walking in that odd straight way, looking so fierce and yet so ashamed?

Celestine's heart was heavy as she walked back from church. It was clear that there was something wrong. What could it be? Lord Bellasis was a Protestant, but what then? In England many people married Protestants and proper arrangements were made. Perhaps Lord Bellasis wouldn't make the proper arrangements. But that wasn't likely, from what she knew of Lord Bellasis. He was far too indifferent to questions of that kind. Still it was possible, but somehow she didn't think that was all. Perhaps it was something to do with another gentleman. But madame had no lover, of that Celestine was convinced. No, probably it had to do with that tiresome Miss Rupert, but then why should that prevent madame going to *la messe du Dimanche*?

Two other instances of madame being upset with regard to religion occurred during the week that followed. That night while Madge was dressing for dinner, Celestine, who was pouring water into a basin, saw her in the looking-glass glance round to make sure that the maid's back was turned, and then take off her scapular, kiss it as usual, and drop it into the fire. It was the scapular about which Madge had always been so particular, and Celestine had heard her say that she had never been without one since she had been invested with it in the convent chapel when she was only nine years old.

The brass hot water can clattered on to the basin and splashed the water on the floor, and Madge began to scold her attendant, who was blushing violently.

On Wednesday when she was going out in the afternoon, Madge suddenly pulled at her skirts and asked why the pocket was so heavy, what was in it? Celestine said that she had put nothing more than usual, the little note-book, the handkerchief, the rosary. Madge pulled the things out and threw down the note-book and rosary on the table.

"Never put them in again, they spoil the set of the skirts."

Then taking up the rosary beads again she said:—

"Keep it, Celestine, it is made of real garnets," and she held it out to the maid, "though garnets are of no value compared to rubies."

"Mais pourquoi, madame, n'aurait-elle pas tous les deux?" cried the poor little woman, her honest kindly eyes meeting Madge's with an imploring glance. But her mistress swept out of the room in silence.

CHAPTER XIV

HILDA UNDERSTANDS

Hilda was dressing for a ball in Grosvenor Place, the second in her whole experience, on Tuesday, 21st March. She was not naturally very much interested in dress, but a ball gown can rouse the most indifferent to animation. It was a soft creamy affair, with little trimming, but it was skilfully made by Madge's own dressmaker, and fitted well. Madge had insisted on having it tried on several times, and her efforts had proved successful.

Hilda was resting on the sofa for a few moments before giving herself into Brown's hands, when a small parcel was brought to her. It was only a book in a wrapper, but Hilda recognised Mark's handwriting in the address. He often sent her things of note which might interest her, sometimes works of the most serious kind, abstract and metaphysical; sometimes a modern poem to which he called her attention; little things, yet they were well chosen and intended to send thrills through the passages of Hilda's poetic faculties to warmer regions in her nature. All this fulfilled her ideal of friendship and satisfied her as to the manner in which she was worshipped.

She tore the cover off the review. It was the *Bi-monthly Review* published that day. She had not known that Fieldes was to have an article in this number. She glanced over the contents. "On the Modern Pessimist," yes, that might be by him. She turned the leaves with haste, and began to read eagerly. The style proved his authorship, and the first quotation was a favourite passage of his. Fieldes had written the article, that was certain. There was no time to study it properly. Hilda glanced through it, and gathered the main idea rather hazily. But she paused and hesitated and blushed as she read one passage near the conclusion. Was it . . .? did it . . .? had it a double meaning? Was it written mainly for one eye alone?

"If there is anything," it said, "which might carry conviction to the saddened doubter and give him hope of a glorious solution of the mystery, it is the development of faith in the best women. To recognise that their moral completeness, the fulfilment of their natures can only come from some real communion with the Unseen becomes in itself an argument. Were the doubter blest with such light habitually shining for him, such constant testimony to the fittingness of the supernatural to humanity at its best, might he not be forced to recognise a divine and infinite paternity for such a spiritual nature? And might he not even extend to all natures the parentage in this case so unmistakable? Might he not at length cry aloud with the poet:—

In te misericordia, in te pietate,

In te magnificenza, in te s'aduna Quantunque in creatura è di bontate."

Hilda read every word of the conclusion, and felt that it had been *written* for her. (This was true, though it had in reality been inspired chiefly by the thought of Mary Riversdale.) Was it wonderful that she put on her ball gown in a tremor of excitement, or that she blushed when Brown spoke to her suddenly? When she was dressed she sat down and began the article over again, while Brown waited on the landing to warn her the moment that the carriage drove up. Madge had been dining out, and was to call for Hilda on her way to the ball.

Hilda had read only two pages when she again turned to the end and looked at the concluding passage. She let the book drop as she finished and gazed into the fire. She made a pretty picture, the brightness of her excited eyes, the tremulous, eager mouth, the touch of sympathy, of a responsive note awakened by what she had read. "Ah! poor man, poor great mind that pined for light and was engulfed in such darkness! Was it not a woman's work to show the light, to supply out of the fulness of her own nature what was wanting to him?"

So mused Hilda. The utter unconsciousness of her ball gown, of her own lovely effect in the creamy softness about her, was in marked contrast to the upright attitude, the anxiety not to be crushed, the scrutiny of glove buttons that occupied Madge at the same moment in the brougham which was driving to pick up Hilda. Yet Madge too had something to think about quite as absorbing as Mark Fieldes' article.

They drove together to a house in Grosvenor Place almost in silence. There a small winter's dance was in full swing. They met one or two men whom they knew on the stairs, and Hilda noticed that Lord Bellasis was standing in the first room they entered. After that she saw him no more and she lost sight of Madge. She fancied he had spoken to Madge, but she was not quite sure. Directly she moved into the ball-room, expecting Madge to follow, Hilda saw Mark Fieldes a few feet from her. She had been thinking much of him; she had been expecting to see him; yet she was startled. He was so close to her; and there was nobody else near at the moment; and he seemed to be presented before her quite suddenly. Hilda felt the colour rising in her cheeks—he should not see it was for him. She turned aside sharply, almost rudely, and at that moment she met smiling and inviting looks from Mrs. Hurstmonceaux who was seated close to the door. She took refuge with her.

"My dear child," said Laura in a tone of tender raillery which showed Hilda that her confusion had been noticed.

Laura was talking to an elderly man and she did not pause. She was using a large feather fan in a telling manner and seemed to be enjoying herself, but she never looked quite as happy in other people's houses as she did in her own. When she was not a hostess, her most congenial occupation was gone.

"Ah," she was saying, "do read it, Sir Edward. It will really repay you. Whoever it is by it must add to his reputation. Here is a young lady who reads everything. Have you seen the article on "modern pessimists" in the new *Bimonthly?* Of course you have. Isn't it striking? Sir Edward was complaining of the feebleness of our literature at present, but here in this article there is real strength. I wonder who has written it?"

Laura as she spoke turned laughing eyes of inquiry on Hilda and glanced towards Mark. Fieldes was standing disconsolately at a little distance. He could not conceive what Hilda meant by her rudeness. What had he done, what could it mean? He was angry and offended. If he had had sense he would have walked away and left her to feel that she could not be rude without producing some effect; but being Mark, he stood near, looking not unlike a snubbed hound.

Laura beckoned to him gaily—but she did not do so before she had had time to whisper to Hilda:—

"My dear child, don't be too *ingénue;* though I own you look lovely with those little airs."

After that Hilda received Mark with contrite meekness and they walked off together a little sheepishly. Hilda had unconsciously half risen before he had asked her to dance. It was surprising that Mark did not dance badly. But after two turns at the valse, the music of which was of a sweet sad description, Mark led her out of the room along the passage at the top of the stairs. As they left the ball-room Hilda saw that Marmaduke was dancing with Madge. For a moment she forgot Mark and watched those two. How pretty Madge looked, and Marmaduke—well, he was one of the finest, most manly figures in the room.

There was a little crowd at the door. Hilda and Fieldes were blocked and she could quietly watch the others. Fieldes always got more completely stuck in a block than other people. Marmaduke and Madge had paused. He was looking down at her speaking little, but listening—his dark eyes bent upon her. Only yesterday Cecilia had said to Hilda: "If you want to be convinced, watch him when he is looking at her." Marmaduke suddenly turned round and saw Hilda fixed in the crowd with an extended hand that clung to Fieldes, who was a little in front of her. He gave a start and began to dance again vigorously, Madge looking very tiny beside him. Fieldes led Hilda across the landing to a farther drawing-room where the band came more faintly to their ears and a low murmur of talk from scattered couples could be heard. They sat down on two arm-chairs which were half hidden by a palm-tree.

A touch of anger added to Hilda's excitement. How could Marmaduke have ventured to propose to her while this treachery was going on? Yes, it was treachery. It was culpable self-deception, he had no right to be constantly with Madge and to have made love to herself. He might pretend it was all over. Hilda knew better.

Mark watched her in silence for a moment.

"You seem preoccupied this evening," he said quietly.

It was Mark's power of sympathy that made it possible for him to make observations on people's moods and ways without giving offence.

"Oh, no," said Hilda eagerly and with confusion, "and yet, yes, I suppose I am a little absent, I have been rather full of an article I read this evening."

Hilda wanted to make amends for her involuntary rudeness when they first met—she did not want to look preoccupied while she was only thinking of Marmaduke. Yet to say that she was preoccupied by thoughts of the article was a little strong. She felt it the moment the words were uttered, yet she was not sure if she regretted them. It was rather exciting.

"Ah," said Fieldes in a tone of feeling. Then he was silent again. At last he went on simply:—

"You understood, you must have understood its meaning, and that is why you were angry when you saw me to-night."

This was not badly said.

"Oh, no," cried Hilda with almost childish vexation, "oh, no, it wasn't that. It was that I didn't see you—didn't know—I mean I was shy."

Fieldes showed no consciousness of any admission there might have been in her words, but he felt himself emboldened by them.

"Ah," he cried, "how dare I tell you how those lines were forced from me as I came to the conclusion of the article. How in the darkness of my thoughts there had come light and almost hope. I felt then more strongly than ever that my whole life lies in your hands, the life of my soul as completely as the life of my heart. Yet I shrank, I shrink now, from letting you see all this. I fear to appeal too strongly to your pity, almost to your sense of responsibility to a fellow-creature who depends so entirely on you."

Fieldes meant and truly felt what he said. He had made a good many proposals in his life. Some had been more impassioned, but none in so high and pure a tone as this one. It added to his admiration of Hilda that she did bring out this better self, so far at least as imagination could carry him. His voice which was metallic and oppressive when he spoke among several people, was peculiarly suited to a *tête-à-tête*. It had a vibration, a sense of pathos when its tone was lowered. Hilda sat absolutely still, her hands joined, looking at the carpet in front of her. The childish love of excitement was strong in her. The sense of the interest of the situation filled her imagination. Here at a ball where other people were flirting and talking nonsense, these two souls, her own and Mark's, were independent of it all, free in a pure outer ether of enthusiasm. This surely was the highest tribute that could be paid her. This was very different from Marmaduke's half-hearted curt inquiry as to whether she would be his wife.

"How is it to be?" said Mark with a tremor in his voice breaking the silence. "Is this wounded man to be left by the roadside? I will not say any more. It is for you to speak to me."

There was dignity in the pathos of this. Hilda had to answer, and, to her own surprise, she spoke straight on as if she had rehearsed her part and knew exactly what she had meant to say.

"Do you know that one must never do wrong that good may come of it—one may not be one's own or anybody else's Providence. That is not clear—but what I mean is this. If the light should come to you, we should know that we have been on the right track; but we could not be sure of that now."

Fieldes felt that things were going well—but it was dangerous, brittle ground.

"I think," he said, "you may trust me. The question is can I become a Catholic?"

"Yes," said Hilda, hardly seeing how he had advanced and defined their position.

"And if I can, if after some time of prayer and of study I can truly say I am convinced, and after urgent self-examination know that it is from no attraction in this world, however holy, then in that case may I come again, and can you promise to receive me then?"

Truth hovered uneasily about Fieldes as the question came to its issue. He could truly weave ideals as to Hilda and the man by the roadside, but he hardly pretended to himself that weeks of theological study and prayer were a practical programme. However, Hilda was not cool enough to make subtle observations. The same excitement still carried her on. The last "yes," though it came more slowly, did not seem very different from the former one. Mark took no advantage of it then. He did not take her hand, he only leant back and murmured: "I cannot but hope that I may be the happiest man on earth." There was nothing to scare her, no engagement that need alarm her. But Fieldes half unconsciously trusted to Laura to make clear to Hilda's sensitive conscience that she was bound, till he could tell her whether or no he could be a Catholic. Why shouldn't that happen, after all? And, if not, Hilda herself might change in many ways under his influence.

While they were still silent there came round the bushy palm-tree a young lady and her partner. She laughed when she saw that the seats were occupied, and nodded to Mark. Fieldes sprang up with unnecessary eagerness, treading on Hilda's gown as he did so. The young lady was an heiress who had been rather kind to him, and Mark never neglected an heiress. He turned round half apologetically to Hilda; but Hilda was still in the clouds, and attributed his sudden movement to shyness at their being interrupted. But it jarred her back to earth that Mark should ask her if she thought the girl pretty, and remark on the number of thousands at which her income was computed. He said this as they walked across the landing where, of course, he must have talked of indifferent things. Perhaps it was because this was an effort that he had spoken of anything so uninteresting as the heiress' fortune.

That was the first false note. But she was not to get to the end of the evening without a much greater discord being struck by Mark, who had become rash and self-confident with success.

Laura drove Hilda home that night, by arrangement with Madge. Mark saw them into their carriage and Mrs. Hurstmonceaux offered to take him so far on the road to his rooms. When they reached the house Mark sprang out before Hilda to help her to get down. In doing so he caught his foot in Laura's gown, and though no damage was done, his descent did not gain in grace. Then it was that he made the mistake which almost undid the results of all his skill. Hilda was springing out when Mark touched her arm to help her, and she could not avoid his assistance. But as she reached the pavement he gave the soft white arm a slight but unmistakable pressure. Hilda turned round, looked back into the brougham with her back to him, bade Mrs. Hurstmonceaux another "Good-night," and then sped into the hall, passing between Fieldes and the footman as if they had equal claims on her civility.

"There are wine and biscuits in the dining-room," said the butler. "Mrs. Riversdale has gone upstairs."

"All right, don't wait," said Hilda, and she walked into the dining-room, not because she wanted wine or biscuits but because it was an open door in front of her. She passed in with her head erect, her cheeks flushed, her eyes shining with anger. She gave a little stamp on the parquet floor as she stood still, just within the screen. Then she started back. She had thought she was alone.

"Oh!" said Marmaduke in a surprised voice. They were both silent. The room was softly bright with lamps, candlelight and a big fire. Marmaduke was standing with his back to the fireplace.

He had his greatcoat on; in his hand was a cigarette. He looked particularly handsome in that coat. Hilda gave a little gasp and held on to the table as if she were giddy.

Turning as he spoke to knock the ash off his cigarette into the fire he broke the silence.

"Well, have you had fun?" he said.

Hilda sat down and leant her head on her hand.

"I don't know," she answered; then suddenly lifting up her head in a tone of superiority she added: "Fun isn't the word for it. It was immensely interesting, quite too exciting"; but her voice quivered a little and she got no farther.

"In fact, you are having a good time," he said, leaning his back against the chimneypiece and looking at her coolly.

"First rate," said Hilda, drumming with her fingers on the table.

"Then why were you so cross when you came in here?"

"I wasn't cross that I know of," said Hilda.

"Then you were cross that you didn't know of," said Marmaduke. "That's a way some people have. They are cross and they are disagreeable and all sorts of things they don't know of."

But Hilda suddenly lifted up a sad little face with a suspicion of tears on the long eyelashes.

"I'm afraid that's true," she said gently.

She was dreadfully troubled, more troubled than she had ever been before. Surely she had not put herself in such a position towards Mark as to give him the right to treat her like that. What had she said, what had she done that evening? The arm seemed to tingle where he had touched it. Her eyes flashed again. She felt humiliated, and that at this very moment she should find Marmaduke and be alone with him was very hard. How could she bear it? There was no use in trying to deceive herself. She seemed to have come at the same moment from Mark in the dark street to Marmaduke in the light room; and from Mark, whom she had turned from with a sudden surprised repulsion, to Marmaduke—whom she knew, with a sudden but far less surprised discovery, that she loved. She let her head fall on her arms on the table before her. She would not look at him and he should not see her face. He hardly dared to allow himself to see distinctly the graceful head bowed down on the table. He smoked quietly on. Whatever this emotion of hers might be it had obviously nothing to do with him.

Suddenly she looked up.

"Is Mr. Fieldes a gentleman?" she said abruptly.

Marmaduke did not answer for a moment.

"In what way do you mean? He is educated and all that. Plenty of men of his extraction are perfect gentlemen. You can judge of Fieldes as well as I can. Personally I think he is a snob."

"You never were fair to him," said Hilda, trying to feel combative.

"Perhaps not," said Marmaduke indifferently. "Well, if Madge isn't coming down again I must be off."

Hilda said nothing—then she raised her head and spoke quickly.

"I want to go home. I wish mother would let me," her voice had a little sob in it.

Marmaduke's face brightened perceptibly.

"Couldn't it be managed?" he said. Hilda felt bitterly that he could not conceal that he wanted her to go.

"No, she won't, because of the scarlet fever. They have not finished disinfecting the house. I will ask if I may go to Skipton."

There was a touch of temper in her manner which made Marmaduke cautious. While he was still silent Madge came in, and the opportunity for further speech with Hilda was ended.

Marmaduke soon left them, and Madge and Hilda were alone. Madge sank into an arm-chair by the fire and gazed silently into the dying embers. Hilda was walking up and down on the farther side of the long table.

"How hot it is, isn't it?" she exclaimed, throwing her opera-cloak off her shoulders.

Madge did not answer.

"It is stifling," Hilda went on, and pausing by the table she tried to uncork a bottle of seltzer water. "Hang the thing," she said, with very unusual vehemence, "it won't open."

"Leave it alone," said Madge dreamily, and a moment later the cork struck against Hilda, as she went on walking. She stopped and drank hastily of the fizzing water.

"Shall we go to bed?" said Madge, rising suddenly and turning towards the light. "Why, Hilda, how excited you look."

At the same moment each had been distracted from herself by the look on the other's face.

"Madge, are you ill?" exclaimed Hilda in horror.

"Ill? No, I wish you would not be so foolish. But your face is so flushed, I think you must be feverish."

Madge, candle in hand, walked slowly from the room with a somewhat constrained "Good-night."

Hilda waited until she heard Madge's door safely shut and then ran noiselessly up to her own room, trusting to feel her way in the dark. Through the open door a welcome sight met her eyes.

"Brown, I told you not to wait," she cried joyfully.

The old maid smiled, she could see that the child was in trouble, and was glad to find her there.

"I have my doubts, Miss Hilda, as to whether that French girl helps you as well as her own mistress, who takes a deal of waiting on."

Brown's voice was combative. She did not hold with any of the household with whom they were staying, in her case unwillingly.

"Oh, yes, she does, when I want her," said Hilda hurriedly, "but it is not like having you to put me to bed."

Brown then plaited the great mass of hair to her own satisfaction, after which Hilda knelt down to pray. Brown would not leave her, and she could hear stifled sobs coming from the bent head. Hilda had forgotten that she was not alone, but when she tumbled hastily into bed, it was very comforting to be tucked up by loving hands. The ugly affectionate little woman bustled round the bed, and Hilda watched her with tearful eyes.

"There now, Miss Hilda; go to sleep, and my room is just opposite, and I shall hear you. The men have done papering the room where that silly girl had the fever. I had a letter to-night, and they won't be long fumigating the whole house, and, please God, we will soon be home again, and everything just as usual," and Brown and her light went away.

Hilda almost laughed at the futility of these suggestions for her consolation.

"Did dear, dear old Brown think I was afraid of ghosts or burglars? And to go home and everything be as usual." A sharp pain came with the thought. Everything to be as if these weeks had never existed, as if she had never known, never loved, never so nearly been happy, and missed it all by her own fault. Yet was that not the very thing she had said to him herself? She turned her face on the pillow, and wept very bitterly at the thought of her own speech, and what heartless frivolity it seemed to show.

"Let us play as the children do," she had said. "Let us play that it never really happened."

"Ah, he couldn't have loved me," she moaned, "I was right to think it wasn't true. If he had loved me, he must have answered me then, and he only looked grave and disapproving. Oh, it is very hard, and I did so try not to love him. I always thought I would never condescend to be the first to fall in love, and now I am, for he doesn't, indeed he doesn't love me. I am sure he cares for Madge. But I can't go away, I can't go home, and be as if nothing had happened. I must stay and see what goes on here. I must stay in London. But then, if I do, there is Mark Fieldes—only, thank heaven, he is going away to-day, perhaps only for one night, but perhaps for more. What did I say? what did I say to him at that hateful ball? I can't remember exactly. I can't get anything clear to-night, but it must have been something very rash, very foolish. Oh dear, I must ask Laura if I committed myself in any way so that he ought to be allowed to hold my arm in his horrid hand. Laura is the only person I can speak to; for I can't and I won't and I won't and I can't go home. How good and beautiful he did look to-night, and how kindly he looked at me, though I have been a brute. And I asked him about Mr. Fieldes. He must think I care about that horrid, horrid Mr. Fieldes, who is such a snob, as he said. Oh dear, how queer it is to be in love."

She sat up now, and leant her chin on her hand, and the elbow that supported it rested on her knee. "The man was right who said that it was better to have loved and lost than never to have loved at all. I quite agree with him. I am glad I love him so and that I would do anything for him, even if he treated me ever so badly, and even if I never never see him again." And she threw herself back on the pillow and sobbed again; the extreme unlikeliness of her never meeting such a near connection as Marmaduke in no way impeding the free flow of her tears.

CHAPTER XV

CECILIA

Cecilia had been to the same dance in Grosvenor Place. She had got back to Charles Street at about half-past two, and let herself in with her latch-key. She then ran noiselessly upstairs, and went into her own room, where the fire was bright and the gas burning.

Cecilia threw off her cloak, and then sat down on the armchair nearest the fire. She folded her hands helplessly and looked vacantly at the burning coals; then she shuddered and gave a low moan. She had had such a long anxious winter; she had had so much to wear her. She was growing very thin. Her ball gown, which had once fitted so perfectly, was quite loose now. She had been really unwell for six months or more. She had lived too hard for her strength for several years past, as Madge had said. Then had come the strain of a great anxiety on the top of a lowered physical condition. In spite of her fears of the autumn, she was for some time conscious of her power over Bellasis when they met. And there had been moments in their *tête-à-têtes* when something of the old sense of fascination, on which she had built so much, reappeared. She had been anxious, painfully anxious, but not desperate.

Back in London, Cecilia had instantly perceived in him a subtle change, and she could not now blind herself. Before she had been long in London, she had felt sure that the fear of the autumn was a reality, that he loved, and loved Madge. Ever since that discovery she had lived in a struggle, a vehement and useless struggle against forces that were beyond her control. She had not despaired. She knew of the impediment which made his marriage with Madge so difficult. But that Bellasis loved Madge was agony to her, and the possibility of their union was an ever-recurring nightmare.

Quite lately, since Hilda's arrival in London, one plan appeared at last to have some hope in it. She seemed to have something more definite against Madge than her own mere dislike. She had resolved to play what she knew to be a desperate game. She would actually speak against Madge to Bellasis himself. She would let him know of the handsome Marmaduke. She would hint as much as she dared. She would try her influence with him, not the influence of a woman whom he loved, but still a woman's influence, in affecting his judgment and rousing his intensely sensitive pride and suspiciousness.

And for a short time it seemed that she had succeeded. For quite three weeks she felt sure that she had kept Bellasis and Madge from having any conversation. She knew from his own lips that he was avoiding Madge. He had been in low spirits, but all the same there had been positive as well as negative signs in Cecilia's favour. It did for a time seem as if for Madge to decrease was for her to increase. Lord Bellasis once more seemed to seek her out, and became more confidential in their talks. It made her nervous, though hopeful, that he seemed to have a growing confidence in her truthfulness. But then about a fortnight before this night of the ball he had left London and she had not seen him since. He had gone down to Bellasis on business—a natural reason; but she was uneasy. Those days while he was away were terrible to Cecilia, coming just when her hopes had risen again. She thought even bad news would be more bearable than this complete uncertainty.

Yet to-night, while sitting by the fire, that ignorance seemed to have been bliss compared to her present feelings. She always loved dancing. Her powers of enjoyment were naturally very great, and she must have been hopelessly far gone in trouble for dancing with good music to fail to soothe and brighten her. Then, too, a ball always showed her well in the eyes of the world, and success was a passion with her. Who did not want to dance with

Cecilia? People are only indifferent to genius because they don't see it. Cecilia's was a genius that anybody with even a faint notion of music and of grace could see when she danced, when she sang, when she recited, and sometimes, but less often, when she talked.

She had been walking about the drawing-room adjoining the ball-room after a dance with a heavy quiet youth—heavy mentally, not physically. Across the end of the room was a large screen, and it was not till she had passed by it that she saw that Madge and Lord Bellasis were standing behind it. She started. She had believed him to be still at Bellasis. But he was here! And he was with Madge. There was nothing particularly private in the spot they had chosen. Madge had been on her way to the ball-room and Lord Bellasis had caught her up. They were saying nothing to each other, but it seemed to Cecilia as if his whole attitude betrayed a complete change in the situation. Madge appeared to be very nervous. Bellasis looked down at her—she was so small—he could never look down at Cecilia like that. There was something protective in his attitude. Cecilia saw no more, and they had not seen her. She went back to the ball-room and she danced; but she danced now with no pleasure, no relief.

"Did you ever," she said to her partner, "wonder why the old painters made all the little damned souls dance, and the blessed sit upright on hard marble seats? It wasn't a bad division of mankind after all, was it? The good are dull and bored, and the others dance even in this world."

A moment after this speech Cecilia saw that Bellasis had come into the ball-room and was standing not far off watching her. She stopped close to where he was standing, but he did not come any nearer. As she started to go on with the polka, she nodded to him—he bowed rather ceremoniously, but that was his usual manner. He affected old-world externals of manner, though he certainly did not submit to old-world restraints. During the evening she was again near him, several times, but he never took advantage of these opportunities.

Seated alone by her fire in the intensely still house which seemed to echo the great silence of the sleeping town, Cecilia tried to think over her position coolly. Was it all a failure? Had he found out that Madge had been maligned, and maligned by her? If this were so, not only had she failed, but it was infinitely worse than if things had gone on without her interference. He would hate her now as a liar. He would despise her for sinking so low for his sake. It was intolerable, life was intolerable. Even before, when she had found out that Lord Bellasis loved Madge, the pain had seemed too great to bear; but this was far worse. This second disappointment, though after slighter hope—for she had only half believed that she could detach him from Madge—was far harder to bear. The strain was telling upon her, she was weaker mentally and physically. Alone in the night she grasped her own arms, she hugged herself in a frenzy of pity. She slipped off the chair on to the ground and she buried her head on the seat where she had been sitting.

Life, what was life now? nothing, nothing but misery. She wailed there alone and nobody answered. She might cry for very loneliness in grief, and nobody would mind. Not only was there no more hope, but there was to be the end of the small sustenance that her love and her life had been fed upon. The sound of Bellasis's voice had been wonderful to her. So had the look in his eyes when he admired her, the almost involuntary startled sympathy when some chord had been struck by her music or sometimes by her talk, oftener by her dancing, something which she had once likened to the kissing of their souls. She had lived on such moments, and one of them would make her happy for days. Now she seemed to be burying all that; all was going from her and what was left?

She shivered. She felt very ill that night; there was an aching pain in her side which came after any exertion now. The fire was getting low, the pain increased. She got up with an effort, took scissors that lay near, and cut through the lace of her bodice rather than undo it and tore the gown off. She turned out the gas, jumped into bed and cowered down among the bed-clothes.

For all the four hours, from four to eight in the morning, she lay there, shaking, thinking, thinking with the terrible vividness of sleeplessness.

"And yet I don't want to die," she said more than once in a kind of astonishment at herself. It was a relief when her maid came with the tea. For almost the first time in her self-centred life she was terrified at being alone.

The hospital nurse who attended the elder Miss Rupert at night was not a little surprised at receiving a visit from Cecilia in her own room at about nine in the morning. Nurse Barnes was very tired as she had only finished the night duty about an hour before.

At the moment Cecilia came in she was getting out her bonnet for the hour's regulation walk before she lay down for the day's sleep.

Cecilia appeared in her dressing-gown and inquired at once how her aunt had slept. The report was not good and perhaps the nurse was not loath to give a bad account of things to Cecilia. According to the nurse's code a woman's whole character is decided by her conduct towards the patient for the time being; and Cecilia was condemned by every standard which Nurse Barnes knew.

Cecilia hardly seemed to hear the details given her, but her next question surprised Nurse Barnes still further.

She had walked across to the fireplace, and was leaning with one elbow on the chimneypiece. She looked ill, tired and worn in the morning light. Her mass of rather coarse hair fell about her face which depended a good deal for its usually classic effect on the arrangement of her locks. Nurse Barnes took a woman's pleasure in reflecting how plain Miss Cecilia could look without adornment. "She will not wear well," she thought.

"Nurse," Cecilia said, "how long do you suppose my aunt has had this illness?"

"Oh, it must have been brewing for a long, long time," said Nurse Barnes fidgeting with her bonnet. She longed to put it on, and get off for her walk.

"For years?" said Cecilia.

"Oh, yes."

"Then in old days when she used to get giddy when she took me to balls, and say sometimes that she was in pain—do you suppose it had begun then?"

"Surely," answered Barnes with satisfaction, "she has been a greater sufferer than anybody would give her credit for."

"And was it one of the symptoms that sometimes she was frightfully hungry and yet couldn't eat?"

"I believe that is a common symptom," said Barnes, trying to remember what she had once read in a medical dictionary on the subject. She had ventured now to begin putting on her bonnet which she did with almost scientific precision. It had been bought at the Stores for sixteen shillings and nine pence, and was generally considered a success at the Nursing Institute.

"Did she ever tell you that years ago she had a tiny lump in her side which she thought came from a blow?"

There was something so curious in Cecilia's voice that the nurse was struck by it.

"What is she at now?" thought Nurse Barnes, "whatever is in her head I wish she would let me go out."

"She did say something of it," said Barnes, "but mostly she tells those things to Dr. Rule and he is not one to tell the nurses much about it. Now if I were working with my own doctor I should have had the whole scientific diagnosis."

"I suppose so," said Cecilia.

"Did you want to say anything more?" said Barnes suggestively.

"Oh, no, thank you," said Cecilia and she walked out of the room.

An hour later and Cecilia was being shown into one of the largest houses in Harley Street. She was very pale, but then so were many of the many patients waiting in the soberly handsome dining-room. Cecilia was not accustomed to the waiting-room of a great consulting physician. The pale-faced youth in one corner, the middle-aged man in another, the young couple sitting together talking in whispers, the old lady reading a novel, all seemed to her to have looks of tragic anxiety on their faces.

She took up a book and tried to read. She succeeded; she became excited. It was a strange piece of modern realism—it was the account of a man having his leg cut off in a hospital. It was ghastly in its reality, yet the art of the poetry was so studied as to give a great sense of calmness in the narrator which added to its force. The description of the man losing consciousness under ether had passages of extraordinary beauty. Cecilia was fascinated. The artist in her was always aroused by a touch of genius. Yet the poem could hardly distract her from herself. It rather seemed to grow into her own state of mind, to intensify her own feelings. She shut the book. It was becoming too exciting, not distracting. She looked about her at the others in the room.

"Which of them," she wondered, "felt as she felt in that room?"

It was all so horrible, so ghastly to think of people looking at illustrated papers who were waiting for their life or death verdict. In her present mood she fancied that they had all come to a crisis in their lives. But after all, she thought to herself, she was not really as they were. She had come with a horrid creepy fear in her mind; but she had come chiefly because she believed that it would be set at rest by the great man. She was stronger now and felt an inclination to a reaction against the misery of the night. Had she not been morbid, overstrained? Was she so very sure that all was over? Might she not have made the most of her momentary glimpse of Madge and Bellasis? Would not their attitude admit of another interpretation? Might it not be due to embarrassment, not sympathy? Madge had looked quite nervous, almost guilty. Then they must have parted at once, and they had not danced together. Madge had danced two or three times and then gone away. Would she have gone so early had she been hopeful of seeing more of Lord Bellasis? Then as to that individual's own conduct—it was always peculiar, his emotions so often took the strangest forms. She had known him watch Madge in silence for a whole evening without speaking to her, at a time when his feelings for her were unmistakable. Why then was his looking at herself last night in silence a bad sign? Cecilia was arguing against her own instincts, but she succeeded in quieting her fears to some extent by the strength of the case she made out against them.

But at length the door opened and the functionary looked in for the ninth time since she had been in the room, and this time she felt almost surprised to see that he was bowing to her in the same mysteriously summoning manner that he had used to the other patients. She went out, crossed the small hall, and was ushered into the presence of the great magnate, the revealer of hidden things, who gave hope or fear to all, and healing to a possible few.

Dr. Rule had taken full advantage of the position of a successful doctor in an age in which health is a mania. He felt himself to be on a platform that commanded an attentive audience. So he discoursed to it, chiefly in the reviews, on many things, on moral, on philosophical questions. But of course science was his strong point, and the heredity of disease was the strong point in his science. He enjoyed the position of a sage and of a confessor to many. He was in the habit of watching character. He had observed Cecilia Rupert during his chance meetings with her at her aunt's. He knew something of her life, and he had noticed that she looked ill.

As she came in, he rose from his desk at which his last patient's prescription had been written, and came one step forward, no more, for the light behind him fell full on her face and he was occupied in looking at her. He said: "How d'ye do?" and there was a pause. Cecilia's courage failed.

"I came," she said, "to ask you what you think of my aunt?"

The voice was hard, cold, indifferent. Dr. Rule hesitated because he had not been thinking of the elder Miss Rupert.

"There is very little to say in these cases," he observed; "it is almost impossible for us to form any idea of what the progress of the disease will be."

"Will it always be painful?" inquired Cecilia, her eyes dilating.

"I hope not," he said. He thought she was showing some feeling. "I sincerely hope not, but it is impossible to prognosticate with any accuracy. Let me see," he said, "how long has she been ill? We might judge a little how affairs have gone so far."

He took up his notes of the case and looked them over. He became interested in them. He was no longer thinking of Cecilia. She had evidently not come as a patient. He told her a good deal from the notes in highly technical phraseology which she could not understand. She listened impatiently for some minutes and then broke in:—

"Where has she got the disease?"

"Oh, of course it is hereditary," said the great man, his face brightening as he got on his favourite topic. "It is one of the most hereditary diseases we know of."

"I remember," said Cecilia, "that years ago she used to have curious health."

"This sort of thing may begin quite young," said Dr. Rule, "but a great deal may be postponed by quiet, healthy living. Take two people with germs of the disease, alike in all other respects, and one may by his own doing avoid years of suffering. Depend upon it, Miss Rupert, in quietness shall be our strength."

"But I am not quiet," said Cecilia, forcing a smile.

Dr. Rule did not understand this sudden self-application. He thought it was a general answer to his text.

"But, my dear young lady," he said paternally, "you must be quiet. It is necessary for everybody. You don't know the irreparable injury that may be done in two or three years, and for a member of your family care is specially necessary."

Dr. Rule thought she needed frightening—he had heard something of her recklessness, of her selfishness; and as a moralist and as a doctor he thought she needed frightening. Then Cecilia suddenly in a calm voice told him of all her symptoms. He cross-questioned her closely, but his eyes occasionally strayed to the clock. When she had finished he said:—

"I wish I could give you more time now, but I have a consultation at twelve. I think that you are certainly not in a right state. Still there is nothing for you to worry over. I should recommend complete change and rest. I think it might be as well for me to see you the day after to-morrow when I come to your aunt. If I could see you then I would examine you just to set our minds at rest—your mind I mean, for I see no cause for present anxiety, only of course one cannot forget the hereditary tendency. But don't worry, don't worry, it can do no good."

The great man shook hands with her, and Cecilia went out.

CHAPTER XVI

MORE ABOUT CECILIA

When Cecilia found herself again in the street it felt to her strangely chilly. She walked on rapidly, hardly knowing which direction she was taking. She seemed to herself to have gone a great step downwards since she entered that house. She had expected to be laughed at by the great man for her fancies. She had known such fears and such reassuring treatment of them before. Ever since she was a child she had had a tendency to nervousness about her health, and she half liked the process of confiding her ideas and having them set at rest. But now instead of being told not to think more about them he said that he would see her again at once and examine her. An examination! She was about then to be drawn into the first circle of the *inferno* of disease and death. Oh, those examinations, when the first fears of her aunt's health were beginning! Those ghastly consultations, she knew it all so well. And then he had told her not to worry, not because he was certain that there was no cause for anxiety but "because it would do no good"! No indeed, nothing that she could do or think would do good any more if the disease were there, if Death's finger had touched her. Her courage of reaction after the night seemed to have gone.

"All, all is wrong," she found herself saying. "Last night my hopes were killed, this is but the carrying out of the programme."

Cecilia never dissociated her hopes and her fears. The *clairvoyante's* prophecy had been too distinct for that. The woman's words seemed always to ring in her ears. Either the attainment of an immense happiness, her heart's desire, or a horrible and painful death were before her. Never had her credulity been shaken by a doubt. Either she should win Bellasis or she should die of her aunt's disease. Life since that revelation had presented only two possible alternatives, perfect happiness or perfect misery. She had read every sign of friendship from Bellasis as throwing light also on her health. She had taken any bad sign in her health as a proof that her love was hopeless. She had thought that the doctor would bring positive evidence to weigh against Bellasis's apparent desertion the evening before, against her strong impression on seeing him with Madge. The sick hopelessness of the night was returning upon her. But it was morning; it was daylight. She could not cower down among the bed-clothes now. She had to live through the day. The *clairvoyante* was away. She could not go to her; and if she could have seen her, had not the medium constantly told her that she could not explain her own words further, that she herself did not understand them any better than Cecilia did?

But this state of things was intolerable. She must find out more about Bellasis. It would be better, infinitely better, to know the worst.

She had been walking fast, almost unconscious where she went, but she had been getting nearer the park. Oh, if only one could get some more light on the question. Hilda might be useful if they could talk alone; but she doubted if it would be possible to manage that in Madge's house. On the whole it was as likely that Hilda would be at Laura Hurstmonceaux', and really it might be easier to find out more of what was going on from Laura than from anybody. Directly this became clear, she called a hansom and drove towards Cadogan Place. But Laura was out. It was intensely provoking. All through the drive Cecilia had become more and more eager to see her. But as Laura was not to be found, she would go straight to Madge. Madge was out too, and so was Hilda Riversdale. It was now getting near lunch time and Cecilia was feeling very giddy. She was engaged to lunch miles away at a great actor's house in Hampstead, a friend of Lord Bellasis. He might be there.

She went home to dress more gorgeously, but while the maid was doing her hair she nearly fainted. She drank some brandy and water, and drove off in the brougham. Bellasis was not one of the luncheon party, and nobody talked much about him—she did not think that he had been asked. The meal prolonged itself endlessly. To Cecilia it was dulness that could be felt physically. She had thought she was very hungry, but she could eat very little. As soon as possible, she got away, and drove again to Laura's, nearly an hour's drive from Hampstead Heath. Mrs. Hurstmonceaux had gone out a few moments before. Cecilia felt half crazy with annoyance as the carriage drove home. On the table in the hall was Laura's card, showing that they had only just missed again. She had not cried at all till now, but the tears came at this slight mischance. It was impossible to keep still, and it would not do to go to Madge twice in the same day. There was a card for a tea-party, where Madge was not unlikely to be, lying on the table. It was worth while to go to it.

She went, and stayed half an hour in vain talking wild nonsense to some of her girl admirers. Then on to the house of another friend of Madge's where at least they were sure to talk of her. Here indeed it was easy to make her hostess discuss Madge, not altogether amiably; but there was nothing definite in what they said, no gossip as to Lord Bellasis, no apparent consciousness that anything special was going on. Still as long as the subject could be prolonged Cecilia stayed. At length, when it seemed impossible to carry it on further, she made her farewells and left. As she was going downstairs Laura Hurstmonceaux was coming up—just too late.

"So provoked at missing you twice to-day," cried Laura. "How are you, my dear? not very well, that I can see. My dear Cecilia, when will you learn wisdom? Your high spirits are quite wearing you out!"

It was so sweetly, so affectionately said.

"Ah!" cried Cecilia, "let them. I'd rather get life's worth in a few years. A woman should live till thirty and then for heaven's sake shoot her. Don't you," with a slight hesitation, "think so too, Laura?"

"Oh, of course," said Laura sarcastically, but wincing a little at the shaft. "But, dear, when shall we meet in this city of confusion? how would eleven to-morrow morning do?"

"Perfectly," cried Cecilia.

Cecilia drove home, trying the while to see if anything could possibly be gathered from Laura's few words. Certainly Laura was in good spirits, and her manner had been caressing, always a sign of ill-nature when she was talking to Cecilia. Then her anxiety to see Cecilia looked bad. She would wish to meet if she could annoy her, on the other hand she would wish to meet if she were afraid of her influence with Lord Bellasis. Though not gauging exactly how much Laura was in his confidence, it was plain to Cecilia that Laura was promoting his flirtation with Madge and eager to interfere with herself. But it was of no use; further light on the question would not come. Her mind went on working with desperate activity, producing nothing but increase of exhaustion.

When she was at home again it was still too soon to dress for dinner, and rest was out of the question. An idea struck her. She went down to her aunt's room. Miss Rupert was lying very still, but a slight moan came from the bed as Cecilia drew near. The girl shuddered, and touched the curtain to draw it aside, when the nurse who was sitting on the other side of the bed signed to her not to do so. Miss Rupert was sleeping. Cecilia moved hastily, almost impatiently away. Then it was of no use. What was of no use? Strange as it may seem, Cecilia had come downstairs to ask her aunt to pray for her happiness. It might do good; any how it couldn't do harm. She would have implored the *clairvoyante* to foretell it. She would have asked her aunt to pray for it. She went back to her room and got through the time as best she could till the maid came to dress her.

The house at which the dinner was to be was a congenial one. It was a home of real musical talent. The family and their food were too simple to be much *répandu* in Cecilia's own world. But some of her friends went there from time to time and always said they wished they could manage to get there oftener.

To-night Cecilia longed for distraction, and although the dinner seemed intolerably long, the music afterwards did help to lull thought.

Having begun with some successful solos they had been drawn on into trying to sketch parts of their favourite operas. They all knew the things well and rather rejoiced in them as in reminiscences, than attempted finished execution. Nobody minded if a note were missed or a few bars only hummed; it was only to revive in their memories moments when the greatest performers had carried them out of themselves into a world that never was and never will be describable in words.

They had come to a passionate woman's solo, and Cecilia was singing it. Her voice was not strong, but she acted as she sang with wonderful force for an amateur. Her whole being seemed to be drunk with the music. The others might have been startled, only that they were all filled with the same spirit as herself. When she stopped a moment's silence followed; and then before the son of the house could take up his part, a voice she knew well startled her. From behind a screen close at hand Bellasis the privileged, who had come in uninvited, had stepped forward and was singing the lover's part, a little crudely but with vigour. For the moment Cecilia was carried away by the conviction that the deep manly voice, the grey slightly sunken eyes were speaking the heart's language for which she had thirsted. Suddenly it overcame her. She knew that she had been confused, that she had blushed deeply and been too upset to sing any more; but it was a delicious trouble, the sweetest, most soul-soothing pain.

After the music was over Bellasis came across the room to where she was sitting. He sat down beside her, but they neither of them spoke. "What a wonderful creature!" he thought, "what an extraordinary being. How she loves me! What a genius and how her genius transforms her! Yet heaven defend one from depending on a creature of that kind. How false, how cruel she could be! And yet well might a man be infatuated by her!"

He was looking at her as he was thinking. She was leaning back, resting—resting body and mind in the light of his countenance. He felt almost as if he were condescending in praising somewhat contemptuously this human creature, lazily taking a sensuous pleasure in the thing that he knew would have given her life for him, and half despising her, manlike, even for her devotion. And she was feeling that the whole sun of her heavens came from those eyes looking at her in a way that was in reality an insult. For it was because he held her so lightly, because he did not believe her to be true, that he could play with her so easily.

"Cecilia," he said in a low voice, and Cecilia almost wished the joy of the silence had not been broken. She was silent. Then he slid his hand under the large feather fan that lay on her knee and covered with his large hand the little fingers clasped tightly together. For a moment he held one of her hands in his. Cecilia was quite motionless. He gave it the slightest pressure. He leant over her and for one moment she looked up at him. In that moment her fate was sealed.

"Good-night," said Bellasis abruptly recovering himself, and he rose up and went away.

"Though she is a liar I oughtn't to have done that," he thought as he made his way out of the room. "But the past has been very pleasant. Nobody has ever amused me as much as Cecilia." He gave a little sigh. "And how exquisitely graceful she is. Madge won't be half as amusing!"

He hummed the tune he had been singing and he talked of Cecilia with a friend he met at the Travellers.

Cecilia went home in clouds of misty glory. She would analyse nothing, she would doubt nothing. "All is well with my soul, all is well," she sang laughingly to herself the refrain of the Methodist hymn. That night the pain in her side kept her awake; but she didn't want to sleep, she wanted to day-dream, and what did the pain matter?

CHAPTER XVII

THE REST ABOUT CECILIA

Laura had quite looked forward to her talk with Cecilia.

"Poor girl," she thought, "one does not wish to be ill-natured, but really she has been so very ridiculous and worse than ridiculous. Her conduct has been unpardonable."

Laura felt quite maternal. She was going to do the girl so much good, and it was much kinder than letting her hear the news by chance, perhaps among a crowd of people. Cecilia looked better this morning. She had quite a colour, and the haggard tension in her face was relaxed. She and Laura kissed, which was an unusual ceremony between them. Laura admired Cecilia's gown. There was something so very clever about the arrangement of the fur. Made by her maid? No, that was impossible. Why the woman was worth her weight in gold. Cecilia admired Laura's flowers. Quite too exquisite and so perfectly arranged. It must be so delightful to be as artistic as Laura.

"They are lovely, lovable things," said Laura, "so different from what one gets in shops—though our English shops are so improved."

"You get them from the country?" asked Cecilia.

"Yes, they come from Bellasis."

Cecilia knew it before she spoke. A very rare kind of begonia was among them, the particular pride of the gardener at Bellasis Castle. Now that the name had been mentioned they were silent for a second. Laura rose and moved to the fireplace and held one foot to the blaze. Her eyes and hands were occupied in keeping her skirts at a safe distance from the flames.

"Talking of Lord Bellasis," she said in a bright tone, "has it ever struck you that he admires Madge?"

"Oh, of course," said Cecilia airily, "months ago I noticed it." Laura was enjoying herself; and her feline instincts made her inclined to dawdle over what she had to say.

"Yes, I think so too," she said in a meditative voice; "and I thought you must have seen it, because you are so extraordinarily quick in all that concerns your friends. I thought long ago 'Cecilia is certain to see this'; but I did not like to say anything. And there was really then nothing to expect, no likely result, I mean."

Cecilia felt herself turning very cold. She was afraid of losing her balance, of saying something that would betray her. Yet she must speak.

"What makes you talk of it now?" she asked.

The simplicity of the question a little interfered with Laura's "play." She turned round with the sweetest smile and looked straight at Cecilia.

"Well, I think people are getting wind of it to-day," she said. "Surely you have heard the gossip as to Madge's engagement?"

Cecilia tightened her grasp on the arm of the chair she was sitting in.

"And is the gossip true?" she said.

Again the directness of the question changed Laura's tack.

"Well, yes," she answered; "I think I may tell you privately that it is true."

Cecilia did not speak. Laura went on.

"You are so quick," she said. "You would see if I did not tell you. You know that I am behind the scenes. Well poor Madge has suffered a great deal—she is so conscientious, so absurdly scrupulous, that she was quite afraid it would be wrong to marry one who was not a Roman Catholic."

"And she has got over these scruples?" Cecilia's tone betrayed bitterness.

"Yes," said Laura sweetly, "at last she has, I almost thought at one moment that the irrational folly would carry the day; and I think it might have, if it had not been for one consideration. And yet she had immense attractions to overcome. I own it astonished me that Madge should be willing to sacrifice so much to religious ideas. Love, position, wealth, power, happiness." Laura dwelt on each word as she summed up. "And especially after all she had suffered."

"And yet," said Cecilia, "you say there has been a consideration greater than religion."

Cecilia looked hard at Laura; but she might as well have given up the struggle to appear indifferent. Laura could read her easily and rather enjoyed seeing the courage that was so futile a disguise. One can conceive a tyrant preferring the victim who did not scream aloud on the rack, as a more delicate source of enjoyment than an ordinary coward.

"Yes," said Laura, "it was a consideration of ordinary plain duty that dispersed the mist of religious scruples. Some one had been trying to make Lord Bellasis believe that Madge had had an old love affair which was not at an end; that this was what made her hesitate to say 'yes,' and that her feelings towards Bellasis were the most sordid and mercenary. She felt it due to herself to explain matters, and the explanation—in this very house—led to her engagement. It is difficult to realise how odious the world can be till one sees its capacity for cruelty."

Cecilia commanded herself with an effort. She felt now that Laura knew all. There was a true ring of righteous indignation in Laura's voice; but there was no answering moral shame in Cecilia. The question of right and wrong had been done with long ago. What she felt at this moment was the utterness of her defeat, the completeness of her humiliation, the stupidity, the gross stupidity of her plans. But she did not blame herself much for her own failures. What she had done had made little difference. This was her fate. She was sinking deeper and deeper. She put her hand to her side for a moment as if she felt pain. She thought of Dr. Rule and the *clairvoyante*. She knew now that she was to die. But the world was still with her—still had its eyes upon her. The instinct of combat rose up. She might be defeated by disease and death, these were greater than she. But Laura or Madge should not defeat her. As Manfred defied the lesser spirits when he knew himself defeated by the greatest, so Cecilia defied these puny spiteful women who, like herself, were after all only subjects of death. She was not silent for as much as a quarter of a minute, but the soul works quickly. She got up quietly and looked at Laura.

"Thank you for telling me all about it," she said. "Will you tell me one thing more? Is this engagement known by people in general?"

"Oh, no," said Laura smiling, "one mustn't say anything about it yet. Only I suppose it must be getting out, but I would not for the world be quoted on the subject. I can trust you, Cecilia?"

"You can trust me perfectly," said Cecilia calmly. Her attitude had a certain dignity. She avoided Laura's kiss, shook hands and went out of the room. She was walking downstairs, not looking in front of her, when she suddenly found herself opposite Lord Bellasis. He was two steps below her, so their eyes met on a level. She looked straight at his face with a searching firm glance. She did not shrink this time as she had done in the delicious joy of the evening before. She simply looked one question with her whole power.

"What do you mean?"

Directly she saw that he shrank from answering it, directly she recognised in his face only a sense of embarrassment, and even that not acute, she looked down again. She ought to have known it. She was not really surprised. She was to him simply a matter of indifference. Her instinct had deceived her. Last night had been nothing—only a sort of unwilling yielding to an artistic attraction.

After that one glance Cecilia did not look up again. Bellasis was in her way but he did not move. He could not see her face hidden under her enormous hat now that she was looking down. He only saw that her little hands were trembling as she pulled on her long gloves. Her hands were thinner than when he had first known her. They were beautifully modelled, white and small. He reflected with annoyance that Madge's were larger and not well formed.

Cecilia knew that she could not deceive him, could not pretend indifference. He had had her soul at his mercy and he simply did not care. Well, she would show no weakness. No sob of pain should escape her. Nothing more should be told by her;—she had shown far too much already. But the thought that she was alone for one moment with the man she loved with the vehemence of a passion she could not control was becoming too much for her. She was ashamed, bitterly ashamed. Laura's rebuke as to the weapons she had used against Madge had awakened no moral sense; but the knowledge that this man thought her to be base filled her with shame for what she had done. Was it nothing to him that it had been for his sake? And had she suffered nothing? Had she not been wronged when Madge had come between them? Had Madge's conduct been any nobler than her own? Madge, a Catholic, had gone against her dearest convictions to wreck Cecilia's happiness! Could she in no way clear herself before Bellasis?

No, all was over. All words would be futile now for ever. No use now to "plumb the salt estranging sea" that lay between them. Half the bitterness of such a parting is the sense of being misunderstood. He did not know her; he did not know Madge; and he was not troubled. Cecilia only was troubled.

At last Bellasis with the British instinct under embarrassment— and he was embarrassed—held out his hand. Cecilia did not seem to see it now. She stepped forward. He was obliged to move to let her pass and she ran downstairs and was lost to sight in a moment.

CHAPTER XVIII

THE TWENTY-FOURTH OF MARCH

Madge had had a troubled night of heavy sleep and bad dreams, intangible and vague, but none the less distressing. She could not rest in the morning. Her brain was tired and yet active, and would not be quieted. She felt better when she had had some tea and dressed and come down to the drawing-room. It was the 24th of March, and she was not sorry that there was still plenty to do to prepare for her leaving home on the 27th.

On the whole, the plans arranged at Mrs. Hurstmonceaux' little over a fortnight ago had been adhered to. There were to be no settlements so as to avoid the necessity of mentioning the engagement to the Riversdales before it was made public. Lord Bellasis had kept away from her for the two weeks, with the exception of a night in London on which a meeting was effected with Madge at Laura's house. During that evening Lord Bellasis had asked her to fix Saturday the 25th as the wedding-day. The talk up to this point had gone very smoothly. They were quite agreed as to keeping to the first plan of arrangements, the engagement should be announced in the papers, and two days afterwards they would be married privately, with no witnesses but the Hurstmonceaux. In that way they would secure the public announcement and would yet avoid any time for interference from Madge's Catholic relations. Lord Bellasis thought himself considerate in suggesting so late a day in the week as Saturday, and Madge said quietly with a little break in her voice, which touched him inexpressibly, that Saturday would do. Madge was so small, so gentle, and there was something pathetic in the delicate feminine reserves and half-unwilling yielding that fascinated the strong man and satisfied his unconscious love of power.

"Then Saturday, little woman, I will take you right away to the south and the sea. You are so pale and tired, darling, you ought to be taken care of."

Madge leant back and looked up in his face with a wan little smile.

"I am not well, you know, and I have lived so much alone. I am afraid you won't find me very bright."

Lord Bellasis knelt down by her side for a moment, leant forward and lightly kissed her forehead.

"Wait and see, little woman, if we can't manage that after March the 25th."

Madge gave a start and looked alarmed.

"The 25th," she cried, "which day is the 25th?"

"Saturday, of course," he said smiling, but a little perplexed.

Madge tried to command herself and puckered her forehead in the effort.

"No, no, the 25th won't do; it is too soon, I can't, no, I can't be ready by then."

"But you know," answered Lord Bellasis a little impatiently, "you told me that if I went away for two weeks we would then put it in the papers and be married two days afterwards. That would make our wedding-day Friday the 24th. It isn't quite fair to turn upon me when I suggest the 25th and say it is too soon."

Madge was exercising great self-control; she had nearly lost her head while she was speaking and had been on the point of crying out that the 23rd or the 24th would do, any day but the 25th. She would have been obliged to tell him the truth if she had gone so far. For on the 25th of March, Lady Day, the Feast of the Annunciation in the chapel of the Sacré Cœur Convent at Montmartre, Madge O'Reilly, aged ten years, had made her first communion. The fact of Lord Bellasis pressing for that special day raised in her mind and heart a sudden paroxysm of fear and awe. Now, all that she could say was that she must have more time, that she could not be ready, she wished to wind up her affairs at home, dismiss the servants, pay the house accounts, arrange for a caretaker, etc.

Lord Bellasis fumed for a few minutes and called it all nonsense, but Madge had recovered her wits and knew how to soothe him. She said that it was important to have everything in order—it made the whole thing look better.

"For my own little reputation," she said, half laughing, "I don't know that I ought to consent to be married only two days after we have taken the world into our confidence."

"Then tell them now," growled Bellasis.

Madge looked really hurt, and one of the tears that had been confined with difficulty rolled out in silvery brightness on her cheek. After that, though the logic may have been indistinct, the conclusions reached were clear. They were to be married on Monday, the 27th, as the wedding could not be on a Sunday, and the engagement was to be put in the *Morning Post* of the 25th.

"Put 'will shortly take place,'" said Madge with a shy smile.

"By Jove, yes, it will be very shortly."

And then, with a very unusual touch of solemnity which became him well, he bowed his head over hers as they stood together before parting.

"May God do so to me and much more also if I do not make thee happy."

Madge clutched his arm for support. The world about her was becoming indistinct.

"Oh, yes, you will give me a very good time," and she hid her face with a little laugh on his shoulder.

All, up to the morning of the 24th, was carried out as had been planned. Madge had been very busy putting her affairs in order. She was not a bad woman of business when she chose. She was one of those extravagant people who know quite well what they are about and get their money's worth to the full value, although much of the money is still unpaid. And in her own house she had housewifely instincts. She owed very large sums to dressmakers and many shops, but the butler and the housekeeper thought her very regular in her payments. She was writing cheques for the wages to be given at the last moment with full directions as to what the servants were to do when she had gone. Yet though unconsciously glad not to have a moment to spare, and throwing herself almost vehemently into all the business she could think of, it was unusually badly done. Sums were added up wrong, and two cheques were put into their envelopes that were not signed at all.

Madge had been at her writing-table by half past nine,—for her an extraordinarily early hour. Celestine kept coming in with a number of questions.

"Would madame take all the new *lingerie*, even to the summer *toilettes de bain en dentelles Russes?*"

"Mais, certainement."

Five minutes later she was sorry to *déranger* madame, but the second opera-cloak had just come. Would madame see it? and Celestine held out a light cloud-like object of blue brocade trimmed with chiffon. Madge turned round to give her full attention.

"Why they have put the wrong ribbons at the back. Those are horribly vulgar; and you know they have all the petticoat bodices to alter before to-morrow night. The tucks are so absurdly exaggerated. What intolerable people they are."

And then a footman interrupted the interview with the opera-cloak bringing a note on a salver.

Friday, 24th March.

DEAREST MADGE,

One detail more—may I fetch you in my brougham on Monday or will you come for me? I am entirely at your disposal, but if my brougham is to be honoured, I should like to order bouquets, etc., to-morrow morning. I feel so much for you at having all this business on your hands. Can I be of any use to-day? I was shown the tea-gowns at Kate Reilly's yesterday in a private room. They are divine. But I must not run on, I will look in this afternoon to see if you want me.

Your loving
LAURA.

P.S.—I told Cecilia of the engagement yesterday as you wished.

The colour rose in a hot flush to Madge's face as she glanced at the postscript, and her hand shook. Having hastily written a line to say that she was most grateful and would much rather be taken to the wedding in Laura's brougham, she turned her attention again to the opera-cloak.

"It isn't right at all. The lining is actually greenish and of the wrong kind of green. Oh, Hilda, is that you, and going out already? Do you like my new opera-cloak?"

"How lovely!" cried Hilda. "But I can't stop; Cecilia wants particularly to see me at half-past ten."

"Cecilia this morning? Why, how tiresome; I want you to come out with me. I think you might have told me last night."

Hilda looked astonished. Madge had seldom shown the faintest interest in her morning occupations before.

"What's the use?" thought Madge, "she must know it soon. It may be as well to get it done to-day," and she made one more effort.

"Oh, do throw Cecilia over; you might, for once in a way, give her up for me," said Madge flushing. "Send her a note to say you can't come."

"But she is so very urgent," Hilda answered nervously.

Then Madge walked in a curiously unsteady yet direct way to the window and clasping her hands in front of her said in a dreamy voice:—

"You won't see Cecilia if you do go!"

"Why not?" said the astonished Hilda.

Madge turned round, walked back to the fireplace and gave a little hysterical laugh.

"Oh, nonsense, I don't know. Go if you want to," and she sank back in an arm-chair.

"Why did I say that? It was odd. I suppose I wanted to stop her going." She shivered. "What a bright day and I want sunshine. I must get out soon and get rid of these horrid thoughts. It won't be pleasant when Hilda knows; but then, after all, she won't know anything more than that it is a mixed marriage, unless Cecilia—but—but how very odd! Cecilia is coming here, coming upstairs. I can hear her!"

And at that moment the door opened and the footman appeared. Behind him was a lady. Madge had almost said "Cecilia," when she suddenly realised that it was not Cecilia but Mary Riversdale who had followed the servant.

Madge was half relieved but greatly annoyed. Marmaduke had not told her that the Riversdales were coming up. And she was feeling queer and ill. She did not feel equal to complications. Still the sight of Mary had brought her back to the realities of life.

"How d'ye do, Mary?" she said, kissing her not more mechanically than usual. "Isn't it cold? Come nearer the fire, won't you?"

Mary said she had walked too quickly to feel cold.

"How well you look," cried Madge, "and what a lovely hat."

Mary smiled; it was so like Madge to admire her hat with a tone of surprise in her admiration.

"Yes, isn't it pretty?" said Mary lightly; "mother bought it for me to-day."

Mary seemed wonderfully well certainly, and bright, quite curiously bright, Madge reflected; there was a sunniness about her that was very observable. She had never seen her so handsome, so well dressed—quite fashionably dressed—before. What could it mean?

"We came up yesterday for a short time and I've heaps to do," Mary went on; "I am to be painted among other things."

Madge had intended to keep as close to the weather line in talk as possible, but this was too much for her.

"Mary," she cried, "what has happened? are you going to be married?"

Madge blushed a deep red as she spoke. A soft tender look came into Mary's blue eyes; and the wells of light in their depths shone brilliantly. Mr. Fieldes had once said that he had never seen eyes that distributed the light as well as Mary's.

"No," she answered with a low laugh. Everything about her seemed to Madge transformed and softened. "No, but I have come to tell you something," for a moment she hesitated and blushed. Madge bent forward eagerly; her face with its dark lines round the eyes looked almost haggard, and her hair was ruffled in the way Mrs. Hurstmonceaux so much disliked. What made Mary look like this? To what fruition had she passed?

Like the reflection of a summer's cloud, a tremulous shadow of feeling passed over Mary's face, a suspicion of emotion.

"Madge, I came to tell you that I am going to be a Sister of Charity."

Madge stared on. She seemed to have lost the power of speech. At last she said very coldly:—

"Have you thought of it for a long time?"

"No. Only—only since that time you were at Skipton."

Madge's face did not change in the least.

"Why did it attract you?" she said in the same hard voice.

"It didn't attract me," said Mary, blushing deeply; "I couldn't bear it."

"But you look happy now."

"Oh, yes," said Mary. "I should think so."

"Where are you going?"

"I hope to China."

"China?" said Madge in the same voice as before. "Why China?"

"Because of the babies," said Mary. "They throw away girl babies there, you know."

"But, Mary, if it didn't attract you at first when did it attract you?"

It was becoming a great difficulty to Mary to answer these hard unsympathetic curious questions. Madge had always managed to hurt Mary. She was hurting her now, but Mary reflected that happy people mustn't be selfish, and Madge somehow looked so very very odd. For a moment the same fear that had once overwhelmed Hilda came to her, that Madge might be a little mad. At that very instant Madge was thinking to herself: "It is sheer intolerable madness. They are all mad and they are all bad, very bad, to let that girl sacrifice herself like this."

Mary had been quite silent for a moment.

"I'll tell you what I can, but it is rather difficult. Do you remember that night Father Clement preached, and the text? Well it came to me then first of all as an idea, but I ran away, I was a coward and I was frightened; I suppose it was the supernatural that frightened me, and for some weeks I was always running away and I was, oh, so miserable. The day you went away and Carlos was killed was almost the worst. My horse died a week later. I was full of horrors, everything seemed so hard and horrible. I couldn't see why I couldn't be left alone. It seemed as if God had killed them both as a message to me, and God seemed hard. Have you ever had that temptation?"

"Yes," said Madge, but the words seemed to stick in her throat.

"And I couldn't bear Mr. Fieldes giving me the Imitation. It seemed as if he too witnessed against me. Then at last one night I suddenly saw God's love clearly, and my life seemed such a little thing to give up. I saw that I was standing in my own way and I gave in. It felt simply as if I could not possibly help it."

"Then were you happy?" said Madge. Her voice seemed to grow more and more negative.

"Yes, but not as I am now. I think it was like a deathbed with all one's consciousness. There seemed great happiness but great sorrow too. It was like dying. It took a week to die."

"And then?" said Madge, moving unconsciously a little nearer to Mary. "And then?"

"I suppose one doesn't know what heaven is," said Mary, "but one may say it has been heavenly—not that I care one bit less for mother or father, only I seem to be always on the point of meeting all I love in heaven for ever."

There was a strange mingling of pain and joy in Mary's face as she spoke; but the suffering appeared to be conquered by some habitual mental state as if a cloud had passed between her and an overmastering vision, and had obscured it for a moment only. She was gazing in front of her as she spoke, when she heard a low sob from Madge. Madge had bent over the side of the chair and had buried her face in her hands. She was shaking with suppressed sobs. Mary knelt down beside her and stroked her hair softly—the elaborately dressed hair she had so often wondered at. At last Madge threw up her tear-stained face almost roughly.

"You won't meet *me* in heaven any how," she said.

"Madge, dear, you mustn't say that," said Mary with tender gravity.

Madge buried her face again.

"Mary, you can't understand," Madge went on, in a low, quick tone, "only you can see that it is of no use to talk to me about religion, about God. You must go now, and you mustn't come here again; you will know soon why not, and you must tell them all that it was not possible, after the life I led with George at Skipton, to refuse happiness now. You know," her voice grew harder and more shrill, and she bent over the side of her chair, "you know it is not possible."

"Madge," said Mary quietly, "I am going." The childlike narrative was over, Mary was the strong girl that she had been an hour earlier, a stronger, more complete personality than Madge had ever seen her before. "I am going now. I cannot tell why you are sending me away, but as you wish to do so, I will go. But I have to say something first which you must listen to, as we may not meet again. I should have had my great-aunt's fortune when I came of age, £4000 a year, now I have settled to give the income to trustees, to pay off the rest of George's debts and to pay you for whatever you have had to pay for him up to now. Then, if you will let me, I should like to clear up anything you owe yourself. After that the rest will go to my father. I am going now, Madge, you will say good-bye?"

Mary was standing over her.

"Good-bye," muttered Madge, without raising her head. Mary walked slowly and sadly to the door and opened it.

"Oh, don't, don't go, Mary! Stay now. How can you leave me? How can you be so unkind?"

It was Madge, Madge holding out her hands, gazing with a longing as if for mercy. Mary went back and put her arms round her. Madge was sobbing and could not speak.

Some moments passed. At last, when Madge's sobs had grown quieter, Mary, who was sitting on the arm of the chair leaning over Madge, spoke very gently.

"Is there something the matter?"

Madge made an effort to control herself.

"Oh, no, I don't know, I am foolish. Never mind, I mustn't keep you, you had better—"

But here she put her hands to her face and sobbed more wildly than ever.

"Don't, Madge," said Mary, "don't behave like that."

"Put your arm round me then," said Madge, "and I won't. You wouldn't touch me if you knew," she whispered, "but you needn't know just yet," and she leant back, keeping very still.

Mary waited with a trembling foreboding for what might come. Then Madge said suddenly:—

"I am not a Catholic any more, Mary, so I suppose we shan't meet again."

"Hush, hush," said Mary, with a sort of motherly reproof.

"It is no use hushing me and soothing me as if I were a baby. It is quite true, and you mustn't suppose you can make any difference. You needn't think I don't know what I am about. I do, perfectly well." She sat up again. "I have thought it all out," she said. "I can't be good. It is of no use. And so I can't avoid doing something very wrong, can I? And so it simply is that I've chosen one big wrong thing to do. Then of course, you know, I shall repent some day. I've not lost the faith, I never shall lose it. Mary, I sometimes wish I *could*. Don't look like that, I don't want *you* to. Oh, Mary, Mary, go away; I am going mad. Oh, why, why didn't God leave me that baby!"

She was standing now facing Mary. "Don't look like the angel in the picture. I have sold my soul, and it is no business of yours. I will, I will marry Bellasis, and his wife whom he has divorced is sure to die, you know, and then we shall be married by a priest. Now I've told you; now go—only—only—there is the door bell—wait till I've told them to say 'Not at home' to Cecilia."

She walked to the bell in the same unsteady and yet direct way that she had done when Hilda was with her in the morning. Then she paused and without raising her hand or pressing the bell she said in a dreamy voice:—

"But it is of no use to say 'Not at home' to Cecilia."

She turned round with a frightened look and saw that Mary had knelt down by the sofa, and she appeared to be praying. A sudden fit of temper seized Madge, and she dashed forward to pull Mary to her feet and force her to go away. But suddenly, how she never knew, the momentary gust of anger passed from her, and as if against her will she knelt down by Mary's side. Then she heard Mary saying in what seemed to her a strangely exultant voice:—

"Hail, Mary, full of grace, the Lord is with thee, blessed art thou amongst women, and blessed is the fruit of thy womb, Jesus". Madge answered mechanically:—

"Holy Mary, Mother of God, pray for us sinners now, and at the hour of our death, Amen."

Mary was saying the Rosary. And Madge was answering her in the words familiar to her day after day in her life as a child and as a school-girl. The Rosary had been said by the girls at the Sacré Cœur every day before dinner. Madge had always said the Sorrowful Mysteries as part of her preparation for confession. Torn by a conflict of feelings she could not understand or explain, the words that had so often given comfort seemed a relief. Another Hail Mary and yet another, and at the end of the decade the "Glory be to the Father," and then another decade.

Dreamily she continued to answer. She forgot that she had told herself it was of no use to pray, she soon forgot that she was kneeling against the sofa in her own drawing-room. She thought she was in the convent chapel at the Sacré Cœur, with the beautiful Notre Dame high on the throne. And the girls were singing a *cantique*, and the warm air was scented with lilies and with incense. And Madge found herself praying, as she had never prayed before, for she knew that she was in some terrible danger. There was a chasm open between her and the altar, and she could not get across it. Then the *cantique* grew fainter, but she was holding up her rosary to show the others that she was praying too.

"Sainte Marie, mère de Dieu, priez pour nous pauvres pecheurs maintenant et à l'heure de notre mort. Ainsi soit-il." "L'heure de notre mort," that was it, that was what she had been saying in English, "the hour of our death." Was this a foresight of that hour? Was that Lady on the throne, turning away from Madge, turning to a little baby who will never see its mother again?

"Glory be to the Father and to the Son and to the Holy Ghost," Mary was finishing the second decade. What was the priest doing in the convent chapel, the same old *curé*? He was at the altar, and the altar was farther off now. He was asking them to pray, to pray for one who was dying, who was once one of themselves, and who was dying without the sacraments; and he seemed to say that he could not reach her across the chasm; and he kneels down and the words come faintly to her:—

"Ave, Maria, gratia plena, Dominus tecum, benedicta tu in mulieribus et benedictus fructus ventris tui, Jesus."

And Madge answered: "Sancta Maria, mater Dei, ora pro nobis peccatoribus nunc et in hora mortis nostrae. Amen."

Mary recalling the scene later on remembered that Madge had finished the Hail Mary once in Latin and once or twice in French.

. . . . . .

The rosary was finished, and Mary had risen from her knees; but Madge did not get up for some minutes. She remained kneeling, her face buried in her hands, no longer praying, but as if dazed and stupefied. At last she got up and said very quietly:—

"Will you take me to Skipton for a little while, Mary?"

CHAPTER XIX

SILENCE

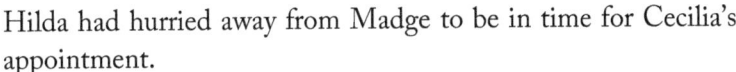

Hilda had hurried away from Madge to be in time for Cecilia's appointment.

"I must see you to-morrow at half-past ten," she had written, "it is important."

It was a bright, sunny, windy morning, and Hilda, who was in low spirits and worried, seemed to herself to be the only exception to the general cheerfulness. Yet the people she met would hardly have thought her a blot upon the sunshine. Her large hat was trimmed with spring flowers; her graceful vigorous figure was well defined by her close-fitting jacket. The look of trouble on the brilliant face was so slight as to be unnoticeable by a chance observer. A young man who encountered her carelessly held parasol, and felt that its point had scratched him, muttered to himself that that beautiful girl must be already in love. She knew her way and did not miss one of the right turnings in spite of her preoccupation. Dreamily she walked up the steps of the house in Charles Street and rang.

The visitors' bell was answered almost instantly. Hilda was still half absent and was habitually shy of servants. She turned round as she shut her parasol saying, "Miss Cecilia Rupert," without looking at the maid. The girl answered quietly—hysterical women servants had already gone out of fashion:—

"We are in great trouble, miss. Miss Cecilia Rupert was found dead this morning. Dr. Rule has just been here."

Hilda stood and looked at her in silence for a moment. Then she said:—

"How awful!"

"I was told, miss, if you called, to ask you to see Nurse Barnes."

"Me?" said Hilda.

She had already turned to the door with an instinctive wish to get away. Cecilia, whom she was to have been with at that moment for the sort of chat she knew so well, which always left her a little shocked at Cecilia, and a good deal ashamed of herself—Cecilia was dead. Dead, why, oh why? Had she been ill? Had there been an accident? She turned to the parlourmaid.

"But," she cried, "she was not at all ill!"

Motionless were the muscles of that admirable person. No butler of the old *régime* could have been more calmly automatic.

"Would you please to see Nurse Barnes, miss?"

Hilda signed acquiescence, and she was led to the little back sitting-room that had been Cecilia's sanctum. Hilda went to the window, and turned her back on the room. It was oppressively full of Cecilia, every object in it was painful to her vision. The writing-table and sofa, the cushions, the swing—Hilda would not look at them.

After a moment the nurse entered. She was a thin woman with hair turning grey. Her manner now was extremely professional. The parlourmaid was exercising great self-control. The nurse required no effort in that direction. She had got over that sort of thing in her hospital days. She shut the door very quietly and came up to Hilda.

"You will be surprised at my asking to see you, and I fear it may be painful, but when I was called to Miss Cecilia's room this morning I noticed two notes lying on the table beside the bed. I would not allow anything to be touched until Dr. Rule had been."

"But why," faltered Hilda, "why did she die?"

Nurse Barnes looked out of the window.

"Dr. Rule has told me to give this to all private inquirers."

She held out to Hilda a scrap of paper, on which she read:—

Miss Cecilia Rupert died from the effects of a large dose of chloroform, death probably taking place about twelve o'clock last night.

(Signed) F. RULE, M.D., F.R.C.P.

Hilda turned quite white and sat down involuntarily on the chair behind her. Her eyes swam, she could not see the address of a note which the nurse now held out to her. Nurse Barnes gave her time, and then spoke a little sternly.

"You must please read that now, in case it should have to be shown to the coroner," she said.

Hilda obeyed. The note was addressed:—

"Miss Hilda Riversdale—To be called for."

Hilda opened it, then let it drop. The nurse picked it up, and put it back into her hand.

"Read it," she said, with authority. Hilda read:—

DEAR LITTLE HILDA,

I don't want to live any more, so you will not see me again. I should any how have died soon, so there is nothing to fash for, even if there were anybody who would mind, which there isn't. But I hope you will live and have a good time. Don't be afraid about Mr. Marmaduke; he loves you very much, and if he ever loved anybody else, he got over it years ago.

Don't imagine that he will be unhappy when Madge marries Bellasis. There will be nobody who will be sorry for themselves when that comes. You good people will be furious with Madge, because he is a divorcee. There, it is out now. A dead woman may surely tell tales. I tried to make you all save her, but you wouldn't, and it is too late now.

Little Hilda, I will tell you that I would be rather different if I had to try living again. But the rest is silence. A hackneyed quotation—still I hope an appropriate one, irresistible under present circumstances.

Yours very affectionately,
CECILIA."

Hilda only half took in what the words meant. Then she looked imploringly up at the nurse.

"Oh, she was mad, she was mad, wasn't she?" she cried.

"That will be the verdict,—'while of unsound mind.' It is always put like that."

Then the nurse did not think that Cecilia was mad. And if she were not mad, then probably that letter was true. There was no sense of comfort out of the note yet. Blank, colourless horror and anguish crushing her soul and her body, was all Hilda knew. Were not the simple facts to a home-bred religious girl sufficiently crushing? Her friend had committed suicide, and Madge, a Catholic and her cousin's widow, intended to make a sacrilegious marriage. And Hilda could not doubt the truth of the assertion, as Cecilia must have had positive proof of it before she destroyed herself. But how far, far more wicked was Madge than Cecilia—Madge who had faith than Cecilia who had not.

Hilda started up, holding the note tightly, and walked blindly across the room. Madge was the wickedest but Cecilia was dead. And she, Hilda, what had she been doing, what had she tried to do? She had been of no help to them, she had been selfish, utterly selfish. Had she ever tried really to help Cecilia? Had she not been full of her own wicked jealousies and rash judgments? Oh, it was very hideous. Marmaduke would never love her if he knew, and he would be right not to. Hilda turned fiercely on herself. The thought of Cecilia was intolerable. She knelt down suddenly, "Oh God, be merciful!" she cried aloud.

The nurse touched her on the shoulder, Hilda recollected herself and rose. Something in the woman's face made her fold the note tightly in her hand. It was not feminine curiosity, but the professional sense that there was a business side to the note. Hilda had not completely lost her head. She rallied.

"Miss Cecilia Rupert believed that she had but a short time to live, and so she took her own life," she said firmly.

Whatever happened that note must not be seen. Come coroners, come doctors, come a whole army of calm commanding nurses, they should not get that note. Hilda glanced at the grate, but there was no fire. Nurse Barnes saw the glance.

"You must not destroy it," she said sternly.

"But then what am I to do? I can't show it, I can't leave it, and, oh, I can't wait in this house for the coroner."

"No, no," said the nurse soothingly, "that would not be fitting; you are too young. You ought not to be here at all. Now listen to me. Pay attention. I can't let that note go. I am too much concerned in it. For I let Miss Cecilia have that chloroform for her toothache, as she called it, and I must think of myself. If there is a good reason for this death, whether it makes a scandal or not, those gentlemen must know it. And if you destroyed the note, you would have to give evidence on oath which would probably bring out something far more awkward. If you give that to Dr. Rule, you can trust him to keep it out of the papers. The brother, Lord Rupert, has been telegraphed for, and he and the doctor and the coroner will manage matters between them. I know how these things are done. It will be settled at the inquest that she was insane, and then, being insane, it will be evident that what she wrote was mere madness. It is a mercy that the poor thing upstairs is past knowing anything about it in this world. I expect Lord Rupert will have to arrange for a double funeral. Just sit down at this table and do up the letter, address it to Dr. Rule, and seal it up. If you like we will post it together."

"No," said Hilda, "I will leave it with you. I believe you are right. Where is the sealing-wax? I have my father's seal."

She spoke quietly, but her hand shook so much that she could hardly write the address—or fix the seal firmly. The nurse helped her, and the moment it was finished, she turned to escape.

"I will put you in a cab," the nurse said kindly; "you are not fit to be alone. But where are you going to; who will look after you?"

"I don't know," said Hilda impatiently, breaking away from the nurse's questions, and leaving the room before the woman could speak again. As she came into the hall she started back. Standing talking with the parlourmaid, with an expression of intense pain on his dark face, she saw Marmaduke, and she heard the maid say:—

"There is Nurse Barnes, sir; Dr. Rule wished her to see you."

Marmaduke at Cecilia's house early in the morning, also commanded to interview Nurse Barnes seemed to be confusing for a moment, but for a moment only. Nurse Barnes had spoken of two notes. Was the other for Marmaduke? and was it also "to be called for"? Hilda's feelings were divided between the strong wish to get away from Marmaduke and a wish to cling to him in this moment of horror amid these calm automatic women.

"Wait for me, Hilda," exclaimed Marmaduke; "what has brought you here?" He was full of horror at the news and much distressed at finding Hilda at that house. But he too was to find that far worse things were to be told him in the little sitting-room than in the hall. Being stronger, calmer, more experienced,—being a man, he was able to get at least good hope of happiness out of the note left to him by Cecilia, with its positive assurance of Hilda's love for himself. Then too the revelation it contained as to Madge's engagement to Lord Bellasis and of his being a divorcee, though a shock, was not quite as astonishing to him as to Hilda. His suspicions that something very wrong was going forward had been growing rapidly stronger during the last few days. This meeting with Hilda was in itself fortunate, though he wished he could have shielded her from contact with the awful tragedy in Miss Rupert's house. He must consider now where she ought to go, as on no account must she return to Madge.

He escaped from the nurse as quickly as he could, after he had sealed up his note also. He said that he would see Dr. Rule himself at once. After a moment's glance into the empty hall, he saw an open door, and through it Hilda was visible, leaning back in an arm-chair, her face absolutely colourless, her eyes large and vacant. But she got up quite quietly and followed him. The nurse had been called upstairs, the parlourmaid was gone—they were alone—but he would speak no word to her and ask no sign from her while they were in that house haunted by the shadow of

Death—not Death ruling as a king, almost gracious in his majesty, but Death as an unwilling guest, grudging his awful pomp to a rebel who had dared to forestall his chosen hour.

Marmaduke and Hilda once in the street, paused for a moment—then Hilda said in a very low but distinct voice:—

"Will you call a hansom?"

He signed to a hansom standing near and helped her into it. She sat down in the middle of the seat. Marmaduke looked at her. Whether she wanted him or not it was clear to him that he must go with her. She was unfit to be alone. And where was she going? She must not go to Madge; that he could not allow. He wished he knew if Cecilia had told Hilda of the engagement. He dared not at this moment risk upsetting her further by speaking of it for fear that she did not know it. He had better take her to Mrs. Riversdale's hotel, that was the only safe thing to do. But before he could decide to tell her that her aunt and Mary had come up to London, Hilda leant forward in the hansom, "Tell him," she said in a louder voice, "to go to Victoria Station—Brighton line."

Marmaduke obeyed, and then got into the hansom without asking her leave. As the horse moved, Hilda said:—

"I am going to mother."

Marmaduke's masculine mind was not prepared for such sudden action—though it was really by far the best and simplest solution of the problem. But that Hilda should drive off to the station, and go down to the country, without Brown and without boxes, was so very sudden. Men instinctively dislike the idea of sudden action on the part of women, it seems a straining of the practicable. Hilda had not even looked out her train. If, on the other hand, she would allow him to go with her how very different that would be! In this time of sorrow and shock would she not be very gentle, and turn to him for comfort? If what Cecilia wrote to him were true,—and surely only an hour before death she would speak the truth,—Hilda really loved him, and only some mysterious misunderstanding, some girlish mistake, had made her hide it so long. Surely, throwing into the scale Cecilia's positive assertion and much in Hilda's conduct that had always puzzled him,—a look in her eyes that seemed so much more kindly than her words, a break in her voice that seemed so much less self-assured than her manner,—might he not hope now, hope with good confidence? What if at the end of that journey he and she went together to her mother? Delicious, glorious conclusion! The simple sweetness, the sweet simplicity of it nearly made him laugh aloud! But he had to rein up those boisterous hopes of his very quickly.

His best plan he thought was to be firm,

"Hilda," he said, "I must go down with you if you want to go now." He trembled with anxiety behind his most masterful manner.

"No, you cannot leave London," said Hilda, "the coroner may want you, and you said you must go and see Dr. Rule."

Marmaduke felt rebuked by these words. This was not the day for his hopes any more than Miss Rupert's had been the house in which to express them. Cecilia would soon be left behind them, casting at most a shadow of sadness, of tragic suffering, of haunting fear on their imaginations. But to-day was too full of her, too dark with the horror of her lifeless body, not to be entirely hers. For to-day at least their own lives must be interrupted, and such mourning and prayer as it could contain must be wholly given to Cecilia. Hilda's words, and Hilda's manner seemed a just reproof for the thoughts of love that filled his mind. It was wonderfully touching to Marmaduke to see such pity and sorrow, such shrinking and pain in the beautiful young face. So would he have fancied an angel to look in the midst of a sinful, sorrowing world.

It was a short drive to the station, and the porter told them that a Brighton train was just starting. Hilda asked Marmaduke to take her ticket instantly. He did so and led her on to the platform. She was grateful for the necessity of haste, for the publicity of their position.

Hilda had hardly taken her seat before the train started. As it moved away Marmaduke saw the white face leaning back against the cushions, and the great dark eyes looking at him with a strange painful sense of entreaty; then she disappeared. There was something in the look so forlorn, so entreating, so humble, that he felt doubly miserable as he walked away at having been forced to let her go alone.

Hilda leant back in the seat of the carriage, looking mechanically first at the dark station and high narrow streets and then at the river dimly seen through the great balustrade of the bridge. But after Battersea Park was passed and the vast monotonous dulness of London suburbs, and the train had escaped into the country, Hilda looking at the fields began to cry. Her only companions were two elderly men seated at the other end of the carriage talking to each other. Hilda turned her head away from them and let the tears flow freely.

She was mourning for Cecilia, mourning for Madge, mourning for herself. She had thought when she left Brierly Cottage in February that in ten days at least she would be home again. It was about seven weeks now since she had seen her mother. And what would she have to tell her to-day? The whole story was infinitely terrible to Hilda. Strong upon her was the childish wish to wake up and find it all to have been a horrible nightmare. She tried to see clearly how the time in London had been spent.

"I wonder," she thought, "how long Madge has been thinking of this horrible thing! I remember she talked of Lord Bellasis that first night in London. I wonder I was allowed to stay with her. Then the very first time Cecilia spoke to me she asked me about Lord Bellasis. I might have seen she was jealous of Madge. How amazingly stupid I have been. But then why did she make me believe that Marmaduke had cared for Madge? oh, dear me, I have believed anything anybody said—what a goose they must have thought me! and Laura—I wonder what she knew about it all? I daresay she has been playing with my stupidity too. But I do not know what about. The fact is that I am very, very stupid and I can't understand anything now except that Cecilia is dead, and Madge is wicked, and I can't ever be happy again—

Marmaduke can't possibly forgive me when he knows how I half engaged myself to Mark Fieldes."

Long deep-drawn sobs shook her. Her head throbbed painfully, her mind worked hard. It seemed as if it were something apart from herself, another voice talking to her that went on far faster than the train did, and that spoke louder than the shrill whistle of the engine. "Some girls," it said, "might think they were bound to Mark, but I am sure I am not, although I have treated him very, very badly—it would only be treating him worse to go on with it. Shall I write to him? Oh, I don't know—I will ask mother—I will never do anything on my own judgment again. If I never marry Marmaduke I shall love him all my life."

Then the horror of the thought of Cecilia came back and the misery of Madge's wrong-doing. "And I did nothing to help them," she said to herself again. Her brain was in a strange whirl of pain and confusion. She pressed her hands on her temples, and her elbows against the little ledge below the window.

She was surprised at suddenly hearing "Broomhurst" called out as the train stopped, and to find that her journey was at an end. She hastily pulled down her veil and thrust her handkerchief into her pocket. There was a strange familiarity in the little station to her in her present state of mind. She was the only thing there in the least altered. Avoiding the friendly porter, who would certainly want to know why she was without luggage and who was happily occupied with some milk cans at the other end of the platform, Hilda hurried through the ticket-office, crossed the broad road on the other side, and took a little foot-path through the fields that led to her home.

The sun was shining brightly, the larches were green, the primroses were thick under the hedges. On such a day, although only just escaped from the dark wood and at the beginning of his terrible journey, Dante felt an irrational cheerfulness owing to "L'ora del tempo e la dolce stagione." Hilda was out of her dark wood of trouble. She was still at the beginning of life, and not like the poet "nell mezzo del camin di nostra vita." In a few moments she would be at home, clasped in her mother's arms. Her life was in reality full of "sweet records, promises as sweet." Although her nerves were thoroughly shaken, and she had had a rude awakening from her ideal of the charms of the world, still as she walks through those fields she cannot but feel that there is much hope in the good air and the beautiful season, a hope and comfort which, with a very new humility and meekness, must bring her the peace that men have been commanded to pray for. Tears started again to her eyes; but this time they were tears of relief and wistfulness, as her parched spirit drank freely of the living nature about her.

CHAPTER XX

MADGE AND LAURA ON THE TWENTY-FOURTH

Laura had lunched with the Duchess of A. on that Friday. There had been a large party, and every one had noticed her unusual animation and brightness. As she drove away to keep her appointment with Madge, her day-dreams were of the pleasantest. All was at last arranged. The wedding would gain a hundredfold from the mysterious secrecy which had preceded it. Bellasis was bound to her by cords of steel. Madge's acceptance of the offer of her brougham was an additional satisfaction. Laura reached Madge's house at half-past three in the highest spirits.

Mary had stayed to luncheon and Madge had given a general order that she would not be "at home" to any visitor. The butler soon after luncheon came in to know if she would make the usual exception for Mrs. Hurstmonceaux.

"No, certainly not," said Madge vigorously; "I am at home to nobody."

"Mrs. Hurstmonceaux insisted upon my inquiring as she particularly wished to see you."

"Is she here? Why didn't you say so at once?"

Madge sprang up, then sat down again. Here was the influence, the personification of all that she was trying to keep behind her mentally. Here was the view in which Mary would be simply the object of a beautiful delusion, and her parents almost criminal for their sacrifice. Here was the view that she, Madge, would be putting an end to her own life, to all that made life worth living, and that she was incurring also the moral condemnation of a world that would not think lightly or without suspicion of a woman that could jilt Lord Bellasis. Was she not risking even her good name, and could that be right?

"Would you rather I went away if you want to see her?" Mary spoke hesitatingly.

"No, no, no," said Madge with a vehemence that startled Mary, but did not startle the butler who knew the state of things very fairly well, as such functionaries generally do. A surprise however was in store for him. He had expected that either Mary or Mrs. Hurstmonceaux would be in the ascendant and the other be sent away—but he had not supposed that they would meet.

"Show her up here, and Mary whatever she says don't you go away. She is rather a bore but she won't stay long."

Laura came into the room with a face of exceeding sympathy, not at all the ordinary expression suitable to an afternoon call. When she saw Mary she composed her features, but she was surprised that Madge had admitted anybody else after the "not at home" which she had herself never met there before. Madge avoided a kiss and then at once said rather solemnly in an unconsciously loud voice:—

"This is Mary Riversdale, my sister-in-law; let me introduce her."

Laura gasped and actually turned pale with astonishment. What could it mean? The announcement would be in the papers next day if it were not forestalled by the evening papers of to-day, and yet Mary, George's intensely Catholic sister, was closeted with Madge, and she had caught a glimpse of the two sitting hand in hand before Madge rose to receive her. Laura's manners failed her for a moment, she only stared.

"Yes," said Madge—it excited her to have some living thing to combat, and she had often rebelled against the subtle influence which she had never been able to resist successfully before—"Mary has come to spend some days with me."

What was Madge's scheme? What could she be meaning? At this juncture to try and keep friends with the Riversdales was idiotic, and nothing would be gained by it.

"I just came in to ask you if you would like to dine with me quite alone to-night? Lady Tempest has to put off her dinner because she has influenza, and so I shall be at home and quite alone, as my husband dines elsewhere."

Laura was too quick not to perceive a difference in Madge's manner. The dull weight that had appeared to oppress her during the past fortnight was gone. She seemed excited and overstrung.

"No," said Madge, looking straight at her, fighting the creeping kind of atmospheric influence which seemed to be growing stronger. "No, I'm so sorry I can't; I'm going to St. Philip's to-night with Mary, it is the eve of one of our feasts, and you know we always go to confession on such eves."

An alarming light began to dawn upon Laura.

"Always, dear Madge?" she said with a touch of irony. Madge flushed.

"The fact is, Laura, that my plans are quite altered by some news Mary has brought me. She is going to be a Sister of Charity. She is going to China to pick up babies." She hesitated, then ended defiantly: "I shall spend the last months with her."

Laura knew quite well what Madge had said, and now she understood plainly what she meant. It was clear that for the moment Madge had reverted to her religious beliefs and meant to give up her engagement. And Laura was wholly unprepared for such a crisis. She wanted to gain time for thought. She turned round, and for the first time looked at Mary. It might have been embarrassing and painful to hear her vocation mentioned in this way; but Mary was far too much interested and astonished by what was passing to think of herself. She laughed a little.

"Perhaps I shan't be allowed to go for the babies," she said.

Laura, for a moment, was lost in studying Mary. She was thinking of Fieldes' account of the fair girl who rode so straight to hounds. She seemed to have no further attention for Madge. She saw now who was the enemy, and she admired her unwillingly. But it was impossible surely for this girl to ruin Madge's life. She must be cautious. What did this Miss Riversdale know of the state of things? It would not be safe to be explicit, yet an instinct told her that she must speak to Madge at once, if she were not to lose her influence for ever afterwards.

"Ah," she said, speaking to Mary, "that is very beautiful, very supporting, you are carried on by wonderful enthusiasms. It is very noble. I congratulate you with all my heart, but I confess I can conceive harder things than that. I wouldn't speak of the work at our doors, of the workers one knows and helps in one's own small way, picking up the gutter babies. I think, if I were called, London would be my China. But I don't mean that. All babies are human,"—she hesitated a moment. She felt that she was in danger of talking nonsense. "But there is something harder than living for babies. That is living without the call, the enthusiasm, without all that makes a glory round you now, having to live in this world and to be supposed to belong to it and yet, in fact, to sacrifice life, hope, joy, to conscience perhaps—or perhaps," she hesitated again, and half kneeling on a low chair by her, looked beyond Mary, and as if speaking only to herself, her voice falling to a penetrating whisper, she concluded, "perhaps to some poor scruple, a futile and tragic mistake."

There was a silence, unbroken by her listeners, and then, with a ring of genuine feeling, she went on:—

"The years of life are much longer than you can understand as yet. There are more days in them as life goes on than in younger years, and more hours in the day, far longer hours in the night. That is why, at my age, one trembles at seeing the young make a life's mistake. I should not feel it for you—if you will forgive a personal allusion from a stranger in a peculiar moment. Your life has had a single purpose, one *motif,* one trend, one current. It may be hard at times, it will never be confused, weary, trivial. I understand your Church providing this high, rarefied, pure atmosphere for you. But for others is she not at times terribly hard? Is it even safe to say to a young woman of keen vitality, with rich human gifts, 'I forbid you from a stern iron law of my own, for which I will give you no reason, forbid you to take love, joy, power, success; I forbid you although—'" She turned towards Madge, and her voice was imploring, "I can't go on like this. I am not a diplomatist. Madge, what will your life be if you yield to this superstitious madness? You can't be as if this had not been. Are you facing in the least what your conduct means? If you had not given your word—but you have, and most solemnly. Why, good heavens, it is too late even for privacy."

Madge did not speak, but she winced for a moment, then lay down deliberately on the sofa and shut her eyes. But Laura detected something besides a suggestion of impertinence in her attitude; it seemed to her that Madge was taking refuge.

"After all you had suffered in the past, you had this year enjoyed your life a little—you had won for yourself a unique social position by your wonderful goodness."

"Or my want of it," interrupted Madge in a sleepy voice, and a faint smile of sarcasm passed over her white face. That last touch of Laura's was a relapse into her ordinary self; it weakened a strong point.

"But," a little impatience helped Laura now, "but the best of us have enemies"—Madge stirred perceptibly—"waiting ready for our mistakes."

Cecilia was the unspoken word that filled both their minds, and Laura trembled. Had she played her trump card too soon?

Madge's head moved restlessly. She opened her eyes to avoid the mental picture of Cecilia, radiant, triumphant; Cecilia, Lady Bellasis. No faint shudder, no warning chill from the spirit world came now. Laura's personality perhaps guarded that moment free. Madge met the glance from Laura's inscrutable long narrow eyes and she felt its power. But her own passed to Mary who stood with an expression of bewildered astonishment, with wide open blue eyes and a slightly wrinkled forehead. The contrast was so marked, and Mary's earnest puzzled effort to understand the extraordinary being in front of her who used words she had never heard of, and who spoke as if Madge were a saint, came with such a new effect on Madge's overwrought nerves that it produced a sensation of smothered laughter.

"Mary," she gasped, holding out her hand, "come here. Will you rub my temples with that *eau de Cologne*. They ache. No, come over this side, and sit on that chair; that is right, only a little harder please. But don't let us interrupt you, Laura. I think I understand so far. You were telling me about my friends, I mean to say my enemies, weren't you? I should like you to say all you want to now, as I don't feel sure that we shall meet for some time."

She hesitated and put up a hand to take hold of Mary's and clasped it tightly.

"You are going to the Riviera, perhaps," there was a break in her voice, "you will yacht with friends in the Mediterranean. I hope," the pressure of her hand was tighter on Mary's, "you will enjoy it. I shall be," her eyes filling with tears looked up at Mary imploringly, "I shall be at Skipton."

Laura rose from the chair she had been kneeling on: no one had asked her to sit down. She stood at her full height and faced the two young women, sternly determined to keep her long-conquered and enslaved temper well in hand now. But her words were not well chosen.

"Good God," she cried, with absolute conviction, "if you do break your word, you will rue it to your dying day."

"But on my dying day itself, Mary? she forgets that, doesn't she?" Madge sat up suddenly for a moment; her voice had risen higher. Mary was afraid she was going to break down.

Laura looked at Mary. It was of no use to do more, unless she could get her away. But Mary was pressing her hand firmly on Madge's forehead just above the closed eyes. Then, to their surprise, in a jerky half-whisper, Madge said abruptly:—

"And you will have a dying day too you know, Laura."

Laura treated this absurd interjection with quiet dignity. It was evidently of no use to stay, as Madge was becoming hysterical, and something might still be done in a letter. She bent over the sofa and kissed her with a mingled severity and tenderness that was almost maternal. She shook hands with Mary over the prostrate form between them and went away.

As soon as she had left the room Madge apostrophised the closed door almost with violence.

"You're gone," she cried, "and never, never, never shall you darken these doors again." But the door remained unmoved as the stately if not graceful figure of Mrs. Hurstmonceaux left the house.

Madge then rang the bell; the butler reappeared.

"No evening papers are to be admitted into the house to-night on any account."

"No, madam," was the solemn answer, and he conscientiously resolved that nobody should see them but himself.

"Madge," said Mary, "that was a very odd woman, wasn't she?"

"Stark staring mad," said Madge, looking up.

"And what made you tell her that I had come to stay with you?"

"Because you have," rejoined Madge passionately.

"But, Madge, I really don't think I can. It would hurt mother."

Madge looked at her for a moment, and then began to cry. A fit of hysterical sobbing followed of so violent a kind that when Mary consented to stay she hardly seemed to understand her.

Mary was peaceful and happy. But there still rested on her mind a shade of anxiety. She felt instinctively that the feelings which had triumphed in the inconstant little heart might hold their place by a fragile tenure. She saw that her presence seemed almost a necessity to Madge. But this could not last for ever. She could only pray that the grace, which had done so much, might yet do more—that feeling and purpose might be deepened and prove constant.

CHAPTER XXI

LORD BELLASIS MEETS MARK FIELDES ON THE TWENTY-FOURTH

Mark Fieldes had been quite upset in the morning by the news. He had met Dr. Rule by accident, and learnt it from him. Fieldes had felt very shaky. He had not been able to write, and—an unusual thing for him—he went to the Reform Club in the middle of the morning, and had a brandy and soda. At the club he met a particular crony of his, a man who was sure to be found there before twelve. The news had not yet reached the club. He confided the tragedy to his crony as a matter that had quite unnerved him. His friend, Barclay by name, was shocked, but also curious. Fieldes was mysterious. An hour passed in this way, and then another man came in who had also heard of the death from Dr. Rule. Cecilia was well known and popular, the sensation was growing.

"What on earth did it mean?"

"Good heavens, what could have driven her crazy?"

"Could it have been an accident?"

"Had there been a scandal?"

The talk was at its height when Lord Bellasis came upon them. There was a sudden silence, and a "Hush" from Fieldes which was unmistakable. Bellasis thought that his engagement to Madge must be getting known. This sort of thing was unpleasant, he had better get away at once. What did that cad Fieldes mean by his "Hush"? It was d—d impertinent. Bellasis took up the paper, but he was too annoyed to read. In a few moments the group round Fieldes had melted away and moved off to another part of the room. Fieldes could not take his eyes off Bellasis. Had he or had he not heard the news? That was the question he wished to have solved.

Bellasis knew that Fieldes was looking at him, and he lost his temper. He was particularly resentful of Mark's part in the stories about Madge. He strode across the room to him in an evident passion.

"May I ask," he said with sardonic ceremoniousness, "if you intend to convey by your persistent glance that you wish to speak to me?"

Fieldes was morally a terrier matched against a Newfoundland in confronting Bellasis. But he had a spite against the man, and he was sure that he had the sting in his own power. Even terriers have their day.

"No," he said distinctly, "I have no such wish, but I own I was wondering if you had heard the news that Dr. Rule told me this morning."

"News!" cried Bellasis who was little accustomed to being confronted by such as Fieldes. "What d—d news do you mean? What is it to me?"

"Nothing," said Fieldes. "It is only that Miss Cecilia Rupert committed suicide last night."

Fieldes, having delivered his fire, moved off. Bellasis was a strong man, and he knew he was being watched, but for a moment he remained rooted to the spot. Then he gathered himself together and walked out of the room. He went downstairs slowly, called a hansom and drove off. He thought he had shown nothing. He was not conscious that he was driving to Grosvenor Square bareheaded.

There was something in his gloomy face which made it impossible for the old hall-porter at Bellasis House, who had known him from a child, to call attention to the missing hat.

Lord Bellasis seated himself heavily at his writing-table, rang for his valet, and stretched out his hand, groping blindly among a mass of papers in front of him. The man ventured to put some telegraph forms within reach. Bellasis buried his face in his hands and remained immovable. Then after some minutes of silence, he muttered:—

"Take the forms, Bennett, and wire to make all ready for me to go on board the yacht to-night. I shall leave you here—to postpone all that was arranged for the wedding."

Then turning round, he concluded with a firm and distinct utterance: "Postpone, not countermand it, and mind, no newspaper paragraphs. You will, of course, after to-day, apply for further orders to Mr. Howman" (mentioning his private secretary).

"Yes, my lord," Bennett had reiterated at every fresh injunction. "And am I to follow you, my lord?"

"No,—yes," said Lord Bellasis in an abstracted tone. "As to the future—" but the sentence was not concluded.

"As to the future, my lord?" at length ventured Bennett.

"The future," said Lord Bellasis with a start, "the future is passed."

"Yes, my lord," said Bennett with decision, abandoning a conversation that was evidently fruitless. Nor did he trouble his master with any further interruption.

An hour later, Lord Bellasis rang his bell and gave a letter for the post, addressed to Mrs. George Riversdale. This letter held the few lines in which he told Madge, in irregular handwriting, that the wedding must inevitably be postponed in consequence of Cecilia's death.

Strangely enough, it was almost at the same moment that Madge, still all unknowing of the tragedy, was writing to him in order to break off their engagement.

Madge wrote the brief note in a firm hand. She asked his pardon, and told him simply, without giving any reason, that the marriage was impossible. He would know well enough why. She stamped it and addressed it to the Travellers' Club. He received the letter in his yacht, off Malta, two weeks afterwards. He looked at it long enough to make sure of the date on the notepaper and on the envelope. "It was just after hearing of the death," he said, "and it crossed mine." Then he folded it, put it inside a novel he was holding, and dropped the book into the blue waters of the Mediterranean.

Had Madge's letter come before he heard of the tragedy, it would have been a very heavy blow. But that news had given him a shock the degree of which he had not yet fully fathomed. His nature seemed dulled; his capacity for fresh pain blunted.

A moody English *"milord"* made his appearance at several towns on the Italian coast during the weeks that followed. He did not stay long at any, but at each he was the object of some curiosity. It transpired through his servant that he had been disappointed in love. To the curious onlooker he seemed restless and very gloomy. He was mourning evidently for the woman he had lost. Was it for a woman he had loved very dearly, but whose scruples forbade her to marry him? Or was it for one who—as he realised all too late—had loved him as he craved to be loved, but was now lost to him for ever?

Fieldes would hardly have been able to eat his luncheon alone that Friday. Fortunately he was engaged to a luncheon party. He was so obviously oppressed that his hostess rallied him on his low spirits.

Fieldes looked round the table and then said in a low tone:—

"I have heard something particularly shocking which has upset me a good deal."

Instantly the company hung upon his lips. He told the facts well and concisely. There was a chorus of comments and astonishment. Fieldes was too mysterious and too languid and depressed, to enter into the excitement. Everybody felt that he knew more than he said. Then under cover of the general discussion he told his neighbour in a low voice how he had had to break it to Bellasis, and how Bellasis had left the club without his hat. The lady said that of course he must feel it after all one had seen and known. One couldn't imagine that Lord Bellasis could be quite callous. The rest of the table gradually became silent in their anxiety to hear more. Fieldes spoke aloud.

"The fact was," he said, "that Miss Rupert had become very hysterical lately, and had had a craze about her health. This very morning she was to have been examined by Dr. Rule. When he arrived," there was the slightest break in Fieldes' voice here, "he certified that she was dead—had been dead many hours. Probably she had taken the chloroform about eleven o'clock. This hysteria is becoming one of the most alarming symptoms in our growing civilisation."

Nobody in the least believed this explanation, and Mark's manner conveyed that he wanted to put them off the true scent.

After luncheon Fieldes had the much coveted honour of being drawn into a *tête-à-tête* with Lady L., a beautiful woman, and undoubtedly the most important person present. It was felt to be only natural that Lady L. should have him to herself. Never before had she shown the least anxiety for his company, and Mark fully appreciated the situation. He told her all that he knew, though he did not let her think that it was by any means all. In Lady L's company, under the light of her earnest beautiful eyes, Mark's own real feelings came out. He had been very much shocked and upset by the news of Cecilia's death.

"I see now," he said, "how much all in her was tending towards this end. You know that Cecilia Rupert was entirely without faith. She was brought up to disbelieve in the Christian dogmas, in Christian ethics, in Christian views of life. She did not, like some of us, grieve deeply over the greatest loss that man or woman can sustain. I think a woman's mind cannot resign itself to dwell among shadows. It craves after a completeness which to us others seems utterly unattainable. Cecilia Rupert would not regret what she could not believe in. If it were not true it was hateful. It is not original in me, Lady L., to think that Christianity is a necessity for such women. It is the old saying of Voltaire, that if there had not been a God He must have been invented. I think that if you will forgive my calling it so, the greatest invention of the world, Christianity, came out of its dire necessity and chiefly from its necessity for women. Cecilia broke down under our present conditions of life. She was developed by all that Christianity has claimed for woman, the highest education and a spiritual equality with man.

Give this highly developed sensitive organisation, and take away from it all that makes suffering endurable and all that restrains the thirst for immediate happiness. Cecilia coolly counted up what was worth having,—love, success, pleasure. I never saw anybody drink a glass of champagne with more anxiety to get every sip of enjoyment out of it. She played her game. She had you know one great wish—you know, too, that it was thwarted. At the same time there grew upon her a suspicion that great bodily pain might be in store for her. Now does it seem to you wonderful that she should choose death rather than wait for it to come? We know now that she was probably wrong. There was in fact, Dr. Rule thinks, no disease; and even on the strongest hereditary disease theory we must remember that there are many cross currents of heredity in any family—innumerable diseases to choose from! We have mothers and grandparents as well as fathers. Then, too, there are so many other things to die of, fevers and accidents. You and I then know that Cecilia was unreasonable. But we are not surprised at her being unreasonable. We are not surprised at her thinking that she should never recover her disappointment, her broken heart as she thought it. We have known many women like that; but we have not known many women who held nothing to be sacred but their own happiness. We shall get to know them, Lady L. Twenty years hence you and I may have met many other Cecilias. Only," he looked at her earnestly and with fervour, "it is to you and such as you that we look to diminish the number, to extend the circle of faith and light, and to prevent such tragedies as that of last night."

Lady L. was too much moved to speak. In that hour of genuine feeling Fieldes had made one of his rare conquests among great ladies. Lady L. had become his friend: and though there were to come days when she thought him almost intolerably wanting in tact, the recollection of the better side he had once shown her kept secure for him the *entrée* into one of the best houses in London.

Fieldes happily for himself after that made his adieux and got himself quietly away.

CHAPTER XXII

LAURA DRIVES MARK TO THE REFORM CLUB

As Fieldes walked away from the luncheon party his own words grew upon him. "Yes," he thought, "it is to Christian women that we owe what peace and happiness we possess."

Hilda's image seemed very beautiful and dear to him to-day. He had secured for himself the love of a Christian woman, one who would idealise her service of himself as a loving, tender wife. She would be such another as Lady L.; and Lady L. and her friends would be in love with Hilda's cleverness and her simplicity, and all the men would be envious of her large luminous eyes. He wished he had hinted to Lady L. that he was engaged to Hilda Riversdale. He had passed by Grosvenor Crescent that morning, and as he went he had dreamed that possibly with Hilda's fortune he might be able to live even there. Inspiring thought! He had not seen her since the night of the ball, as he had been obliged to leave London early next day.

Little did he imagine what a reprieve his absence had been to Hilda. Strangely enough he had been quite satisfied with that night's work. He had been too much pleased with their conversation at the ball to attribute her abrupt "Good-night" to anything but maidenly embarrassment. He was dwelling on that night now, while he walked along by the river in the direction of St. Paul's, when he saw Marmaduke coming towards him. Marmaduke appeared grave and anxious, and even Fieldes' perceptions were not subtle enough at the moment to see that in reality he was not looking as gloomy to-day as he had been of late. Fieldes' bearing towards Marmaduke in these days betrayed the consciousness of a successful rival. Fieldes asked him at once if he had heard about Cecilia.

"Yes," was the answer, "I had a note from her last night telling me to go and see her. It must have been written just before she did it. I went to the house and I found she was dead."

Marmaduke did not care to speak further on the subject to this man. Fieldes was beginning again, but Marmaduke checked him. "I have a bit of family news to-day," he said, "Mrs. Riversdale and my cousin have come to London and my cousin is going to be a Sister of Charity."

"Indeed," cried Fieldes, "how very interesting."

"It is curious," said Marmaduke, speaking on a sudden impulse and eyeing him keenly, "that the heiress of the family should go into religion. I hope she may be allowed by the trustees to leave a little to help Hilda and her mother, as they are hard up."

Fieldes' face was a study. He quite lost his head and said with the greatest simplicity:—

"I thought Miss Hilda Riversdale was an heiress also."

A faint smile came over Marmaduke's face. The man really was delightful! Was it possible, was it conceivable that Hilda had ever cared for him? Marmaduke nodded and passed on, leaving Fieldes standing.

Mark recovered himself, and walked on, at first rapidly: then his pace slackened. It was not worth while to walk quickly any more than to do anything else, quickly or slowly.

It was all over then between him and Hilda—she was not what he had supposed. The golden aureole was not about her—she was in fact actually poor. He breathed a sigh of relief as he remembered that they were not engaged, but the relief was only on the surface of the gloom he was feeling. Had he been in love with her? Undoubtedly yes, and he was thankful to give her up because she had no money. He was not even sure if the news of her poverty had not taken off the bloom of his personal feeling for her. That quivering, sensitive mouth, those eyes that lit up with a light he knew so well how to call into them, would he enjoy them now? Hardly: for they had become so interwoven with a future of luxury, ease and success, in his fertile fancy, that he could not tell how much his enjoyment of them had depended on what he believed she could give him. Oh! how he scorned himself as his pitiless analysis went forward. He could imagine such high ideals of love: he had painted to Hilda such a pure noble courtship of which he was in reality entirely incapable.

All day long in the background of his mind he had been threatened with one of the fits of deep depression against which he had often to struggle. The thought of Cecilia had been near him. He had tried to drown it in talk. He had often drowned other strong impressions by talking of them, but this one would not be dimmed. He and she had spoken together so often of their weariness of life. They had said extravagant things, they had piled up horrors, so that their fancies might make them laugh at each other's wit to prevent their feeling each other's sadness. They wanted to make it all feel unreal by force of exaggeration. And now that beautiful, brilliant woman had gone down before it, had been defeated by sorrow and suffering. And what was there to prevent defeat? What was there to save himself from such a defeat as Cecilia's? It was true that he could not love as she had loved. But would that save him from suffering? It was not only love that had made her kill herself, it was the agonised fear of physical suffering, the distorted vision of an all-absorbing egotism. And had not he too to suffer some day? As she used to say, "Life is a mortal illness." Suffering lay in wait for him too; and even if he had no morbid imaginings of present disease, must it not come in time? did not each hour bring it nearer? Yes, the gloom was about him, was gathering thicker and closer. It was a darkness to be felt. What was there to cheer him? He had lost Hilda—he had lost hope of the domestic hearth whose light and sweetness would have made a charmed circle, within which these demons of nervous sensation could have been kept at arm's length. He had not even the wholesome lover's sorrow, the tender pathos of which would have been warm and consoling compared to his present state of mind.

And in this particular fit of horror he turned to the thought of religion, reflecting on what he had often described, and described eloquently, the mystery of the conquest of faith over pain.

But to-day the curse of his own fluency seemed to have spoilt such thoughts for his own use. He was dwelling on his latest articles on the religious ideal, when a more acute, more clear thought seemed to come out of them;—the thought, not of sweetness, light, enthusiasm, "of the stream of tendency that makes for righteousness," but of the other side of the shield; the sense not of a subjective notion, but of a possible objective power, with retributive menacing complete sway over himself and his destiny. Strangely enough there was something in this which was almost a relief. Such a fear was more human, less void, less lonely.

"I once met a man who said he would rather be damned than be annihilated," he said to himself with a wan smile. "I don't agree, for that would end it all. But it is awful to be alive and to be alone as I am! If it were true that there were a Judge who really existed, He would approve as well as condemn. Love would grow near to fear. And the human instinct to value life which failed Cecilia would not be part of a great illusion. We should gain in hope as well as in fear."

But Mark was very tired.

It had been an hour of acute mental suffering. It had begun in disappointment, self-disgust, discouragement as to worldly success. It had led him on to the questions that lay at the root of his very existence, and the pain had been intense. Suddenly a tall footman became visible to him, and his highly civilised bowing figure gave a sense almost of physical comfort. He was still in a world in which were luxury and smart footmen—in the best conceivably fitting coats, and with the most intelligently deferential bows. He pulled himself together—he must be worthy of the footman.

"Mrs. Hurstmonceaux is in the carriage," the man indicated a brougham at the other side of the wide pavement.

More light, more consolation, the sight of Mrs. Hurstmonceaux in her beautiful *demi-saison* cloak, looking eagerly towards him out of that perfect brougham.

"Come, Mark, get in," she said, when he came within earshot. "I want you."

"And I want you," he said, with a poor attempt at a sprightly manner.

The moment Mark had fitted himself into Mrs. Hurstmonceaux' brougham she began to speak:—

"Have you heard the news?"

"Yes," answered Mark with a shiver.

Laura was too full of her own train of thought to notice his face.

"But I am entirely puzzled," she went on. "I think it must all have been stopped. It is madness."

"Stopped," said Mark; "do you mean hushed up?"

"It is too late to hush it up," said Laura impatiently; "that is what is so annoying."

"But you can't keep a thing of that kind dark, Mrs. Hurstmonceaux. It is out of the question, it always comes out through the doctors. And then there must be an inquest."

"Inquest—doctors—Mark, what are you talking of?"

"That," said Mark, pointing to a news-boy, who was carrying a bundle of papers. On the placard was written between two other announcements:—

STARTLING DISCOVERY.
SUICIDE IN HIGH LIFE.

"Who is it?" said Laura. "But I have no time for other people's affairs to-day. Haven't you heard of Madge's engagement to Lord Bellasis? And I have just been to see her, and she is closeted with Miss Mary Riversdale and is talking of going to confession to-night. It is maddening."

Mark was silent for a moment. He knew now what Laura had been working for. He pitied her when she should know the first fruits of her success.

"Hadn't you heard of it?" Laura repeated.

"And you have not heard who it was who killed herself? It was Miss Cecilia Rupert."

Mark looked out of the window. Laura sank back and they drove on in silence. A few moments later she leant forward and let down the window near her, as if in want of air. As she did so, she said in a very quiet voice to Mark:—

"How very foolish of Cecilia. This explains Madge's conduct."

Such calmness entirely surprised Mark, but it was a relief to him. He returned to his ordinary manner, but before he could speak, Laura began a sharp quick questioning as to all he knew, as to what Dr. Rule had said, and as to who else knew of the death. She cross-questioned him as to the exact moment at which Lord Bellasis had received the news, at what moment Dr. Rule had been called to the house, and what Marmaduke had said.

At last she went on:—

"I cannot quite understand it. I suppose Madge must have known this before I saw her just now, and that either she or Lord Bellasis has broken off the engagement in consequence of Cecilia's action." She shivered.

"When was the engagement to be announced?" he asked.

"It was to be in the papers to-morrow; and yet she has just told me that she is going to Skipton for some weeks, whereas they were to have been married privately in three days by special licence."

"Special licence?" inquired Mark.

"Yes, it is far the best plan with a marriage like that; there is such a fuss about even an innocent divorcee being married now."

"Lord Bellasis a divorcee?" cried Mark in astonishment.

Laura did not seem to notice that she was being indiscreet. She talked on mechanically.

"Yes, and that was of course the whole difficulty. This is why Cecilia's conduct so much puzzles me. Knowing what objections and difficulties there were, I wonder she didn't wait to see if the marriage would take place at all. If she had told the secret of his former wife's existence, all the Roman Catholics would have done their utmost to prevent the marriage. This very unpleasant violence of hers may have put a stop to it; I think it has. But what good has it done her?"

"Strange," said Mark, "it must have been from some notion of honour I think, or perhaps—yes, I think that is most likely," his dramatic interest in the story growing upon him. "She felt that it was no use to separate them if he really loved Madge; she was capable of a kind of complete despair, of a sense of fate that is unusual. And you think it has divided them already? Her spirit has come between them. How indeed could they meet over such a hecatomb?"

"I don't know; don't be dramatic, for goodness sake! All I know is that Madge met me as if we had had no secret, no plans in common; that she seemed devoted to her ultra-Catholic sister-in-law, who is going out to China in some sisterhood, and that they are going to their confession at St. Philip's Church to-night. Yet nothing about Madge suggested that she knew of Cecilia's death."

"I suppose that she does not know of it," said Mark. "Depend upon it, Miss Riversdale has come up to stop this engagement—you know they would think it a most shocking sin—and has succeeded. Mary Riversdale is an angel; it is a beautiful idea."

"Mark, you are insufferable," cried Laura in a voice of more natural wrath than he had ever heard her use before; "how can you talk of beautiful ideas to-day?"

Mark reverted to Cecilia.

"I wonder when she first heard of the engagement," he said.

There was a moment's silence, then Laura spoke, turning her face full upon him.

"I told her yesterday morning."

never forgot the look in that subtle, hardened face, as it
ed towards him; the pain in it froze him. Whatever had
been the history of the soul which showed itself to him now,
whatever moral cruelties it had hitherto inflicted without shrinking, it was at this moment a prey to agony; and it asked for no
help, looked for no comfort.

"Good God," cried Mark, and shrank back in the brougham.

"Shall I drop you here?" asked Laura and she pulled the check
string. She had noticed, as he had not, that they were just opposite to the Reform Club.

He went upstairs mechanically and crossing the library stood
at a window; his eyes vacantly following the gay crowd as it
passed along Pall Mall, glittering in the spring sunshine.

"What a queer fellow that is," thought an acquaintance who
watched him as he stood there. "I wonder what he is muttering?"
Mark was repeating to himself a verse that often haunted him:—

> Bright else and fast the stream of life may roll
> And no man may the other's hurt behold,
> Yet each will have one anguish, his own soul,
>   Which perishes from cold.

It may seem strange that throughout that afternoon no news,
no rumour, reached Madge of the death of Cecilia Rupert. And
yet who was there intimate enough to tell her, among those who
knew of it, except Marmaduke? In fact he was the one person
who did mean to do so, though he shrank from the task. He
could not imagine what her state of mind would be. Now that he
had heard that she intended to make a marriage that he knew she
must believe to be sacrilegious, Madge had become a new person,
a stranger in his eyes. She was not in the least what he had supposed her to be. And he was filled too with a great sense of indignation at wrong done to Cecilia. He felt that Madge was to blame,
was horribly to blame, for her death. He felt towards Madge the
repugnance he might have felt towards an actual murderer. If he

must go and tell her, and he thought he ought not to leave her to the chance of seeing it in the papers, he had no intention of sparing her. Yes, he would go and let her know what she had done, what were the first fruits of her unhallowed engagement. It might be possible that the shock of such a death would save her from destruction, would change her heart even now. But he felt at the time as if it were almost unfair that Madge should be saved by such means. She didn't deserve much grace, he thought, as he made up his mind to go and see her and get it over.

But then he remembered that he had promised to see his aunt early in the afternoon, and he thought he would go there first.

After he had met Mark and left him standing bewildered in the street, Marmaduke called a hansom and drove to the little hotel in Dover Street where Mrs. Riversdale was staying. He found her sitting by the round table in the middle of the stiff, gaudy room, upright as ever in a red velvet chair, with her perpetual needlework in her hands. She raised a sad yet peaceful face to Marmaduke's darkened countenance, and he experienced a sudden relief and comfort in her presence, such as he had never felt before. It was not merely a certain sister's likeness to his mother that struck him: it was the sense that comes over most of us at times when we are with people who, with however many tiresome faults, in the main have never failed consciously to live for duty and for conscience' sake. With his horror at Cecilia's death, his disgust with Madge, his utter contempt for Mark, the world seemed, with the exception of his love, to be a black and hateful place, where men and women were greedy and cruel, and fate was dark about them. Thus this quiet figure of his aunt, reminding him of the long record or her life at Skipton, was grateful to him. That quiet dull action of her sewing was suggestive to him of duties done and of an habitual patience which had schemed little for others and grasped at nothing for herself. It had been a long education in patience that had made possible her last and greatest sacrifice—for there was a heroism in her readiness to give up Mary that could have sprung out of no thin or poor soil.

Not quite so explicit as this, however, was Marmaduke's thought as he sat down by his aunt and asked when she had got back from the convent at Mill Hill?

"At two o'clock," she replied, "and I expected to find Mary."

"Where can she be?" asked Marmaduke.

"There is a note from her," holding out as she spoke a sheet of paper on which Mary had written in pencil:—

DEAR MOTHER,

I must stay here to-day. Madge is in great trouble and danger, and I can't leave her. It makes me so unhappy to think that you came back to the hotel tired and found me not returned. I do hope I shall get back to you this evening after I have taken Madge to St. Philip's as she wishes to go to confession.

There was no signature to the hastily folded piece of paper.

"Then Madge does know," thought Marmaduke, coming to the same conclusion as Laura's had been when Mark told her the news.

He leant his elbow on the showy tapestry cloth that covered the table and rested his head on his hand. Mary was with Madge, and he would not be wanted. It was an immense relief.

Mrs. Riversdale looked at him in silence for a few moments, then she said a little irritably:—

"What does it mean?"

Marmaduke was not intimate with his aunt—he never had been. She was not sympathetic to youth in general, and in Marmaduke's case she had always felt a little unacknowledged jealousy, not so much because she had heard him praised more than George could ever be praised, but because she had known in her heart that he was the better man of the two. A moment's reflection made him conclude that she ought to be told all, and it was easier to him to speak out with the softer impression he had just received of her, and of the peace that seemed to be about her.

It was easier after the start than he had expected, and he told her the whole story from beginning to end. After all, secluded though her life had been, and unreceptive as her faculties might be compared to others, she had lived many more years than Marmaduke had, and he felt as if instead of her being startled out of measure with the tale of a sacrilegious marriage—now he hoped no longer thought of—and an actual suicide, she was more able to locate them in her life's philosophy than he was. He would have expected her to be prepared for more iniquity on Madge's part than he had been, but she said quietly:—

"She wasn't a good wife and she was a misfortune to us. Mary has saved her now, or this poor crazy girl's death has. But she has the faith, and in any case she would never have gone through with this marriage. And as to poor Miss Rupert, if she wasn't crazy as she seems to have been, she did commit a great sin. But these unfortunate people know so little about God."

Then seeing the pain in the young man's face deepening as she spoke openly of what he had shrunk from in thought, she made one more effort.

"You don't know," she said, trying to remember Father Clement's words to her after her son's death, "you don't know what God may have done in her soul at the very end. Of course she must be punished in purgatory, you know, for her sin in killing herself: but you needn't think of anything worse, and we will all pray for her. She may have made an act of contrition when she felt death coming. God knows—if I didn't think that of—" she had broken down in the little disconnected sentences, and George's name remained unspoken as she turned away to put her handkerchief to her eyes.

Marmaduke knelt down beside her in silence. Presently she turned round, and her white face betrayed little emotion. Marmaduke had told her enough to start another train of thought in his aunt.

"You are right," she said, "to send Hilda home, she ought never to have stayed with Madge, but I hope—in fact I feel sure—"

"But perhaps it is a mistake, Aunt Helen; I have understood so little to-day."

"No, I feel sure it is all right, Marmaduke, and I will say—but we won't talk of it again after this—that I would rather you and Hilda had Skipton after we die than anybody else. Your marriage would be a comfort."

Marmaduke bent down and she kissed him a little stiffly; he kissed the hand that held her work and rose.

"I think," she said, "Benediction at Farm Street is at four o'clock, and I will go to it. We must leave Mary and Madge to themselves."

Marmaduke then left her and turning into Piccadilly met the boys carrying the placards of an evening paper: "Suicide in high life." He shivered and walked on quickly. He was glad to think that Madge would not learn it from the papers. She evidently knew it already. That was clear from Mary's note.

CHAPTER XXIII

THE EVE OF LADY DAY

It was getting late. Father Gabriel was tired. He wondered if it would be safe to leave the confessional now. He had heard a good many confessions, for it was the eve of the Annunciation; and he had been in his "box," as he called the carved confessional, for nearly two hours.

St. Philip's Church was dimly lighted, and in the side chapel where stood Father Gabriel's confessional it was difficult to see whether any kneeling figures were still hidden in the dark corners of the marble piers. In the depths of the low chapel under the organ-loft stood the three great crosses of a life-size Calvary, and before it hung three tiny red lights. Gaunt and terrible as it might appear to unaccustomed eyes, this Calvary with its awful realism of suffering was a favourite object of devotion.

Father Gabriel leant forward over the door of his confessional and peered into the dark spaces about the Calvary.

"I wish," he muttered to himself, "that little lady would come to confession now if she is coming at all, or would finish her prayers and go away. She has been there for more than an hour and it is past half-past nine."

He sighed impatiently; he had told his nephew, a young officer of whom he was very proud, that he would be able to see him at half-past nine.

He smiled affectionately as he thought of the handsome young soldier, of whom he was always talking, until Father Gabriel's nephew and his wonderful perfections had passed into a proverb among the younger fathers of the community.

Need he after all stay any later in the Calvary Chapel? There were several other fathers still left in different parts of the great church. She would have no difficulty in finding a confessor, if indeed she wanted one. But he dismissed the thought and composed himself to patience.

It would be better to be doing something he thought; so he struck a match and lit the candle in a little tin sconce by his side. Instantly the confessional appeared in the dark church to be a blaze of light. Father Gabriel's white hair and bent head, his cotta and even the books on the tiny shelf by his side, made a vivid picture in the distance. He looked out cautiously. The little lady had stirred, and had for a moment turned a very white face in his direction.

Yes, she evidently did mean to come to him and he must wait her convenience, and let Charlie kick his heels impatiently in his uncle's room. Father Gabriel sighed again, drew a pair of pincers and a half-made rosary and a roll of wire out of the pocket of his cassock, and set to work.

Nobody could make rosaries as well as Father Gabriel. Each twist of the silver wire was so strongly and firmly done; each link was so cleanly cut off by the tweezers; there was not a weak point throughout. No wonder they lasted for a lifetime, and that dying hands long after he had left this world clasped the rosaries he had made for little children. Swiftly and dexterously the old fingers, though crooked and almost deformed from rheumatism, worked at their task. He wanted to finish the rosary that night. It was to be a present for a little girl who was to make her first communion on to-morrow's feast, the Annunciation. He smiled gently as he thought of the child's earnestness and sweet anxiety over her preparation. "And that fool of a mother of hers kept talking to her about how well her white frock had been made. That's the sort of woman that ought to be stifled."

Yet though he spoke fiercely to himself and was fond of strong words, and used to say that he was sorry "he couldn't help swearing," yet he was very patient with wrong-doers, and he was noted among the younger fathers for his love of any real big sinner. The old man's experience of the catalogue of sin was large. He had sat in that confessional "so sedately" year out and year in for more than forty years. There were crowds of people whom he had only known in this way coming time after time with much the same story, for we may suppose that it was not a very large number who showed marked changes of character, great improvements. Then there had been some, too, who came there weighted with great sins, horrid cruelties, moral and physical, murders of the body or murders of the soul. All this had been poured into his ears. He knew of things stranger than any fiction has imagined; he knew the secret sins of the respectable; he knew the secret remorse of the speculator haunted by his victims; he knew the secrets of women of every kind and sort.

He must have been often saddened at the half-hearted repentances, the self-delusions, the deceptions of those who came to satisfy their own consciences, to persuade themselves that they had repented. Had he not trembled in pronouncing the words of absolution for fear they were not ratified in the heavenly courts? Were such the occupations, was such the knowledge which should produce a sunny old age, almost exuberantly bright, almost childishly gay? Yet though he could not have denied the long catalogue of which we have spoken, the old man stoutly maintained that every year of his life he had grown in that confessional to think better, more highly, of human nature!

He had seen so much of goodness, he would say, so much of heroism, such high aspirations,—at the word "aspirations" perhaps he would smile a little. "The women have the highest aspirations, but are the most inclined to self-deception and delusion. Yet I've known very grand women." Then he would shake his head and tell the hearer to "get along" and take care of *himself.*

The rosary was nearly finished, and it only needed the addition of a little silver crucifix which Father Gabriel had left upstairs. He looked at his watch,—ten o'clock, twenty more minutes had passed and the church would soon be shut.

All the other fathers had gone now; he had heard them all shut and lock their confessionals one by one; some quite faintly from the farthest chapels in the great church. The old men left slowly and with feet dragging; the young men with long strides impeded by their cassocks. They were all gone into the house, shutting the door that communicated with the church more or less loudly behind them. It would be best to resort to diplomacy and pretend to go, and then the little woman would have to make up her mind. Otherwise the bell would ring and she would be obliged to leave at the closing hour.

He opened the low doors in front of him and rose; he made a noise with his books and blew out the candle. In a moment she had moved quickly to his side and spoke in a low, hurried voice:—

"I want to go to confession," Madge said, "but I'm afraid I shan't be ready for some time."

The priest smiled at her:—his old face was a very gentle one.

"Why, you have been preparing for nearly an hour!"

"But I can't get clear!" said Madge, "it is so long since I've been."

"How many years?" he inquired, still smiling.

"Oh, not quite a year."

"Come along," he said, laying a hand on her arm, "come along; can't you see, my dear child, that you will only muddle your brains by this?"

There was a slight touch of eccentricity in the old man's manner: a sense of humour seemed to lurk in the overflowing kindness. But his fatherliness suited Madge just then and seemed to make matters easier.

How natural it was to Madge to be kneeling on the narrow footboard, with her mouth to the little grating and a crucifix hanging just above her. Mechanically she was soothed by the priest's blessing, and by repeating herself the first half of the *Confiteor*. Then she began:—

"It is about nine months since I last went to Confession." Then a pause.

"Well," said Father Gabriel.

"I was engaged till to-day to marry a divorcee." The words were jerked out abruptly.

"How long had you been engaged?"

"A little more than a fortnight. I broke it off to-day."

"Thank God. And now, my child, you loved this man very much?"

"No," Madge faltered. "Somebody else did," she stopped.

"How did it come about? Mind, you needn't tell me unless it would be a help."

"I had been getting worse and worse," came in a childish, broken voice, "I often didn't go to Mass, and I played cards and didn't pay my bills, and read bad books, and I felt I couldn't be good, and, and I wanted to marry him because he is rich and great, and I knew nobody would know he had a wife living as—"

"Yes, yes, I see, and now how were you saved to-day, eh?"

"I don't know how it happened. My sister-in-law who has brought me here to-night came to tell me that she is going to be a Sister of Charity, and it startled me. I felt she would go to heaven and I never should, and when I told her she must go away and she said 'Good-bye,' I couldn't let her go. It seemed—I don't know why—as if she was taking away my dead baby with her. Then to-morrow is the day when I made my first communion in the convent school in France—and I remembered it was the Eve of the Annunciation—and Mary was going to heaven and I was going to hell—and—" her voice faltered.

"Don't hurry," said Father Gabriel,

"And I had been frightened all night. I don't know why, somebody seemed to be in the room with me. I am sure something has happened. I haven't even been good in giving him up. I was frightened. I had an instinct—"

"Never mind those feelings, child." Father Gabriel was a little alarmed at a sort of wildness in her tone. "Thank God that He has saved you and brought you to His feet. Now try to recollect a little more about your sins. The world got hold of you and you just did what others were doing. Let us try now to sift a little. When did you stop going to Mass?"

And so, in a few moments it was all told and Madge was surprised to find how clear her story had become—how by "seeming venial genial fault" she had passed to worse, more cruel sin, merciless towards others, merciless to her own soul. No self-excuse, no blame to anybody came out in her story—she had always been by nature candid, and she had been too well trained to be tempted to dim the simplicity of her confession. At last "that is all I can remember, father," came in a low murmur, and Madge bowed her head below the crucifix. "Then for your penance you will say one decade of the Rosary, the Mystery of the Annunciation, tomorrow's feast—and, my child, let us think a great deal of the love of God. He came down to this unhappy sinful world and He became a little child for love of you," and so he spoke on for a few moments,—nothing much more than that, no word of death or of the judgment or eternal punishment. But while he spoke balm fell on Madge's bruised spirit and shaken nerves, and when he concluded those few words thus: "Now, child, make an act of sorrow whilst I give you absolution," the tears of penance flowed freely and the words of pardon came upon a deeply contrite heart.

As soon as Madge had gone Father Gabriel rose, took his breviary off the shelf, left the confessional and locked the folding doors behind him. Then he passed across to the middle of the church and walked a little way up the central passage. The custodian was walking round the chapels to be sure that nobody was left before he locked the outer doors. Father Gabriel signed to him, and when he was near enough, whispered to him not to disturb the lady who had just been to confession for another five minutes. The man sighed sleepily but did not venture to object.

The spacious building was dark and still. One jet of gas in the far distance near the door, a few lamps hanging before statues and pictures in the side chapels, and the distant line of still radiance from the sanctuary lamps hardly did more than reveal the great size of the church. But one brighter spot there was in front of the Lady Altar—a stand of votive candles lit by the faithful for their own private intentions. It was a favourite object with Father Gabriel; and he would glance that way, thinking with pleasure that each golden spot of light, each taper consuming itself there, carried on the prayer of some faithful soul now sleeping after the day's toil. As he came in front of the Lady Altar he glanced, as he ever did, at the marble statue enthroned above it, shining in the yellow light of the votive candles. Then he raised his biretta, and whispered a good-night to the Blessed Mother. As he turned from the altar to move towards the sanctuary for a moment's adoration, he saw that there was another lady still in the church. In a corner formed by the red marble base of the pier knelt the light upright figure of a young girl whose eyes gazed straight across the wide space of the sanctuary to the gold door of the tabernacle. The wax tapers cast a faint mellow light on the young face. Those who loved Mary had seen that face lit with the high spirits of pure childlike enjoyment riding or playing with the dogs: they had seen too that face spiritualised and awestruck with suffering. Now its beauty was wonderfully intensified by the spiritual beauty of the King's daughter that is from within.

From the moment she knelt there, all that tried Mary had been left behind—the dreary anxious day with Madge, the sense of a blind moral struggle, the oppression that might be compared to the difficulty of finding her way in a thick fog. All day the vision of her soul had been interrupted and disturbed; but in the evening she had found her way to the Blessed Sacrament, and in the evening there had been light and peace.

A less sympathetic observer of men and women's faces than Father Gabriel might have paused for a moment to look at and to understand Mary's as he passed her. What a contrast between the pale face of the overstrained, repentant, little woman of the world, with her elaborate bonnet and cloak and unmistakable air of wealth, and this fresh, fair, strong, active, young and typically English girl, in her happy unconsciousness and mysterious peace of soul. "My sister-in-law told me that she was going to be a

Sister of Charity." The words came in a flash to Father Gabriel, and he bowed his head reverently and muttered a *Deo gratias* as he went. This was one more of the heroisms that filled his humble soul with a tender and thankful surprise. He turned again for a moment ere he reached the door leading into the house, and looked back. He could still see the golden hair, the high narrow white forehead; the adoration of her attitude, the complete sacrifice so strongly suggested by every line of the vigorous young figure. He saw the little lady come up to her, kneel by her side for a moment; and then they went away together.

He gave a faint sigh and then checked himself. A figure rose before his imagination such as he had often seen. A young Sister of Charity clothed in a peasant's blue gown, or, worse, if still a novice, in a singularly hideous kind of black alpaca, her hands red with household toil; the figure bent as if habitually tired, the white cap on the head and the golden hair gone for ever. Nor was it likely, he reminded himself, that this great sense of joy, this flood of mystic happiness would be unbroken—"God fulfils His purpose in many ways, and He sends times of darkness even to the simplest of His children," thought the old man as he shut the door into the house behind him with a little bang, and slowly made his way down a dark and narrow passage. He knew so well what lay before Mary in her new life—the trials from superiors, the inevitable class differences between herself and her companions, the longing for loved faces left at home. Yet the sigh had been but a superficial one, and the deep joy rose in his heart, the heart of a brave soldier of the cross, who has grown old and is deeply rooted in God's peace, as he recognised a young novice soon to be promoted to a post of danger but of glory.

Father Gabriel's was not a mind much addicted to abstract thought or to philosophy; he troubled himself little about the infidelity or the agnosticism of the day. But of one argument in the face of modern thought he was almost fatiguingly fond—he was always saying that none of "those fellows" could explain away the beauty of the soul: and to-night he muttered to himself as he lifted one rheumatic knee after the other up the high staircase: "What would they make of a girl like that, I wonder?—bother my old knees!—she has given up everything—I suppose she has a father and a mother and she is young and beautiful. Almighty God always takes the best of them. Well, and she is giving up fun and joy and life and home. And what do they suppose is left in their place?"

He was unconsciously assuming his pulpit manner as he spoke.

"Just a sentiment, a feeling, an echo from no voice, a response, to no call! Do they think it is a sacrifice for mere love of sacrifice? Dear me, I am up at last, but Charlie is gone, of course, I couldn't expect anything else at this hour"—for he saw before him that the room was dark.

He went in and fumbled for his matches on the table. Then he struck a light and went on talking to himself:—

"A good thing I've only got to put the cross on the rosary now. It is too cold here to use one's fingers properly—yes, yes, a sacrifice for the mere love of sacrifice, that will do for a sermon. Then they think there is something hard and cruel underneath it all, and that this sort of joy the child has in giving up herself to Our Lord is a sort of—let me see—sort of hectic flush brought out by a spiritual disease, a humbug disguising some dark mystery in a cruel system of religion."

He was rather pleased with that sentence; he took up a notebook that lay near him and wrote it down. Then he turned over the pages to look for a passage he had copied from Montalembert, written by the great orator in a time of suffering, when his daughter was about to leave him and go into a convent.

"Quel est donc cet amant invisible, mort sur un gibet il y a dix huit siecles, et qui attire ainsi a lui la jeunesse, la beauté et l'amour? Est-ce un homme? Non, c'est un Dieu."

"That is the only explanation of the mystery!" he muttered, "the answer to this riddle of life offered by crowds of such young girls. The Creator has undertaken to fill the hearts of His creatures if they give up all to Him. No wonder they are happy!"

But Father Gabriel was getting very cold; the day's work was done and he was glad to go to bed.

Early next day, before the dawn of a March morning had done more than penetrate the darkness of the great dome with a few shafts of light, or had sent more than one clear ray from the eastern window to gild the statue of the Madonna, Father Gabriel said his Mass at the high altar. He had given her first communion to the little girl for whom he had finished the rosary the night before, and for her he had offered the Mass. After the joy of giving her Lord to the little child, he had passed down a row of communicants and had noticed with half-conscious surprise at her being up so early, the little lady who had kept him waiting the night before, and by her side the tall girl he had seen praying in the church.

But what had happened to them both? Mary's face had the peace rather of a Mater Dolorosa than the joy of a spiritual bride, and Madge lifted a face of such haggard agony and anguished longing when he gave her Holy Communion, that the old man was troubled. After Mass he knelt in one of the benches of the church to make his thanksgiving, and during that time he prayed earnestly for the little stranger. Presently rising to go back to the house he turned to look for her again, and saw that she was leaning forward almost as if she were falling over the bench in front of her. The tall girl was not by her, but kneeling a few benches behind. Father Gabriel walked across the church, made a genuflexion by Mary's side, and touched her on the shoulder:—

"Did you come with that lady?" he asked, indicating Madge.

Mary raised a tear-stained face and answered "Yes" in a broken voice.

"Listen, child," said Father Gabriel, "you ought to take her home and send for a doctor, she is going to be ill, very ill."

"Yes," said Mary with a grateful look, "I am sure she is. I wanted to have a doctor last night, but she was afraid he would not let her come to communion. We have not been to bed at all. We heard last night that a girl my sister-in-law knows well has," tears broke her voice for a moment, "has killed herself—because—because of something my sister-in-law had done;—no, I mean, something she nearly did, meant to do."

Mary could say no more. The perplexed face of the old priest showed now a look of understanding. Father Gabriel knelt down in the bench in front and buried his face in his hands.

Then he rose and went back to Mary. "Child," he said, putting his hand on her shoulder, "remember that He died for each one of us. Take her home now and get a doctor at once. Comfort her, but don't speak of it more than—But look, she is going to faint, be quick!" A sudden movement of the little figure as if sinking backwards in the front bench had alarmed him. Mary moved quickly. Madge was not actually fainting, but her eyes betrayed no consciousness. Father Gabriel followed them at a little distance as Mary led her down the church, till he saw that they were safe in a brougham which was waiting outside. Then he turned back.

He thought of the happiness of Madge's face when she left the confessional the day before. He had seen the penal suffering now. "It was best so;"—but Father Gabriel's eyes had filled with tears;—"let sin bring its own punishment here."

A few minutes later and the work of the day had begun. An old Irish woman in distress, an impostor of an Italian beggar, a lady who was not sure if she ought to dismiss her under housemaid, and another lady who having been at a ball most of the night had called to ask whether St. John of the Cross or St. Theresa would suit her best for spiritual reading, a tailor out of work, and a man who had invented a new method of lighting the House of Commons and wanted his invention to be used by the fathers of St. Philip's, an earnest but tactless district visitor—all these soon occupied Father Gabriel's mind to the exclusion of Madge and Mary. He never saw those two again, and he did not so much as know their names. But from time to time their faces rose in the kaleidoscope of memory, and the old priest would commend their souls with so many others who had passed by his way, to the care of the "Mother of Sorrows" and the "Queen of Heaven."

CHAPTER XXIV

A POSTSCRIPT

Nearly a score of years have passed since that 25th of March. Hilda Riversdale and Madge Fitz-Wygram will next season be bringing out their girls—who are great friends.

For Hilda is still Hilda Riversdale. Marmaduke took his uncle's name when he came into the Skipton property at old Mrs. Riversdale's death. Lady Fitz-Wygram and her only girl are frequent visitors at Skipton, of which, under the new *régime*, Madge has become very fond. Some people think there is a kindness already growing up between the tall, blue-eyed Arthur Riversdale, who is just going up to Oxford, and Mary Fitz-Wygram—and they are *not* cousins, so that no one much minds it, while Madge certainly likes it.

It is only fifteen years since Mary Riversdale went to be a nun, and five years since her death. After she had nursed Madge through the severe illness which came a few days after the news of Cecilia's suicide, and spent some weeks of her convalescence at Eastbourne, they went together to Skipton only to find old Mr. Riversdale seriously ill. He was attacked by a paralytic seizure on the very day of their arrival, and although he rallied to some extent it was clearly the beginning of the end. Mary stayed with her father during the few years of life which remained, and he died a very peaceful and holy death, without being called upon to make the sacrifice the thought of which had helped to break him. The father and daughter used often to talk of George's widow, whose life now seemed so blank and aimless, and for whose future they could not but be anxious.

Her nature seemed to have lost its buoyancy, and from time to time there was an expression in her eyes which once made Mr. Riversdale exclaim "She looks as if she had seen a ghost"

"Whom has she to care for—what has she to look to—is what one feels," the old man would often say.

And even when old Lord Fitz-Wygram fell in love with her at a country house party, and gave her an unexceptionable Catholic home, they could not be quite free from anxiety. Some of her former restless love of excitement was still there, and the position of an old man's wife did not seem to them to solve the problem of her future satisfactorily. Mary's most stable consolation was the negative one—that the intimacy with Laura Hurstmonceaux had never been renewed.

But when, two years after her marriage, Madge brought her baby girl of six months old on a visit to Skipton, Mary and her father soon became very happy indeed. Peace and new life seemed at last to have come for Madge in devotion to the child she idolised.

"I am much happier about Madge," was all that the Squire said to Mary two days after his daughter-in-law had arrived, and Mary answered: "Oh yes!" in a tone and with a look which more than satisfied her father.

Mr. Riversdale did not live long after this. In his will he left the property to Hilda after his wife's death.

Marmaduke had been already returned as member for the county before he succeeded to Skipton, and Mark Fieldes—owing to an accidental meeting while he was canvassing his constituents—had helped him a good deal in the election.

They became decidedly better friends, and Mark still pays an annual visit to Skipton. He goes less frequently to visit the Benedictines and Carthusians than he used to—though he stayed so long at Father Clement's monastery in Warwickshire, soon after Cecilia's death, that his friends said he had become a monk. He reappeared however with the MS. of *Phidias Redux* completed.

If he goes less to monasteries, he also cares less for his country house visits and his London season. But he goes through with both in a rather perfunctory manner. Some people say that his heart is more than ever in his work; but Lord Tim declares that he is growing lazy and fond of his dinner. His visit to Skipton is, I think, the greatest pleasure of the year. He contemplates the happiness of Hilda and Marmaduke with a sympathy unclouded by any jealous memories, and is a great favourite with their children. He still studies the signs of the times, and owns that he was wrong in his prophecy of a general decay of faith on the lines suggested to him by the story of Cecilia Rupert. He is not sure that he understands the intellectual outlook of the dawning century; but he is determined that he will understand it before he leaves the problem alone.

Mary Riversdale's death, after ten years of devoted work among the poor in the East End—for she was not, after all, sent to China—was a great shock to him, the degree of which was indeed almost inexplicable; and Hilda told Marmaduke that she thought they should soon hear that Mr. Fieldes wished to be received into the Church. But no such event has yet happened.

Old Mrs. Riversdale survived her husband five years, and was then laid to rest in the vault by his side. And now the schoolroom at Skipton is occupied by a generation of Riversdales who have a good deal in common with their predecessors, though there is a difference. Arthur, the eldest boy, is held by the old villagers and tenants to be the image of Mr. Arthur, his grandfather. "To see the young squire on his horse, you would think it was Mr. Arthur himself come back again."

But Hilda thinks him more like her mother's father. And in tastes he represents both impartially—for he is an excellent sportsman who nevertheless loves his books, and is keenly looking forward to his first year at Balliol.

And now we bid them farewell and commit their fate to the coming century.

Milton Keynes UK
Ingram Content Group UK Ltd.
UKHW040954050923
428080UK00004B/122